"You don't believe in love?"

Beatrice paused, drafting her response carefully. "Really, Mr. Barrow, I believe true love is exceedingly rare and . . . probably overrated."

"Well, how do you expect your niece to learn about love and marriage unless she has some experience with it?"

"She can learn by watching others' mistakes, by listening to sound counsel, and by remaining unmarried long enough to—"

"Nonsense," Connor moved closer and her skin prickled with anticipation. "How will she know the pleasure of a man's body pressed against hers?" A gentle pressure spread up her back and shoulders.

"How will she know the thrill of a well-tutored touch on her skin?" His hand settled on her shoulder and slowly followed the slope of it toward her neck.

"How will she know the ache of a need so deep that there are no words to describe it?" He ran his hand slowly up the side of her neck. A hot chill raced up her spine. Her responses weren't her own as she sank back against him. . . .

BANTAM BOOKS BY BETINA KRAHN

SWEET TALKING MAN

Betina Krahn

BANTAM BOOKS
NEW YORK · TORONTO · LONDON · SYDNEY · AUCKLAND

SWEET TALKING MAN

A Bantam Book / July 2000

ISBN 0-553-57619-4
Published simultaneously in the United States and Canada

Bantam Books are published by Bantam Books, a division of Random House, Inc. Its
trademark, consisting of the words "Bantam Books" and the portrayal of a rooster, is
Registered in U.S. Patent and Trademark Office and in other countries. Marca
Registrada. Bantam Books, 1540 Broadway, New York, New York 10036.

PRINTED IN THE UNITED STATES OF AMERICA

OPM   10   9   8   7   6   5   4   3   2   1

For
Nathan and Kristine.

May your love deepen
and grow richer
with each passing day.

SWEET TALKING MAN

ONE

New York, 1892

THE DARKNESS HAD become their friend. The deep purple of the late summer nights hid them in its shadows and muffled the rustle of her skirts, the scrape of his shoes on paving stones, and the pounding of their earnest hearts.

She found him in the sympathetic shadows of the arbor at the rear of the garden, waiting among lush cascades of gloriously overripe roses.

"Jeffrey?"

"Prissy . . . here!"

She located him, then paused to adore him with her eyes. Tall, fair, and undeniably handsome, he was everything a girl's heart could desire.

"I was afraid you wouldn't be able to come," he said in a tense rush, holding out his hands to draw her close.

"Nothing could have kept me from coming to you," she said, sinking against his shirtfront and sighing as his arms folded around her. "Even if she had locked me up, I still would have found a way."

"Locked you up?" Jeffrey gasped and pulled her tighter against him. "I wouldn't put it past her, the old witch. She's nothing short of a tyrant—ordering you about—forbidding us to—"

She reached up to stop his words with her fingertips. "Let's not waste precious time on my poor, wretched aunt. What could she possibly know of love? She's so old and lonely and miserable—she must be thirty years old. . . ."

"At least," he muttered.

She ran her hand reverently across his cheek.

"You are my whole world, Jeffrey."

"You are my moon and my stars, Prissy." He drew a deep breath to counter the constriction in his chest. She was so lovely. He felt a familiar ache begin deep in his loins and groaned softly. "Oh, if only we could marry, sweetness, and be together." He pulled her head against his shirt and closed his eyes. "Forever and ever."

"And ever," she echoed wistfully, closing her eyes as well.

"I would be able to touch your—hands—whenever I please, and hold you like this . . ." His more explicit longings were buried in a passionate kiss pressed on her cool, delicate fingers. "We're like Romeo and Juliet. Forbidden to love."

"And my parents, who were forbidden to love, too. *They* found a way." She lifted her head, her eyes shining. "We'll find a way, too, Jeffrey."

"Your parents?" Jeffrey set her back just enough to see her face clearly.

"My grandparents forbade their love, so they eloped

and fled to Italy." Her voice grew warm and impassioned. "My mother said that they lived as free as gypsies at first . . . on nothing but wine and love." She pushed back farther in his arms and her eyes lighted. "We could do that."

"What? Live on wine and love?"

"No. Elope, like my mother and father."

"Elope?" For a brief moment the possibility was tantalizing. Then a draft of reality blew through his heated senses. "And flee the country?"

"No, we wouldn't have to do that." Her face glowed as she envisioned it. "We could . . . stay with your family until we get a house of our own."

"With my mother?" He envisioned it and winced in spite of himself. "Mother would never countenance such a thing. I mean, she's always planned a huge, society wedding for me . . . it would break her heart if . . . no, no, it can't be an elopement."

"You wouldn't elope with me?" she asked, surprised by his reluctance.

"There's the future to think about." A trace of anxiety crept into his voice. "Elopements are terrible scandals. We have to think of something else."

"But what?" She made fists around handfuls of his sleeves. "We'll grow as old and decrepit as Aunt Beatrice if we wait for her to change her mind." Then she paused, caught by another idea. "Unless we change it for her."

"Change a Von Furstenberg's mind?" He snorted. "We'd have better luck jumping off the Brooklyn Bridge and trying to fly. She despises me, Prissy . . . she acts as if I'm still in short pants. When I asked my father to plead our case with her, she wouldn't even see him. Now he's afraid that if he pushes the matter . . ."

There was no need to describe his father's fears. They both knew that her aunt and guardian, Beatrice Von Furstenberg, could wield her money and power like a sword and mace.

"If she only knew you as I do . . . knew how generous and honorable and brilliant you are." She loosened her grip on his sleeves to caress the arms inside them and lowered her voice. "How manly and brave you can be." She studied his face in the dimness and felt a surge of defiant passion. "She must be made to see it. Jeffrey, we must show her that you are a man to be reckoned with . . . that despite your youth, you are a force in the world of men."

"And how do you propose that we do that?"

She scowled, thinking, and the logic became inescapable. "I suppose . . . she would have to see you doing something daring or courageous."

"Courageous? You mean like . . . fighting a duel or something? Saving you from a burning building? Fending off a band of robbers?"

"Exactly."

She beamed.

He stiffened.

"Dueling is against the law—not to mention deadly. It takes hook and ladder companies to battle fires. And robbers run in packs and carry *guns*."

"Well, if a building were on fire, you would rescue me, wouldn't you?"

He blinked. "O-Of course."

"Then that's what you have to do, 'rescue' me." Then her eyes flew wide with another burst of inspiration. "No! Even better—rescue *her*!"

"Rescue her?" He was truly horrified. "What would I rescue *her* from?"

"Jeffrey." She pulled away and crossed her arms.

"Be reasonable, Prissy. Where is your aunt likely to get caught in a burning building or be held up by a gang of thieves?"

"Well, I don't know, but . . ." Mounting frustration caused her to blurt out: "I bet it could be arranged."

His hands and his jaw both dropped. "Prissy! You want to arrange for your aunt to be set upon by some thieves and cutthroats . . . so I can rescue her?"

Phrased so bluntly, the idea set Priscilla back for a moment.

"It does sound a little crazy." Then her inherited determination asserted itself. "But think about it, Jeffrey. If you rescued her from danger, she would owe you a debt. And you know how fanatical she is about debts—paying them as well as collecting them. She would have to let us see each other. And once we've begun to court, I'm sure we could convince her to let us marry."

"But *thieves,* Prissy . . ."

Her gaze again swept that mental tableau and her fertile mind began to work again.

"Well, they wouldn't have to actually *be* thieves or cutthroats. Surely with all of your knowledge of gaming houses and manly pursuits, you could find some men who would *pretend* to rob her. We'd only need two or three."

He stared at her, finally grasping that she was serious. It was a mark of his respect for her quick wits that he actually considered the idea.

"It wouldn't be *real* danger, then." He rubbed his chin, wishing he was as adroit in assessing the potential pitfalls of the scheme as she was in spinning it.

"Of course not." A gleam appeared in her eye. "But Aunt Beatrice wouldn't know that. She would think you

were the most courageous young man she's ever met."
She fixed him with a somber look. "And she would never
again mention that wretched convent school in France."

"Convent school? In France?" He pulled her against
him and wrapped her in his arms. "But, I couldn't bear it
if she sent you away."

"I couldn't bear it either," she said with a sudden
catch in her voice. "I wouldn't want to go on if I had to
be parted from you."

For a few moments they clung fiercely to each other
in the light of the sympathetic moon. Then, when the
longing in his chest became too much, he cleared his
throat and spoke with reluctant resolve.

"All right, I'll do it."

"You will?" She looked up and wiped her wet cheeks.

"If you think it will change her mind about me, I will."
He took a deep breath and gazed off into the distance . . .
glimpsing the start of a plan. "I have a cousin—actually
it's my mother's cousin—who is Irish. He's in with all
sorts of lowlifes and riffraff. I'll talk to him. Maybe he
can find us a couple of men willing to be 'thieves' for a
few hours."

"Oh, Jeffrey, I just know you can do it." She threw her
arms around his neck and beamed. "You're the bravest,
smartest man in the world!"

IN A DARKENED window, far above the tryst in that
garden bower, a pair of eyes searched the couple's dim
outline, then darted uncomfortably to a ladies' brooch
watch, held out in the moonlight streaming through the
panes. A moment later, the couple broke apart and the
girl's pale figure darted back up the garden path toward
the terraces and house.

A heartbeat later, Beatrice Von Furstenberg joined her secretary at the window and squinted over her shoulder at the watch.

"How long this time?" she demanded.

"Just over ten minutes," Alice Henry replied, closing the watch and allowing the cord to rewind to her shoulder.

"Damn." Beatrice peered out the darkened window, following her secretary's pointing finger. "Each time they stretch the bounds of decency and my patience a little more. They think they're being so clever. I'd march down there and catch them red-handed, if I didn't think they'd just find a more devious way to meet and satisfy their rampaging urge for romance."

She kicked the train of her dress around, hiked her skirts, and sailed back down the hall.

"Damned nauseating adolescents. 'But we're in *lov-v-ve*, Aunt Beatrice,'" she muttered in falsetto. " 'But he's so *won-n-nderful*, Aunt Beatrice. He's so *smar-r-rt*, Aunt Beatrice. So *sen-n-nsitive* . . .'"

She paused at the top of the sweeping mahogany staircase of her grand country house, causing Alice to have to stop short to avoid bumping into her.

"He's a spoiled, overbred, pimple-faced moron," Beatrice declared hotly. "And eighteen." She continued on down the stairs, speaking partly to Alice, who hurried along beside her, and partly to her own conscience. "What the hell does he know about anything at *eighteen*?

"He hasn't a clue what life is about. Making your way in a tough and daunting world . . . pitting your wits, nerve, and stamina against the odds and opposition . . . that's what it's about. You have to be prepared to recognize every opportunity and seize every advantage. And perhaps—just perhaps—if you're very, very lucky, you'll be able to build something or change something for the better, and make a lasting mark on this world."

She realized she had paused again and was jabbing a finger at Alice . . . who was scowling and leaning back to avoid being poked. She reddened, jerked her hand to her side, and continued down the steps, muttering.

"What the devil would an eighteen-year-old boy know about such things?" Halfway down she paused again to clarify her course and justify her actions.

"And what does a sheltered sixteen-year-old girl know of the tests and obstacles life has in store? Or even of the responsibilities that a marriage would thrust upon her? Claiming a place in a large household, forging a place in society, dealing constantly with a husband's temperament, expectations, and demands. At seventeen, even *I* found it all—" She bit off the rest.

Crushing. She had found it all damned near obliterating. Even without the ever-present threat of childbed.

"The simple truth is that women have a hard time of it, even in the most affluent of households," she continued, starting down the steps again. "And they have damned few rights and privileges to compensate. The longer I can postpone the trials of marriage for Priscilla the better. Someday, when she is older and wiser, she will appreciate how I have protected her freedom."

By the time they reached the floor of the main hall, they could hear Priscilla running from the morning room, which faced the east terrace, into the drawing room. Beatrice planted herself between the drawing-room door and the staircase, folding her arms.

Priscilla entered the main hall gripping her fluttery silk organza skirts with both hands, and stopped dead at the sight of her aunt. Her face grew rosier and her lashes

lowered to hide the guilt and resentment in her huge
brown eyes.

"And just where have you been, young lady?" Beatrice
demanded.

"O-Out for a walk. I wanted to take a bit of fresh air
before retiring." Priscilla tensed, collecting herself behind her excuse.

Beatrice gave a tight smile. "You've become quite a
devotee of 'fresh air' in recent days."

" 'Fresh air and exercise are good for a young woman's
constitution,'" the girl countered. "Isn't that what *you* always say?"

Beatrice considered the rebellion involved in Priscilla
quoting her own words to her.

"Night air, however, can be downright dangerous."
Her expression took on a taut, clear warning. "I hear that
the air in *France* is quite healthful."

Priscilla's eyes flew wide. "I won't go. I won't be
shipped off to any old convent school in France. I'll fling
myself in the duck pond first!"

A potent threat indeed. The duck pond was all of
three feet deep.

"You will go where I send you, young lady," Beatrice
declared with determined calm. "And you will comport
yourself with decency, integrity, and whatever modicum
of intelligence you possess."

"Well, I won't go to France," Priscilla declared as
crimson edged into her face. "If you send me there, I'll—
I'll—run away and find my father. He would understand.
He would let me marry Jeffrey!"

"Marry? You are only *sixteen,* Priscilla." Beatrice was
quickly losing what was left of her sense of humor.

"You were sixteen when *you* were married," Priscilla
said, ignoring the glint in Beatrice's eyes.

Beatrice stepped closer to her young charge and lowered her voice to its most compelling register.

"I was married on my seventeenth birthday. *Not* by choice. I will not allow you to destroy your life by handing it over to a randy eighteen-year-old who hasn't a clue what to do with his own idle, overprivileged existence. I have told you: When you've learned who and what you are and have enough experience of the world to judge wisely, then and only then will I sanction a marriage for you." Her eyes now burned like bright stones. "If, after learning the ways of the world and of men, you still want to marry."

Some of the high color in Priscilla's face drained as she finally caught the reined anger in her aunt's response, and her brashness dissolved into a puddle of adolescent uncertainty. Her chin began to quiver and her voice grew constricted.

"But I love him, Aunt Beatrice." Tears collected once again in her dark eyes. "I will always love him. With all my heart. Nothing you make me do will ever, *e-e-ever* change that." Choking back a sob, she jerked up her skirts and dashed for the stairs.

Beatrice watched her charge fly from her, up the steps. When a far off door slammed, she closed her eyes and tried to scour her niece's youthful passion from her mind. For an instant, she had glimpsed in Priscilla's big brown eyes—so very like her beloved sister's—the pain of longing. Real pain. Real longing. For one moment, Beatrice allowed a part of her pragmatic heart to open to that raw emotion. What if she were wrong? What if this truly were Priscilla's best chance for happi—

She caught herself and looked up to find Alice watching her with a discerning eye.

"Let me guess," Alice said. "We're heading back to the city."

"Clever woman. Have I given you a raise, lately?"

"Just last month."

"Well, put yourself down for another." Beatrice kicked her bustle train out of the way yet again and headed for her library. "And have Williams bring up the trunks straightaway. I have to be back in the city in a few days anyway to review Consolidated's quarterly report before it goes to press and to attend the suffrage association executive committee meeting. We'll leave first thing tomorrow morning. I want to be well away from moonlit gardens and back on Fifth Avenue by this time tomorrow night."

Throwing open the library door, she flicked on the electrical light and went straight to her desk, with its neat piles of documents, stacks of ledgers, and legal folios. Staring down at those reassuring reams and sheaves of paper, her gaze fell on the pamphlet she had been composing for the National American Woman Suffrage Association, and she felt her inner calm returning. This was *her* realm, her dream, the mark she would someday leave on the world.

"*Love*," she muttered as she began to collect and pack the documents. "What has that got to do with anything?"

TWO

EVERYONE IN NEW York knew that if they wanted to find someone Irish in the city, O'Toole's was the place to go.

The restaurant, located in the middle of the city's sprawling Eighteenth Precinct, was one of three places where the burgeoning Irish community and rising political power met. Sooner or later every former resident of County Cork who landed in New York walked through those heavy glass and mahogany doors, stood on that checkered marble floor, and marveled at the polished wooden paneling, the giant gilt-framed mirror over the bar, and the heights to which an Irishman in America could aspire.

Seated around the remains of a hearty dinner that night, at the rear of the dining room, were a half dozen men who by virtue of moxy or muscle had burrowed deep into the marrow of the city . . . so deep, in fact, that their Irish organization "Tammany Hall" had become synonymous with city hall.

Each man there had worked his way up the ladder of

Tammany's political organization, from "precinct runner" to "ward heeler," to minor city official to officeholder. And it was that record of achievement that entitled them to be present for the election campaign strategy session now in progress.

"It's set then, lads," declared the barrel-chested leader, Richard Croker. The Tammany Hall boss removed the cigar from his mouth and tossed back a healthy draft of brandy. "We'll have a round of debates with th' reform party's 'willie.' Murphy and McFadden, here"—he gestured to his two handpicked under-bosses—"will make sure the crowds are proper friendly. And we'll pass the word to our friends in the papers, suggestin' they'd be showin' a bit of foresight if they was to declare our boy the winner early on." He paused to smile at their youngest member. "Not that you'll be needin' much help with the papers, Connor lad. Not a word drips from your lips that isn't just beggin' fer print."

Connor Sullivan Barrow smiled back. It was a bold slash of a grin containing a bit of rakishness, a bundle of charm, and an unmistakable bit of invitation. Its effect on the men seated around him was immediate. Nods and approving winks appeared as the election committee congratulated themselves on their candidate's appeal.

"I hear the reformers may bring in William Jennings Bryan to campaign for Netherton," Connor said.

"Doesn't matter who they bring in." The boss clamped down on his cigar. "The voters get one look at that sweet Irish mug of yours, my boy, and you'll be sittin' under a landslide."

There was a murmur of agreement.

"A pity th' women ain't got the vote," declared a wavery voice from the rear of the table. "We could schweep ever' ward in th'—"

The political planners turned on the speaker with looks that ranged from mild disgust to out-and-out horror. The well-lubricated alderman pulled in his chin, blinked, and then had the grace to be appalled by what he'd said. After a moment, the others mercifully allowed him to sink back into oblivion.

"Give the women the vote," Croker muttered in disbelief. That had to be the whiskey talking. No man in his right mind believed in females voting. Not even the reform-minded *one-man-one-vote* mongers.

Then he turned to underboss Charles Murphy, on his left. "See to it. Set it up. I'm puttin' you in charge, Murphy. I've got my hands full runnin' Gilroy's campaign for mayor."

"Excuse th' interruption, Mr. Croker," a voice inserted, causing all present at the table to turn. "But, the lad here's been waiting for a spell." It was one of the Fourth Ward's burly heelers holding a tense-looking young man by the arm.

"We got business." Croker turned back to the others. "He'll have to come by city hall tomorrow mornin'."

The petitioner wrung his frayed tweed cap and looked a bit frantic as the heeler dismissed him with a jerk of the head.

"Wait." Connor examined the young man's weedy frame, thinking that he was much too young to have shoulders so rounded. There were only two things that weighed that heavily on a man: sorrow and responsibility. "What's your name, my friend?"

"Grady, sir. Thomas Grady."

Connor cocked his head to eye the young man at a slant. "Any relation to a fellow named Mick Grady over in Firth Alley?"

"My pa," the young man said, straightening his spine.

"He died Tuesd'y last. That's how come I need a better job. Ma's got six little ones still at home an' my wife . . ." He looked down and twisted his cap. "She be carryin' our first."

He scarcely looked old enough to be married, much less to have been thrust into the role of breadwinner for two households. Sorrow *and* responsibility. A deadly combination.

"I knew your pa," Connor said, his voice taking on a bit of a lilt. "A fine, solid block of Cork stone he was. Could lay brick from dawn to dusk and then tell ye stories all the way to sunup." The pride that mingled with wary hope in the young man's eyes was wrenching. "A loyal supporter of Tammany, too. I heard he voted for Mayor Grant in the last election . . . *twenty-eight times!*"

The others hooted with laughter while the young man reddened and grinned shyly.

"Then by all means, lad, we must see to your problem," Croker said, wiping his eyes.

Connor sat back and watched with a smile as the young man was given the name of a builder who had just received a sweetheart of a contract for some waterworks.

This was the true business of government. This was the way things truly got done. The people elected the men of Tammany Hall to provide for them and provide they did: public works, public safety, public services, jobs, and sometimes even the bare necessities of life. It was the system within the system, the informal agreements and tacit cooperation that kept the city—the entire state—running like a well-oiled machine. And that was precisely what the muckraking journalists and fiery-eyed reformers called it: *machine politics*.

Soon they were interrupted by another petitioner, another young man. But, unlike Thomas Grady, this one was dressed in the height of fashion: black-tie evening clothes with an ivory silk scarf hanging around his neck.

"Which of you gentlemen is Connor Barrow?" The young fellow's voice was barely a few years removed from a soprano.

"I am." Connor turned in his chair to face him. "Who is asking?"

"Your cousin, sir. I am the son of Alicia Barrow Granton . . . Jeffrey Granton."

Connor straightened. The boy clearly expected the name to work some sort of magic and it did. The sound of it, pronounced in those aristocratic tones—*Baaarrrow*—was enough to capture Connor's undivided attention. No Barrow had claimed him as kin or contacted him in ten years; not since his wealthy grandfather disowned and disinherited him. Since then, he'd been a Sullivan in all but legal surname, and even that residual bit of "Barrow" was omitted on occasion, depending on his audience.

Now the Barrow side was reaching out to him in the person of this green kid, who was at the moment sizing him up with what Connor recognized as the fabled Barrow squint. That expression, perfected by his iron-willed grandfather, was seen by the rest of the world as evidence of great sagacity and superiority, when in fact, it was simply the result of the Barrows' dogged refusal to wear spectacles, no matter how poor their eyesight.

"What can I do for you?" Connor asked.

"I would like a few minutes of your time," Jeffrey Granton said, looking defensively at the others. "In private."

Connor very nearly told him to get lost. Curiosity, however, got the better of him. He rose and waved the young man over to an unoccupied table in the corner.

As they settled into chairs opposite each other, he realized the boy was younger than he had first supposed. There was a fine blond fuzz on his upper lip.

"Something to drink?" Connor asked, beckoning to an apron-clad waiter.

"No . . . thank you."

Apparently Jeffrey wasn't a shaving man or a drinking man.

"How is your mother? I haven't seen her in—oh—ten years at least."

"She is fine." The youth tugged at his collar as if the mention of his mother had somehow made it contract. "Busy. Her charities, you know." Connor didn't know, but it made sense. All women of social standing had *charities*. "She's taking my sister on a tour of the capitals this fall. London in September, Paris in October, and November in Venice, of course."

Connor smiled. It had been years since anyone from society's vaunted Four Hundred had "of coursed" him. The kid was buttering him up.

"What can I do for you, Jeffrey Granton?"

"I've come to ask . . . to see if you can put me in touch with some people who might be willing to . . . um . . . work for me."

"Work?" Connor frowned. "You're in business?"

"Well, it's not so much *work* as it is"—Jeffrey squirmed—"a *job*."

"A job," Connor mused, taking in the boy's guilty flush. "And you've come to me because . . ."

"You know people. And I need a certain sort of man for this job. Someone with experience . . . and . . ."

"Muscle," Connor offered.

The youth wilted slightly. "Yes. And a bit of . . ."

"Daring?"

"Exactly."

Connor stiffened. It was now clear why the kid had sought out the Barrows' black sheep. He needed help with something dangerous, disreputable, or at the very least, distasteful. He was tempted to tell Precious Jeffrey what he could do with his dirty little "job." But curiosity again got the better of him.

"What kind of trouble are you in?" he demanded. "Gambling debts? An insult that cannot go unanswered? A servant girl in the family way?"

"Nothing like that!" Jeffrey's voice cracked. "It's just . . . a romantic matter."

"Romantic?" Connor nearly choked on the word. It was so improbable it just might be true.

"The young lady and I wish to marry, but there is some interference." Jeffrey lowered his voice. "I simply wish to . . . to . . ." He paused as if gathering the courage to say it.

"Elope."

Jeffrey's eyes widened then, after a moment, he nodded again.

"Yes, that's it. I have to elope."

Connor studied him, deciding that the situation must be desperate indeed for the youth to risk approaching a scapegrace of a cousin he'd never laid eyes on.

"There must be at least a dozen ways to arrange an elopement, none of which involve burly henchmen." Unless the "delicate situation" involved more than just the garden variety of parental disapproval, he realized. "Who is this young lady you have your heart set on?"

Jeffrey looked away. "Someone from a wealthy and powerful family."

"*Your* family is wealthy and powerful," Connor observed.

"Yes, but . . . she is young."

"How young?"

"Sixteen."

Connor drew a deep breath and contained his urge to bolt from the chair. Sixteen. What the devil was he doing listening to this? He was running for the United States Congress, for God's sake. But the blend of longing and desperation in the boy's expression took on a strangely poignant appeal, and he couldn't seem to raise himself out of the seat.

"You can't be much older than that."

"Old enough." Jeffrey sat straighter and squared his shoulders. When Connor narrowed his eyes, the boy declared: "Eighteen is plenty old enough." With a stroke of defiance, he added: "*Irish* marry at eighteen all the time."

Unbidden, the memory of Thomas Grady materialized in Connor's mind. The young Irish lad was scarcely older than Jeffrey here, and was already a father-to-be and a breadwinner burdened with eight hungry mouths to feed. Precious Jeffrey had no idea what responsibility was. Well, it might do him good to find out, starting with this marriage he was so dead set on plunging into.

"Is she that special?" Connor asked. Instantly, the youth grew so earnest and impassioned that Connor felt a surprising pang of guilt.

"She is the moon and the stars to me. She is so lovely and bright—if they send her to that convent school in France my life is over."

"I see." And against his better judgment, Connor remembered as well. It had been years since he had felt such fervent and all-possessing . . . That twinge in his chest, he realized irritably, was some part envy. "I take it she reciprocates."

Jeffrey's manly resolve dissolved.

"I am her moon, too."

It was all Connor could do to keep from groaning aloud.

"Then, by all means, we must do what we can to get your blessed 'moons' together."

"You mean it? You'll help me?"

"I'd be pleased to help a fellow 'romantic' achieve the goal of his heart." Connor looked to the tavern side and down the long, polished bar, where men with drink-reddened faces and arms too big for their sleeves were playing darts.

"Well"—Jeffrey sat forward—"I have a plan that—"

"No, no." Connor raised a restraining hand. "Don't tell me. It's not wise for too many people to be privy to such a plan." Much less, people who are running for national office. "I'll put you in touch with some fellows and you take it from there." He again scrutinized the men at the far end of the bar. "What you need is somebody with plenty of muscle and a dearth of ideas." His mouth quirked up. "Too much thinking can ruin a perfectly good elopement."

He spotted, in a far corner of the tavern side, two men who seldom showed their faces in O'Toole's. They generally frequented places where the lighting was as bad as the whiskey and a man could go largely unrecognized. Dipper Muldoon and Shorty O'Shea weren't bad fellows; just a bit too fond of drink and too unlucky at dice.

"I'll put you in touch with two fellows. The rest is up to you."

It was very simple, really, Connor thought as he sent Jeffrey out the side door to wait for Dipper and Shorty. Sooner or later everybody had a need they couldn't fill for themselves, even society's almighty Four Hundred. It was then that they turned to government. To the well-oiled machine of Tammany Hall. To him.

His famously effective grin reappeared as he sent a waiter to fetch Dipper and Shorty to his table.

It was always a pleasure to be of service to the people.

THREE

ONE WEEK AFTER her arrival in the city, Beatrice
Von Furstenberg was again hurrying . . . this time down
the stairs from an upper-level meeting room at the ven-
erable Osterman Hall. Around her the members of the
Executive Committee of the National American Woman
Suffrage Association were arguing in muted, ladylike
voices and fierce whispers, carrying the heated discussion of their recently adjourned meeting down the steps
and out into the street.

Once again the women of the organization had refused to acknowledge a simple political reality: that securing the vote for women meant moving *men* to action.
And motivating men with the power to make things happen would require that suffragists use the same tools as
men: money, coercion, and compromise. When Beatrice
pointed this out, the reaction had been heated.

In the ensuing chaos, the NAWSA's leaders,
Elizabeth Cady Stanton and Susan B. Anthony, declared
that they would never stoop to "unsavory male practices

of persuasion." Deal-making and vote-buying would reduce them to little more than "men in skirts."

As Beatrice donned her gloves and manteau and exited the first-floor cloakroom, Lacey Waterman, a liberal-minded socialite and Beatrice's longtime friend, fell in beside her with a grim expression.

"You tried, Beatrice. God knows you tried," Lacey said, jerking on her gloves. "They're determined to march into obscurity with their heads held high."

"Hell-bent on being rational and noble minded and utterly doomed to failure," Beatrice responded as they stepped out onto the pavement in front of the meeting hall.

"I still say we should publish the names of their light-skirts in the newspapers," said wiry, frizzy-haired Frannie Excelsior, the resident civil agitator on the committee. "Or chain ourselves to their office doors until they agree to vote for suffrage. Or march arm in arm—*buck naked*—down Fifth Avenue!"

Beatrice couldn't help a wry laugh. As she gave Frannie a one-armed hug, she caught sight of the graying, rail-thin Susan Anthony behind them, descending the stairs amidst a covey of matronly activists.

"Most of the committee don't have a clue what they're up against," she said with frustration. "But, you'd think Susan would know. After all these years, she *has* to know."

After all these years. As Beatrice climbed into her coach and settled back into the seat, the words haunted her. It had been over forty years since the convention at Seneca Falls, and what did women's rights advocates have to show for all their hard work? Mostly fatigue, tears, and broken promises. It was a wonder that the older campaigners like Susan Anthony and Elizabeth Cady Stanton had the will to keep going after so many disappointments.

She was right, Beatrice told herself. The leadership just didn't want to face it. Truth be told, who could blame them? Who would welcome the difficult conclusion that all men had their price and were motivated primarily by self-interest. She certainly hadn't wanted to believe it.

Married off to the wealthy Mercer Von Furstenberg at such a young age, she hadn't known what to think of men, even her own father. She had been raised by a governess and then disposed of as a family asset before she had a chance to form opinions on much of anything.

Seventeen years old on her wedding day, she had been little more than a curiosity in her husband's house for the first year. She was largely ignored by her aging husband, who had no idea what to do with a nubile young wife once he acquired one. And she was superfluous to a household that ran like a well-tended clock. The staff weren't intentionally thoughtless or cruel; they simply didn't think of her as someone who needed to be considered. In that, they merely followed the lead of their employer, who treated her as a lovely thing that provided him a primarily aesthetic pleasure whenever he thought to take it down from the shelf.

What engrossed her husband, she soon discovered, was his businesses. Acquisitions, mergers, closing deals, putting one over on the competition, finagling a bit of legislation . . . those were the things that made his aging heart race. It was only when she began to show interest in his businesses that he began, with wry surprise, to take more than a dim and confusing carnal interest in her.

She had gradually become more a pupil than a wife to him. And it wasn't until she turned her first thousand in profit from a stock transaction that he began to regularly take meals with her and to introduce her to his skeptical peers.

Over the seven years of their marriage, she acquired quite an education in both business and men. She came to understand their motives, their thinking, and even— she winced to admit—many of their attitudes toward women. She had also come to understand that unless the women of the suffrage movement were content to wait another fifty or seventy-five years for access to the ballot box, they were going to have to change their tactics.

What the movement needed were a few politicians in its pocket: men who could be persuaded by a satisfying "exchange of interest" to support women's suffrage. And what the executive committee needed was a demonstration of the practical acquisition of influence and power.

She burrowed back into the seat as a light appeared in her eyes.

They needed a politician in their pocket.

Well, why didn't she just buy them one?

BEATRICE WAS SO absorbed in her thoughts that it took her a few moments to realize that the carriage had come to a halt. Looking at the window, she saw nothing but darkness outside. That in itself was not unusual. Many of the main thoroughfares were undergoing electrification, and there were frequent interruptions of lighting during the changeover.

There was a thud outside and the coach swayed heavily, as if Rukart, her German-born driver, had just climbed down from his seat. After a moment, she heard voices outside and tried to make out what was being said. Nothing in the short bursts of verbiage seemed to resonate with Rukart's rich Teutonic bass. She pressed her forehead against the glass of the window to see what was happening.

Two dark shapes hovered near the horses, but she couldn't hear what was being said. She sat back for a moment, frowning. What was happening?

Accustomed to taking situations in hand, she seized the brass handle and pushed open the door. Two startled male faces drew back to avoid the swinging door. Their gasp of surprise equaled hers.

"What's going on?" She looked the men over in a glance, finding them to be thickset and roughly clad . . . nothing remarkable or worrisome.

"Nothin,' ma'am." When the one who spoke received an elbow in the ribs, he muttered, "Well—he ain't here yet."

"Where is my driver?"

"Ummm . . ."

"Well . . . he's . . . he's . . ."

The pair glanced anxiously at each another.

When she grabbed the edge of the door and ducked out onto the step, she spotted Rukart sprawled against a nearby wall with his chin on his chest.

"What on earth?" She looked back at the pair with a dawning awareness of peril. She called to Rukart over their heads, but he didn't respond. "What have you done to him?"

"He ain't hurt bad," one said, pulling his chin back and glowering at her.

"Hand over yer val-u-ables, ma'am," the other

demanded, extending his hand and lowering his voice mid-threat. "An' you won't get hurt neither."

"Get away from me," she ordered, her anxiety rising as she tried to step down from the coach and found the way blocked. She froze. Her coach had been waylaid, her driver rendered senseless . . . and she was being *held up*!

"We said, 'give us yer val-u-ables' an' . . . an' . . ."

"We mean it," the other one finished for him, glancing nervously at the end of the alley, where increased light from the main street warned of increased traffic and the threat of discovery. "You best hand 'em over, ma'am."

"Never!" Someone else seemed to be in control of her as she clasped her purse to her breast with both hands . . . bringing it straight into their view.

"Don't make us get ugly," one warned, bringing a club from behind him.

"I think someone's already beaten me to that," she blurted out, dismayed by her own defiance.

One of them grabbed for her purse, growling "Gimme that." She jerked it back, lost her footing on the narrow step and fell . . . straight into the hands of the other one.

"No! Let me go—" She twisted and shoved, trying to steady and then free herself. But, between the two robbers, she was soon overwhelmed. She panicked at the feel of their hands on her and did something she had never done in her entire life . . . gasped for air and screamed for all she was worth.

The earsplitting sound galvanized the pair of thieves. One cinched both arms around her, pinning her arms to her sides while the other clamped a hand tight across her mouth, and both began to shush her like a pair of steam boilers that had sprung leaks.

"Shhhhh! Don't scream—"

"Shhhh—hush lady—we ain't gonna hurt ye none—honest!"

Above the scuffling and muffled screams, there came the clear, piercing sound of a whistle in the distance. Her attackers froze and looked at each other in horror. The whistle sounded again. Louder.

"Coppers!"

They panicked, dragging her first one way and then another.

"This way—over here!" one rasped out, pointing behind the coach.

"No—no—they'll see us over there—this way!"

The one with his arms around her dragged her farther down the alley, while the one covering her mouth scrambled to keep up. They spotted a small footpath between two buildings and headed for it, glancing over their shoulders. When her resistance slowed them down, one took out a handkerchief and stuffed it in her mouth . . . not, however, before she got out a "He-elp—help me!"

The pair hesitated, listening. Heavy footsteps echoed down the brick-lined alley toward the carriage and then halted, followed by several shrill blasts from a police whistle.

"Dipper, they found th' coach an' driver."

Beatrice stilled for a moment, trying to hear above the sound of their panting and of her blood rushing in her ears. She focused desperately on the end of the narrow passage between buildings, praying for a glimpse of a dome-shaped policeman's hat.

"Aghhh!" gasped the one holding her, as the sound of footsteps and voices grew louder. "They're comin' this way!"

She was suddenly frantic to make noise—anything that would draw notice. She began to stomp her feet on the pavement and to try to call out through the cloth in her mouth.

"Hush, woman"—one slapped his hand over her mouth again and whispered frantically— "we won't hurt you!" In the next instant, she was being hauled by shoulders and feet, like an uncooperative hammock, back through the foot alley and into a niche in the brickwork.

The sounds coming from behind them suggested the police were hot on their trail, and the pair began to panic. Between puffs and stifled groans, they hauled her back out into the alley, retreating from one darkened doorway to another, pausing only to listen and then lurch, wide-eyed, into desperate flight again. It was during one of those stops that the one carrying the majority of her weight ordered the other to take off his belt and bind her hands. She fought as best she could, but breathless, frantic, and disoriented, she soon found her hands bound in front of her. A moment later she was slung, bottom up, over a brawny shoulder.

The pause had cost her abductors dearly. Fatigue and the sounds of pursuit both closed in on them. "We gotta run for it!" the one in charge ordered. They hadn't gone a dozen jarring strides when the one carrying her stopped abruptly.

"My pants!" he gasped out and she managed, through the red flooding her gaze to realized that his trousers had slid enough to bare a decrepit expanse of underwear.

"Damnation!" The other one rushed back to jerk up his partner's pants and then drag him around a bit of wooden fence. As they panted for breath and peered around the fence, checking their pursuers' progress, the leader declared, "We got to get rid o' her."

The one carrying her made to shift her from his shoulders, but was stopped. "No, ye ninny—we got to stash 'er somewheres—till we can get 'er rescued. We'll never get paid if she ain't 'rescued.'"

"Where, Dipper?" Shorty O'Shea whispered, straining under her weight.

Dipper Muldoon, the brains of the pair, rubbed the wheat-colored stubble that covered his chin. If only their fancy employer had put in his "heroic" appearance like he was supposed to . . . He stuck his head around the corner, pulled it back, then stuck it out again to stare at something he glimpsed at the end of the alley. His face lit with inspiration.

"I know where we'll stash 'er. Come on." He dragged his partner by the arm toward the end of the alley and a well-paved street in the more fashionable part of Manhattan. They paused in the shadows, staring at the glow coming from a grand-looking house across the way and at the well-dressed men coming and going from it.

"That's the only place in th' city where another woman screamin' won't matter!"

SOON DIPPER AND Shorty were in the Barrel & Shamrock, a tavern on the Lower East Side, bracing themselves with shots of whiskey chased with pints of dark ale as they tried to figure out what their next move should be.

They didn't have the name or address of their employer, had no idea who they had just abducted, and were only now realizing that at this rate, they might never get paid for the job. Things took another drastic turn for the worse when Shorty looked up and saw a face that made the blood freeze in his veins. He elbowed Dipper and pointed. Dipper's throat closed midswallow.

Across the smoky, gas-lit tavern stood Black Terrence Hoolihan . . . so called for the black armband he habitually wore, a reminder of the wives he'd sent into mourning during his career as a cardsharp, bet maker, and high-risk financier. Gaunt, narrow-eyed Terrence and his pair of beefy escorts stood blocking the door, surveying the evening's crowd for delinquent debtors. And chief on his list of blokes due for a bit of anatomical rearrangement were Dipper Muldoon and Shorty O'Shea.

Fortunately, they had spotted him first and were already headed for the alley door when one of his henchmen noticed them.

"Hey you—Muldoon! It's Muldoon and O'Shea!"

Dipper and Shorty lunged for the door and burst out the back of the Barrel & Shamrock just seconds ahead of Black Terrence's men. As they ran pell-mell down the alley, Shorty was frantically invoking every Irish saint on the books and one of them must have responded. A beer wagon came rumbling into the alley between them and their pursuers. While Hoolihan's men cursed and resorted to climbing over the wagon, Dipper and Shorty made it to the end of the alley and took off across a narrow square teeming with sailors on leave and women and barkers touting fleshly wares.

"We gotta lay low!" Dipper yelled as he ran.

"But wot about '*er*?" Shorty panted, trying desperately to keep up. "An' wot about our money?"

Dipper cast a frantic look over his shoulder and

spotted Hoolihan's bone breakers emerging from the alley and searching through the crowd behind them. Now was no time to worry about the pesky details of a make-believe robbery gone wrong!

"She'll just 'ave to fend fer herself!"

FOUR

JEFFREY GRANTON ARRIVED half an hour late and one alley off target for his date with heroism. Alarmed by the empty pavement, he charged back out to the street and caught the sound of voices coming from the next alley. He sucked a deep breath and rushed to the rescue. But instead of a quivering woman being menaced by two burly "thieves," he found an empty coach and groggy driver who was being questioned earnestly by a pair of uniformed policemen.

Police!

"Dear God," he breathed, jerking back around the corner and shutting his eyes as if hoping to erase the sight. But when he turned to look again, the coach was still empty and one of the policemen spotted him peering down the alley.

"Hey—you!"

In the moment it took for Jeffrey to decide whether or not to flee, the policeman had covered much of the distance between them and running would have done him no good. He managed to exhibit a bit of composure and

demanded to know what was happening. A woman had
been abducted, he was informed. A Mrs. Von Furstenberg. His shock was so obvious that the officer glowered
and asked him what was wrong.

"I—I know Mrs. Von Furstenberg," he responded,
with genuine horror.

The minute they dismissed him, he headed straight
for Fifth Avenue and the kitchen door of the Von
Furstenberg mansion.

With the help of a kitchen maid who had assisted
their clandestine meetings before, he sent word to
Priscilla to meet him in the butler's pantry. She arrived
flushed with excitement.

"Your aunt"—he grabbed her by the shoulders—"she's
gone!"

"You mean she's late coming home from her meeting.
You should know, silly. You—"

"No, I mean she's *gone!*" His fingers dug into her upper arms.

"What do you mean 'gone'? What happened? Wasn't
she there?" Even in the dimness of the pantry she could
see that he was pale and his eyes had a feverish quality.

"It all went wrong—everything. I was a little late getting there and when I arrived—"

"You were late?"

"I couldn't help it." He released her and turned aside,
stewing in humiliation and guilt. "My mother caught me
on the way out the door and made me sit down and . . .
have a sherry with . . . her dinner guests."

"Your mother?" She shook her head in disbelief. "You
mean you just sat there with your mother's guests while
you were supposed to be . . . while my poor aunt was
being . . ."

"Abducted," he said hoarsely. "When I got there she was gone. Rukart had been knocked senseless, and the *police* were there. They questioned me!"

"The police? You didn't tell them any—" Her eyes widened as the full impact of what he'd said registered. "Abducted? You mean those men *took* her somewhere? Jeffrey, you have to go and get her back—right now!"

"I can't."

"But you have to!" She tried to shove him toward the door.

"I don't know where she is," he blurted out. "I don't have a clue where they might be—I barely even know their names."

She stared at him, praying that he would burst out laughing and tell her he was joking. When he didn't, she began to tremble. *They had taken her . . . he didn't know where she was . . .*

"She's been *kidnapped*," she whispered, horror mounting. "Jeffrey—you have to do something."

"Yes, but what?"

"You have to find her . . . get her back!"

"But I told you—I haven't a clue where they might be."

"Well, there has to be some way you can locate them. Where did you find these awful men in the first place?"

"My cousin put me on to them," he said miserably. "I should have known that no good would come from getting involved with him and his Irish mob."

"Then that's where you have to go. Your cousin—he must know how to find them—maybe even where they've taken Aunt Beatrice." She pushed him toward the door. "Go and see your wretched old cousin. He arranged the entire thing—*he's* the one responsible for this mess. Make *him* find my poor aunt!"

CONNOR KNEW THE minute he saw Jeffrey Granton standing in the entry of O'Toole's, that something had gone wrong.

He had just concluded a strategy session over dinner with underboss Charles Murphy and the boys from Tammany Hall. He had been looking forward to calling it an evening and heading home. But there was no avoiding his red-faced cousin.

"Cousin Connor!" Jeffrey called out, hurrying toward him.

Connor rose quickly and steered the youth through a draped rear door. Once in the hallway, out of sight of prying eyes, Jeffrey turned and grabbed his sleeve.

"You've got to help me. It's all gone wrong—she's missing—and I've got to find those two lunkheads you hooked me up with before it's too—"

"Slow down. What do you mean? Your bride is missing?"

Jeffrey winced. "Not my bride. Her aunt."

"Her aunt? Dipper and Shorty brought you the wrong bride?"

"No—they were supposed to rob her and I was supposed to happen along—only my mother made me have a sherry with her whist club and I was late. When I got there the carriage was empty and the police were there—and I've got to get her back before—"

"Police? Your bride's family sent police after you?" Connor scowled.

"I don't *have* a bride," Jeffrey blurted out. "I'm not eloping—I never was eloping."

"You weren't?" Connor braced, seeing in Jeffrey's anguish something far more serious than mere matrimonial passion run amok. "Dammit!" He'd had a bad feeling about this mess at the beginning and had overridden his own good sense to help the kid—no, if truth be told, to teach him a lesson. "Then just what the bloody hell were you doing?"

Jeffrey looked down. He was having trouble swallowing. Red crept into his ears.

"Pro-o-o"—his voice cracked and he had to clear his throat—"proving how grown up and capable I am."

Connor bit his lip to keep back an involuntary hoot of laughter.

"And how does hiring two thugs to—" He sobered abruptly. "Just what the hell were they supposed to do?"

"Pretend to rob my fiancée's stubborn old aunt." Jeffrey couldn't meet his cousin's incredulous stare. "I was supposed to happen along and . . . rescue her . . . to show her how brave and manly . . ."

"Of all the stupid . . . the same stubborn old aunt who disapproves of you romancing her niece, I assume," Connor said, recalling the reason Jeffrey had given for taking such drastic action in the first place. The girl's family was wealthy and powerful. The turmoil in his stomach began spreading to his chest. "Whatever possessed you to come up with such a harebrained scheme?"

"I didn't!" Jeffrey protested. "It was Priscilla—she made me do it."

Connor ran a hand through his hair. He was embroiled in a plot hatched by a love-struck sixteen-year-old chit and bungled by an eighteen-year-old clot who tripped over his own ballocks and was just too gullible to live.

"Who is she—this 'Priscilla,' who beguiled you out of

every shred of your common sense?" When the boy drew
back and looked uncertain whether he should divulge
such a weighty secret, it was all Connor could do to keep
from strangling him. *"Who the bloody hell is she?"* he
roared.

"Priscilla Lucciano," Jeffrey whispered.

Connor found his anger oddly cheated. Not an Astor,
a Vanderbilt, a Morgan, or a Cabot. A Lucciano? What
the hell was a "Lucciano"?

"Never heard of 'em," Connor was relieved to be able
to say.

Jeffrey took his reaction as something of an insult.

"Her aunt is *Beatrice Von Furstenberg*."

There it was; the kick in the gut Connor had dreaded.
Beatrice Von Furstenberg. To describe her as rich would
be a gross understatement. In wealth she was right up
there with the Morgans and Astors! He scratched his
head, trying to recall what he'd heard—other than the
fact that she was old Mercer Von Furstenberg's widow
and that she was reported to have improved upon his already shrewd business practices.

"Dear God." It was something of a prayer. Only divine
intervention could save them now. "You sent Dipper and
Shorty to pretend to rob Beatrice Von Furstenberg . . . so
you could impress her by rescuing her?"

The boy nodded.

"But now she's *gone?*"

His nodding became desperate. "They must have
taken her somewhere. You've got to help me find out
what they did with her and get her back."

Connor stared at his young cousin, putting one and
one and one together and coming up with "catastrophe
on the way."

"You're a lunatic, Jeffrey Granton. And a doomed one. Condolences to your dear mother on your upcoming demise."

He turned on his heel and was at the door to the main dining room before Jeffrey realized he was being abandoned.

"Wait—stop! You have to help me!"

Connor paused and looked over his shoulder. "You got yourself into this, Granton. Prove just how 'capable' and 'manly' you really are . . . get yourself *out* of it."

"B-But you can't just leave me—leave her—"

"Watch me." Connor turned and parted the curtain that covered the doorway.

"I'll tell mother!" Jeffrey said, lurching after Connor. "I'll tell the police! I'll tell them it was all *your* fault!"

Connor froze. Police. He had forgotten about them. The implications of legal involvement now struck him forcefully. Jesus, Mary, and Joseph—if he didn't do something the damage would just keep spreading!

He turned back, sorely tempted to thrash Precious Jeffrey within an inch of his worthless, overindulged life. Not a jury in the world would convict him. But on second thought . . . a trial for assault, following allegations that he had helped kidnap one of the wealthiest women in New York, could conceivably dim his chances for election to Congress. . . .

Then he caught the quiver in the boy's chin. Precious Jeffrey was trembling all over. Manfully blinking back tears. He was terrified.

"Dammit," Connor muttered. The kid had landed them both down a privy hole and *he* was going to have to get them out. He'd have to find old Mrs. Von Furstenberg and see that she was returned home safely . . . without revealing Jeffrey's ridiculous plot and his own boneheaded participation in it. First, he had to find those idiots Dipper and Shorty. . . .

He stalked back to an office door, shoved it open, and ordered Jeffrey inside with a furious gesture.

"Get in there and wait—no matter how long it takes."

"But I have to be home soon. Mother will expect—"

The I'm-a-heartbeat-away-from-murder look on Connor's face apparently made Jeffrey reconsider his priorities. Now seemed to be as good a time as any to start acting like a man. He stepped inside the office, but panicked one last time when Connor started to shut the door.

"Wait—what are you going to do?"

"Locate your victim," Connor declared furiously, "and save your worthless hide."

FIVE

BEATRICE HAD LOST all sense of time and location. Shushed and trussed and upended over a shoulder for what seemed an eternity, it was all she could do to simply continue breathing. Blood had pooled in her head, and her hands and arms were going numb. Worse yet, the gag had wicked up every drop of moisture in her mouth and she was half crazed with thrist. By the time her kidnappers carried her into a building of some sort, she was in no condition to resist.

She blinked against the gaslight of a hallway filled with foreign smells . . . a strange perfume . . . expensive floral covering an earthy musk mingled with cigar smoke. A woman's voice directed her kidnappers and they labored up a set of steps with her, then down a dim hallway lined with flocked red wallpaper, heavy gilt-framed paintings, and doors . . . lots of doors. At the end of the hallway, they trudged up another set of stairs—narrower, with two landings.

It was on one of these landings that they paused to

tie her feet together and she caught a glimpse of the woman in charge. She could have sworn the creature was wearing nothing but a corset, silk stockings, and a shawl.

Moments later she was trundled through a narrow doorway, heaved onto a bed, and left without light or explanation. At least the bed was well sprung and smelled of clean linens. She was able to turn so that she lay on her side with her head on a pillow. Her initial panic subsided and her mind began to work.

She'd been abducted by common hoodlums because she wouldn't hand over her purse. Why, when the police approached, hadn't they just taken her valuables and fled? Why had they taken *her*? It didn't make sense . . . unless . . . something or someone else was behind it . . . someone wanted her abducted. But who? A business rival? Could George Jay Gould, William Vanderbilt, Harry Winthrop, J. P. Morgan, or Archibald Lynch be capable of such underhanded dealings? She went through the list of her current business projects and couldn't think of any competitors desperate enough to engineer a kidnapping.

Some time later, when the door opened and light bloomed around her, she found herself in a sizable room that was decorated in a nautical motif. There were portholes, an oversized captain's bed, replicas of a mast, rigging, and a ship's wheel . . . all set against a length of railing with an ocean painted behind it.

Standing over her, dressed in a corset and stockings and holding an oil lamp, was the young woman she'd glimpsed earlier.

"What's that idiot gone an' done now?" the girl muttered in what sounded like an Irish accent. Then she pulled the handkerchief from Beatrice's mouth.

"Wa-ter," escaped Beatrice on a parched moan.

After helping her drink, the girl untied the scarf used to bind her feet. Beatrice was able to sit up and rub circulation back into her limbs.

"Let me go. Untie my hands—free me—and I'll see you're not charged with anything criminal," she croaked out.

The girl set about lighting a hanging lantern overhead, apparently untempted by Beatrice's offer of clemency. She seemed perfectly comfortable walking about in her corset, black silk stockings, and high-button shoes, showing everything the Almighty had given her. When she came back to the bed, Beatrice noted kohl around her eyes and rouge on her cheeks and—Dear Lord!—the tips of her breasts!

She'd heard whispers of such things. Standing before her, Beatrice realized with deepening shock, was one of New York's legendary *filles de plaisir*—a genuine soiled dove. Glancing wildly about, she sensed that the strange decor must have something to do with the woman's shameful profession—though, honestly, it was hard for her to imagine how a ship's wheel and a cargo net might be pressed into salacious duty.

Then it struck her: She'd been brought to a house of ill repute! Why on earth would they bring her to such a—unless—

Dear God—she'd been kidnapped by white slavers!

For the second time that night, she filled her lungs and began to scream.

THE NEXT EVENING, Connor Sullivan Barrow emerged from a cab half a block away from the Oriental Palace and walked the rest of the way.

He entered through a side door reserved for gentlemen who required more discreet access to New York's premier house of pleasure. After handing off his hat to the ancient butler, he headed up the steps and through the busy card room, nodding to acquaintances along the way.

In the main salon, wine-colored velvets and shimmering brocades imported from France draped long windows, chaises, and sinuously curved banquettes. Gilded mirrors reflected and re-reflected scenes of sensual dalliance bathed in subdued golden light, producing an illusion of endless pleasures. In an atmosphere laden with expensive cigars and Scotch and even more expensive perfume, a bevy of scantily clad females entertained the well-heeled pleasure seekers of New York with receptive smiles, provocative poses, and the promise of delights to be had for a price.

At one end of the salon, overseeing her employees and patrons with the aplomb of a royal overseeing a cotillion, sat Mrs. Charlotte Brown, the proprietress. She was dressed, as usual, in a lavish crimson gown that matched her henna-enhanced hair and provided a vivid contrast to her powdered white shoulders and abundant bosom. Her elaborately coiffed hair was decorated with red and white ostrich feathers, and for jewelry she wore sumptuous strands of pearls. In her younger days, she had been an actress of fiery beauty and somewhat incendiary reputation.

Charlotte Brown saw the services her Oriental Palace provided for the elite of the city as something of a civic duty. Furnishing discreet, private pleasures to men of power allowed them—drained of bothersome urges—to focus their public attentions on weightier matters. The

wealthy and powerful men of the city were happy to accommodate her reasoning and had long afforded her a
quiet protection.

Even now, two of the city's aldermen were seated to
her right, dallying with two of her prettiest girls. One alderman spotted Connor, and the other followed his gaze.
Connor's jaw clenched. It seemed like everything he did
these days had a damned audience.

Charlotte rose to meet him and extended her hand.

"Why, if it isn't the next congressman from the Fourth
District," she crooned. "It's been too long, Congressman
Barrow."

Connor hoped his wince would pass for a smile as he
drew her close and whispered for her ears only: "I understand you have an unwanted guest."

"You? You're the—" She drew back slightly, tension
showing through her smile as she caught the warning in
his eyes. "Well, then, we'll just have to catch up on all
your doings, dearie."

She slipped her arm through his and chatted pleasantly as she steered him out the door and toward
the grand stairs. The minute they were out of view of
the grand salon, she dropped his arm and turned
on him.

"You've got a heap of explainin' to do, Barrow."

"I can't really . . . I'm not at liberty to—"

"Who the hell is she?" Charlotte jammed her fists
on her hips and dropped all pretense of ladyhood. "Besides a screechin' demon from the backwaters of hell
itself?"

"It's best if you don't know. I'm here to take her—"

"Look, you." Charlotte advanced and began to punch
his shirt and the chest beneath with one long, red-tipped

fingernail. "She's all but deafened Punjab . . . disrupted my trade . . . an' generally behaved like a devil on holiday! How dare you bring that earsplittin' baggage into my—"

"Me?" Connor shrank back as far as the railing behind him would allow and tried to shield his chest. "I had nothing to do with it!"

"Right. And my old granny died a flamin' virgin." She advanced again, choosing another spot, nearer his stomach to punch. "My girls all vow they have no idea who she is or where she came from, and I don't believe a word of *that* either. Who is she? Some lightskirt you're tryin' to shake?"

"I don't have 'lightskirts.' And it's better for you if you don't know."

"Yeah. My innocent ears. Connor sweetie"—she smiled suggestively—"you ought to know by now that there ain't no part o' me still a virgin."

Under the heat of her stare, Connor became aware of the sweat popping out on his face. He could see that Charlotte had noticed it, too.

"Suffice it to say—she's important. And it's critical that she be returned to her home safe and sound. And *soon.*"

"Oh?" Charlotte's kohled eyes narrowed cannily.

When he scanned the doors of the nearby hallway and tried to sidestep her, she blocked the way and folded her arms under her ample breasts, thrusting them up even farther.

"If she's as important as you say, she could bring a heap of trouble down on my head. That damned 'Purity League' would like nothing better than to hear I'm keepin' a society woman prisoner in my house. She's not goin' anywhere until I learn who she is and get her promise she won't report me to the police."

Connor studied Charlotte's determination, seeing in it some part defensiveness, and some part pleasure at being in on a scandal of sorts. Damn. Why had those two idiots chosen to deposit their victim on the one woman in all New York who used iniquity and indiscretion as her own private currency?

"Her name, Barrow." Charlotte advanced on him and he again retreated. "Or she'll be my guest 'til you can't tell 'er tits from 'er liver spots."

She had backed him into the corner of the stairway landing.

"Dammit, Charlotte." He ran his hands down his face. "All right. She's Beatrice Von Furstenberg."

"Von Furstenberg?" Charlotte blinked. "Old Mercer's wife?"

"The same."

"I don't mean to limp your timber, sweetie, but are you sure?" Charlotte scowled. "I mean, I knew old Mercer—in the biblical sense—and he was a withered old cod even when he was young. It took me half the night to wring one good twitch out of him. And she hisses and spits and scratches like a she-cat in heat." She grabbed him by the arm and dragged him down two steps. "Maybe it's not the same—"

"Come on,"—he pulled her to a stop—"I have to get her out of here."

"She's not upstairs." Her next words struck terror into his heart. "I had to put her in the Dungeon."

"The Dungeon?" He allowed himself to be pulled along. "Are you crazy?"

"I told you"—she reeled him closer and lowered

her voice—"she was disrupting my trade. Got lungs like a damned set of bellows. Had to put her downstairs, where the noise wouldn't make my regulars too edgy."

"But the *Dungeon* . . ." He groaned, thinking of the one and only time he'd seen that particular chamber. Even three sheets to the wind, he'd been astonished by what passed for implements of "pleasure" there.

"It was either that or the Inferno. And I had a party of the city's finest scheduled in there for last night. Couldn't afford to disappoint the boys in blue."

As Charlotte led him down a set of carpeted steps beneath the main staircase, he tried to think of the effect Charlotte's pleasure Dungeon must have had on old Mrs. Von Furstenberg's ladylike sensibilities. Maybe they could drug her and convince her she'd been asleep . . . that it was all just a nightmare . . .

They arrived at the forbidding ironbound doors to the Oriental's Dungeon and reality descended; he'd need both equipment and help. "I'll need a rope and . . . a bag to put over her head . . . somebody will have to help me tie her up and carry her out to the carriage in the back alley."

"A bag?" Charlotte's hands were on her hips again. "Honey, she already knows where she is. One of my girls—the blabby little tart—let it slip when she carried in some food and water. Old Furstie's widow knows she's in a bawd house and she knows it's run by me. Your job, Barrow love, is to get in there and convince her to forget both things. She has to agree not to press charges and sign a paper to that fact before she gets out."

Connor was speechless. "You must be kidding."

"I've never been more serious in my life. I don't know

how, but I have a feeling it was *you* got me into this." She stabbed that blood-red fingernail into the dent in his shirtfront. "So *you* can get me out."

"And just how do you suggest I do that?"

"You're a lawyer, aren't you?" Charlotte smiled wickedly and jerked her head toward the door and the woman imprisoned behind it. *"Negotiate."*

BEATRICE WAS HUDDLED with her knees drawn up under her chin, in the middle of a huge leather ottoman that was black, like the other furnishings in the brick-lined chamber. She had a massive case of chill bumps, brought on by both the cool temperature and what the flickering torches in the iron brackets revealed in the room around her. A cage built of iron bars . . . a huge wooden table with iron shackles at the head and foot . . . a well-used set of wooden stocks . . . something that looked like a bizarre hobbyhorse, only with iron hand shackles instead of reins . . . chains hanging from the walls . . . and a rack containing all manner of implements of discipline . . . whips, rods, shackles, harnesses . . .

She shivered. She was in big trouble . . . kidnapped by the infamous "white slavers" and held against her will in a house of ill repute. She looked around her again. A *fortress* of ill repute. Complete with dungeon.

Thus far, she'd suffered only deprivations of freedom, dignity, and clothing. She looked down at herself and ran her hands up and down the exposed upper parts of her arms. They'd taken her clothes after she'd managed to dart out a door and down one of the long hallways, nearly reaching what looked like an outside door. But it wouldn't be long, she sensed, before the violations would begin as well. She'd had a foretaste of her fate when that monstrosity of a man—Punjab, they called him—had slung her over his shoulder and fondled her bottom as he carried her from place to place.

This was her fourth place of imprisonment. After the nautical room, they had trundled her into a Moorish harem complete with a bathing pool and silken veils. When her screams created a stir there, the turbaned giant carried her to a schoolroom, complete with desks and inkwells, a huge globe and map stands, and a chalkboard and stacks of most unusual schoolbooks. She wasn't there long enough to do any reading, however. When she climbed up the bookcase, threw open a small window, and screamed for help, that "Punjab" creature had captured and carted her down to this wretched corner of perdition.

She looked down at her hands. Her palms were red and fingers were sore and puffy from pounding on doors and walls. Then her gaze slid to her half-bared breasts and she realized with horror that her black satin corset with its pink ribbons and her white silk knickers were an appalling match for the garments the unfortunate females imprisoned in this place were forced to wear.

Well, she thought, hugging herself, they might be able to make her look like the others, but they'd never make her behave like the others. She'd die first. And if she died, she was determined to take a few of her captors with her.

The sound of a key scraping in the iron lock sent her bounding up from the ottoman. The prickles on the back of her neck told her that the time she dreaded had finally come. She looked wildly around for a place to hide.

The door swung open just enough for one person to

enter, then closed again with a bang. But it was not the bottom-fondling giant nor one of the corseted unfortunates who'd been imprisoned along with her; it was a man in a gray business suit. Tall. On the younger side. Her relief rebounded into anxiety. If he wasn't part of the staff, he was undoubtedly one of the patrons. Here was her first abuser!

Looking about for something with which to defend herself, she spotted that rack of fiendish disciplinary implements and grabbed a leather whip in one hand and a bamboo cane in the other . . . reasoning that they could be wielded in a defensive manner as well as an offensive one.

"Stay right where you are." Every word had to be forced through badly strained vocal chords. "Don't you dare come near me."

The man blinked, seeming shocked by the sight of her brandishing a whip and a rod. Apparently, he had expected to be the one wielding the weapons.

"Don't move a muscle," she ordered.

"I wouldn't dream of it."

"I mean it! If you move, I'll flay every inch of skin from your body!"

Intent on proving herself a force to be reckoned with, she advanced two steps, stopped, and braced with her feet apart and her weapons poised to strike. In the pause that followed, as she stood there, prepared for battle, she could feel his gaze roaming her half-naked body and taking in every exposed mound and crevice. Humiliation washed her skin crimson. There were far worse things than being naked, she told herself, forcing her chin up. Being ravished, for instance.

"Perhaps I have the wrong dungeon," he said, recovering.

"Undoubtedly." She raised her whip and cane another inch, frustrated that she couldn't shield herself from his gaze and maintain her grip on them at the same time. "The Inquisition is down the hall."

His eyes widened briefly and his mouth twitched at one corner. Her gaze fixed on that suppressed smile, and details flooded her mind in distracting waves. A full mouth. Strong, square chin. Face framed on high cheekbones. Dark, curly hair. Deep-set eyes . . . crinkling just now at the corners. Apparently he found the notion of her defending herself amusing.

"I was looking for the Dungeon with a 'Mrs. Von Furstenberg' in it."

He knew her name. Panic threatened to bloom as she tried to think what it meant. Whoever was responsible for abducting her must have sent him to . . . When he took a step forward, she lurched back.

"Stay where you are—don't you lay a hand on me!"

"Really, Mrs.—you are Mrs. Von Furstenberg, are you not? You seem to be under the misapprehension that I am here for some nefarious purpose. I assure you, madam,"—he raised and spread both hands—"you are in no danger."

"That depends on what you call 'danger,'" she said, her volume increasing with each word. "I've already been abducted and stripped of clothing and imprisoned in chambers furnished for depraved carnal assignations. That certainly qualifies as danger in my book. Not to mention being carted bodily from place to place and fondled rudely by that menace in a turban!"

"Punjab?" He allowed his smile to escape. "I assure you, madam, Punjab is not equipped to inflict the sort of harm that you seem to fear."

"He's as big as a mountain," she insisted.

"He is also a eunuch."

The pronouncement startled her so that she lowered her whip and cane.

"Really?" She'd read of such things . . . harems, eunuchs, and the like . . . but never imagined running into them in person. "Are you quite certain?"

"If you mean, have I made personal observations, no. But, I have been reliably informed by several of the 'employees' here that Punjab is physically powerful, but—alas for him—not the least bit potent."

His knowing smile and the way his eyes kept dipping to her corset aroused both disbelief and outrage. Up came the whip and cane again.

"If you didn't come to ravish me, then what are you doing here?" she demanded, advancing another step.

"The proprietress of this establishment sent me."

"I knew it!" She brandished her weapons and saw his gaze dart from whip to cane. "Look, you—you'll get nothing out of me but trouble!"

"No doubt," he said, holding his ground. "I repeat, I haven't come to sample your"—he gestured to her exposed form—"*charms*. I've come as Mrs. Brown's agent."

Beatrice scowled. She wasn't sure what she expected, but this wasn't it.

"Her agent? In what?"

"Certain *legal* matters."

"You're a lawyer?" Her mouth dropped open in surprise, then she snapped it shut and scowled. "I should have known. Conspiracy. Criminality. Depravity. *Lawyers* couldn't be far behind."

It was his turn to redden.

"There has been a mistake," he continued, his voice

suddenly a bit deeper and smoother. "Mrs. Brown sent for me the moment she learned you were in her establishment. She wants no difficulty. In fact, she is eager to free you."

He had evaded the question of his role, Beatrice thought, as she struggled to ignore the way his attention strayed from her face. Blue, she realized. His eyes were a vivid blue.

"Well, she *has* difficulty, whether she wants it or not. And if it was all just a mistake, why doesn't she let me go?" she demanded, annoyed at the way she couldn't seem to find a word to describe the exact color of his eyes. Sky blue . . . powder blue . . . turquoise . . . kerry blue . . . cornflower . . . azure . . .

"Well, there *is* something she insists on having first," he said, moving to the side, strolling deliberately toward the far side of the ottoman.

She turned to follow his movement, momentarily absorbed in the way he moved . . . easily, naturally . . . with consummate male confidence . . . as if he were used to being scrutinized. Only men at the top of their game moved as he did; only men who knew what they wanted and fully expected to get it. The question was, what *was* his game?

"A fat ransom, no doubt," she declared, pulling her wandering attention back under control, intent on staying a step ahead of him in this . . . this bizarre interview that was taking on the tenor of a business negotiation.

"Not at all." He had the gall to chuckle. Aloud. "Mrs. Brown has no need or desire for your money. What she wants is your written agreement not to press legal charges against her or her establishment." He shrugged. "That is her only condition for your release."

Was it possible that the creature who ran this place

really had sent him to negotiate her release? She couldn't imagine white slavers employing lawyers to placate their victims or cover their mistakes, but the tide of power did seem to be turning. The questions were: how far and why.

SIX

"GIVE ME YOUR coat," Beatrice ordered.

"What?" The lawyer was genuinely taken aback.

Much better, she thought, feeling as if she were finding her legs in this unthinkable bit of commerce. If twelve years in business and trade had taught her anything, it was that you had to keep your opponent off guard.

"I refuse to discuss your client's wishes until I have your coat."

Clearly reluctant but at a loss to proceed otherwise, he removed his coat and offered it to her. She extended the bamboo rod like a scepter, motioning for him to drape it over the end. With a wary eye on him, she slid both of her arms, still holding the whip and cane, through the sleeves.

A disconcerting wave of body heat enveloped her as the garment settled against her skin. But now that he had literally given her the coat off his back, she was certain that she could get more.

"The moment I am free," she declared, "I intend to

see your client and everyone else connected to this outrage prosecuted to the fullest."

"I know this has been a trial for you, Mrs. Von
Furstenberg." His voice acquired a deep, rolling quality.
"But punishing my client makes no sense. She and her
employees had nothing to do with your abduction."

"They didn't?" She tossed the whip and cane onto the
ottoman and folded her arms. The relief that flickered
through his expression surprised her. For a lawyer, he
was surprisingly easy to read. And to lead.

"How can you know with any certainty that they had
nothing to do with it . . . *unless you know who did*?"

He blinked, his chin tucked, and he stiffened. Common signs of surprise. Or guilt. "My client has no idea
who was involved."

"You say you know nothing about it, and yet you're
sure it was a mistake. How can that be, Mr.—what did
you say your name was?"

"My identity isn't important. I'm here only as an in-
termediary," he protested. She could see a sheen of
sweat developing on his features. He knew more than he
was saying. "If anyone here knows what happened, it is
you. What do you remember about how you came to be
here?"

Clever. Turning it back on her. As if he didn't know
every little detail. She wrapped his coat tighter and
folded her arms over it.

"I was on my way home from a meeting when my carriage was stopped by two men—Irish from their thick accents and even thicker heads." She turned her head
away from his unsettling gaze and felt her hair scraping
the coat collar. It was dangling in disarray around her
shoulders and she squashed the impulse to tuck it up

and make herself more presentable. "They demanded my valuables, and when I refused to cooperate, they hauled me bodily from my carriage. Then as the police approached, they dragged me off with them, bound and gagged me, and brought me to this abominable place."

"There you are, then. A simple robbery gone wrong." He inhaled deeply, inflating his chest and running his hands down his vest. Her eyes followed in spite of herself. Large hands . . . muscular, neatly tapered. "We may never know what possessed those idiots to abduct you. But it's clear that they realized they were in over their heads and they had to find a place to leave you. The Oriental enjoys something of a reputation for upper-class premises and personnel. No doubt they thought you would be more in your element here."

Connor cringed inwardly as he watched Beatrice Von Furstenberg's nostrils flare and her gaze narrow like a poised scalpel. Now was *not* the time for double entendres—either intended or accidental. He tensed as she reached for the whip and began to fondle it, tracing the braided leather and testing the flexibility of the shaft with long, capable fingers.

But, truth be told, she did seem to be in her element. Shockingly so. She was altogether brazen . . . standing there in her corset and stockings, her body boldly displayed, her eyes blazing, her abundant hair in tantalizing disarray . . . She was testing the whip with a slow, alluring hint of determination. He swallowed hard. She was clearly in charge and had been from the moment he walked through the door and found himself facing a woman thirty years younger and a hell of a lot more attractive than expected. Not to mention, nearly naked. Charlotte had neglected to mention that he would be negotiating with a half-naked woman.

"There was a woman who helped the pair carry me upstairs and lock me away," she said tautly. "It shouldn't be difficult to find her. She was dressed like one of the poor creatures forced to work in this place . . . no doubt an accomplice. I suggest you set about finding out who it is. What law firm do you work for?"

His hands clenched at his sides. "That is not important."

"Oh?" She looked him over. "What if *you're* an accomplice, too?" She smacked the tip of the whip on her open palm.

He was sure he paled; he could feel the blood draining from his face.

"I assure you, I had nothing to do with your being here."

"Tell me who you are."

"That is irrelevant."

"I'll be the judge of that."

"Just accept my client's proposal and walk out of here a free woman."

"And let whoever did this to me remain scot-free? Never."

Suddenly they were toe to toe, virtually nose to nose, and he hadn't a clue how they'd gotten that way. Her warmth spiraled upward and on it, he caught a sensual blend of fading perfume, scented talcum, and feminine musk. His heart began to thud. As he looked down, his gaze dropped of its own will to the line between her breasts and his coat, then rebounded to her face. Torchlight reflected in her eyes like sentinel fires. He could almost feel the contained outrage, the battle readiness in her. And he sensed one more thing . . . something else . . . something . . . not quite so angry.

"You won't need that," he said, taking hold of the whip.

She searched his face, openly considering him. Her chest seemed to rise and fall faster and the fires at her core burned hotter. Then as he began to slide the whip from her hands, she suddenly grasped it tighter and lurched back out of range.

"Tell your client"—her voice seemed constricted—"I won't sign anything until I have names and proof of who was behind my abduction."

"You're determined to be unreasonable, then." He fell back a pace, then another, irritation growing with each step. "Perhaps another night of the Oriental's 'hospitality' will change your attitude."

He heard her sharp intake of breath, but before she could protest he escaped out the ironbound door.

HE LURCHED INTO the corridor feeling as if he were just a step ahead of the jaws of disaster . . . only to find Charlotte Brown waiting for him.

"Well?" she demanded, stepping squarely into his path.

"She has to think it over," he said, trying to slip past her.

She countered his move, trapping him against the wall and subjecting his bare shirt and vest to her discerning scrutiny. "What's there to think about? It's a simple straightforward deal. What happened in there, Barrow?"

"Damned infernal female. You should have let me throw a bag over her head and dump her in a woods somewhere," he said gruffly, shouldering past her and heading for the stairs.

She grabbed his sleeve and fixed him with a warning glare.

"She's mad as a wet hen and swearing vengeance on

everything on the premises that sweats and moans," he said. "Does that clear it up for you?"

Charlotte pursed one corner of her mouth. He had the unsettling feeling that she was looking straight into his thoughts.

"Then I'd say you have your work cut out for you," she said, shrugging off the news and adopting a maliciously cheery determination.

"Me?"

"You're the one who has to sweet-talk her into leavin' the law out of this."

"Why me?"

She lowered her chin and narrowed her eyes, a look that said they both knew better. He was involved now because he had somehow been involved from the very start.

Frustration and recrimination rasped his conscience like grit on a grindstone. How the hell had he gotten himself into such a mess? He stepped around Charlotte and headed up the steps muttering to himself. But as he retrieved his hat from the old butler at the side door and jammed it down on his head, Charlotte's voice stopped him.

"I'll expect you at eight tomorrow night." It was not an invitation; it was a command. "And bring your smoothest line of blarney, Barrow. Sounds to me like you're going to need it."

TWO HOURS LATER, Beatrice was pacing back and forth in the Dungeon, clutching the whip with one hand and rubbing her stiff neck with the other. He'd left her there . . . just left her . . . to endure yet another night in this miserable rat hole in Perdition's Pantry. At least her virtue seemed to be safe . . . for whatever that was worth. She tossed the whip onto the ottoman.

At least someone knew who she was and had the sense to beware her wrath. She shivered and pulled the coat tighter around her. They'd sent a smooth-talking lawyer to persuade her to forget the pain and indignity she'd suffered; they either seriously underestimated her or greatly overestimated him.

Her thoughts turned yet again to the man sent to deal with her. Tall, elegant, and educated, with arresting blue eyes and a manner as silky as his dark hair. She'd seen his sort before, though she generally saw them across a crowded boardroom table, while flanked by a pack of legal beagles and—she glanced down at herself and blushed—while fully dressed.

It was her lack of clothing that had caused her unprecedented reaction to him, she told herself. Her heart had raced, her head had gone all spongy, and her body flushed hot on the side facing him . . .

A key rattled in the iron lock. The door swung open and in charged that moving mountain in a turban, *Punjab,* making straight for her. She gasped and scuttled back, looking for the weapons she had used to defend herself earlier. But the huge Indian was already between her and the ottoman where the whip and cane lay.

"Come, mamsab." His broad, eager grin appeared.

"Don't you come near me!" she choked out, backing around the ottoman, hoping to make it to the door.

But his bulk was fully equaled by his agility. In one deft movement, he bolted across the ottoman and grabbed her by the arm. In her struggle to get away, she yanked her arm from the sleeve and struggled out of the lawyer's coat, leaving the giant holding an empty garment as she dashed for the door. He tossed it aside and lunged for her—grabbing her just as she reached the doorway. Instantly she was lifted up, thrown over his shoulder, and borne out into a dimly lit corridor.

"Put me down, you brute!" she yelled, bashing his ox-like back as he trudged up the stairs. "I'll have your guts for garters!"

"No, no, mamsab," her huge captor assured her in heavily accented tones as his fleshy hand patted the back of her thigh and slowly worked its way upward. "Pretteee mamsab. Veddy nice."

As they mounted the steps, he continued to pat and fondle her upturned bottom. She screamed, shoved, and tried to twist off her humiliating perch, all to no avail. Then, as they reached what appeared to be a huge marble-lined entry hall filled with well-dressed men and scantily clad beauties, Punjab paused to announce his findings in a booming voice to any and all who might be interested:

"Veddy fine bottom!" He demonstrated with a cupped hand and a jiggle. "Yes, yes . . . veddy nice."

Laughter buffeted her from all sides. Through the blood pooling in her head, she managed to make out the fact that people were collecting along their route, clucking and calling out ribald bits of advice. Men in evening dress came rushing out of various rooms to see what the commotion was about, and several of the better lubricated patrons imitated Punjab's example . . . hauling the closest available female up on their shoulders and charging up the stairs to squeals and coy shrieks of terror.

By the time they reached the upper hallway, hearing was the only one of her senses still fully functional. She managed to catch a blur of red as Punjab paused, and she heard a woman's voice.

"Sorry about this, lovey, but I need my Dungeon for an

important client." Someone patted the back of her head. "You understand."

Shortly thereafter, she was plopped into the middle of what seemed to be a prodigiously deep feather bed and she heard that same female voice issuing orders as the door slammed. Fighting her way up through a tangle of hair, engorged senses, and pillowy mattress, she surfaced to take stock of her surroundings.

She had been dropped into a veritable jewel box of a room. Richly colored velvet and shimmering gilt covered every visible surface; walls, curtains, bed and table, mirrors, settee, chaise, and chairs. The furnishings were French—Louis Quatorze—and thick Persian rugs covered the entire floor, except for a broad marble hearth on the far side. Light came from polished brass candelabra on either side of the huge bed, and over her head hung a stately half canopy bearing what appeared to be Louis XIV's royal crest.

At first the abundance of color, form, and texture bordered on sensory assault. But as she looked around, that impression softened to one of unabashed luxury. She was loath to admit: It did seem to grow on her.

She fought her way out of the monstrous bed and walked around the room, examining the place while keeping an eye on the door. It wasn't long before two young women arrived with a linen-draped cart laden with silver service. Behind them stood Punjab with his arms crossed, blocking the exit, his gaze fixed on the lower half of her anatomy. One of the girls saw Beatrice glaring at him and shooed him back outside, closing the door.

"Brought ye some food," the girl said, turning back to lift a silver domed cover and reveal a steaming plate of what appeared to be prime rib.

"And some hot water," the other girl added, stooping

to pull a pitcher and toweling out of the bottom of the cart.

Beatrice stared at the pair and recognition flooded her. One was the same girl who had assisted her abductors and tended her the first night she was here! Suddenly she was desperate to get the girl alone and ask her some questions.

"It looks lovely," she said, her mouth watering as she ventured toward the cart and inhaled appreciatively. "But you know what I *really* need . . ." She melted with a longing that was all too real. "A bath."

The young women looked at each other, shrugged, then asked matter-of-factly: "Milk or champagne?"

OUTSIDE IN THE hall, where Punjab stood forbidding entry or exit, a gentleman with graying temples and a well-heeled appearance slowed to give the door and its turbaned guard a look. Then with a sniff of dismissal, he adjusted his tie, checked his cuffs, and sauntered on down the hall, giving the impression that he had just quitted one of the nearby rooms.

But in fact, the slight disarray of his garments had occurred as he raced up the steps behind Punjab and his indignant passenger, riveted to the sight of the screeching, thrashing woman on the eunuch's shoulder. When the big Indian tossed Beatrice onto the bed in the Sun King chamber, he had been in the hall, craning his neck for a glimpse.

Now as he descended the main steps, he developed a calculating grin. It was her, he thought. In the flesh. Not a doubt in his mind. He arrived in the card room, paused in the doorway to search the gaming tables, then hurried to one of them and bent to his partner's ear.

"You won't believe what I just saw," he said.

"Not now—" The squat, balding man waved as if trying to rid himself of a gnat. "Can't you see I'm about to make a killing?"

"This is worth a dozen killings!" He yanked the cards from the player's hand and tossed them facedown on the table, telling the others: "He's out."

"How dare you, Lynch?"

"You'll thank me for this, Winthrop." He pulled the sputtering card player to the side of the stairs, out of earshot of others. "You'll never guess who I just saw here."

"It better be the damned archbishop of New York," Winthrop snarled.

"Better than that." Lynch glanced furtively around them, savoring the revelation. "Beatrice Von Furstenberg!"

It took a moment to sink in. "You've gone stark raving mad. And just when I finally had a hand that—"

"You had a pair of eights; you'd have lost your arse." Lynch held him back as he tried to leave. "I'm telling you, I saw the Indian carrying her upstairs, kicking and screaming. I couldn't believe my eyes, so I followed them for a better look and there she was—standing there in her cincher and socks—bold as brass. It's *her*, I tell you. Beatrice Von Furstenberg—on the hoof." His eyes began to glow. "Caught smack in the clutches of sin."

Financier Harry Winthrop stared at his fellow Consolidated Industries board member, Archibald Lynch, letting the ramifications of that astounding news unfold. He could scarcely count the times he had locked horns with Beatrice Von Furstenberg over business deals and been forced to bend to her righteous attitude and canny maneuverings.

"Good God, if it's true—"

"It's her, believe me." Lynch's smile bore the taint of malice. "It appears the high-and-mighty Mrs. Von Furstenberg has a secret taste for a bit of depravity."

"Then we've got her—at last!" Winthrop's fleshy face reddened as he threw back his head and laughed. "As of the next board meeting, Consolidated will finally be free of her damned 'tyranny of skirts'!"

IT WAS WELL into the next day before Beatrice got her bath or a chance to talk to the young woman who might be able to shed some light on her abduction. She had spent an uneasy night curled on the very edge of the mammoth bed, catnapping, trying to keep one sense alert at all times. She awakened tired and aching all over from the strain of her uncomfortable sleeping position, the constant tension of her situation, and her unsettling bouts with Punjab.

Worse still, she had no sense of whether she had been asleep for an hour or two or ten. When food arrived some time later, it was poached eggs, bacon, fried potatoes, biscuits, and coffee. She asked the old butler who brought the tray what the hour was and he surprised her with: "Noon." They always had late nights at the Oriental, he mumbled, and even later mornings.

Her bath arrived some time later, brought by two older women in maid's uniforms and the very girl she had hoped to interview. While the maids were filling the hip bath with water, Beatrice tried to draw the girl into conversation . . . starting with her name and how she came to be at the Oriental.

"Mary Katherine," the girl answered in an Irish brogue, tossing her thick auburn hair back over her shoulder. "Mary Kate, like half o' Ireland. I come here on th' boat when I was but a babe. Me ma had half a dozen mouths to feed, so she put me out in service soon as she could. Barely fourteen years I was, but looked a sight older." She grew thoughtful. "Caught men's eyes, I did. Wasn't long before the master an' his son was both creeping up the back stairs to me bed. The ol' lady found them out an' beat *me* black an' blue for it. I went home and me ma stood in the door, sayin' I was an evil girl who tempted men to sin. She wouldn' have me around no more, an' I had no place to go . . . no money . . ."

Beatrice sat on the edge of the velvet chaise, watching the girl dangle her fingers in the bath water, and she glimpsed in Mary Kate the pain that was usually hidden behind a saucy demeanor. Mary Katherine, like many girls of her class, had been used callously by men of wealth and privilege. When discovered, she had been condemned as the cause of her own corruption and turned out into the streets by her mother—when only fifteen or sixteen, Priscilla's age. There were still traces of that vulnerable young girl beneath the powder and henna.

"I figured, if I was such a almighty temp-ta-tion, an' my vir-tue was alwus in peril, I might as well get paid fer it." Mary Kate lifted her head and squared her shoulders, with a defiantly lascivious grin. "And I get paid right handsome. I'm uncommon good at makin' men hot and desperate, then makin' 'em all cool an' satisfied." The girl's pride in her carnal abilities dumbfounded Beatrice.

"But they keep you here—to let men vent their basest urges on you."

"Keep me?" Mary Kate looked puzzled, then chuckled. "Nobody *keeps* me or *makes* me to do anything." She jerked a thumb toward herself with her jaw jutting stubbornly. "I'd like to see a son-of-a-bitch who'd try!"

"But that Punjab creature—"

"Punny? He's our protection. Grabby, but not a bad sort once ye get him to keep his mitts off yer arse. Got a thing for the old bum-cheeks Punny does." She grinned, showing a healthy set of teeth. "But then, wot man ain't? They all want to grab, don't they? Punjab, he just *does* it." She shook her head. "Nobody keeps us here. Nobody'd have to. Where else could we go?"

"You could be a shop girl . . . or a seamstress . . . or work in a . . ."

Beatrice halted at the scornful look on Mary Katherine's face.

"Shop girls don't eat steak every night an' drink French champagne." She held up the alençon lace on her flowing peignoir. "They don't get fine silk clothes an' French perfume. Nor presents from aldermen an' congressmen . . . even full-blooded English noblemen. And yer seamstresses . . . they go blind by twenty-five, then to an almshouse . . . if the bloody place'll have 'em."

Beatrice resisted the girl's logic, but was unable to refute it.

"Come on. Into th' water with ye—what's yer name again?"

"Mrs. Von Furstenberg," Beatrice said, rising and submitting when Mary Kate turned her to get at her laces.

"Nooo, I mean *yer* name, not yer old man's. Yer Christian name."

"Beatrice."

"Beeeatrice?" Mary Kate laughed. "Sounds like some old prune of an auntie." That was annoyingly close to Priscilla's view of her. "I'll call you . . . Bebe. Yeah, I like that better. Step in and have a good soak, Bebe."

The girl's familiarity should have affronted her. But it had been a decade since anyone had called her by the name her beloved sister had given her in childhood. Bebe. She was so distracted by the realization that it didn't occur to her to take offense at the girl's familiarity. She stepped into the tub.

"How about if I scrub yer back?" Mary Kate seized a sponge.

"No, that's not necessary."

"Oh, come on." The girl jerked her dressing gown out of the way and knelt on the carpet beside the tub. She grabbed the soap, pushed Beatrice forward, and began to scrub her back. "This is one o' my specialties. I give gents baths all the time." She lowered her voice to a conspiratorial whisper. "An' afterward I have to give some o' them a nappy an' a bit o' the tit to get 'em ready for a right old tumble." She gave a naughty giggle at Beatrice's stunned expression. "Ye'd be surprised what some o' yer fancy society men *fancy.*"

Beatrice was ready to wrestle the sponge and soap from her when she continued: "An' anyway—I reckon I owe you—after what them two idiots went an did—kidnappin' you and hauling you in here. The Muldoons ain't never been long on brains. Ma always said that whole side of the family wus dumber than dirt. That Dipper— he must have got dropped on his head when he was a babe."

Beatrice tried not to make her shock or her interest too obvious. "Dipper Muldoon. And what is his friend's name?"

"Shorty? He's an O'Shea. The O'Sheas—now there's a lot destined for the hind tit of life." She shook her head with a wry expression. "More than just a few fish short of a barrel. You weren't in no real danger. Them two wouldn't swat a fly even if it was bitin' 'em. Say, Bebe, you got a real nice set of—"

"I believe I can take it from here!" Beatrice snatched the sponge from her enthusiastic source and turned away. "You've been most helpful, Mary Katherine. But, do you think perhaps you could find my clothes?"

Mary Kate scowled. "You won't be needin' clothes here."

"I'm afraid I will. I'm supposed to meet with someone tonight and I'd rather not face him without proper clothing."

"Him?" Mary Kate studied Beatrice a moment, then she apparently remembered something she had heard. "It's true then. The congressman's comin' to see ye."

Beatrice was suddenly upright in the water and all ears.

"Congressman?"

"Ever'body calls 'im that. He ain't been elected yet, but 'e will be, next ballot. Congressman Connor Sullivan." She gave a wicked wink. "A prime piece o' bully beef. Can stay up an' in the saddle all night." She laughed at Beatrice's blush. "I'll talk to th' girls—we'll find ye somethin' proper to wear."

It wasn't long before Beatrice's room was filled with a bewildering array of half-clad women bearing garments. Mary Kate introduced them as they offered up garments suited only to titillating the upper-crust male, and sundry items better categorized as equipment.

The young women, Millie, Jane, Pansy, Eleanor, Annie, Tessa, and Diedre, represented the entire gamut of female form and appeal. Millie was buxom and sturdy and offered up a corset and drawstring chemise of the sort worn by tavern wenches. Jane—blond, ladylike, and elegant—had brought a seductive open pelisse of Mediterranean blue moiré. Pansy—dark, chatty, and ebullient—had brought a lace-drenched dressing gown as purple as the corset and stockings she wore. Eleanor was a golden-eyed sphinx who spoke with a French accent, and insisted Beatrice wear her shimmering iridescent chiffon made in the old empire style . . . which bared the breasts entirely. Annie was a tough and boisterous westerner whose deerskin bustier and boots fascinated Beatrice—though not to the extent that she would consider wearing her bottom-baring buckskin chaps and western boots. Tessa was another exotic—from the West Indies—with black eyes, dusky skin, and a sultry Creole accent that was harder to resist than the leopard-print dressing gown she suggested Beatrice wear. And Diedre, a tall, severely beautiful brunette with a dangerous look in her eye, offered to share her black leather gherkins, body harnesses, and glistening thigh-high boots:

"In my experience," Diedre declared in crisp, authoritative tones, "congressmen need to be shown who's in charge."

Her comment unleashed a torrent of advice on handling men of power and importance. Story followed upon story; the brigadier who insisted his partner wear a saddle, the alderman who had to wear a corset, stockings, and rouge in order to perform, a Protestant preacher who fancied nuns in wimples, and a Roman bishop who insisted on ravishing Puritan lasses. Some men insisted on being in charge; others were more than pleased to put control in a knowledgeable woman's hands. Some wanted to be pampered, others deprived. Some came to indulge themselves; others came to purge.

Beatrice sat on the chaise, wrapped in a sheet of toweling, staring at them. These were the "scarlet women" she had heard pitied, condemned, lamented, and derided by the moralists and thinkers of the day . . . even by the women in her own women's rights organization.

These were the females who were alternately labeled victims and opportunists . . . sometimes declared products of immorality and sometimes denounced as the cause of it.

As they talked about their trade and the peculiarities of the men who patronized them, it became clear to her that they did not consider themselves the "oppressed sisters" of femininity any more than they perceived themselves as wicked and depraved. They were surprisingly matter-of-fact in their approach to their trade, and had strong opinions on hygiene, health, and the worth of their particular specialties. But most of all, they knew men . . . had studied them even as they pleasured them.

It struck Beatrice that she shared something with these women: both she and they knew men in ways that most women did not. She knew men as they were among themselves; competitors, cronies, opponents, resources, allies. And these women knew them as creatures of passion and need, as revelers in the sensual. For a brief, insightful moment, she wondered how much more there might be to know about men. What other sides were there to be studied?

As she surfaced from those astonishing thoughts, Mary Kate leaned close and chuckled. "Men ain't so tough," she explained to Beatrice. "You just got to figure out what it is they really want. I spend half my time listenin' to 'em talk . . . about how their wives spend 'em blind and how their kids hate 'em and how their competitors is eatin' into their profits . . . and about how they ain't got a single soul to talk to about it all."

"Men," Annie sagely summed up their observations, "are just like ever'body else. There's some worth their weight in gold and some not worth th' powder an' lead to blow 'em up." She grinned. "An' we get both kinds here."

"Problem is, you can't alwus tell which is which," Pansy said with a thoughtful frown. "It ought to be a law or somethin' that a man has to look like what he's really like inside."

"Yeah," Annie said, nodding. "Like my hoity-toity 'banker.'" She raised her chin to a combative angle. "I been savin' for four years. Got a tidy little sum to buy me a place of my own when my looks go. This 'client' of mine . . . this *banker* . . . he says he can take care of my money for me. So I dress up on my day off an' go down to his bank to get me one of his 'accounts.' The bastard acted like he'd never laid eyes on me before. Asked me for ref-er-ences. Said he couldn't accept money from a woman unless he knew where it come from." Her eyes crackled with righteous fury. "Like he didn't know where it come from—the slimy little bastard. That was the last time he set foot in my room, I tell you."

"I told you—you ought to buy gold jewelry with your tips," Tessa declared, pulling up her generous sleeves to reveal wrists covered in spectacular gold bangles. "You can wear it now and sell it later, when you need the money."

"Yeah, well you can do that . . . until some customer three sheets to the wind decides to bash you over the head and make your jewelry *his* retirement."

There was plenty of nodding and bitter agreement.

"Well, I have my money hidden safely away," Eleanor said with a superior air. This prompted the others to respond in chorus: "In your mattress!"

Her jaw dropped and the others broke up in raucous laughter.

"I had me three hundred dollars saved up," Millie declared bitterly. "It got stole out o' my room by a 'client.' Later, when Punjab caught up wi' him and beat th' tar outta him, he said it wasn't stealin'—since he took it from a whore."

There was no laughter at that, no smart remark or saucy retort. Silence descended for a time. They knew too well that comfort and security were commodities in short supply for women like them. It seemed that their earnings and savings, while substantial, could prove just as transitory as their youth and charms.

"My next life," Annie said after a moment, shoving to her feet and striking a pose, "I'm gonna be a banker. An' every cent that gets put in *my* bank will be one some poor sister earned on her back!"

With the tension broken, the women laughed and began to file out of the room . . . many of them giving Punjab a teasing pat on the rear as they passed him outside the door.

Beatrice watched them go with a strange mixture of insight and compassion. Who would have thought that in a house of ill repute, she'd find herself surrounded by a bevy of frustrated *businesswomen*?

SEVEN

CONNOR ARRIVED AT the Oriental at eight o'clock that evening, freshly shaved and determined to convince his unwitting victim to forego taking legal measures. He could be very persuasive when the occasion called for it and there wasn't a woman alive who wasn't susceptible to a bit of persuasion now and then. A look of admiration, a heartfelt compliment slipped into the conversation, a wayward glance that resulted in an appreciative smile . . . it was simply a matter of finding the right approach.

Charlotte Brown met him in the front hall, gave him a thorough visual inspection, then told him that her "guest" had been moved yet again. As he turned to follow Punjab up the stairs, she reminded him that she wanted an agreement in writing and produced a document, a pen, and a bottle of ink, which he shoved into his pocket. When Punjab reached the appropriate door, he paused and turned to Connor with a grin.

"Veddy fine bottom." The giant made a suggestive squeezing motion with his muscular hand. "Veddy fine indeed."

The last thing he needed in his head as he negotiated with the outraged Beatrice Von Furstenberg was an image of her "veddy fine bottom," Connor thought. He was having enough difficulty ridding himself of the memory of her breasts spilling from her black satin corset.

Thus, when the door opened and she was standing in the middle of the room wrapped in a voluminous sheet torn from the rumpled bed, his reaction was an unsettling mixture of dread and relief.

"You," she greeted him.

"Mrs. Von Furstenberg." He nodded, then motioned to their surroundings. "And in much better circumstances than when we last met."

She fixed him with a stare.

"They needed the Dungeon."

He took a deep breath and used it to buttress his good humor.

"Well, I'm sure it's hard to find a high-quality dungeon these days." Then he spotted a table set with snowy linen, fine china, and fresh flowers, and strolled toward it with genuine curiosity. "I see we're having dinner." He ran his hand down his stomach. "They have an excellent chef here. Brought over from Paris. Does a magnificent Beef Wellington and an unparalleled Trout Almondine." He glanced up and struck a tone of indignation as he looked her up and down. "Ye gods, is that all they found you to wear? A bed sheet?"

"They found me something else. I'd rather wear the sheet." She faced him with her arms crossed to hold her covering in place. "It's not going to work, you know. Plying me with luxury. Trying to bribe me to forget the pain and indignity I have suffered."

Her irritability only fueled his determination to bring her around.

"I assure you, Mrs. Brown is not so naive as to expect that a few comforts could erase the unpleasantness of the last two days. She simply means to see to your welfare, to treat you courteously . . . while an understanding is reached."

"While an underhanded business scheme is being carried out, more likely! While you are holding me here, my stocks may be plummeting, my boards may be splitting and selling off assets, my competitors could be stealing my markets, and my futures contracts could be withering away. The longer I am here, the more damage can be done to my fortunes . . . which, I am coming to think, may be the whole purpose of this outrage. But bear in mind: the more I lose, the more liability your Mrs. Brown will have to bear."

"Plots and schemes. You have a suspicious mind, Mrs. Von Furstenberg."

"A pragmatic mind."

He skimmed her swathed form with a look and gave her a wry smile. "I'm certain your 'stocks' are in fine shape."

"You won't mind if I don't take your word for it," she said, tightening the tuck of her arms, "Mister—or should I say 'Congressman'—Sullivan."

His body went taut and his senses came to a razor's edge of alertness.

"I am not a congressman," he said, racing to imagine how she could have learned his name and that he was running for congress, and what kind of trouble this was going to cause. "Where did you hear such a thing?"

"One of the girls who works here told me. She seemed quite confident of your ability to carry the upcoming election." She tilted her nose. "The question is: Who will you be carrying it for? Whose man are you?"

"An unpleasant assumption," he said as calmly as possible.

"Sullivan is Irish," she declared. "Tammany Hall, perhaps? Are you their man? Their—what do they call it—*mouthpiece*?"

"I am no one's man, Mrs. Von Furstenberg, except my own."

"And Mrs. Sullivan's."

"There is no Mrs. Sullivan." Spurred by her superior air he added: "Nor a Mrs. Barrow. The full name is Connor Sullivan *Barrow*."

"Barrow?" She frowned, searching her memory. "No relation to Hurst Eddington Barrow, the dean of New York's bankers, surely."

"My grandfather," he said, fighting a fleeting temptation to claim the right of condescension that went with a blood connection to one of the richest families in banking. "However, he relinquished all claim to me some years ago. Since then, I have made my own way on my own merit."

She studied him openly.

"You're part Irish."

"The *best* part Irish," he said, letting the Gaelic in him surface to speak for itself. "The part that works hard, lives free, laughs often, and loves well. The part that lives on honest terms with all other men and gives respect and allegiance where it is due . . . especially to this fine, fair land that has sheltered so many of the beleaguered and starvin' children of Erin."

The lilt and the passion that crept into his voice were all too genuine. The United States had saved a million shattered Irish lives during the famine, and the refuge the Irish had found in America was a subject on which no son or descendent of Ireland could remain unmoved.

After a moment's pause, he relaxed enough to give a self-mocking chuckle.

"I do get exercised on the subject. But enough of politics. I've always heard it said that any business done on an empty stomach is bad business. And I do not intend to do 'bad business' tonight."

He pulled out a chair at the table and waited for her to take it. She hesitated, frowning, still contemplating what he had said, but after a moment, accepted. He seated himself opposite her and lifted the cover of the largest dish on the food cart.

"Ahhhh." He smiled as he inhaled the aroma of slow-roasted beef. "There's only one chef in New York that can begin to compare with the Oriental's Pierre. You know, of course, who that is."

He uncovered the bread and butter, then a bowl of cold raspberry salad and put it down before her with a wave that indicated she should serve it.

He had lured her to the table and if he could get her to cooperate at dinner, he might just succeed in getting her to cooperate in other ways.

"Michael of the Waldorf," she said, staring at the salad as if it might bite. "Unless you're a devotee of Eduard of the Ritz."

He paused in the middle of plunging a corkscrew into the wine bottle and gave her a pained and pitying look.

"It's Mary McMurtry of O'Toole's Restaurant. Sweet Mary is Ireland's gift of gratitude to America." He shook the cork, still attached to the corkscrew, as if it were his finger. "She's a miracle in the kitchen, that woman. What she can do with a shank o' lamb has been known to make grown men weep. The priests down at St. Patrick's Cathedral give abstinence from Mary's cookin' as a penance."

When she gave him a disbelieving look, he straightened and went on with exaggerated sincerity. "I swear it's true. Though, I hear the archbishop has declared that they must reserve such punishment for only the worst offenses . . . like ax murderin' or breakin' a bottle of good Irish whiskey.

"I'll have no scoffin', madam. You cannot judge until you've tried her cookin', especially her pie." The longer he talked the more of an Irish lilt crept into his voice. "Sweet Mary has 'the gift' for makin' pie . . . bakes a miracle of a crust that is so rich and buttery . . ." He leaned toward her and lowered his voice. "There's talk that she has conjured a way of stealing sunbeams and weavin' 'em into her crusts. Which would explain why it's always cloudy on the East Side on Thursdays . . . that's her bakin' day. And they say that when she runs short of berries, she just plucks a few from the glow of her cheeks to finish the filling . . ."

Beatrice sat clutching her sheet together in front, immobilized by the seductive cadence of his voice and the outrageous claims he was making. When he poured the wine and lifted his goblet, she found herself oddly drawn to meet it with hers.

"To home and hearth, and a quick return to both for you," he declared.

It was bad form to refuse to drink a toast raised in one's honor, Beatrice reasoned as she raised the glass to her nose. A spicy oak-rich aroma filled her head. She knew how it would taste just from the vapor and when she took a sip, she nearly groaned. There couldn't be a more complex or sophisticated burgundy this side of the Atlantic. Her mouth began to water. The marvelous smells of the food and the unexpected amicability of the company were melting the starch in her spine.

A body has to eat, she told herself. And if appearing to cooperate caused him to lower his guard and divulge more of what he knew about her abduction, then she might as well eat, drink, and . . . serve the blessed salad.

"I'm right, am I not?" he said, moments later, smiling over the rim of his glass. "About Pierre."

"Ummmmm," she mumbled, her mouth full of tender greens and plump raspberries and almonds that had been drizzled with a sweet vinaigrette. After a moment she swallowed. "It is quite . . . acceptable."

"You're a hard woman Beatrice Von Furstenberg," he said, pointing with his fork. "Hard but fair, I believe. You'll come around."

Then he smiled at her.

It was a broad, beaming beacon of goodwill . . . a bold and brimming expression that invited her to reciprocate. She stared at his features, studying the change in them. That smile was pure alchemy. In that simple release of pleasure, granite had been transformed into vibrant flesh and "stranger" had become "person."

She came to herself, moments later, with odd ribbons of warmth circulating through her body and a strange, boneless heaviness in her limbs. She was staring fixedly into those sky-blue eyes across the table, while her fork drooped in her hand and her body had gravitated forward until her bosom was practically lying in her salad plate.

Straightening sharply, she reached for her wineglass and drained it, and tried unsuccessfully to recall what he had just said.

"Beg pardon?" she said.

"I was commenting on the color of the sheet," he said.

"White?"

"I was thinking along the lines of 'pale,' actually. Life-less"—he stared intently at her shoulders—"especially against your skin. Now, the leopard skin . . . that has real possibilities. Type running to type, I suppose."

"Leopard?" She frowned. The appropriate association refused to connect in her mind until she followed his gaze to her chest. The sheet had fallen away and she sat, exposed, in Tessa's leopard-print silk dressing gown that bared far more of her breasts than it concealed. Startled to find so much of herself exposed, she dropped her fork with a clang and fumbled to cover herself.

"Very nice skin, Mrs. Von Furstenberg," he said in that teasing brogue. "Punjab forgot to mention it. Truth to tell"—he lowered his voice—"I don't think he got past your lower half. What was it he said? Oh, yes. 'Veddy fine bottom.'"

"Really, Mr. Barrow—"

"*Tsk, tsk*"—he waved her protest away as he refilled her wineglass—"a fine bottom's naught to be ashamed of, Mrs. Von Furstenberg. A good bottom can be a right old comfort . . . when yer tired and sore and need to give yer feet a rest. But a *fine* bottom . . . well, that's another story altogether. A *fine* bottom is a thing o' beauty. Many's the young Irish lass who's said to herself . . . 'If I only had a *fine* bottom, I could make somethin' of meself, I could.'"

She was staring again . . . jaw slack and shoulders rounded . . . like some shoeless bumpkin glimpsing city lights for the first time. She snapped upright.

"It is bad enough that I must endure that human mountain taking liberties with my—" She couldn't make herself say the word. "I will not countenance you speaking of my lower half with such familiarity."

His mesmerizing smile broadened.

"I'll take that to mean you won't mind if I mention yer upper parts. Because, I can assure ye, they're every bit as worthy of notice." Just as she opened her mouth to protest he continued: "Your mind, for instance. You're a clever, managing woman, keen on observin,' an' not easily taken in." Having effectively undercut her protest before it was uttered, he went on. "Lovely eyes, too . . . green as a meadow on a summer's day. Hair like sable fire." Each word was like the twist of a stick in dry tinder; the friction they created inside her made her feel alarmingly combustible. "I was always taught to beware a touch of red in a woman's hair. It bespeaks a strong will. But, speakin' personally, I like a strong bit of *will* in a woman. Always a site more enjoyable than a strong bit of *won't*."

He waggled his brows and poured them both another glass of wine.

Beatrice sat with smoke from the fires he was igniting in her swirling through her head and curling around the edges of her gaze. She was trembling as she reached for her glass and downed a good bit of whatever was in it. Warmth cascaded through her limbs as if she'd poured the wine directly into them. What was happening to her?

She looked up and her gaze met his. Those blue eyes. Those handsome lips. That tongue made of pure sugar. Never in her life had she encountered anyone with the ability to turn words into eighty-proof liquor. She was beginning to understand the intoxicating impact that sensual male persuasion could have on a woman's better sense.

Thinking of it in such terms jolted her back to a firmer footing in reality. She plopped her wineglass on the table and made one last, frantic grab at sanity.

"You're quite a sweet talker, Mr. Barrow." She reached for her knife and fork and sliced into the braised beef tips he had placed on her plate. "Is that how you got

Dipper Muldoon and Shorty O'Shea to kidnap me? Sweet-talking?"

He froze with a helping of beef halfway to his plate.

"I beg your pardon. I had nothing to do with your kidnapping." He finished serving the beef then sat for a moment contemplating her charge. "How did you find out about Dipper and Shorty?"

"I listened." She mustered an air of triumph. "It's surprising what you can learn that way. The young woman I told you about—the one who helped them that first night—is Dipper's cousin. She works here. You were right on one point, at least. They seem to have brought me here because they had no idea what else to do with me."

He leaned back in his chair, looking properly discomforted. "All right, I confess. I knew about Dipper and Shorty. After Charlotte Brown sent for me, I asked some questions and it wasn't especially hard to uncover the truth. That's how I knew it wasn't some grand conspiracy to ruin your businesses."

"You might have told me what you knew . . . who was to blame."

He raised his brows and looked down at his plate. "Would you have believed me? Worse yet, would you have been receptive to a plea for mercy?" He leaned forward and engaged her eyes. "Because that's what I'm asking you for . . . clemency for the pair of them. They're shiftless, feckless, and dumb as bricks, but they're not bad fellows. They had no idea what they were doing. They're just day laborers with a yen for Irish whiskey and the sound of rolling dice." There was a bit of wistfulness in his smile. "You can't blame them for being confused . . . they don't often run across women like you, Beatrice Von Furstenberg." His voice lowered. "None of us do."

It might have been the candlelight or the wine or the glow of his dark-centered eyes, or the skin-tingling vibration of his voice . . . something caused an opening, sinking sensation in the middle of her. It was like a hunger. And she knew in the depths of her being that it had nothing to do with food.

Picking up her glass of wine, she fled the table to pace the far side of the room. But she had risen so quickly that for a moment her head swam. When she collected herself and turned, he was standing behind her, looking at her. Shivering, she gave a panicky glance around. There was nothing to sit on, to hide behind, or even to put her glass down on. When she shivered again and looked down, she realized that she'd left her sheet at the table. There she stood in a silky leopard-print dressing gown that bared the top of her corset and much of her breasts. She looked up.

A wry, appreciative quirk lifted one side of his mouth. Her gaze fixed on that tantalizing half smile, and she suddenly had difficulty recalling what she'd been about to say.

"I'm sorry they brought you here," he said. The earnestness of his voice filled her mind like a mélange of heat and wine vapor and smoke from the flames igniting along the sinews of her limbs. "You don't belong in a place like this. Let me take you home," he said quietly. "Forget you were ever here."

"Would you forget it?" she asked.

His smile faded and the reflection of the candle flame in his eyes seemed to flare. "Would I forget that I've seen your bare shoulders? Could I forget the decadent way you spill over your corset and the smoothness of your legs above your stockings? Forget the way the light turns to fire in your hair and the way your lips glisten with the color of the wine?" He took her goblet from her and as she relinquished it to him, she felt an alarming surge of anticipation. "I'll try.

"And you," he said after he'd set her glass aside, "will you forget being bound and dragged halfway to Jersey and imprisoned and inconvenienced? Will you forget being held against your will in a brothel and deprived and insulted? Will you forget everything and everyone you've seen here?"

"I'm . . . not sure." She tried to swallow against the weakness in her throat.

"Well, try," he said inching closer, settling against her. "And while you're at it, try to forget this as well . . ."

He lowered his mouth to hers and brushed it over her lips . . . once, twice . . . She held her breath, waiting, sensing that this was exactly what those tinglings and peculiar weaknesses were leading to. Then his arms closed around her, lifting, drawing her hard against him, and her breath left her in a whoosh. His mouth closed on hers, teasing, caressing, unexpectedly gentle. He was exploring the shape of her, the taste of her, the possibility of response in her.

And she did respond.

From somewhere deep inside her came the instinct to slide her arms around him, to tilt her head and arch into him, meeting his kiss and taking it deeper. She parted her lips and fitted them to his, searching out a number of pleasurable angles, each of which seemed just a bit more delicious than the last and beckoned her to still greater pleasures. Then he began to trace her lips with his tongue and she felt a new liquid heat sluicing through her body and pooling between her legs.

She couldn't catch her breath—her head was spinning—her body seemed boneless as it melted into his. He was so big and firm and warm. . . .

A nearby noise penetrated the steam shrouding her senses and a moment later she pushed back even as he released her, and they broke apart.

Standing at the table behind them was the aged butler, bearing an unopened bottle of wine.

"Guess ye won't be needin' this," he muttered, turning and shuffling out.

In the doorway, arms primly crossed, stood a red-haired woman dressed in a dramatic black and crimson gown. She gave the pair a thorough visual inspection, collecting every detail of their appearance to add to what she'd already observed of their behavior. A tart smile appeared on her rouged lips.

"I take it we've reached an agreement," she said. "I'll send for a carriage."

Shame washed Beatrice's face crimson as she struggled for both breath and composure. The knowing look the woman shot Connor Barrow spoke of his duty to her and of its successful fulfillment. It struck Beatrice like a slap.

"I haven't signed your wretched agreement," she declared, her chest heaving. "And I won't."

"Oh"—Charlotte Brown's smile broadened as she stepped out the door—"I don't think we need one *now*." Then she was gone.

It took a moment for Beatrice to parse out the meaning of her declaration. Charlotte Brown no longer needed a written statement because she no longer feared legal reprisals. In succumbing to Barrow's devious charm, Beatrice sensed she had played right into the madam's hands. Now, whatever she might say about her presence here, Charlotte Brown could counter by asserting that her presence had been voluntary . . . in pursuit of an assignation.

She looked up at Connor Barrow, whose shoulders were braced and expression was grim. Struggling with an impulse to introduce her fist to his aristocratic nose, she faced him with her head high and her eyes blazing.

"You . . . miserable . . . lawyer!"

"Mrs. Von Furstenberg—Beatrice—I assure you—"

"I believe I've had all of the 'assurances' I can bear from you." She pointed to the door and her voice shook with anger. "Right now, I wouldn't believe you if you said the sky was blue."

His eyes narrowed and she could almost feel the effort he had to exert to contain a furious response. But a moment later he gave her a sardonic nod, and strode out.

Within minutes, Mary Kate appeared with a hooded cloak for her to wear and ushered her down the back stairs to a waiting carriage.

She was going home.

IN THE DARKENED carriage, clutching her cloak tightly about her, she began to shiver with contained emotion. Free—she was finally free. But instead of relief, she felt anger and humiliation. They had sent Connor Barrow to talk her into a forgiving frame of mind, and when it hadn't worked, they sent him back in to charm her into cooperating. She didn't know what made her angrier: the fact that he'd tried to charm and seduce her to serve another's ends or that she'd actually succumbed to it!

For a brief moment she felt a liquid surge of memory that left her body tingling and made her touch her suddenly sensitive lips. He'd kissed her in a way she'd never been kissed before. Tenderly. Provocatively. With a clear desire to give as well as receive pleasure. And she had kissed him back with an urgency and excitement she'd never felt before. In seven years of marriage she'd never experienced anything like the deliciously sensual tumult he stirred in her body. Confusion, excitement, pleasure, longing, surrender . . . it had been all of that and . . . it had also been manipulative, right down to its devious sensual core.

She shuddered away those remnants of warmth and sensation and stuffed those memories back into the farthest, most forgotten corner of her being. Appalling. Humiliating. There was no room in her life for such weakness; the fact of her kidnapping had made that abundantly clear. There were forces in her world that would use the slightest hint of vulnerability on her part to ruin her. Despite Mrs. Brown's and Connor Barrow's protestations, she was far from convinced that her stay at the Oriental wasn't the result of a broader conspiracy against her.

The more she thought about it, the more determined she became to find out if her kidnapping had indeed been the idiot whim of two incompetent "bag men" or if it had originated in something more sinister. There were ways to learn such things, she knew, and starting tomorrow morning, she was going to use every resource at her command to uncover the truth.

When she arrived in the darkened entry hall of her Fifth Avenue mansion, she was greeted with a flurry by her butler, her secretary, and her niece.

"Madam!" Richards called joyfully, rushing to flip on the electrical lights.

"Aunt Beatrice!" Priscilla rushed out of the drawing

room to hug her with an enthusiasm that would have been unthinkable only three days before. "Where have you been? Are you all right?"

"A bit shaken . . . otherwise, whole and sound," she said, holding Priscilla by the shoulders and noting with surprise the anxiety in her eyes.

"Thank God!" Alice Henry wrapped an arm around Beatrice's shoulders and squeezed. "We've been frantic ever since the police brought word that you were missing. What happened? Where have you been?"

"I was accosted by robbers and then abducted."

"Robbers?" came a male voice that startled her. "Who abducted you?"

She turned to find a nice-looking young man in a gray suit standing in the drawing-room doorway. He strode toward them with a grave look of concern.

Alice explained: "This is Detective Blackwell, of the police department."

Beatrice's knees buckled. She was ushered instantly to a chair in the drawing room and handed a glass of sherry. She refused to let them send for a doctor or take her cloak, which she pulled tighter around her.

"Are you sure you're all right?" Priscilla knelt by her knees. "We were so worried when Detective Blackwell brought Rukart home and said you were missing." She glanced up at the detective, then quickly lowered her eyes.

"I think we should send for a doctor," Alice declared.

"No, truly . . . I'm fine."

"Then perhaps you feel up to telling us what happened, Mrs. Von Furstenberg," Blackwell said in carefully modulated tones, taking out a notepad and pencil. "The sooner you can give us the details, the better the chance we will have to catch the men who accosted you.

Can you describe your assailants? Was there anything distinctive about them? Have you ever seen them before?"

What could she tell them? Beatrice was so absorbed in sorting out the disgraceful and humiliating facts of the last two days, that she barely felt Priscilla seize and squeeze her hands.

"My poor aunt. Can't this wait, Detective?"

"No, no, Priscilla, I must cooperate. I want these men found." Beatrice gave her niece a grateful smile, then squared her shoulders and turned to the detective. "I'm afraid I can be of little help. I was coming home from my suffrage meeting, when my carriage was diverted into an alley and my driver was knocked senseless. Two men seized me and demanded my valuables. They were rough and coarse . . . they spoke with heavy Irish accents." She winced as if distressed by the memory. "Beyond that . . . it was so dark and happened so fast . . ."

"I understand." He wrote on his pad. "What happened next?"

"I heard a police whistle and the next thing I knew they were dragging me down one alley and then another. They tied my hands and put a cloth in my mouth . . ." She closed her eyes and prayed that whatever came out next would be believable. "I was taken somewhere . . . a warehouse, I believe. They put me on a bed of some sort." She opened her eyes and looked away, scrambling to think of a few convincing details.

"They didn't come back. By the next night, I had managed to loosen my bonds and was able to crawl out a window." She astonished herself with how easily the story came. "I hid until it was light and I realized I was somewhere near the docks. I remember the calls of gulls and the foul smell of old seawater . . . and there were sailors . . ." She pressed her temple. "I stumbled into a boardinghouse and I believe I must have fainted. When I awakened, the woman who ran the place was good enough to hire a cab to bring me home."

"You mean they abducted you and just left you there?" Blackwell asked.

She nodded, then suddenly recalled something. "Wait! I seem to remember . . . they were arguing about . . . waiting for someone . . ." She sat straighter, her eyes widening. "There must have been someone else, someone I didn't see."

"Really, Detective," Priscilla said with alarm, popping up. "This is much too horrid. My aunt has just been through a terrible ordeal . . ."

"Of course." Blackwell gazed for a moment at Priscilla, then cleared his throat and put his pad away. "You've given me enough for a start, Mrs. Von Furstenberg. If you remember anything else, please send for me." He glanced again at Priscilla. "I'll come at a moment's notice."

"Detective," Beatrice said with delicacy, "I would be forever grateful if you could manage to keep this inquiry confidential. I couldn't bear for my ordeal to become a public curiosity."

"You may count on me, ma'am."

As he turned to go, she realized that this earnest young civil servant might be the key to unlocking the mystery of what had truly happened to her. Weighing the risks, she waited until she was halfway up the stairs and he was halfway out the front door before calling him back.

"I just remembered!" she said breathlessly. "One of

them used a word—I think perhaps a name. 'Dipper.' "
She thought about it for a moment. "Yes, I'm certain it
was *Dipper*."

"An Irishman named 'Dipper.' " Detective Blackwell
seemed pleased as he tugged the brim of his hat. "Rest
well, Mrs. Von Furstenberg, Miss Henry, Miss Lucciano.
These men are as good as caught."

By the time Beatrice reached her rooms, the fatigue
she had feigned earlier had become real indeed. She
asked Alice to join her as she prepared for bed, and as
soon as Priscilla was out of the room, she turned to her
secretary.

"Tell me what has been happening here. Any inquiries
from the Consolidated board? Any word from my
bankers?"

"Not a peep," Alice said, suddenly uncomfortable. "I
confess . . . I didn't report your disappearance to anyone
at the offices." When Beatrice just stared at her, she
winced. "Well, I was afraid that if word got out that you
were missing . . ."

"Alice, you're a perfect genius!" Beatrice threw her
arms around her secretary, nearly bowling her over. "You
couldn't possibly have handled it any better. Have I given
you a raise, lately?"

"Just last week," Alice said with a relieved smile.

"Well, put yourself down for another—I've got to have
a bath," she declared, heading for the bathing room.

As hot water poured into the big porcelain tub and
steam curled around her in scented spirals, she stood
with her eyes closed, luxuriating in the comfort and feeling grateful to be back in the security of her own home.
She was suddenly so relaxed that she didn't object when
Alice removed her borrowed cloak from her shoulders.

At the sound of Alice's gasp, she opened her eyes to

find her secretary staring at the scandalous leopard-print silk she wore underneath. Shock transformed slowly into a frown of suspicion.

"All right. Where have you *really* been?" Alice demanded.

Beatrice thought about it for a moment and it came to her.

"I've been learning about how the 'other half' lives."

Alice's look expressed some doubt.

"Which other half?"

Beatrice laughed.

"Men, my dear Alice. *Men.*"

EIGHT

"WHAT IS IT—what's happened?" Jeffrey's face was ashen as he stepped into the dim light of the butler's pantry.

"She's home," Priscilla said anxiously. "She returned last night saying she'd been abducted by some men who tried to rob her."

He blinked, taking in the news.

"That's all? She didn't say anything about me or us?"

When she shook her head, he groaned "Oh, thank God!"

"Nor did she mention your awful cousin, who was supposed to *find* her."

"What does it matter how she got home? The nightmare is finally over. Look at me—I'm a wreck!" He held out his hands to show how they trembled. "I've hardly slept a wink in three days. Mother has noticed I'm off my feed and keeps insisting I take that hideous tonic she puts such stock in."

"Jeffrey!"

"Well, your aunt's none the wiser, right?" He gave a giddy laugh. "It couldn't have turned out better."

"It certainly could have," she declared irritably. "You could have rescued Aunt Beatrice as we planned in the first place. Then she wouldn't have had to endure heaven-knows-what at the hands of those vile, vicious criminals."

"You're *sure* she hasn't said anything about who nabbed her?" He grew anxious again until she nodded. "Then she must not know anything. If she did, you can bet she would be lopping off heads by now. That means we're clear!" He planted an exuberant kiss in the vicinity of her lips, then headed for the door.

"Where are you going?" Priscilla asked, stunned by his abrupt departure.

"Home—to sleep for a week!"

Priscilla stood in the dimness, staring at the open door and wrestling with a disappointment she couldn't explain. Minutes later, she hurried up the stairs behind Richards, who was carrying her aunt's morning tray, and slipped through the door of her aunt's suite after him. She was surprised to find Aunt Beatrice not only awake, but already dressed in her customary dark skirt and white blouse with leg-of-mutton sleeves.

"Fresh raspberries this morning, madam," Richards said, depositing the tray on the tea table and lifting a silver lid. His professional demeanor cracked enough to permit a rare smile. "Did a bit of early shopping for Cook."

"My favorites." Aunt Beatrice abandoned her writing desk for the tray and melted at the sight of the berries. "Richards, you're a treasure."

"As are you, madam." Richards gave a curt nod and withdrew.

"Priscilla." Aunt Beatrice spotted her standing by the door, smiled, and beckoned her to the table. "What do you want, dear?"

"Aunt Beatrice, are you all right . . . really all right?" She searched her aunt's face for signs of duress.

"I'm well enough. It was a great relief to be back in my own bed." She developed a faraway look. "I suppose that is one of those things it is easy to take for granted: the security of your own bed and good night's rest."

"So, you're really all right? They didn't do anything horrible to you?"

"Do I look as if they did?" she said, came back to the present and busied herself pouring coffee. "It was horrible, I won't deny it. But I made it through, and it's over. People have to learn to endure and to persevere in life, Priscilla. Trials and difficulties come to us all, sooner or later. The real test of a person's character is how she meets those difficulties, whether she bests her problems or is bested by them." She softened and met Priscilla's troubled gaze with a quizzical look as if pleasantly surprised by Priscilla's concern.

"I've seen a good bit of life, and I've learned that sometimes difficulties are just opportunities in disguise." She creamed her coffee, then studied Priscilla over the rim of her cup as she sipped. "Does any of that make sense to you?"

Confused by her aunt's composure in the wake of so traumatic an experience, and annoyed by the fact that her imperious aunt had seized her expression of concern as an opportunity for yet another lecture on Life, Priscilla scowled.

"I'm not a child, Aunt Beatrice. I do know a few things about life."

She stalked from the room and down the main steps,

where Richards was admitting a familiar face to the entry hall. Surprised, she paused on the landing to smooth her hair, then proceeded down the stairs to greet Detective Blackwell.

"Good morning, Detective." She extended her hand with ladylike aplomb. "We certainly didn't expect to see you this morning."

The young man's eyes brightened as he pressed her hand.

"I didn't expect to be here so soon. But when I left here, my men and I spent a good part of the night checking taverns and waterfront gang haunts. I believe I have uncovered the identity of your aunt's assailants."

"You have?" Priscilla drew her hand back abruptly.

"My goodness, Detective, you're not only dedicated, you're efficient," came Beatrice's voice from above. They turned to find her coming down the steps. "Who are they?"

"Mrs. Von Furstenberg." He smiled and nodded to her. "A pair of Irish day laborers who do a bit of 'night work' on the side. Your recollection gave us a head start. One seems to have been Dipper Muldoon and the other was most likely his partner, Shorty O'Shea. We're searching for them now." He glanced back at Priscilla, who managed a sickly smile, and then he assured them: "It's only a matter of time."

THREE DAYS AFTER his disastrous dinner with Beatrice Von Furstenberg at the Oriental Palace, Connor Barrow still was not himself. He rose each day at the usual hour, had his customary breakfast, and spent the morning seeing clients in his law office on Fourteenth Street, just around the corner from Tammany Hall. Each

afternoon, he had dinner with a client, a precinct captain, or a city official, then he spent much of the afternoon in election meetings and walking the streets,
talking to shopkeepers, craftsmen, and city workers who
were registered in the Fourth District. Supper found him
at O'Toole's, sampling Mary McMurtry's delicious fare.

But dogged adherence to a well-established routine
was the only normalcy in his life. He frequently came to
his senses on the street and discovered he had walked
well past his destination or missed a cab or trolley because he was staring at the pavement or scowling off into
space. He left his food half eaten, had difficulty falling
asleep at night, and had to ask everyone to repeat what
they'd said. His law clerk chanced a remark on his uncharacteristic lack of attention to details, and he erupted
in an uncharacteristic explosion.

But it wasn't until a message written in a feminine
hand and bearing a Fifth Avenue address arrived that he
recognized that for the last three days he'd been waiting
for the other shoe to drop. He had unfinished business
with Beatrice Von Furstenberg and when he read the
high-handed summons she had issued him, he was on
his feet in a heartbeat and reaching for his hat.

It was the rancor of their last parting that had plagued
him, he told himself. He felt unjustly accused, and the
contempt in her face as she ordered him out the door
had lodged like a nettle in his pride, preventing him from
putting the whole damnable incident behind him. Now
she had asked him to call on her and he intended to use
the opportunity to set her straight.

As the cab rumbled along the brick streets, uninvited
memories materialized in his mind: Beatrice in a black
corset and black stockings, wielding a whip by torchlight . . . Beatrice wrapped in a tousled sheet . . . her

green eyes wide with surprise . . . Beatrice, with her breasts spilling out of a leopard-print gown, looking like the brazen huntress she was at heart. Every image seemed to raise the temperature in the cab. His mouth went dry.

It was only when the cab rolled to a stop in front of the imposing Fifth Avenue mansion that he managed to get around to the reasons she might have for insisting that he come to her home straightaway. As he stood on the doorstep fiddling with his cuff links and picking imaginary lint from his sleeves, a host of unpleasant possibilities descended on him . . . including the prospect that she'd somehow learned the truth.

What the hell was he doing here?

Before he could escape down the steps, the door opened.

"Mr. Barrow?" An efficient-looking butler waved him inside with one gloved hand and reached for his hat with the other. "This way, sir. Madam is expecting you."

Connor followed, tugging down the bottom of his vest and taking in the white marble entry hall, crystal chandeliers, and gold-framed portraits lining the sweeping staircase. Everything about the place spoke of wealth and power and of the owner's willingness to use both to gain the advantage in everything she did.

As the butler showed him into the drawing room, he felt himself bracing.

"Good afternoon, Mrs. Von Furstenberg."

She was standing on the far end of a large, rectangular chamber decorated in a style that could only be called "palatial cozy." Oak paneling, arched windows, and imposing gothic marble fireplace were balanced by plush, overstuffed chairs and settees upholstered in color-drenched damasks, abundant still lifes and landscapes, oriental vases and screens, thick floral pattern rugs, and a storm of pettipoint pillows. Settled serenely amongst that profusion of color and pattern, dressed in a forest green silk with leg-of-mutton sleeves, and a scooped neckline, she was the set piece of the room and she clearly knew it.

"Do come in, Mr. Barrow." She waved with regal authority toward the nearby settee. "And be seated."

The huge doors behind him closed with a bang and he had to control a powerful urge to turn and make a run for them.

"Will whatever business you have with me take that long?" he said with more geniality than he felt.

"That depends, Mr. Barrow."

"On what, Mrs. Von Furstenberg?"

"On you, sir."

"Determined to be mysterious, I see." He strode forward and took the seat she had indicated, determined to show no indecision or undo concern.

"On the contrary, Mr. Barrow. I am determined to dispel a mystery. I have spent some time and energy inquiring into the cause of my abduction. And I think you may be surprised at what I have found."

"Very little you do would surprise me, Mrs. Von Furstenberg." Every part his body seemed to be tightening, even his throat.

"Well, then," she said with a smile, moving toward a cleverly disguised door on one side of the ornate fireplace, "you won't be shocked to learn that I've located the men who kidnapped me." She turned the handle and the door swung open into a small sitting room, where two bedraggled male figures were perched uncomfortably on the edge of a dainty floral settee.

Dipper and Shorty.

Connor sprang to his feet, feeling as if his stomach stayed behind and now rested somewhere in the vicinity of his knees. How the hell had she found them?

"Mr. Barrow!" and "Gov'ner!" They greeted him with a flare of hope that died as they perceived the horror in his face.

"They tell a most interesting tale. And your name figures prominently in it." She crossed her arms and prodded the pair with an arch look. "Repeat for Mr. Barrow what you told me, gentlemen."

"Well," Dipper rose anxiously and rubbed his sweaty palms on his coarse trousers. "I said we were plenty sorry fer th' inconveenyence we caused 'er. We wasn't supposed to kidnap her."

"We was supposed to rob her like," Shorty put in.

"The congressman here . . . he told us there was a gent needed a job done an' that we'd get paid right well for it. The young gent told us he wanted us to make believe we was robbin' some old lady. Said we was to scare her real good and then he'd come an' rescue her. Only he was late an' the coppers showed up. We figured we wouldn't get paid if she didn't get 'rescued' . . . so we took 'er with us."

"We owe Black Terrence money . . . an' he wants to break our heads," Shorty inserted. Dipper's glower silenced him.

"The coppers kept gettin' closer and closer . . . we had to stash her someplace safe and I spotted the Oriental. My cousin, Mary Kate, she works there, and I figured she'd help us out." He shrugged. "So, we stowed th' Missus there and laid low 'til that de-tective come nosin' around and put the pinch on us." Dipper jammed his hands into his trouser pockets and tucked his chin.

"Sorry, gov," Shorty said with a wince of apology.

"And who was this other 'gent' who was supposed to join you, only never came?" Beatrice demanded.

"Don't know, ma'am. We jus saw 'im that once. Young fella. It wus dark," Dipper said. Shorty echoed that with a vigorous nod.

"And what was he supposed to do when he arrived?"

Dipper shrugged and glanced at Connor. "Rescue ye, is all I know."

"From your foul clutches," she clarified.

"Yes, ma'am," Shorty answered with a despondent nod.

"Thank you. Sit down, gentlemen," Beatrice ordered. The pair sank as if someone had dropped lead weights into their trousers. She closed the door on them and turned again to Connor. "So, *you* are the one who recruited those two for the purpose of robbing and menacing me. Don't waste breath denying it. What I want to know is the identity of the person responsible for this plot. Who hired these wretches and what were they truly supposed to do with me?"

"I haven't a clue," he said, folding his arms and hoping that grit and bravado might win out where logic and sanity had already failed.

"Don't you?" She advanced on him, her eyes narrowing.

"Revenge is a vastly overrated pleasure," he declared. "I strongly suggest you forget it and cultivate more improving pastimes."

He turned sharply and headed for the door. With a sputter of outrage she rushed past him in a storm of swishing silk. She reached the door ahead of him, huddled for a second over the door handles, then turned, holding an iron key with an air of triumph.

"Just what do you think you're doing?"

With a cool smile, she plunged the key inside the rounded neckline of her dress, until only a small spot of iron was visible between the mounds of her breasts. He reddened all the way to his ears as he stared at that bit of metal.

"You can leave when I have the information I need," she declared.

"Don't be absurd." He jerked his gaze from that disturbing sight. "Open the door." He took a step forward so that he loomed over her as she stood with her back against the door. She looked up with a determined set to her jaw and a shiver raced through him, accompanied by palpable memories of the feel of her warm curves pressed hard against him and the pleasure of her soft mouth opening under his. Very bad move, he realized. Stiffening, he dropped back a step, then another, and struggled to right his derailed train of thought.

"Look, you have the word of those two numskulls that no harm was intended. And you have their word, my word, and Charlotte Brown's word that your being at the Oriental was a mistake. Why can't you leave it at that?"

She studied him for a moment, then pushed off from the door and strode back to the center of the room, where she rested her hands on the back of a chair.

"I am a businesswoman, Mr. Barrow. I don't know if you can appreciate what that means in the New York business world. I am President of Consolidated Industries Corporation and sit on the boards of several other large business concerns. I compete on the open market to buy and sell, to manufacture, to transport, and to franchise. I buy and sell stock for profit and enter into hundreds of financial transactions each year. Many of those transactions cost someone something . . . a stock loss, a forfeited supply of materials, a legal injunction, an option that will never be exercised . . . and I am seldom the one who pays. I am good at what I do, and there are many people in the business world who don't like losing to a woman, whether it occurs in a fair contest or not."

It took a moment for him to connect what she had just said with a comment she had made while at the Oriental. She truly was concerned that the entire episode might have been initiated by a business rival. That put him in something of a quandary. To reassure her would be to reveal his knuckle-headed participation in something that showed abysmal judgment . . . not to mention identifying himself as a party to a criminal action.

"If you are protecting someone, I'll find it out."

"I am protecting no one." His conscience groaned.

"Except perhaps yourself?" she said, striking perilously close to the mark. "Tell me the name of the man who came to you and why he wanted to frighten me."

"I can't imagine anyone with half a brain trying to frighten you, Mrs. Von Furstenberg. That should eliminate the more intelligent of your business rivals. Quite honestly, I had no idea what the fellow was planning when I—"

"When you matched him with the two lackwits in the next room?" she finished for him. "Ahhh. We are getting somewhere. You admit you were involved from the beginning."

He flinched. She had him dead to rights and they both knew it.

"I admit no such thing." He backed up one step, then another. "A fellow approached me at O'Toole's one evening and said he needed a couple of men for a job. I spotted

Dipper and Shorty in the tavern side and I sent them out to see him. That was the extent of my involvement."

"Who was this 'fellow'?" She folded her arms and leveled a glare at him.

"I had never set eyes on him before that night."

"I don't believe you," she said.

"It's true."

"Why would you do such a favor for a perfect stranger? More importantly, why do you continue to protect him?"

Connor tucked his chin and considered her words. Why indeed? He might be able to make up something plausible, but his own disgraceful part in this debacle had already been discovered. What was the point of protecting a spoiled adolescent whose entire problem was that he was already overprotected . . . from decisions, from responsibility, and from consequences . . . the very things that forced a boy to grow into a man.

He strolled back to the settee and sat down, contemplating his course of action. Revealing his reasons for helping Precious Jeffrey could actually work to his credit . . . might even mitigate his participation in the scheme.

"Very well," he said, looking up at her. "The whole truth. Unvarnished."

"It's about time," she responded, taking the chair across from him and focusing intently on him.

"The person responsible for your kidnapping . . . the person who originated the plan . . . is your niece, Priscilla Lunaticcio."

She stared at him for a moment as the information penetrated several layers of incredulity, then crossed her arms in disgust. "Firstly, it's *Lucciano*, not Lunaticcio. Secondly, that is the most preposterous thing I've ever heard."

He stared at her, then blinked. It hadn't occurred to him that she wouldn't believe her niece capable of initiating such a scheme.

"Your niece fancies herself in love with a young man named Jeffrey Granton, does she not?"

"Well, yes." Some of her indignation faded and she sat away from the back of the chair. "But I fail to see—"

"The young man who came to see me that night . . . the man who hired Dipper and Shorty to try to rob you . . . was none other than Jeffrey Granton."

The name broke over Beatrice like cold water and she drew a sharp breath. Priscilla's beloved "Jeffrey" was behind the horrors she had endured? He would have been the very last person on her list of possible suspects . . . about as likely to engineer such a thing as William Shakespeare, Abraham Lincoln, or St. Francis of Assisi!

"That is absurd." She searched his face. "Jeffrey Granton is scarcely capable of dressing himself properly. He could never have come up with such a plan." She was struggling to discredit his charge with the facts already in her mind but found they supported his version of the story all too well. The pair who kidnapped her said the young man hadn't wanted her harmed, just scared . . . he was supposed to join them, but hadn't arrived in time . . . they had mentioned a "rescue" of some sort . . .

"I believe he had a bit of help in the creative department." He spread his arms so that one lay on the arm and the other on the back of the settee, his mood expanding with his posture. "They say behind every successful man, there is a woman. And while the 'successful' part is arguable, the woman behind young Jeffrey was undeniably your niece. According to him, she came up with the idea and insisted he carry it out. To impress you."

"Robbing me, kidnapping me, and imprisoning me in a house of ill repute was supposed to *impress* me?"

"Well, it would have worked better if Jeffrey hadn't been late and missed rescuing you. Dipper and Shorty were supposed to 'rob' you and he was supposed to happen along, defend you and yours, and save the day. You, of course, would have been grateful and impressed enough with his bravery that you would have granted him immediate courting rights with your niece."

Much as she hated to admit it, the story was sounding more credible by the minute. She could almost see Priscilla's absurdly romantic mind at work in such a scheme. Her face flamed as she thought of her grim imaginings and the vehement accusations she had hurled in her mind against sundry of her competitors. Thank heaven she hadn't aired those suspicions.

She jerked her head up to focus on him, her cheeks on fire. In characteristic fashion, she chose the moment she felt the most vulnerable to launch an offensive.

"And you, *Congressman* . . . what could you have been thinking . . . agreeing to help a total stranger with a plot to rob and kidnap a woman?"

"Not a total stranger, I'm afraid." He drew in his arms and sat forward, looking decidedly less smug. "While it is true that I'd never set eyes on him before that night, Jeffrey Granton is my second cousin. Alicia Barrow Granton's son. He sought me out because of my 'unsavory' connections in the Irish community." His smile was self-deprecating. "Every family has a black sheep, and I am the designated 'Barrow' scapegrace.

"In my own defense I must add that he led me to believe he needed help with an elopement, not a pretend robbery or kidnapping. I am, after all, running for a seat in congress. I would never jeopardize my future political career to appease an idiot eighteen-year-old's thirst for intrigue. Had I known what he was truly planning, I'd have thrown him out of O'Toole's on his pampered arse."

"You agreed to help him because you thought he was eloping with my niece?"

"I had no idea who the young lady was." He came to the edge of his seat. "He was reluctant to reveal her name, would only say that her family had money and influence, and that he and she were desperately in love." He grew more serious. "He was so obviously in love and true love being such a rare and precious commodity . . . I confess, I found it impossible to turn him away."

"True love." She could see the scorn in her tone surprised him, and she rose and went to look out the window. "He's eighteen, for God's sake. And she is sixteen—did he tell you that?" She didn't allow him time to answer. "She believes in 'happily ever after' and all manner of romantic drivel. She wants to marry him grandly and ride off into the sunset on a white charger." She turned back briefly. "She hasn't a clue what life is about. Or marriage. Or men. Her 'dearest Jeffrey' knows even less. He wouldn't know a white charger if it rode up and bit him in the—"

"Not much of a romantic, are you?" He rose with a wry laugh.

"Romance is synonymous with *illusion,* Mr. Barrow. Thankfully, I have none of those regarding relations between the sexes."

"You don't believe in true love?"

She paused, drafting her response carefully.

"I believe true love is exceedingly rare and . . . probably overrated."

She watched as he assessed that statement and stored it away.

"Well, how do you expect your niece to learn about love and marriage unless she has some experience with them?"

"She can learn by watching others' mistakes, by listening to sound counsel, and by remaining unmarried long enough to become a person in her own right."

"Nonsense."

"What?"

"That's nonsense," he said, his voice softening and acquiring that alarming trace of Irish that caused her ears to burn for more. "Love is not somethin' you learn by watching others do, it's somethin' you learn by doing yourself. And how would I know, she asks. I know because I've done a bit of lovin' in my day."

"Really, Mr. Barrow." She glared and turned back to the window. "I don't care to hear about your escapades with those poor creatures at the—"

"*Really*, Mrs. Von Furstenberg. How will your niece learn what marriage is like unless she marries? No amount of watchin' or tellin' can do it justice." He strolled up behind her as he talked and she soon felt his breath stirring the hair at the nape of her neck. "How will she ever know the sweet communion of a longin' look in the midst of company or across a proper dinner table. How will she know the deep, silent joy of watchin' her beloved as he sleeps in the misty light of dawn? How will she know the solace to be had in a beloved's embrace when the whole world seems to be dead set against you?"

He moved closer and her skin prickled with anticipation.

"How will she know the pleasure of a man's body pressed against hers?"

A gentle pressure spread against her back and shoulders. She held her breath as the warmth of him began to seep through her clothes.

"How will she know the thrill of a well-tutored touch on her skin?"

His hand settled on her shoulder and slowly followed the slope of it toward her neck. When it reached bare skin she was tortured by, but resisted, an urge to shiver.

"How will she know the ache of a need so deep an' such a part of her blood and marrow that there are no words to describe it?"

He ran his hand slowly up the side of her neck. A hot chill raced up her spine and spread out into tingles along her limbs.

"How will she know the sweet terror of trustin' all that you are and all that you have to th' care of another?"

He traced the outline of her ear and slid his hand from her temple downward across her cheek. It felt as if her skin was melting beneath his touch, as if her nerves were bared to his caress. And it was a caress . . . meant to give pleasure. It was only her resistance to it that produced this tension and discomfort. Then his voice rumbled at the edge of her ear.

"How will she discover the pleasure of small, wayward kisses dropped on her neck . . . for no reason other than a moment's overwhelmin' happiness?"

As she drew a long, erratic breath, it came: a gentle, moist pressure on the side of her neck, just below her ear. Then another just below it. Then another further down. So tender. Her head sagged to one side, allowing him access. Then it came again: a stronger, more urgent pressure on her collarbone. She was scarcely aware that she had closed her eyes until she opened them later and saw his dark head bending over her shoulder and the side of his face as he pressed kisses along her shoulder.

His arms slid around her and he nudged the fabric of her small bustle aside to press more fully against her.

Her responses weren't her own as she sank back against him, curling instinctively into the curve he provided, feeling sheltered in a way she hadn't imagined possible. The melting sensation she had experienced at the Oriental returned, twice as potent. Her knees were weakening, her skin was burning beneath his kisses. Something was stirring in her . . . something hot and powerful . . . rising up from her depths . . .

Her lips were beginning to burn. She turned her head toward him just as he raised his head from her shoulder. There was a dark glimmer in his eyes and his lips seemed thicker and softer. His smile was nothing short of rakish.

"How will she learn such things, Beatrice darlin'? How did you learn them?"

NINE

ALL BEATRICE COULD do was echo his last words.

"How did you learn them?"

"Experience." He gave her a sly smile. "How else?"

He backed away unexpectedly and she had to grab the heavy velvet curtain for support. She was reeling, scrambling for footing in her usually sane and rational inner foundations, and was so occupied with the struggle that it took a minute for the meaning in those words to register. Experience? With marriage? Her heart all but stopped.

"But you said there was no Mrs. Barrow."

"There isn't." His expression remained oddly heated. "She died."

Suddenly the feelings and sensations he had just evoked in her felt shameful. What was it about him that continually diverted her reasonable faculties and waylaid her most high-minded intentions? Sweet-talking wretch. Politics was the perfect place for his glibness. It was that thought that jarred her wits back into operation.

"I'm sorry to hear that," she said, collecting her

composure. "It has nothing, however, to do with my rebellious niece and her brainless excuse for a suitor. Your arguments have merely pointed up how unprepared Priscilla is for a commitment as weighty and grueling as marriage."

"That's what marriage is to you? Weighty and grueling?" His eyes were searching. "Then I should think marriage would be the perfect punishment for her crimes against you. Why not give her what she wants and let her marry her precious Jeffrey?"

"Let her marry a boy so immature and incompetent that he can't even be on time for a crime he is supposed to commit?"

"I admit, he doesn't exactly appear to be a prime specimen. But then, few of us show the true depth and range of our potential at that age. And your niece doesn't seem to mind his deficits."

"Of course she doesn't. She has nothing to compare him to. No male acquaintances. No experience. Not even common sense."

"Try thinking about it this way: his youth can be counted a point in his favor as much as against him." He cocked a wry grin at her. "He can only improve with time."

Something began buzzing in the back of her mind . . . an idea forming. "Improvement over time . . ." She began to pace, letting the movement jog the tumblers of her mind and open her most creative thoughts. It was also possible that he could *worsen* over time, at least in Priscilla's opinion. After a few moments, she stopped and turned back.

"I believe you may have something there, Mr. Barrow. Personally, I have favored the notion of a convent school in France, but this might be even better. Spending time together under the right circumstances could open their eyes to the realities of who they are and of what this marriage they believe they want would be like. If I could give them some real work to do . . . make them experience something of the world outside their privileged existence . . . then perhaps they'd learn something about themselves and each other."

She ran an index finger over her lips, thinking, as she focused on a vision well removed from that elegant salon. Priscilla in an apron stained with cooking spatters . . . Jeffrey with his sleeves rolled up and his hands full of blisters . . .

"Work is the best tuition in the school of life," she said. "It makes for a considerable amount of maturing in a short period of time."

"Have them work together somewhere?"

"Someplace where they would have close contact, but no time to dally. A business or a large household . . . someplace busy, with a variety of work to be done . . . someplace occupied by a number of people. Oh! I know just the place."

"I bet you do." His smile contained a bit of wonder.

"Woodhull House." Her eyes darted back and forth as if she were previewing her solution. "It's a large settlement house on the Lower East Side. They have women and children, operate a school, and always have more work than they can do. The director is a friend of mine." She didn't care that a certain vengeful delight slipped into her smile. "I can't wait to see their reaction to the 'courtship' I have planned."

"Well then, why wait?"

When he raised his hand, it took a moment for her to register that he was holding something . . . something small and round-headed and metallic.

The key.

She glanced down at her bosom, finding it empty, and her face caught fire. While she was at the window . . . while he was pouring honeyed words in her ear, he had . . .

He went to the door, unlocked it and flung it open, positioning himself in the doorway with his shoulder against the door frame and his arms casually crossed. His smile was pure insolence.

"There's no better time than the present," he said smugly.

In the entry hall outside, Richards hurried over to see what his employer needed. The sight of him and his customary "Do you need assistance, madam?" released her from the paralysis of deep humiliation.

"Ask my niece to join me here," she ordered Richards. "And send a messenger to the Granton household for Jeffrey."

As the butler hurried off, she put the length of the room between herself and Connor.

How had the scoundrel—in a few short days—managed to invade both her life and her innermost senses? He had just romanced the key right out of her bosom, literally under her nose, without her even noticing!

In ten years of business and trade, she had never had anyone even attempt such liberties with her, much less take them. To stop her hands from trembling, she seized the nearest parlor chair and squeezed its wooden back until her fingers ached.

Her determination to see everyone connected with her abduction punished—which had recently wavered—abruptly stopped wavering. She suddenly wanted nothing more than to bring his male arrogance under her heel.

"Now, Mr. Barrow"—she had to clear the shame clogging her throat to continue—"the time has come to redress your part in this unsavory little drama."

That brought him up straight.

"Redress what?" He strolled into the room, looking a good bit less smug. "I have already explained—"

"Confessed," she corrected. "What remains is for me to announce the price I have decided to exact for your appalling lack of judgment."

"I believe I have more than compensated for any error on my part."

"Spoken like a lawyer." She smiled coolly. "Imagine how those words would fall on voters' ears. Especially when they've already heard the horrific story of my abduction and agonizing trials in captivity."

"You slept on Belgian linens and drank French Champagne!"

"I was bound and gagged, abducted, stripped of clothing, held in the dungeon of a house of ill repute, humiliated, and forced to endure all manner of assaults on my person . . . every word of which could easily find its way onto the front page of the newspapers . . . along with the charge that *you* helped arrange it."

He reddened and stared furiously at her, trying to read her intentions.

"Unless . . ." he prompted her.

"Unless I am persuaded to forget those vile occurrences."

"Persuaded? By what?" His eyes narrowed, as if he were finally seeing where she was leading.

"By your agreement to promote legislation giving the vote to women."

"Votes for women? You're a *suffragette!*" he exclaimed, shocked.

"Suffra*gist*, thank you."

He gave a snort of disbelief. "You cannot honestly expect me to run for Congress on a woman-vote platform. Why don't you just demand that I put a gun to my head and pull the trigger? It would be a good bit quicker and a whole lot neater! I'd be laughed out of the race."

"And you'll be hounded out of it if my story reaches the newspapers." She directed his gaze with her hand across imaginary headlines.

"CANDIDATE BARROW INVOLVED IN SOCIETY
KIDNAPPING.
BARROW DENIES RESPONSIBILITY; PLEADS POOR
JUDGMENT.

Or, better yet:

BARROW MASTERMINDS KIDNAPPING TO AID
ILLICIT LOVE."

"You have a real talent for muckraking," he said through gritted teeth. "Perhaps you should apply for work in the newspapers."

She accepted that with a nod of amusement.

"Sweet-talking will get you nowhere, Mr. Barrow. Cooperation, however, may get you everywhere, especially to Congress. There are a number of generous persons who believe strongly in votes for women and who would be pleased to support you as a prosuffrage candidate."

"In the Fourth District?" He gave an incredulous half laugh.

"Women everywhere deserve the right to vote," she said, refusing to be diverted by typical male obstructionism. "Even in the Fourth District."

Connor turned away, his fists clenched with frustration. Conniving witch. He could see it all now, as clear as Irish crystal. He had seriously understimated her. *Again*. All the while she was wailing about her mistreatment and plotting the punishment of a couple of lovestruck kids, she was secretly planning this juicy bit of political blackmail for him. Votes for women—of all the insane things she could demand of him!

He turned back and studied the triumphant curve of her mouth. She knew, with predatory feminine instinct, just how much this election and a seat in Congress meant to him. She knew he would have to capitulate to keep his name out of a scandal.

He thought of how he hadn't been able to resist the urge to tease and tempt her and taste her . . . of the way he couldn't help reacting to her as a woman, no matter how strident or condescending she seemed. There was his first mistake, he realized. She wasn't just a woman, she was an arch female . . . a suffragist . . . a renegade of her sex with no domesticating ties to a man . . . a cool, nervy force in the high-stakes game of big business. In short, she was a living, breathing argument for *never* giving women the damned vote!

"All right," he said abruptly, desperate to put distance between himself and her. "If you want a candidate you have to blackmail and coerce every step of the way . . . then I suppose you've got one."

"You'll go on record—newspapers and all—as supporting votes for women?"

"Only when I can no longer avoid it," he said, barely containing his anger.

"Then I shall do my best to see that you cannot avoid it for long."

The triumphant angle of that elegant chin, the emerald glint of those feline eyes, and the prim, knowing smile on those provocative lips were nothing short of a taunt. She knew she had him right where she wanted him.

He was suddenly trembling, poised on the edge of an explosion. If he moved a muscle, he knew, he would either strangle her or kiss her. The odds on which were dead even.

"Well then, I believe we have a deal." Her delicately folded hands and calm countenance were nothing short of maddening. "It will be a pleasure supporting you, Congressman Barrow."

He opened his mouth, but all that came out was an inarticulate rumble. The sweet-talker, it seemed, had just run out of words.

Just then Priscilla appeared at the door.

"You sent for me, Aunt Beatrice?"

She turned to confront her niece with the same deceptively unruffled air.

"Come in, Priscilla. I believe Mr. Barrow was just leaving."

AN HOUR LATER, Jeffrey and Priscilla were sitting side by side on a settee in the drawing room, staring miserably at their own feet. Priscilla sniffed and dabbed at her reddened eyes with a handkerchief her aunt supplied, while Jeffrey sat rigidly and gripped his knees with whitened fingers.

"I've half a mind to turn you over to the police." Beatrice—hands propped on hips—hovered over the pair.

"We're sorr-rry, Aunt Beatrice," Priscilla said, her shoulders twitching as she drew jerky breaths. "We never meant any harm. We just wanted you to let us be together."

As Beatrice turned away, she caught sight of Jeffrey giving Priscilla's hand a covert touch of reassurance. It was a small thing, really, but it lodged in her mind alongside the anguish in Priscilla's huge brown eyes. An annoying spot of warmth developed in the middle of her chest . . . the same traitorous sort of melting she had felt when Connor Barrow practiced his sweet-talking wiles on her. A gooey little puddle of sentiment.

Bridging that spongy emotional ground with resolve, she crossed her arms and forged ahead.

"I can only pray that your callousness resulted from youth and inexperience, not corruption of character." She stole a look at them from the corner of her eye, and they seemed suitably miserable. "Rather than turning you over to the authorities for the punishment you so richly deserve, I have decided to give you a chance to redeem yourselves. Together."

Her last word worked like an incantation. Both of them sat up straighter and looked at each other.

"T-Together?" Jeffrey said, daring to look up at her.

"Together, Aunt Beatrice?" Priscilla's face so filled with hope it was painful to witness.

"You are hereby sentenced to one month's labor and learning . . . at the Woodhull House . . . to begin in three days and continue on for thirty more. You will depart from my front door promptly at six o'clock every morning. For each morning you are late, you will serve an additional two days of obligation, so it will behoove you to be responsible in your approach to your duties. This is, I remind you, a merciful alternative to disgrace, infamy, and prison.

"Together you will help the staff and residents of the

settlement house with whatever is required of you . . . cooking, cleaning, marketing, laundry, teaching . . ."

"Cooking?" The light in Priscilla's face dimmed. "But I don't know how to cook. Nobody *cooks*, Aunt Beatrice."

"Someone always cooks, Priscilla. And if it is required, that someone will be *you*." She turned her relentlessly calm demeanor on Jeffrey.

"*Both* of you. In addition to lifting, mending, book work, baby-minding, soliciting donations . . . whatever they may require of you."

"Book work?" he said petulantly. "But numbers give me a headache. And, anyway . . . I'm no good at them." Under her determined glare, he finally lowered his gaze. "Where is this place? I shall have to know where to have the servants deliver my—Oh, no. This will never do." He lurched to the edge of the settee. "I shall have to go home each day for luncheon—I always have luncheon with Mother. And what if she insists I pay calls with her or sit in as a fourth in her card group? I simply can't—"

"You will take all your meals with the residents of the house . . . eating what they eat and when they eat. And as for your mother . . . I believe you have only two choices: grow a spine and tell her the truth, or lie like the proverbial rug." She tucked her chin and narrowed her eyes. "Close your mouth, Jeffrey."

She stepped back for a moment, looking at the wilted pair before declaring the last condition of their punishment.

"One final thing: while you are there, you are to refrain from all physical contact. Talking is permitted, but touching is strictly forbidden. Is that clear?"

"Really, Aunt Beatrice, that is—is—" Priscilla began, blushing.

"Inhuman," Jeffrey blurted out, turning to Priscilla in distress.

"Call it what you will, it is my rule."

"But it's so unfair," Priscilla said with a hint of a whine.

"You see?" Beatrice smiled triumphantly. "You're learning already. Life is chock-full of unpleasant but unavoidable restrictions. And if you have two brains in your heads you will abide by the restrictions and get on with what you must do." She looked pointedly at Priscilla. "Without weeping." She looked to Jeffrey. "Or sniveling. Now, on your feet." They hesitated, uncertain what she intended, and she grabbed them by the wrists and hauled them up.

"You have two minutes to say whatever you have to say to each other."

When she left the room and closed the door behind her, Priscilla threw herself into Jeffrey's arms.

"Oh, Jeffrey!" She hugged him with all her might. "Can you believe it? She's letting us be together."

"She is not. She's forcing us into slave labor for a month. It's danged criminal, that's what it is."

Priscilla drew back to look at him with disbelief. "How can you say that? She could have had you clapped in jail. Instead—"

"She's turning me into an indentured servant." He snorted irritably. "I've a good notion to tell the old dragon what she can do with this 'labor and learning' nonsense."

"Jeffrey, don't be foolish." She swiped her damp cheeks with the sides of her palms. "Don't you see? She's giving us a chance to prove the strength of our love, to show that we're old enough to marry."

He glowered as she smiled and tugged coquettishly on his sleeves.

"Come on, Jeffrey, we'll be together. You said that if we were together, nothing else would matter." Seeing that her wiles had less effect than expected, she grew instantly serious. "Didn't you mean it when you said that?"

He stared down at her soft hair, feathery lashes, and berry red lips, and felt his indignation dissolve in a stew of adolescent male longings.

"Sure I meant it. You mean more to me than . . . than . . ."

"Than sitting a fourth in your mother's silly old card game?"

He flushed.

"More than *anything,* Prissy."

They embraced and had time for a kiss before the door reopened and the dragon reappeared with smoke on her breath and fire in her eyes.

"Good day, Jeffrey." The dragon stood in the doorway with her arms crossed, and watched him untangle his feet from the parlor rug fringe. "My best to your poor mother."

BEATRICE WAS MIDWAY through a solitary dinner that evening when Richards appeared in the dining-room doorway.

"Sorry to interrupt, madam, but those two men in the private parlor were knocking and asking when they will be let out."

"Good Lord, I forgot all about them." Her fork hit her plate with a clang.

When she opened the door of the private parlor and

flipped the electrical light switch, the two miscreants shrank back and shielded their eyes.

"In the interest of confidentiality, I have convinced Detective Blackwell to leave your 'correction' in my hands."

"What are ye gonna do with us?" Dipper asked, blinking.

What indeed? They were without a doubt the most deferring and apologetic criminals she had ever met. Not to mention the most inept. What was it about them that made her want to yank them up by the ears and send them to bed without supper?

Still, if they were of use against her, they could probably be of use to her. She turned to Richards, who stood in the doorway regarding them with a dubious expression. She was probably mad to even attempt it . . .

"Take them up to the third floor and give them a bath, a meal, and a bed."

"Madam?" Richards look at her as if she'd lost her mind.

"Ma'am?" and "Eh?" The miscreant pair seemed to share his opinion.

"I believe I have a job for you gentlemen. Something perfectly suited to your talents." She watched their eyes widen. "On one condition."

"What's that, ma'am?" They didn't even ask what she wanted done. It was little wonder they got themselves into trouble.

"That you never, *ever* gamble again."

Horror bloomed on their faces and they looked at each other.

"Aw, please, ma'am . . . not that," Dipper pleaded.

"Gambling or whiskey," she said, shifting her strategy slightly. "Take your pick. One has to go."

"No whiskey? Ever?" Shorty licked his lips with a hint of desperation.

"Much obliged, ma'am, but we can't accept yer offer," Dipper said, pressing his crumpled woolen cap to his chest.

"That's fine," she said, turning toward the drawing room. "Then just stay where you are until Detective Blackwell and his police arrive." She was fairly certain they would see the light before she reached the door. They did.

"Wait!" Dipper lurched toward her with Shorty hovering at his shoulder. With one last, agonized look at his partner, he surrendered for both of them. "All right. No gamblin'."

"Excellent." She looked to the long-suffering Richards. "Get them some decent clothes. I'll see them after breakfast tomorrow to explain their duties."

"I ALREADY KNOW about Priscilla; the whole house is buzzing with news of her impending servitude," Alice Henry declared that evening as she settled on the bench at the foot of Beatrice's canopied four-poster. "You could probably forget Christmas bonuses altogether this year and nobody would care a whit." She dumped the stack of papers and leather legal folios on the bench beside her, propped a stiff arm on either side of her on the edge of the bench.

"What I want to know is how it went with the congressman."

"Better than expected," Beatrice said as the laces of her corset gave and she felt the sweet release of blood rushing back through her skin. Rubbing her middle soundly, she slid into a dressing gown of frothy cream silk and issued a sigh. "He agreed. Not without a struggle, however. By now, he's probably wishing he'd never met me or his rotten cousin."

Swinging by the tray on the table, she picked up a cup of chamomile tea and headed for a tufted silk chaise. She sank into the thick pillows, kicked off her shoes, and closed her eyes to savor the comfort.

"While I was at the bank, I asked a few discreet questions," Alice said.

Beatrice popped one eye open and Alice smiled reassuringly.

"My friend Mrs. Hoolihan, the one I took the typewriter course with, she works in the back office and hears all sorts of things. Like about old Mr. Barrow, Hurst Eddington Barrow, that's your congressman's grandfather."

"I believe I knew that." Her eye closed.

"Did you also know the old man disowned him—and him the only grandson—because he married against the old man's orders?"

Both eyes popped open this time. Beatrice was instantly alert.

"That I didn't know. Who did he marry?"

Alice frowned. "I don't know her name. Only that she was from the Lower East Side, poor as a church mouse, and Irish as shamrocks." Alice paused, her eyes and voice softening markedly. "Defied his old grandfather and gave up everything for love of a woman."

"Ye gods." Beatrice squeezed her eyes shut and flung an arm across them. "*Romance* again. It's an epidemic of late. Alice, you must tell me the instant Richards starts to look good to you. I'll get you the best help available."

Alice's voice contained a bit of a nettle. "Well, I thought it was wonderful. It is a rare man indeed who gives up a fortune for the woman he . . ." When Beatrice lowered her arm and leveled a pointed stare at her, she halted. "Just because *you're* not a romantic . . ."

"Back to the bank, Alice," Beatrice said in a chastening tone. "Did you deliver the papers to Mr. Chase?"

"He wasn't in so I had to deal with Mr. Eckles, the vice president, who always feels compelled to define every two-syllable word he uses in my company, as if he's convinced I have probably left my brains in my other purse." She shuddered with annoyance. "Then, to make matters worse, I stopped by a teller to make a deposit in my own account and the wretch refused to take the money."

"Refused?" Beatrice sat up abruptly, sloshing tea into her saucer.

"He insisted that the bank had never issued account numbers that begin with a letter. When I finally got him to look it up, he had the gall to suggest that I wait and allow my husband 'Henry' to transact the business for me."

It was too horrible. Beatrice laughed in spite of herself. "Henry?"

"Don't laugh," Alice said, obviously still stinging. "It took me a full five minutes to explain that 'Henry' was my last name, not my husband. He called over the head teller and, after some checking, they *finally* allowed me to make a deposit into my own account." She began to pick up the folios and papers, then paused and looked at Beatrice. "It made me wonder what I'd have to go through if I ever tried to take money *out* of their blasted bank!"

Beatrice's smile faded.

Alice's words haunted her as she climbed into bed that night and lay in the moon-brightened shadows cast by the lace bed drapes. . . . *what I'd go through if I ever tried to take money out of their blasted bank!*

It was Alice's money, in Alice's account, but it was certainly not under Alice's control. It was so much like what that girl at the Oriental—Annie—had said happened to her that it was a bit shocking. She scowled, vowing silently that President Harold Chase and every other man in the Chase-Darlington Bank would hear and heed Alice's story.

She wished Connor Barrow could have heard it, along with every other politician in the state. Perhaps then it wouldn't take another fifty years to pass a suffrage bill and achieve some level of equal rights for women. Fifty years? She held her breath for a moment. Well, it had already been forty. The thought of all of the fruitless years and work that lay ahead made her feel drained and dispirited.

If Connor Barrow came out strongly for women's suffrage and was elected tomorrow, what difference would it make? It would take a hundred Connor Barrows in every state in the union to get the vote for women. Did that mean Alice had to wait fifty years before she could deposit and withdraw her own money without a man's endorsement?

Not if she had anything to do with it. The Von Furstenberg name and fortune carried influence and she could use it to eliminate the offensive policies and practices at one of New York's leading banks.

And then what? Another bank; another loathsome policy? Was that what her life was meant to be? The possibility left her feeling strangely bereft and empty . . . until Connor's dark hair and sizzling blue eyes edged into her mind, and the ear he had poured honeyed words into earlier began to hum as it had in the drawing room.

That hum slowly condensed to whispers that teased the edges of her mind. There was more to life than causes and politics, it said. There was more to life than winning and losing, than being right or being in charge, than making a profit or even making a mark on the world. There were other things . . . to experience, to explore, to know, to delight in, and to share. Chief on that list were the tingles and lingering warmth that his lips . . .

She turned over onto her stomach, punched the fluffy bolster down into a hard little knot, and plopped her cheek down on it, feeling even more awake.

Romance. She groaned. It really was a contagion of some sort. And sweet-talking, blue-eyed Connor Barrow was a potent carrier.

TEN

SIX O'CLOCK CAME all too early on Monday morning. Priscilla stalked downstairs wearing a sleepy look and a yellow organdy overlaid by a matching linen overdress embroidered with tiny purple pansies. It was all Beatrice could do to keep from sending her straight back upstairs to change into something more sensible. But, reminding herself that learning to be more sensible was the entire point of this exercise, she withheld her comments and offered her niece a glass of freshly squeezed orange juice instead.

"Oh, no." Priscilla winced. "I couldn't possibly. Not *this* early."

Beatrice smiled, drank her own juice, donned her hat, and ushered her niece out the front door just in time to greet Jeffrey, who arrived on horseback, wearing jodhpurs, riding boots, a fitted tweed coat, and a silk top hat. He explained that early riding lessons had been his excuse to his mother for leaving the house. He tied his horse on behind the coach and climbed aboard, greeting Priscilla with a martyred smile and Beatrice with a nod.

A silent half hour later, they pulled up in front of a three-story brick structure with walls studded with windows of various styles and vintages, stuck in unusual places. Woodhull House was a former boardinghouse that had been enlarged several times to accommodate the ever increasing numbers of women and children who needed its services. The result was an eccentric but eminently approachable bit of architecture.

"This is it?" Priscilla said, holding her scented handkerchief ready as she peered out the carriage window.

"It is." Beatrice put out a hand to keep Jeffrey from bolting out the door. "I expect you to work hard at whatever you are assigned and to give the residents of Woodhull House the respect and assistance they deserve. In return, you may find that they have a great deal to teach you."

The carriage door opened and there stood two ruddy-faced men wearing painfully new clothes and hair brilliantined to a high gloss. "Oh, and these gentlemen, Mr. Muldoon and Mr. O'Shea, will be monitoring your work and reporting your progress to me on a daily basis."

Jeffrey looked at Priscilla in horror, then back at the pair, pointing.

"I know them—they're—"

"Your *former* employees," Beatrice said. "Who now work for me."

"I will not be spied on by a pair of—this is intolerable!" Jeffrey cried.

Beatrice's eyes narrowed. "No more intolerable than being brought up on criminal charges and prosecuted to the full extent of the law."

As they entered the building, they were met by a tall, sturdy woman wearing a simple gray dress and harried look. "Mrs. Von Furstenberg, thank heaven you're here. And these must be our new volunteers."

"Priscilla Lucciano, my niece"—Beatrice introduced them—"and Jeffrey Granton. This is Miss Ardis Gerhardt, the director of Woodhull House."

"You're an absolute godsend." Ardis beckoned them along with her toward the rear of the hall as she explained: "We're in dire straits this morning. One of our kitchen staff eloped last night and two others have children who've been taken ill. We're desperately shorthanded. Normally, I would pitch in to help, but I've got a board meeting this morning and an important tea for contributors this afternoon."

She led them through a large dining room filled with long tables that were even now being cleared and washed down by children in smocks. As she turned to tell them about the meal schedule, her gaze fell on Dipper and Shorty, tagging along at the rear.

Her puzzled expression prompted Beatrice to explain: "Mr. Muldoon and Mr. O'Shea. They're volunteers, too." When Beatrice scowled at them, they finally took the hint and nodded.

The minute they stepped into the kitchen, the magnitude of the emergency became clear. Bowls and platters, trays of bread fresh from a bakery, and bags of potatoes, onions, and carrots were stacked all over the long worktables—in the middle of more dirty pots, kettles, and endless stacks of dishes from breakfast. Steam roiled up from giant kettles on the huge cookstoves on the far end of the long room and there was muttering and clanging from behind the tables.

"Nora!" Ardis called to a rotund, red-faced woman engaged in lashing orders at a wincing crew of two young women and a boy. "I've brought you some help!"

Beatrice retreated with Ardis Gerhardt to the safety of the door, where she stayed just long enough to see

Priscilla and Dipper ordered to begin slicing bread and stuffing it with cheese, and Jeffrey and Shorty assigned to dishwashing detail.

Yes . . . she smiled as she carried away with her the picture of delicate Priscilla and coarse, blocky Dipper Muldoon being stuffed into aprons. This should prove to be quite an experience for her niece.

LATER THAT SAME evening, Beatrice announced her acquisition of a prosuffrage candidate to some fellow members of the executive committee of the National American Woman Suffrage Association.

"It's nothing short of amazing," Lacey Waterman said as the small group of women sipped after-dinner coffee in Beatrice's drawing room. "How on earth did you manage to find a candidate willing to stand for women's suffrage?"

She and the others eyed Beatrice's satisfaction, sensing that there was more to the story. No one simply distributed a tract or served a cup of tea and convinced a promising congressional candidate to support women's rights, though, they had to admit, if anyone *could* perform such a feat, it would be Beatrice Von Furstenberg.

"To tell the truth, he sort of 'found' me," Beatrice said with a smile that withheld as much as it revealed. "As I told the executive committee the other evening, one just has to learn what a politician wants and supply it."

"And just what does this 'Connor Barrow' fellow want?" Frannie Excelsior asked, sitting forward, her spectacle-magnified eyes fixed on their hostess.

Beatrice laughed quietly. "Why, to be elected, of course. He will expect us to help, and he has promised, in return, to go on record as supporting votes for women. A simple, honorable exchange of interest. No filthy lucre involved."

"And just how did you meet him, again?" Lacey's polite inquiry cloaked a raging curiosity. She had always had an uncanny ability to detect even the slightest hint of personal interest in a situation.

"I don't believe I said." Beatrice leveled a matter-of-fact look at her, while searching frantically for some plausible explanation. Then it struck her: "Actually it was at the Unified Charity Organization offices. He was there doing a bit of politicking and I was there . . . to help the Magdalene Society director develop a fund-raising event or two."

"The Magdalene Society?" Esther Rose asked. "Isn't that the group that tries to 'rescue' prostitutes?"

"It is," Beatrice said. It wasn't a complete untruth. She actually had met recently with the Magdalene Society director, along with the heads of several other charities, to work on financial planning and fund-raising.

"I didn't know you were interested in rescue work," Lacey said, canting her head to view Beatrice from a skeptical angle.

"It's not something I noise about," Beatrice said, feeling her face heat. "I believe in helping women in all circumstances."

"When do we get to meet him?" Frannie rubbed her hands together.

"The first in a series of debates is scheduled for three days from now . . . Thursday evening. I thought we'd invite Susan Anthony, Elizabeth Cady Stanton, Carrie Catt, and a few other members of the committee to attend with us."

Just then the sound of the front doors opening and slamming shut again drifted into them. "A bath. I need a bath!" was followed by sounds of things slamming onto the marble floor. Beatrice rose immediately and hurried out into the hall, and the others followed to see what was causing the commotion.

Priscilla—hair unraveling and yellow linen badly stained—stood in the middle of the entry. Her picture-book hat lay some distance away on the floor, along with her heeled slippers. As they watched, she ripped off her ruined overdress, crumpled it up, and flung it furiously aside.

That violent action seemed to use up the last of her energy and she turned to Beatrice with her shoulders sagging and her chest heaving.

"They swarmed in like locusts"—she held out her much-abused skirt—"gobbling an' slopping . . . thought I was going to be sick . . . then we finally got it cleaned up . . . here they came again . . . wolfing an' swilling." She made quaffing and chomping sounds to accompany her wild-eyed demonstration. "Stinky old onions an' potatoes . . . an' more onions and potatoes . . . an' *more* onions . . . mountains of them . . . always *onions*!" She jabbed a bandaged finger at them for emphasis, then halted and held it up, looking as if the sight of it jolted her anew.

"See-e-e?" She brandished it, as if the mere fact of it explained all.

Then, grabbing up her bedraggled organdy and what remained of her dignity, she staggered up the stairs in her stockinged feet, muttering to herself. When she disappeared from sight, the others turned to Beatrice with no little shock. Beatrice gave a deep sigh and turned her stunned guests back to the drawing room.

"Cooking lesson," she explained. "Her first."

THE INITIAL DEBATE in the Fourth District congressional race was held that Thursday evening in the

Cutters' Hall on the East Side of the city. The main auditorium seated one hundred and fifty strangers, as the management was wont to say, or two hundred people friendly enough or liquored up enough to get cozy.

Beatrice and her delegation, which included Susan Anthony, Elizabeth Cady Stanton, Carrie Catt, and Belva Vanderbilt, as well as Lacey, Frannie, and Esther Rose, arrived early to secure good seats. Nevertheless, they had to hang onto their hats as they were jostled by sleeveless stevedores, lift their skirts as they navigated a row of heavy boots belonging to construction workers, and hold their breaths as they excused themselves through representatives of tanneries, butcher shops, and taverns. Politics in the Fourth District was a most pungent undertaking.

They made their way to the front of the hall and seated themselves to one side of the bunting-draped stage. The seats around them were soon filled with shopkeepers, pipe fitters, omnibus drivers, union officials, carpenters, teamsters, and bank clerks. Nearby sat a clergyman accompanied by a committee of women wearing "Temperance" buttons. On their right were a number of "nativists" with pennants proclaiming: "Save America for the Americans" and "No More Immigration." At the rear, stood the latecomers, coarsely clad men with beet-red faces, slurred speech, and heavy Irish accents, accompanied by flashily dressed women.

Beatrice was unprepared for the impact of Connor Barrow when he arrived, confidently greeting everyone he saw by name. Dressed in a black suit, pristine white shirt, and gray silk tie, he seemed to light up the hall as he entered. When the other members of the committee nudged her and inquired if he were their candidate, she could only respond with a nod.

The moderator, well-known newspaper publisher Charles Anderson Dana, of *The Sun,* called the meeting to order and introduced both of the candidates for the Fourth District congressional seat.

"We need election reform," Netherton declared in professorial tones.

"He wouldn't say that if he expected to *win,*" Connor countered with a grin, drawing laughter.

"The country needs professional politicians, not men with one hand in their own business and the other in the public till," Netherton asserted.

"He'd like to sit around with one hand in the public till and the other *in his own pocket?*" Connor said with astonishment, then wagged his head in disbelief.

And so it went; Connor punched holes in every point Netherton made. Susan Anthony frowned at Elizabeth Cady Stanton, who passed it on to Frannie Excelsior, who gave Lacey Waterman a dubious look. Beatrice, seated beside Lacey, caught their bewilderment and grew increasingly uncomfortable.

Then the minister with the temperance committee, in the very front row, shot to his feet and called out: "Temperance should be the country's *first* priority. The federal government must pass an act of prohibition to put an end to the evils of drunkenness and alcoholism!"

The outburst was greeted by catcalls and booing, countered only by a pitiful few "here, here's" from the minister's own delegation.

"Now, now . . . the good reverend has raised a most worthy topic," Connor said, making quieting motions toward the rowdy element in the back. "Drunkenness is the cause of many ills. But no law passed in Washington can take a bottle or glass from a drunkard's hand in Haggarty's Tavern." He looked down at the minister who was still trying to sort out whether that meant Connor was for or against prohibition. "Isn't that right, Reverend?"

The minister hesitated, then started to agree.

"Well, yes—"

"What words inscribed into dusty old law books in Washington are going to change what a fellow does down at Murphy's or the Barrel & Shamrock?" He glanced at the group at the back with a cajoling wink. "The Good Lord wrote the Ten Commandments, and yet they get broken every day of the week. If the Almighty can't make people quit doing things by passing a law, what chance do we have?"

Laughter erupted around the hall, all but drowning out Netherton's attempt to mollify the good reverend, who turned—red-faced—to trade words with a detractor several seats away. Beatrice looked down the row of her fellow committee members and found them frowning at her. The more they heard, the less likely he seemed to be a candidate to support women's suffrage. She shot to her feet.

"Tell us, Mr. Barrow . . . how do you feel about the vote for women?"

The noise level seemed to drop dramatically.

"Votes for women?" Connor stepped around the podium, leaned his elbow casually on it, and gazed down at her and her banner-wearing companions. "Now, that is a most interesting subject. Mrs. Von Furstenberg, I believe. I take it *you* want to vote."

"Of course I do," she said, hastily beckoning the others to their feet, too. Frannie, Lacey, Susan, and Elizabeth . . . they rose and stood together, shoulder to shoulder, a united front, waiting for his declaration of support for women's suffrage. "We all want to vote. We are all citizens of this country and we deserve to have a say in how it is governed."

He studied her and her friends, then broke into an infuriating smile.

"I would certainly approve of *you* having the vote, Mrs. Von Furstenberg. In fact, I'd probably vote to give you *two* votes . . . six votes . . . a dozen." He glanced at the men around the hall and winked. "Wouldn't you, gents? Wouldn't you like to see Mrs. Von Furstenberg, here, put her ballots in your precinct box?"

Beatrice reddened as laughter and blatantly personal invitations to do some "ballot-box stuffing" rolled around the auditorium. How dare he use his tawdry personal innuendoes to expose her and her cause to such ridicule? How low could the man sink?

"I have asked a civil question, Mr. Barrow," she declared hotly. "I expect a civil answer. Do you or do you not favor the vote for women?"

"Women in general, you mean? *All* women?"

"Of course, *all* women. Don't parse words with me, sir."

"So, you're asking if I would support giving the vote to . . . oh, say . . . Pearly Quinn back there?" He pointed to the back of the crowd and an older woman with a heavily painted face, dressed in faded satins and feathers. Hearing her name, the old girl squealed with delight— showing several gaps from missing teeth—and began to flap her tatty boa in the laughing faces around her.

Anger seized Beatrice. He was reneging on their agreement in front of Susan and Elizabeth and the rest of the committee!

"Does that estimable specimen of American manhood beside her have the vote?" She pointing to a grizzled old fellow standing near the eager Miss Quinn.

"Shore do!" the old gaffer declared, sticking out his chest. "Fact is—I voted *nine times* in th' last elec-tion!"

Another burst of laughter erupted, drawing an indignant response from her suffrage-supporting group.

"Then Pearly Quinn deserves to have it as well," she called out when the noise subsided. "What do you say, Miss Quinn? Don't you deserve to vote?"

"Shore do!" Pearly echoed her male counterpart's response. "I'd vote fer Connor Barrow, there." She turned to the old fellow beside her. "*Ten* times!"

This time when the laughter subsided, it was Connor who took the offensive.

"And what would women *do* with the vote, Mrs. Von Furstenberg? What could women possibly do with their votes that men do not already do for them?"

The colossal gall.

"First of all"—she propped her hands at her waist and glared—"they could elect honest officials and represen-tatives who *keep their promises!*"

A murmur went through the crowd at that blatant challenge, and for a long moment, she stared at Connor with her eyes blazing, deciding whether to reveal his promise to support suffrage or women. Then there was a subtle change in his expression.

"I can't imagine any man not keeping his promise to you, Mrs. Von Furstenberg. You seem to be a most de-termined woman."

She felt a shiver run up her spine. Righteous indigna-tion, no doubt.

"If nothing else, you are perceptive, Mr. Barrow," she responded. "I *am* determined. Do you or do you not sup-port women's suffrage?"

"I might . . . if I could be persuaded that women could do something with the vote that men can't do for them." He looked her over with a broadening grin. "What about it, Mrs. Von Furstenberg? Do you think you could *persuade* me?"

Desultory male laughter wafted through the back and then expectant silence descended.

"Fine." Her face was aflame. "If you want to know what women will gain by the vote, I challenge you to accompany me to the Woodhull Settlement House and learn firsthand about the women in your district."

Booing came from the rear of the hall, along with calls of "Get yerself a man" and "Go home an' fetch me some dinner, woman!"

Connor held up his hands for quiet, but the time of evening and the length of the meeting were taking their toll on the crowd. He nearly had to shout to be heard.

"I am always willing to learn about the people I intend to serve. I accept your challenge, Mrs. Von Furstenberg. I assume it is meant for my opponent Mr. Netherton as well."

The reform candidate seemed as startled as everyone else at the reminder that he was present.

"But of course I'll come," Netherton said quickly. "The reforms we seek go to the very heart of the issue of proper representation. One man"—he held up a finger—"one vote!"

"Ye hear that, sister?" came voices from the far side of the hall. "One *man*, one vote!" "Women got no bizness votin'!" "Go home to yer stoves an' kids, where ye belong!" Even the temperance-demanding reverend turned on them, shaking an accusing finger.

Trembling with anger, Beatrice hardly felt it when Lacey and Frannie took things into their own hands, snatched up her purse, and shoved her down the row toward the nearest exit. It took some doing, but they made their way up the packed aisle, jostled their way through the rowdies at the back, and escaped.

The night air filled Beatrice with a cold blast of reality. She paused on the pavement just outside the hall, righted her jilted hat, and braced for the censure she was sure to receive from the committee. But when Susan Anthony appeared, she reached for Beatrice's arm and gave it a reassuring squeeze.

"So much for the promises of politicians," she said with a wan little smile. "It's an old story, my dear. Don't lose any sleep over it. Did you see who he arrived with? Richard Croker himself and a pack of Tammany's wretched ward heelers and 'shoulder hitters.' Barrow is Tammany's lap dog." She wagged her head sadly. "He'll never be a friend to women."

Beatrice winced as one by one Carrie Catt, Elizabeth Cady Stanton, and Belva Vanderbilt squeezed her hand or pressed her cheek with theirs before departing for their carriages and cabs. But their unexpected understanding and consoling words only scored the humiliation of his betrayal deeper into her pride.

"How dare he do that to me? Promise me his support and then—"

"Damned *man*," Lacey growled, looping her arm through Beatrice's.

"Hanging's too good for him," Frannie declared, snagging her other arm and helping to propel her toward her carriage.

"He'll pay for this." The depth of her anger surprised her; it felt too intense and too personal to be caused just by the political sleight of hand he had performed tonight. "I'm going to make him change his mind and support women's suffrage in public or my name isn't Beatrice Von Furstenberg!"

"Give it up, Beatrice," Frannie said, pulling Beatrice to a halt. "It'll just be throwing pearls before swine."

"A handsome, sweet-talking swine," Lacey said with a twinge of jaded interest, "but a swine, nonetheless."

"Yes, well . . . you know what happens to swine," Beatrice responded with narrowing eyes. "Sooner or later they become somebody's bacon."

TWO HOURS AFTER the debate ended, the congratulations were still ringing in Connor's ears.

Brawling, colorful Boss Croker had indeed been in the audience . . . along with mayoral candidate Thomas Gilroy, Big Tim Sullivan, the so-called "Baron of the Bowery," and Connor's dapper campaign manager Charles F. Murphy. They had spirited Connor off to O'Toole's for a celebratory drink.

"I doubt you'll need three more debates," Boss Croker declared. "One more should pretty much finish old Netherton off. Did you see him tonight? So green around the gills, I thought he was going to be sick."

"And what you did to that suffragette," Big Tim Sullivan added, "that was brilliant. I thought I'd bust a gut laughin' at that old Pearly Quinn!"

Boss Croker laughed, too, then grew more serious. "You can't ignore these vote-crazed women, Barrow, but you can't give them much attention either. Can't have people thinking you're soft on this 'suffrage' nonsense."

"You know I'd give my right arm for you and the party, Boss." Connor laughed. "But asking me not to give women attention . . . well, there are some things that are just beyond a man's control." He waggled his brows and they responded with ribald laughter.

"I'll go see this 'shrieking sister' settlement house," he

continued, flashing his infamous grin, "show some concern . . . listen to the ladies . . . kiss a few babies. I can take a news reporter or two along and see we get some good press out of it."

Croker clapped him on the shoulder. "That's our boy. Always thinking."

Now, as Connor climbed into a cab and headed home he allowed himself a quiet moment to savor the night's victory. Closing his eyes, he laid his head back against the worn leather seat, listened again to the applause and once again felt that invisible flow of power from the audience that always energized him.

Then into that brief pleasure blew a draft of uneasiness. *She* materialized in his mind, looking just as she had tonight, standing in the audience. Proud. Headstrong. Womanly. With extravagant curves, a lush red mouth, and smoky emerald eyes that betrayed the passion burning in her.

He had known instantly why she was there—he should have expected something like that—could have prevented it if he hadn't been so angry three days ago when he left her house. All he had wanted to do that afternoon was put distance between him and her. It didn't occur to him that she expected an instant, full-blown declaration of support for women's suffrage at his very next public appearance . . . in front of Boss Croker and half of Tammany Hall. Didn't she know anything about politics?

The cab stopped and he opened his eyes, expecting that they were at his brownstone. When he reached for the door handle, it turned before he touched it and the door swung open.

A male form sprang into the cab, knocking him back against the seat.

"What the hell—"

A second man barreled in and Connor was suddenly pinned to the seat by two sets of shoulders and knees. They grabbed his arms and though he struggled, he couldn't seem to gain enough purchase against the floor or seat to fight back. Then a hand clamped over his mouth, and a familiar voice with an Irish brogue stilled his resistance.

"Sorry, gov—" The pair thumped on the roof and the cab lurched into motion again. Light from a streetlamp fell across one of his assailants' faces and Connor recognized Dipper Muldoon.

"She sent us to get ye. Said not to take 'no' fer an answer."

He looked at the other man and found Shorty O'Shea nodding earnest confirmation.

He didn't have to ask who "she" was.

ELEVEN

WHEN THE CAB finally came to a stop, Dipper and Shorty pulled him from the carriage. They had brought him to a broad alley lined with tall wooden fences and doors to carriage houses, and now ushered him across a service yard and into the rear door of an imposing brick house. A turn or two and a glimpse down an elegantly appointed hallway confirmed his suspicion.

When the two opened a pair of imposing mahogany doors and shoved him inside, there she stood, on the far side of a large, richly furnished library with her arms crossed.

"Thank you, gentlemen," she said, dismissing the pair. "If you will wait just outside . . ."

As the doors closed, she looked Connor over with a critical air.

In the soft light of a desk lamp, her eyes glinted and her skin glowed golden. She was wearing the same fitted navy suit she had worn earlier, at Cutters' Hall: prim standing collar, leg-of-mutton sleeves, narrow waist, and a gently flared skirt that finished in a modest bustle. He had no damned business noticing that her hair was slipping from its Gibson-style coif or that it gave her a lightly mussed and eminently touchable appearance.

"What the devil do you think you're doing dragging me here by force?" he demanded, annoyed by his wayward thoughts.

"I doubt you would have come any other way." She lowered her arms and advanced to the edge of the nearby mahogany desk. "Why did you renege on your promise this evening? I want an explanation and a timetable for your announcement of your support of women's suffrage. And I will have both"—she pointed sharply to the floor—"before you leave this room."

"Or?"

"I should think that would be obvious. *You won't leave.*"

"Going to lock me in again?" he said, lowering his gaze pointedly to her chest. "As I recall, that wasn't overly effective."

He wasn't sure if the increased color in her face qualified as a blush.

"I'll depend on my new employees to see that you stay."

"Dipper and Shorty? What makes you think they would raise a hand against me? We go back a long way . . . Dipper, Shorty, and I."

"Well, we have an arrangement . . . Dipper, Shorty, and I."

"Similar to the one you have with me, no doubt. 'Do as I say or face ruination and disgrace.'"

"Jail, actually," she said with an arch smile. "But that is hardly the issue."

"I beg to differ." He started toward her, but stopped after only a few steps. "That is exactly the issue here.

What the hell gives you the right to go around extorting and bullying and using any and every underhanded tactic known to man—"

"Precisely. Every tactic known to *man*," she declared with a calm that infuriated him. "I am doing nothing to you or Dipper and Shorty that men don't do to each other all the time. Nobody cries foul when a man exerts a little 'leverage' on a rival. I do it and I'm called wicked and unnatural . . . a harridan, a heathen, or an amazon."

Beneath the anger in her eyes, he glimpsed a deep well of resentment. Her crusading on behalf of women, he realized, was not a sentimental bit of "do-gooding" on her part. Her determination came from something far more personal. He tilted his head to view her from a fresh angle.

"Tell me. What's your stake in all of this 'suffrage' and 'women's rights' rigmarole? What do you get out of it?"

She seemed surprised by the question, but quickly generated what sounded like a well-rehearsed response.

"The satisfaction of knowing that I've done something worthwhile, something that will have a lasting impact on the world, something that will make women's lives better."

"Yes, yes . . . but what do *you* get out of it? Suffragettes complain about women being downtrodden"— he strolled around the room, touching a polished marble bust on a shelf, stroking the mahogany desktop, and running his fingers through the hand-cut crystals hanging from the lamp shade—"but you are probably the least downtrodden woman in the entire state of New York. You have everything a woman could ever hope to have . . . money, position, and power. Whether you want to admit it or not, you already have the vote in one of the most powerful places in the country . . . the boardroom.

Better yet, you don't have to ask permission of anyone to do anything. You're a widow. You have married respectability without the mess and bother of a husband. What could having the vote give you that you don't already have?"

"You honestly haven't a clue, do you?" she said, returning his scrutiny. "You've never had someone tell you your opinions and ideas are worthless just because you're a man . . . that you can't deposit money in a bank, that you can't purchase a piece of property or sign your name for a—"

"And you have? Was it your husband? Did he make your life such a living hell that you're now determined to return the favor to the entire male sex?" The subtle stiffening of her shoulders made him think he'd struck a nerve.

"My marriage has nothing to do with my belief in women's rights."

"What colossal—and I mean this in the nicest way possible—*bullshit!*" He approached her in a deliberate prowl, his eyes narrowed as if trying to peer straight into her. "Let's see"—he tallied the points on his fingers— "you've said marriage is a great weight and a burden, you complain that men dismiss and ridicule women, you detest vulnerability, think romance is illusion, and believe real love is so rare as to be virtually nonexistent."

He halted and gave her an insultingly thorough look.

"Taken together, that can only mean . . . Mercer was a dried-up old cod, decades older than you, who treated you like a child, except on those rare occasions when he wanted you to be his accommodating toy. You were required to hold your tongue, to decorate his parlor, and to make certain his food was hot and his bed was warm." The sparks struck in her eyes made him reconsider that last duty. "Ahhh. Old Mercer didn't even bother with that." He broke into a wry grin. "He *was* old."

He thought for a moment that she might explode. Instead, she reasserted control and tightly refolded her arms.

"If you're trying to divert me from my purpose in bringing you here, you're doomed to disappointment. I want to know why you refused to declare your support for suffrage."

"Some would say that a woman who marries for money should know enough to be satisfied when money is all she gets," he continued, trying to imagine her with the doddering old fellow he'd seen briefly, some years ago.

"Let's see if my powers of deduction match yours," she said. "You're a glib, smooth-talking politician—which means you'll say whatever is expedient at the moment—hang the consequences. Your singular goal in life is getting elected to office, no matter what it takes. You think women are basically subhuman, and thus, any and all promises made to one are nonbinding. Taken together, that can only mean that you never *intended* to keep your promise."

She was starting to annoy him; no doubt about it.

"I *did not* break my word to you this evening. I said I would support the passage of suffrage legislation for women, and I will."

"Oh, yes?" She took a step closer. *"When?"*

When I damned well please . . . somehow didn't come out. He found himself standing over her, staring down into a pair of fiery emerald eyes, breathing in the fragrance wafting up on tendrils of warmth.

"When you've persuaded me," he declared with heat rising up the back of his throat and invading his voice.

Her eyes widened and she took a step backward.

"Even if that were possible in a mere human life-time . . . 'persuasion' was not a part of our deal."

He took a step forward.

"Did it never once enter that devious mind of yours that it would have been political suicide for me to walk into that debate tonight and out of the clear blue declare that I'm prosuffrage?"

She took another step back and was suddenly trapped with her back against her desk, more accurately, with her bustle squashed against it.

"Typical politician." She sniffed. "As soon as you make a promise, you set about proving it's impossible to keep. 'I'd love to, my dear, but my cronies simply won't allow it.'"

"I didn't say it was impossible. I said it wasn't possible *tonight*. If I change my platform, I have to have good reasons. People have to be prepared . . . change can only be accomplished in small increments."

He paused to let that sink in and when he spoke again, his voice was softer.

"That means you have to educate me . . . enlighten me. And while you're publicly persuading me, I'll be privately persuading Boss Croker and Charles Murphy and campaign contributors and city officials."

Everything he was saying sounded so cursedly reasonable. How could she be sure he was speaking in earnest? She could barely be sure of her own name with him only an inch away.

"I must hand it to you . . . you really are good at this," she said, clinging desperately to her skepticism. "You could almost convince me that you mean it."

He raised his arms as if demanding the universe witness the outrage of her behavior toward him, and then dropped them to his sides.

"You are the damnedest female I've ever—you're determined to make me into a lying, greedy, underhanded heel, aren't you? Why is that? So you can bury me in the same box with old Mercer and every other man who dared cross you? Well, I don't think so, darlin'."

He seized her by the shoulders.

"I'm alive and well and I'm not going into any box. If you really want support for your women's suffrage, you'll just have to deal with me"—his gaze dropped to her mouth—"and whatever it is you feel whenever we do this. . . ."

His lips touched hers and the tension that had been growing in her burst, sending a surge of desire along the underside of her skin. This was what she had dreaded, this power he seemed to have over her senses and responses. A soft flame ignited and raced along the nerves of her limbs.

"Did you forget?" he murmured against her lips, his voice slipping into that cozening Irish lilt that always dispelled her anger and indignation. "I couldn't. The feel of your lips against mine, stirring my blood . . ." He nipped her lips with his, tasting, tempting. She ran her tongue over them to assuage the tingling it caused and he gave a throaty laugh and kissed her deeply again.

"Did you forget how my body comes alive against yours?" he whispered, seizing her waist and pulling her into the bend of his body. Alive was a pale description of the energy and vitality that engulfed her as his arms closed around her. She arched into him and slid her hands around his waist and up his back.

"Did you forget the feel of my arms around you, and how you lean into me when your knees go weak?"

Each word added to the heat building inside her and she felt that melting beginning again. Knees first, then spine, then will. She was suddenly pliant, yielding . . . an overwhelmed observer in her own hungry and receptive body.

"No," she whispered, looking up and seeing halos of light around everything in her vision, "I didn't forget." She blinked, but the light remained. "Not overly smart of me . . ."

"It's not a matter of being smart, Beatrice darlin'. It's a matter of trusting the wisdom of your heart." He drew back enough to run a finger down her chest to her heart. "It's a matter of trusting yourself as much as another . . . of knowing that when it's right, you'll *know*."

"And when you think you know, what then?"

"Ahhh." His smile filled with invitation. "Then, when every particle of your body and every thought in your brain is screaming out for you to reach out and grab that pleasure with both hands . . . you do it. And you hang on for dear life. True pleasure's a great gift, you see. Not something to be taken lightly."

He trailed kisses down her jaw line to the side of her neck, where he was stopped by a pair of prim collars. He slid a hand up the front of her jacket and began expertly dispatching buttons. Her skin seemed to hum everywhere he touched it. She arched her back to meet those soft, scandalous kisses.

Suddenly she was perched on the edge of the desk with her jacket and blouse unbuttoned to bare her white satin corset and thin chemise. He drew back enough to study the way she looked and moaned appreciatively as he ran his fingers over the creamy curves of her breasts. She closed her eyes, trapping in her head the sight of him touching her. More, she wanted . . .

More?

She began to surface from her submersion in that sea

of pleasure. The closer she rose to the surface, the greater the sense of urgency that possessed her. What was she doing? Taking his face between her hands, she looked at him with rising alarm. The blue of his eyes was now mere rings of color around dark pools of desire. She pushed him away and stumbled from the desk.

Her heart was hammering. Her head felt disconnected from her body. She forced herself to breathe deeply and slowly. With trembling hands she worked to right her garments, waiting, desperate for the rise of those inner walls that had long ago ceased to be a barrier and had become, instead, a comfort.

"Don't do that," he said quietly.

"Do what?" she said tautly, lifting her chin.

"Run away."

His gaze held hers for a long moment. She bore it just long enough to salve her pride, then looked away.

"Maybe I just learned what I needed to learn."

"Which was?"

She busied herself fastening the buttons of her jacket.

"That you're as smooth with your kisses as you are with your words. And that I need to beware of both."

He reddened and his eyes narrowed.

"I'm afraid you have it all wrong, Mrs. Von Furstenberg. I'm not the one you have to worry about. When *I* kiss a woman it's for one and only one reason. You, on the other hand, seem to have a whole host of ugly little reasons for kissing a man." He headed for the door.

"Wait just a minute," she commanded. "We haven't settled things, yet."

"Settled things? You mean your nasty little bit of blackmail?" He strode back toward her. "Fine." His eyes were suddenly hot and luminous. "This is how it's going to be: you're going to meet me at this settlement house . . . show me the place and introduce me to some of the inmates. I'm going to watch and listen to it all with noble concern. I'm going to be sympathetic, thoughtful, and then visibly moved. Afterward, I'll make a statement to the news writers present that the women there deserve better justice and better representation.

"When they ask you about my comments, you're going to praise my fairness but say that I still have much to learn. I'll be damned annoyed, and you'll issue another challenge. Something suitably educational, I'm sure . . . a visit to a factory, perhaps . . . someplace where women workers are greatly 'oppressed.'"

"Good Lord—you have it all planned out," she said, astonished.

"Just thinking on my feet." His anger was still rising. "That's what we shifty, underhanded, smooth-talking politicians do best . . . *think on our feet.*"

She tried to find in his eyes some assurance that he meant what he said.

"What guarantee do I have that you'll go through with it?" she demanded.

"Lady, I'm fresh out of guarantees. But it's always been my experience that you get what you pay for."

CONNOR BLEW THROUGH the front doors and out into the autumn night with his pride and his passion both on fire. He couldn't remember when he'd been so angry. He was desperate to put his fist through something . . . preferably something that would shatter and make one hell of a mess.

Damnable woman. Why couldn't she just want him, clean and simple? Why couldn't she—just for one infernal hour—forget she was the widow Von Furstenberg?

That she'd had a rotten marriage with a decrepit old man who had no clue how to appreciate or even enjoy her? That she resented men and disliked her attraction to one of them? Why couldn't she forget for a few blessed moments that he was a "man" and she was a "woman"? Why the hell couldn't he just be Connor and she just be Beatrice?

There were no answers to those questions, but the exertion of walking gradually cleared his head and the rush of angry energy that accompanied his thoughts subsided. By the time he reached his office, he was left with a stream of vivid impressions that were freed from the emotions that had originally accompanied them. Beatrice in command. Beatrice soft-eyed and playful. Beatrice warmed and melting. Beatrice terrified.

He stopped in the middle of turning on a light, scowling, concentrating on that last image, seeing again her trembling frame and hasty retreat. For just a few frantic moments, she had been truly frightened; he would stake his life on it. Of all of the aspects of her he had absorbed during their encounter, that was the one that truly surprised him.

He flipped the switch of his desk lamp and sat down in the pool of light it created. What was it about her that made him so determined to have her, to feel her responding, to make her admit she wanted him as a man? Was it as simple as pride or curiosity? Or was it something more?

His features slowly relaxed.

What did it matter, as long as he had her?

She disdained and distrusted his gifts of persuasion, even as she tried to harness them for her own purposes. But in order to harness them, she had to stay closer to him than she knew to be wise. There wasn't a human born who could resist temptation forever.

He smiled, licking his lips slowly, anticipating, already enjoying the sweet rewards of victory. She was every bit as trapped as he was, and in a scheme of her own devising. His smile broadened.

It served her right.

TWELVE

TWO EVENINGS LATER, Beatrice and Alice were in the drawing room going over the official agenda for the Consolidated Industries board of directors meeting when Priscilla arrived home. The last week had been anything but pleasant for her niece, she knew. The girl was generally too angry or exhausted to say so when she returned home, but Beatrice had received nightly reports from Dipper and Shorty on her activities.

Beatrice put down her board reports and watched from the settee as Priscilla dragged herself up the steps. The girl had given up silk and embroidered tulle in favor of cotton blouses and wool jersey skirts, but her clothes still took a shocking amount of abuse. Today was no exception; she looked like she'd been caught in a cannery explosion.

"How did it go today, gentlemen?" Beatrice said when Dipper and Shorty appeared at the drawing-room door.

"She ain't much of a cook, I can tell ye," Dipper confided in dismay. "Acted like she never seen a chicken plucked in her life. Dang near lost her dinner when I showed her how. An' Cook sent her down to the market . . . she didn't know th' first thing about hagglin' a proper price ner checkin' to see she weren't shorted. They like to robbed 'er blind."

"She shoulda let Jeff hold th' money," Shorty said, mostly to his partner. "He'd 'ave seen to it they paid proper prices."

"Oh, he'd have paid, all right," Dipped declared with indignation. "Through th' nose. Like them beef steaks he had to have."

"They was good meat," Shorty responded, scowling. "And he's right—ye get tired of stew and watery soup day after day."

Dipper turned to explain to Beatrice: "We was sent to get chickens from the market. Only him and her"—clearly Jeffrey and Priscilla—"had a bit of a set-to over buyin' beefsteaks. She wouldn't let him have the money Cook gave 'em . . . said it wouldn't feed enough. He went stalkin' off . . . and we still had potatoes and carrots an' onions and such to buy."

Beatrice pictured Priscilla at a Lower East Side market, amongst the gamey hanging birds, bushels of sprouting potatoes, piles of wilted greens, and baskets of seeping tomatoes. "Jeffrey didn't stay to help her?"

Dipper looked uncomfortable and began to knead the brim of his cap.

Beatrice scowled and turned to Shorty. "Mr. O'Shea?"

"He went on out to th' market stalls and found some turnips and tomatoes," Shorty answered with a sidelong glare at Dipper.

"Yeah . . . to throw at her when she come out of the butcher's," Dipper charged with no little indignation.

"Well, he didn't hit 'er," Shorty said. "She didn't need to get all huffy."

"It wasn't right—him leavin' her with the shopping and runnin' off," Dipper declared. "He was supposed to help."

"He did help."

"Did not," Dipper countered. "You an' me an' Miss Priscilla carried most of it back ourselves."

"Well, his boot was hurtin' him. Got a right big old blister—saw it meself."

"It wouldn't have been hurtin' him if he hadn't been runnin'—"

"Thank you, gentlemen," Beatrice said. "I believe I have the gist of it."

She watched them heading for the kitchen, arguing about who should have listened to whom, and saw in their quarrel a reflection of her niece's straining relationship with Jeffrey. Clearly, things were moving along.

"She might need a sympathetic ear," Alice suggested.

"Just what I was thinking. I believe the rest of these can wait until tomorrow." She set her papers aside and headed for the stairs.

The sound of muffled sobs stopped her outside Priscilla's door. The worry that was never far from her mind returned with a vengeance. What lesson was Priscilla truly learning from all of this? What if the work and the world she had been plunged into were too harsh? It struck Beatrice that her niece would need help in order to draw useful insights from the experience, and there was no one to provide it but her.

A shaft of light from the hallway cut through the darkened room, illuminating Priscilla's lace-draped four-poster. She was lying facedown across the bed, still dressed in her ruined blouse and skirt, crying her heart out.

Beatrice steeled herself against a massive wave of guilt and sat down on the edge of the bed.

"What do you want?" Priscilla's voice was muffled by bedclothes.

"To see how you're doing," Beatrice said.

"Fine—I'm just *fine*."

"You don't look fine, Priscilla. Sit up and let's talk."

After a minute, Priscilla pushed up from the bed and gave her damp face a swipe with each hand. "I guess you're happy now . . . ruining my life . . . making me miserable," she said in the grip of anguish, "like you."

"You think I want you to be miserable?"

"Misery loves company, doesn't it?" Priscilla's eyes glittered with tears.

"I am not miserable, Priscilla. On the contrary, I am quite content with my life."

"Then why are you always so angry?" Priscilla heaved a settling breath. "You're always saying that life isn't fair and talking about how things are so terrible for women. You're always going to meetings about how men are so vile and awful."

"Is that what you really think? That I believe men are vile and awful?"

"You hate men. Everybody knows it, even Alice. That's why you can't stand that Jeffrey and I are in love. Just because you had a rotten old man for a husband doesn't mean all men are bad."

The picture Priscilla painted was neither flattering nor fair, but it was brutally accurate as a picture of how her niece saw her. How had they grown so far apart in recent years? When Priscilla first came to her, at age nine, they spent many happy days together and enjoyed each other's company. Each understood full well that the other was the only real family she had.

"I don't believe all men are loathsome, Priscilla, especially not my late husband, Mercer. He was a good man.

Too old for me, true, and not much of a romantic, but he was honest and trustworthy. He tutored me in business and finance and made me the businesswoman I am today. I will always be grateful to him."

"But you didn't love him, did you?" Priscilla said in accusatory tones.

"That's a complicated question that requires a very complicated answer." She felt a jumble of emotions rising and suppressed them. "I cared for him a great deal."

"But he didn't make your heart pound, or make you melt all over with just a smile, or make the sun shine brighter just by being near you, did he?"

The hurt and anger in the question stung Beatrice. "No, he didn't."

"Then you've never been in love. You don't know what it's like."

Oh, but I do, was on the tip of Beatrice's tongue before she stopped it. It astonished her that in the last week she had indeed experienced that heart-racing, melting-all-over, the-world-is-a-brighter-place sort of feeling. And it further astonished her that—enthralling as it was—she knew that it had precious little to do with real love.

"I won't debate my life or my experience with you, Priscilla. My point, in requiring you to work at Woodhull, is that you have a lot to learn about life."

"Oh? And how is boiling up gallons of gruel and haggling with dirty old men at the market going to teach me anything?" Priscilla demanded.

Beatrice studied her niece's resentment and resistance.

"How many of the Woodhull residents have you met?" she asked.

Priscilla scowled. "I don't know . . . maybe four or five . . . the ones who work in the kitchen."

"Tell me about them."

"Why?" Priscilla's eyes narrowed.

"I'm curious. Aren't *you* curious about the people you work with?"

She drew a long-suffering breath, as if resigning herself to the fact that she was in for another *lesson*. "Nora's the head cook . . . Estelle is her assistant . . . Mary Alice just came there and got assigned to the kitchen, like me. There's Tad, he does scullery work . . . he's twelve. And there's Rita . . . she's in a family way. She gets sick every morning . . . you can hear her . . . it's disgusting." She made a face.

"Do you know much about them?"

Priscilla gave her a resentful look from the corner of her eye. "I know Nora bellows and Estelle gossips and I think Mary Alice has a husband somewhere out West looking for gold. Rita's not married and she's scared they'll turn her out onto the streets. And Tad's mother died two years ago at Woodhull and they let him stay on, instead of sending him off to an orphanage."

"Is that all?" Beatrice asked.

"Isn't that enough?" Priscilla averted her gaze.

Beatrice sighed quietly.

"I'll tell you what. Tomorrow, I'll be showing some gentlemen around the Woodhull House. I'd like you to come with us and see more of what goes on there . . . meet a few more of the people."

Priscilla straightened. "But I have to work in the kitchen again tomorrow."

"I don't think they would mind if you were gone for an hour or two in the afternoon. I'll talk to Ardis

Gerhardt tomorrow morning and arrange it. What do you say?"

Priscilla curled one side of her nose. "If it gets me out of that stinky kitchen for a few hours, I say *yes*."

THAT SAME EVENING, in the oak-paneled smoking room of the exclusive Pantheon Club, Harry Winthrop and Archibald Lynch were lighting up expensive cigars with three more of the nine members of Consolidated's board of directors. One after another, the directors blew out long streams of pungent smoke and settled back into their deep leather chairs. As generally happened, the conversation came around to business and to the latest stock tips and investment opportunities.

"Jaeger, at the German Savings Bank, put me on to some sweet little opportunities the other day," Lynch intoned, pausing to collect the attention of the three board members. "He says that American Telephone and Telegraph is set to expand fast. A couple of German fellows back in the homeland—Daimler and Benz—have invented a new engine that burns petroleum of some sort. Another horseless carriage, but it's worth looking into. And there's a factory on the Lower East Side called Flegler and Fain that's going on the block."

"Flegler and Fain? Never heard of it," one of the directors declared.

"Profitable little place—sturdy building, plenty of cheap labor," Winthrop informed the group. "They make hooks, grommets, and those new zip-cross fasteners. Supposed to be the coming thing for clothes. I checked it out."

"And?" Another director sat forward, clearly interested.

"The place is ripe for the taking. They're cash starved. They've got to have capital to expand and start production of the new fasteners."

"Sounds interesting. But there must be a hitch." The third director, who had intercepted an exchange of glances between Lynch and Winthrop, put his goblet down with a huff of disgust. "There's always a hitch these days."

Lynch studied the three board members. "There might be some resistance at Consolidated."

"From the president, no doubt," the board member responded. "And what would cause her to object to such a plum? She likes a profit well enough."

"That cheap labor?" Winthrop said. "It's women and kids."

There was a general groan and the others reached for their glasses and sat back.

"That again," one of the directors said, downing his drink and setting his goblet down with a clang. "I'm damned sick and tired of passing up deals and losing money because something offends her female sensibilities. She's got no business being in business if she hasn't got the stomach for it."

"Or the balls," Lynch added slyly.

The laughter his comment produced had a purposeful edge.

"Maybe it's time Consolidated Industries resigned from the bleeding heart society," Winthrop declared. "Maybe it's time our president moved on."

"That won't happen," the third director declared, stubbing out his cigar in the nearest crystal ashtray. "You're wasting your breath and our time."

"What would you say if we told you we have the leverage we need to make her decide to 'retire' from office?"

Lynch said with a cryptic smile. "That we can virtually guarantee that after the board meeting, she won't be a factor in the management of Consolidated Industries at all?"

The three directors looked at each other and came to the edges of their seats. "What have you got?"

Lynch glanced knowingly at Winthrop and his smile turned wicked as he turned it back to the others.

"*Dirt*. What else?"

CONNOR ARRIVED AT Woodhull House the next morning looking rested and confident and abominably handsome . . . with reporters from three of the city's major newspapers in tow. Beatrice was waiting in the front hall of the bustling settlement house, with Priscilla, candidate John Netherton, and Woodhull's director, Ardis Gerhardt. The minute he stepped through the door, she found herself examining his charcoal gray coat, his pinstriped trousers with their precise crease, and his impeccable silk tie . . . feeling oddly irritated at his visible perfection. Pansy from the Oriental was right; it ought to be a law that men's outsides and their insides had to match.

He looked up, caught her staring, and smiled. She turned her head and refused to look directly at him again.

The women staying at Woodhull House needed food and clothing as well as shelter, Ardis Gerhardt explained as she began the tour. Meeting the daily needs of nearly a hundred individuals required organization and the concerted effort of staff and residents. Each woman admitted to the house was assigned tasks on a rotating basis; cooking, cleaning, laundry, sewing, and child care.

They entered a large linen room lined floor to ceiling with shelves stocked with sheets and blankets and toweling. The director paused by the large, sunlit worktable in the middle of the room and spoke to a sallow-faced woman mending some donated linens.

"We have some visitors, Wynnie," she said. "Would you mind telling them how long have you been here?" Wynnie thought for a moment.

"Two months now."

"And how did you come to be here?" Beatrice asked.

"An angel come and plucked me out from under the bridge . . . me and my three kids." She gave Beatrice a timid smile. "My husband, he had a barber shop over on Tenth Avenue. When he caught the consumption and died, that miserable landlord—he took the shop and all my man's razors and shears and barberin' tools for rent. Then we lost our place and lived on the street . . . until we got robbed. We had no place to go." Tears appeared in her eyes and she blinked them back. "I'll never forget the sight of them hot biscuits at supper that first night. My kids acted like they'd never seen 'em before—ate till they was sick. We had a safe, clean bed in a room to ourselves . . . it was pure heaven. Miz Gerhardt here . . . she's our angel."

Beatrice stood to one side, watching Connor's face and taking a certain satisfaction in the uneasiness she glimpsed in it. Men should feel discomfort when faced with the inequities and deficits of the society they shaped and controlled for their own benefit.

As they continued the tour, Connor walked with his head bent and his hands clasped behind him, and she found herself wondering what he was thinking . . . besides how soon he could get away from this place. What would it take to convince him to be an advocate for women, to really believe in the cause he was being co-erced into supporting?

Their next stop was the kitchens, where they encountered Jeffrey . . . who glared at them from behind a massive pile of unpeeled potatoes.

"Well, well," Connor said, strolling over to have a look at Jeffrey's handiwork. "You're a man of many talents, cousin."

"Master Jeffrey, here . . . he's learning," Nora, the rotund head cook, declared with a broad smile as she placed a proprietary hand on the youth's shoulder. "If we could just get him to quit flirtin' with the girls . . ."

Jeffrey reddened from his collar up. "I—I . . ." He glanced at Priscilla, who looked stricken. "I'm just being friendly—I can't help it that I'm friendly."

Connor glanced at Priscilla, who was staring at Jeffrey, then at Beatrice. "Well, we all have our cross to bear."

Nora chuckled and ushered them into the dining room, where she continued explaining their procedures: "We make three meals a day . . . feed two shifts at each meal. Not a woman goes through here that doesn't take a turn at peelin' and pluckin' and kneadin' . . ."

From there they visited the large sewing room where clothing pieces were laid out and being cut on large tables and treadle sewing machines were humming.

"Audrey is our head seamstress," Ardis Gerhardt said, introducing a thin, sad-eyed woman with an air of faded gentility. "She came to us a few months ago with nothing but the clothes on her back. Since then, she's set up this sewing room and sees to it that everyone here has proper clothes." Ardis smiled at the woman, who returned a nod. "But, she's about to leave us . . . to work for a clothing manufacturer, where she will help design women's ready-to-wear clothes. She's one of our great successes."

Audrey's brief smile faded. "I won't be a 'success' until I get my children back."

"Your children?" John Netherton asked. "Where are they?"

The seamstress regarded them with pained expectation.

"With my *ex*-husband."

There was a moment's silence as all realized they were looking at a divorced woman. John Netherton took an involuntary step back before he caught himself. Beatrice, seeing Audrey wince at his reaction, stepped forward and extended her hand.

"Beatrice Von Furstenberg, Audrey. Tell me about your children. Perhaps I can help."

"Not unless you're rich as Croesus." Audrey looked at her elegant clothes and aristocratic bearing, and added: "*And* have a few judges in your pocket."

"Close enough," Connor said with an arch look at Beatrice. "If you wouldn't mind . . . please tell us how you came to be here."

"It's a story, sir, and not a happy one. I was married to a well-to-do businessman in Poughkeepsie. After my father died and left me a goodly sum of money, my husband decided I was no longer *cooperative* enough to suit him. Everything I inherited became his legally, and all it took to get rid of me was the affidavit of a rummy old doctor saying I was mad and the complicity of a judge who was a friend of his." She took on a faraway look, as if seeing a familiar horror once again.

"I was in the backyard with the day girl, beating rugs

when they came. I remember thinking: 'he's home early for dinner and he'll be furious it's not ready.' But he'd brought two policemen with him and they put me in irons, right there in front of my children. I begged him . . . pleaded . . ."

She wiped a tear, then closed the door on that disturbing memory. "He had me committed to the state mental asylum and was granted a divorce." Her bitter smile was haunting. "I was so *insane* that they put me in charge of the hospital's laundry. They would have released me sooner, but they needed someone competent to oversee the work.

"Six months later I made my way home to find that I no longer had a home or a marriage. I wrote everyone I could think of, but no one replied. If I had only had money for a lawyer . . ."

There was another moment of silence before Connor asked, "What could the government have done?"

She looked squarely up at him. "What gave my husband the right to say I was crazy and put me away? And why is there justice in the courts only for men who have money? Have I no rights at all?"

"Yes, you do," Beatrice said quietly, stepping in to put an arm around her. "And someday we'll make the government recognize it."

It was a somber group that left the sewing room and exited a rear door into a yard filled with children. Youthful shouts and laughter were a welcome change from the grim story the group had just heard. The children spotted Ardis Gerhardt and came running. Engulfed by a boisterous tide of enthusiasm, Beatrice put her hands out to touch as many of the children as she could reach, and Connor quickly accepted their invitation to toss a baseball with the older boys. John Netherton, watching the news writers scribbling descriptions of Connor's participation, allowed himself to be pulled into helping some of the younger children build a tower of wooden blocks. Priscilla gravitated to a more sedate group of older girls who were cutting and stitching flour sacks into rag dolls for the younger children.

When Ardis Gerhardt called the group to go on to the next stop, they were reluctant to leave the sunny yard and the sounds of the children. But they were soon immersed in viewing the classrooms, the laundry and hanging yard, the dormitories for single women, the rooms for small family groups, and the chapel. It was there that they met the last of their storytellers.

Inge Zeiss was an immigrant from southern Germany, daughter of a goldsmith. In heavily accented English, she told of her decision to come to America and of meeting some charming but unscrupulous men outside the new Ellis Island Center. They promised to find her a place to open a business of her own, but absconded with the money she gave them for rent.

It was an old story: the confidence men at the docks, taking advantage of immigrants, promising them help and giving them only grief.

"I go to a bank to borrow. They say I am only woman . . . must have a man to sign for me. But I am not married and my vater is dead." She looked down at her work-reddened hands. "I sell my tools to eat. I have nowhere to go . . ."

"Blasted bankers," Beatrice said under her breath.

"We're trying to help Inge arrange a business loan, but we've had no luck so far," Ardis said. "If you know of any investors who might be interested . . ."

"I think I might," Beatrice said, searching her purse for a printed card and tucking it into Inge's hand. "If you go to these offices and say that Mrs. Von Furstenberg sent you, I promise you'll get a fair hearing and the chance for a loan *without* a man's signature. Do you have samples of your work?"

"I do!" The woman threw her arms around Beatrice, all but toppling her. "I bring, I bring!" Then she hurried down the hall to share her good fortune.

"Thank you, Mrs. Von Furstenberg," Ardis said, her face glowing with pleasure. "I don't know what we'd do without the support of women such as yourself." Then in her quietly forceful way, she turned to Connor and John Netherton. "We could certainly use the support of men such as yourselves, as well . . . men who are willing to listen and learn about the problems women face. After all, women's problems are all of society's problems."

The news reporters who had been trailing laconically after them now closed in and began to watch and scribble on their notepads.

"I am sympathetic to the plight of the women here," Connor said with a grave expression and a sidelong glance at the reporters. "A man would have to be made of lead not to feel pity after hearing such heartrending stories." That telltale lilt of Irish crept into his voice. "But I must confess, I fail to see what their problems have to do with the woman vote."

"It has everything to do with women voting," Beatrice spoke up. "Every one of these women's stories involves a matter of justice, of equitable treatment before the law . . . each involves a matter of political power."

He folded his arms and leveled a penetrating look on her. "It seems to me they all involve matters of money. They don't need a vote—they need a bank."

"But can't you see that if women had the vote, there would be changes in the laws that would allow all women to control their own money and to deal with it properly . . . to inherit, to succeed their husbands in business, to enter into legal contracts, to acquire loans at . . ." Beatrice halted, staring at him, caught suddenly in the grip of insight.

A bank. It was true. Her immediate and total absorption in the idea eclipsed her irritation that he had been the one to see it first. All she could think was that the pain these women had suffered could have been ameliorated by access to funds . . . borrowed funds. If Wynnie could have taken out a loan, she might have been able to keep her husband's barbering business. If Audrey had had access to funds, she might have retained legal help to protect herself and fight for her children. If Inge had been granted the loan she applied for, she would be a happy and productive goldsmith, in her own shop.

Then it struck her—the "girls" at the Oriental with their desperate savings, her secretary Alice's problems accessing her own account—it wasn't just the women at Woodhull House who needed financial help. And it wasn't just that women needed a way to obtain money; sometimes they needed a safe place to keep or to invest the money they already had.

Her heart began to pound. Less than a week ago, she had wondered what could be done in the short range to make women's lives better while they worked toward the larger issue of full suffrage. Well, here it was. Why bother trying to change things at the Chase-Darlington when she could create a new bank . . . one that would be a friend to women . . . one that could set an example or even a whole new standard?

A hot new light appeared in her eyes.

"You know, Mr. Barrow, you are absolutely right."

"I am?" He seemed truly caught off guard.

"A *bank*. What a wonderful idea! How creative of you. Women are much more adept at handling money than they are generally given credit for. They have been managing household money for centuries . . . and . . ."

She turned to Ardis. "Who does the budget planning and keeps the books and records for Woodhull House?"

"Why, I do, along with several volunteers." Ardis sensed where her argument was going and smiled. "All women."

"And who does the ordering and purchasing?"

Priscilla spoke up. "We—the women who live here do." Her chin rose. "Sometimes women are more responsible with the money than men are."

There were a few snickers and sardonic rumbles from the reporters, but Beatrice ignored them to smile at her young niece and turn back to Connor.

"There, you see! The evidence is everywhere, when you look for it. Women are quite capable of managing money when they're given the chance. And at your suggestion and with your help, we can give women that chance. We could even employ women as tellers and loan officers." She faced the reporters with an air of triumph. "How wonderful, gentlemen, that you're here to witness the start of"—her mind raced—"*The Barrow State Bank*."

"The Barrow Sta—" Connor's jaw loosened visibly and he began to scramble for grounds to protest. "But that's absurd."

"What is absurd about honoring the man who is responsible for the first bank in New York that welcomes and even seeks the accounts of women?"

"All I said was—"

"That you believed many of women's problems had to

do with money . . . and that what women need is a *bank*. What finer way to show your support for the women of New York than to create a bank to serve them?"

She was beaming. "It is forward-thinking public officials," she continued, "who will be the salvation of the women's rights effort in our country. Thank heaven we have men like you, Mr. Barrow, who in your heart of hearts truly believe women are your equal."

She looked up, straight into his fiercely focused gaze, and read his wildly conflicting urges to laugh and to throttle her within an inch of her conniving hide. She wasn't sure if she should push ahead or run for her life.

"I certainly believe *you* are my equal, Mrs. Von Furstenberg." There was a steely resonance beneath the velvet and shamrocks in his tone. "Especially when it comes to talking. Your gift of gab is so remarkable, I might even be tempted to conclude that you were part Irish."

For a long minute they stood staring into each other's eyes . . . immersed in tension . . . the air around them fairly crackling with electricity.

A murmur from the news writers and a snort of confusion from John Netherton brought her forcefully back to the present. When she looked around, she saw Netherton, Priscilla, Ardis Gerhardt, and the reporters staring at her with looks that ranged from mild surprise to deep shock. She reddened and scrambled to get back on track.

"There will be a great deal of legal work, and if we're to get a state charter, there will be legislators to convince. I could think of no better person to shepherd our woman-friendly bank through the legislative process than Mr. Connor Barrow. He does, after all, come from a banking family."

Veins became visible in his neck.

"I have no intention of—"

"Abandoning your campaign? No one would expect that. We certainly wouldn't want to interfere with your chances for election." She fairly glowed with pleasure. "Women's suffrage needs all of the friends in Congress it can get."

Netherton cleared his throat, clearly peeved by the praise and attention being lavished on his opponent. "Really, Mrs. Von Furstenberg, I think there should be some equity here . . ."

"As do I, Mr. Netherton," she responded, with a smile. "We'll be pleased to have you serve on the first board of directors."

Netherton started to protest, but thought better of it when he glanced at the news reporters who were staring expectantly at him.

"I cannot speak for my party, I can only say *I* am sympathetic to the plight of women."

Beatrice looked at the reporters with an unmistakable glow of triumph. She had backed Connor Barrow into a corner and come up with everything she wanted: a sponsor, however reluctant, for her bank, publicity for women's rights, and even a bid of support from his opponent.

"Well, gentlemen, I believe we've accomplished quite a lot here today. Thank you so much for coming."

As the news writers scrambled for the door, Netherton donned his hat with a grim nod and excused himself to a pressing appointment. Priscilla watched her aunt with a dubious look until Ardis suggested she might be needed in the kitchen.

Beatrice was only vaguely aware of their departure. All she could see for the moment was the impending explosion visible in Connor's face. It came as no surprise when he grabbed her by the arm, dragged her into the nearby office, and slammed the door behind them.

"What the hell did I ever do to you," he demanded, seizing her by the shoulders, "to make you so determined to ruin me?"

THIRTEEN

"I AM NOT ruining you," she declared, standing her ground.

"Oh? What do you call hanging a 'women's bank' around my neck?"

"It won't be just a women's bank . . . it will serve men as well."

"A fact which will be lost on virtually everyone who hears about it," he roared, "from the state banking department to Tammany Hall!"

"Then we'll just have to remind everyone of it . . . make certain they all understand that we're building a bank for all people . . . male and female."

He stared at her for a moment, then released her abruptly. "Jesus, Mary, and—you're serious."

"Absolutely."

"I have two words for you," he said, shoving his face irritably into hers. "*Frying pan* and *fire*."

She couldn't have held back the smile that particular image elicited, if her life depended on it, and his reaction was nothing short of alarming.

"Look, sweetheart"—his voice dropped to a growl and his hands curled into fists—"the state banking department has to examine and approve every petition for a state bank charter before the legislature can vote on it. And if you think Tammany Hall is tough, you should see these old birds. They're living, breathing gargoyles. They feed on the bones of people who sponsor proposals like this. This is no longer just blackmail, it's homicide . . . death by bureaucracy . . . paperwork at fifty paces . . ."

"You may find this hard to believe, Connor Barrow, but this *isn't* about you." She braced, refusing to shrink from his intimidating stance. "Not about making you pay or even making you miserable. It's about not waiting forty more years for justice and reason to finally prevail. It's about helping women now . . . directly and immediately . . . about setting an example of how things should be."

"You want to talk about how things *should* be?" He released her and lurched back, running his hands through his hair, causing it to stick out slightly on each side. He was the very picture of exasperation. "I'll tell you how things *should be*, Beatrice, darlin'." He advanced until only a few critical inches separated his nose from hers.

"You *should be* married and busy at home in that big house of yours . . . instead of out trampling the business world underfoot and torturing the male populace for what your old husband did and didn't do to you. You should have half a dozen rambunctious children to look after and a husband who comes home every night and kisses you until your knees give out . . ." He grabbed her and hauled her roughly against his chest. "Like *this*."

The minute his mouth touched hers, she shoved against his chest and twisted in his arms—doing her best to escape what was little more than a brute attempt at domination. How dare he inflict his primitive male instincts on—on—

The second minute she stilled in his arms and braced, desperate to hold on to her anger while feeling it disintegrating all around her. She became aware of the softening, the supple coaxing of his lips . . . began to absorb the warmth radiating from his arms and chest . . . began to feel alive and hungry for sensation. . . .

The third minute, she gave a soft moan and slid her arms up his chest and around his neck. Opening to his kiss, she surrendered to the waves of perception breaking over and within her. The saltiness of his lips, the tension of his arms around her, the breadth of his shoulders, the heat that seemed so tangible that it carried a scent as it filled her head and chest and slowly seeped into her bones.

"Don't you want to be kissed and held like this?" he murmured against her mouth. "Don't you want to wake up each morning nestled in the curve of a big warm body?" He slid his lips down her throat until they came to the hollow at the base of her throat. "Don't you want to be surprised by arms slipping around you from behind as you brush out your hair each night . . . by a shower of rose petals into your bath . . . by a sexy wink in the middle of a board meeting?"

Her throat was so tight with desire that she was unable to speak.

"Don't you want to hold hands beneath the dinner table . . . to stand beside someone as you listen to children's prayers at night?" He took her hand from around his neck and kissed each finger. "Don't you want someone to know every inch of your skin and to love it with his breath, his lips, and his body?"

He touched her face and waited for her to open her

eyes. She had trouble focusing until he spoke again, in a whisper so raw and intimate that it seemed to come from her own aching heart.

"Who does such things for you, Beatrice? Who holds you in the night and fills the darkness around you with sounds of delight? Who absorbs your tears when life gets too hard to bear? Who joins you in laughter when you just can't resist life's silliness anymore?"

Who echoed in the profound stillness he had created inside her, finding no answer until it reached her defenses. It was another minute before she realized she was molded to him bodily, pliant with yearning . . . beyond both modesty and pride, but not beyond the reach of hurt. To have someone to share her life . . . to work and dream and play beside him . . . to no longer be alone . . . She had been so guarded and contained for so long that it was almost physically painful to open herself to such possibilities. She looked up.

Did he truly want to know? Did he care about her answers, or was this just sweet talk to make her forget her plan and release him from his obligation to her? She searched the desire in his eyes, desperate to learn if it was his desire or merely a reflection of hers. With a man like him—glib, charming, sensual, and opportunistic— was it ever possible to know the truth?

Retreating sharply from that intimacy, she ducked out of his reach and steadied herself on the back of a chair. "You never cease to amaze me." There was a lingering huskiness to her voice. "I believe you could talk green shoots from walking sticks." She summoned all of her reserves and looked directly at him. "Which is precisely why I need you to help me establish this bank. You'll find the right thing to say at just the right moment, and we'll have a charter in no time."

For a moment she thought he would launch into another diatribe on her deficits as a woman, but he hesitated long enough to master that visible impulse.

"Answer me," he demanded, his voice so unexpectedly quiet and compelling that she suffered a shiver.

"I'm not certain what the question was." She fixed her gaze on the papers littering the desk, while her ears strained for his slightest movement.

"You know damned well what it was. Don't you want those things in your life? Love, passion, a home, children. Didn't you ever want them?"

"Why do you insist on being so indecently personal with me?"

"Because I'm a nosy bastard." She heard him approach and stop at the edge of the desk. She didn't look up. "And because you don't kiss like a woman who despises men."

"If I kiss and how I kiss are irrelevant," she said as crisply as she could manage with the blood draining from her face and vacating her hands. "I was destined early on for a very different sort of life than most women."

"Bullshit."

That brought her head up. He was standing with his arms folded, staring at her with eyes now silver with heat.

"It's true. If I lack romantic impulses it's because I've seen firsthand the results of a great romantic passion. My older sister got the romance in the family, and I got the duty. She got the passion, I got the security. She got a child and I got . . . the responsibility of raising that child." She shook her head with a fierce little smile. "I used to envy my sister her great love . . . until I learned that she lived in a hovel and often went without the barest necessities . . . until she died in an epidemic that she might have escaped if she had had the few dollars needed to flee her contaminated village. I can live very nicely without such penniless, powerless rapture, thank you."

"You chose riches instead of romance."

She shot him a withering look.

"A very male deduction. Young girls don't get to *choose* anything. After my sister eloped, my parents decided not to take a chance with their only remaining asset. They arranged a wealthy marriage for me straightaway. I was only sixteen. Priscilla's age. I was immediately plunged into a sphere where feeling and affection and passion were inconsequential. It was difficult at first, but over the years I have come to appreciate the lack of emotion business decisions involve."

The intensity of his gaze made her uncomfortable enough to withdraw toward the door. "You asked me why I work for women's rights . . . what I get out of it. I don't expect you to understand, but I truly want to do something good, something lasting, something that will leave the world a better place. Other women give the world children. I can give other women a bank and a vote."

She paused, wondering how much she had revealed to him and how he might use it. She had to know, now, whether or not she could count on him.

"I am prepared to reconsider requiring you to support suffrage . . . to free you of that obligation, if you help me charter and found this bank."

"You need more than politics and paper to start a bank," he said, irritation rising again as she transformed back into cool, efficient businesswoman. "You need money. Lots of it."

"Leave the money to me. Your job is to draw up the paperwork and to cajole and sweet-talk the Barrow State

Bank through those gargoyles at the state banking department."

"That's another thing . . ." He strode closer and seemed annoyed when she coolly backed to the door. "You have to find another name for this bank."

"It's already been announced to the press. Besides, Barrow is a name long associated with banking in New York." She folded her arms and forced a smile. "Give it time. It will grow on you."

His shoulders inflated with outrage, his face reddened, and for a minute she wondered if she had pushed him too far.

"That's the damned point," he declared forcefully. "I spent seven long years shedding an association with that name, and I'm not going back to it now . . . not for you, not for anybody."

She flinched as he reached for her, but he merely set her out of the way and stormed from the office and from the settlement house.

With a hand splayed over her pounding heart and her eyes closed, she waited for that brief spurt of panic to dissolve away.

Was that a *yes* or a *no*?

IT WAS QUIET in the carriage as they drove home from Woodhull House that evening. Beatrice had spent the rest of the afternoon helping Ardis Gerhardt plan fund-raising activities, holding at bay the turmoil she felt over her encounter with Connor.

She should be flushed with the success of the candidate tour and even more so with the idea of a bold and exciting new venture to help women. Instead, she found herself dwelling on the fact that Connor had once again stirred emotions and responses in her that she would rather not deal with. She didn't want to suffer bouts of anticipation and attraction and longing. She didn't want to go weak in the knees when he touched her or melt under his kisses so that she felt liquid and languid and saturated with desire. How could she be so vulnerable to a man so obvious in his deficits and his designs?

"So, are you angry you didn't convince them that women should vote?"

Beatrice looked up and found Priscilla studying her from the other seat.

"Not really." She realized she was frowning and stopped. "Do I seem angry?"

"Not angry exactly." Priscilla gave her a puzzled look. "How do you know that one man . . . that Mr. Barrow? He looked familiar."

"You've seen him before. He's the Democratic candidate for Congress in the Fourth District," she said. "And he's Jeffrey's cousin."

Priscilla's eyes widened in recognition. "He's that Irish one." Then her eyes narrowed. "Aunt Beatrice, he's a crook."

"Oh?" Beatrice was surprised by Priscilla's vehemence. "What makes you say that?"

"He's in with that Irish mob. He's the one that got Jeffrey and me in so much—" She halted and looked resentful. "He can't be trusted. Didn't you hear the awful Irish accent he put on when he was staring at you? He's a wooden nickel, for sure. Some men will say anything to get on your good side."

Out of the mouths of babes . . . Beatrice thought as they rolled to a stop at the front door and she watched Priscilla climb down out of the carriage. She was inside and handing off her hat to Richards when it occurred to her to wonder how Priscilla had come by such a rare bit of insight.

TAMMANY HALL, THE seat of Democratic-Irish control of the city, was bustling the next morning when Connor arrived. He had a full day of campaigning and politicking ahead, and the last thing he wanted to do today was shake hands, make hundreds of hurried promises, and kiss squalling babies.

Bracing himself, he made a congenial circuit through the reception hall. Then he looked in on the Society of St. Tammany Ladies Auxiliary meeting and found them planning victory celebrations for the coming balloting. His smile and his gut both tightened.

By the time he made it up the main stairs to the offices, word of his presence had spread and a group had gathered in one of the main conference rooms.

Del Delaney, one of Croker's beefy ward heelers, snagged his arm and steered him into the meeting room. There, a battle-scarred table was littered with copies of *The Herald* and *New York World* newspapers. As Connor entered, underboss Charles Murphy and half a dozen city officials lowered copies they were reading and settled searching gazes on him.

When Delaney closed the door behind them, Connor realized that something was up.

"So, you made your visit to that settlement house yesterday," campaign manager Murphy declared, gesturing to the papers. "Got a bit of ink, all right."

"Oh?" Connor strolled to the table with a stubbornly cheerful smile and picked up a paper that had been opened to a headline declaring: BARROW FLIRTS WITH WOMEN'S RIGHTS. His smile froze.

Scanning the article below, he glimpsed a few key phrases: "Candidate Barrow . . . visibly moved by the plight of the unfortunate . . . attentively and compassionately . . . development of *a bank for women* . . ."

He quit reading and groaned silently.

Upon a nod from Murphy, the beefy Del Delaney picked up that paper, chose a spot and in his whiskey-hoarse voice, read aloud.

" 'The visit was arranged by Mrs. Beatrice Von Furstenberg, widow of industrialist Mercer Von Furstenberg and a major contributor to the Woodhull Settlement House. The handsome Mrs. Von Furstenberg, who was considerably younger than her late husband, cleverly teased agreement from Mr. Barrow on several key points . . . including a request that he help secure a state charter for a new women's bank to be named in honor of his well-known banking family.'"

Delaney paused and trained an accusatory look at Connor over the top of the paper. Connor looked around and the others' expressions ranged from disbelief to disappointment to outright disgust.

" 'It is not known whether or not his statements represent a major change in Tammany Hall's opposition to female suffrage,'" Delaney continued reading. "'Either way, Mr. Barrow's flirtation with women's rights may draw interest back to what had promised to be a one-sided race.'"

Connor felt as if his collar were shrinking. "Well, that just goes to show," he declared with a desperately casual air, "if reporters don't have something real to write about, they'll make up something."

After a tense moment, there was an audible sigh and several of the men sat back in their chairs. Others, however, remained huddled over the table.

"You're saying you didn't declare yourself a 'suffra-gette'?" Murphy asked, rubbing his chin as he regarded Connor.

"You and Boss Croker were both present when I was challenged to go to this settlement house and listen. *Listen* is precisely what I did. A man would have to be made of stone not to respond to their stories. Even so, a bit of sympathy is a far cry from declaring support for suffrage."

"Yeah, well . . . if we weren't sure, you can bet the voters won't be," Delaney said with a glower. "Not a man in th' Society o' St. Tammany would stand fer havin' women at th' polls. Flirtin' with suffrage is flirtin' with disaster."

"And what's this about a bank?" underboss Murphy spoke up. "The *Barrow* State Bank."

Connor looked at the mistrust in faces around the table . . . the same faces that only a few days ago were beaming with confidence in him.

"It's a scheme this Von Furstenberg woman cooked up while we were looking the place over. The women's talk upset her and she started talking about doing something to help them. I never said I would be involved, and I certainly didn't give permission to put my name on the damnable thing."

Murphy studied him for a moment. "So you've got nothing to do with this *women's bank*?"

Connor looked back at that damning headline.

"Not a thing. I will confess to a bit of flirting, gentle-men." He prayed there was a libidinous glint in his eye. "But, it sure as hell wasn't with *women's suffrage*."

They looked at each other, then at the insinuating look he wore. They followed his gaze to the articles spread before them and one by one, their eyes began to widen in comprehension. One of them snatched up the

Herald article and read aloud: " 'The handsome Mrs. Von Furstenberg.'" Another read from another paper, " 'The stately and elegant Mrs. Von Furstenberg.'"

"You dog," another said in apparent horror. "You'd use the sacred trust of the votin' public to get next to a bit of skirt?"

There was a long pause in which his heart all but stopped.

"That's our boy!" Delaney crowed, slapping him on the back.

Laughter broke out and smiles returned. Several of the men were on their feet and shaking their heads as they made for the door. They clapped him on the shoulder and, as they exited, muttered to each other about the lengths some men would go to for a slip of muslin. But Connor noticed visual exchanges between several of the departing men and Charles Murphy. Clearly, he was being left in the underboss's capable hands.

When the door closed, he braced, sensing that what had just occurred was only a preliminary round. Now came the main event.

Murphy, generally taciturn, sat looking at Connor for a while, examining him, considering his version of what had occurred at the settlement house. Then he glanced at Delaney and rose to look out the window.

"What the hell were ye thinkin', lad?" Delaney stalked close and ripped an unlit cigar from between his teeth. "You've got a platform an' a party that can carry ye straight to Congress. Take a bit o' advice, man. Ferget women 'til *after* the election. Save yer sweet talk for th' voters."

Connor studied the threat in Delaney's opaque eyes and bulldog-tight jaw. Then Murphy turned from the window and sent Delaney out to have a word with some of the news vendors in the area and buy up the rest of their papers. When he was gone, Murphy crossed his arms and sat back against the windowsill.

"I was assigned to oversee your campaign, Barrow," he finally said. "And I'll do my best to get you elected. But you have to cooperate. No more visits to almshouses or hospitals or settlement houses. The people in those places don't vote."

"Haven't you ever wondered if maybe they should?"

Murphy's scowl deepened. "They got to you, didn't they?"

He considered his words carefully. "They made a few points."

The underboss issued an irritable sigh. "Don't be thickheaded, Barrow. You have to know that you haven't risen this quickly in the organization's ranks just because of your charm and political instincts. Boss Croker's been grooming you for office because you're something of a compromise. You've got the blue bloodlines and Harvard credentials to satisfy the swallowtail coats in the party and the common touch that makes you acceptable to the beer-drinkin' regulars in Tammany clubhouses. We need both sides to win an election. But neither side will support a candidate that's soft in the center. Don't let your heart run away with your head, or you'll end up throwing away a promising future."

Again, Connor chose his words judiciously.

"I'm no bleedin' heart, Murphy." His smile had a boldness to it that passed for determination. "The fact that I listen doesn't obligate me to act on everything I hear. That's the first principle of politics: listen to everything, promise nothing. I have no intention of throwing this election or my future away."

Soft in the center. The words hung in Connor's mind

as he left Tammany Hall with Murphy, headed for his first campaign stop . . . an association of small, independent merchants. Between reminders of whom to remember and what issues were likely to come up, he tried unsuccessfully to purge the tension caused by his dressing down.

He had worked in Tammany-led Democratic party committees for years. Tammany had taken him in when he had nothing and had sent business and influence his way. They had groomed and developed him into a candidate with major political potential. What the hell was he doing letting his attraction to Beatrice Von Furstenberg interfere with his political obligations? How could a promise to a woman he'd met barely two weeks ago possibly compete with his long association with Tammany Hall?

Soft in the center.

At first, he had told himself he had agreed to Beatrice's bit of blackmail to keep her from going to the newspapers. But it was painfully clear to him now that the true source of his cooperation was an unabashedly personal interest in Beatrice herself. How had the boys in the upstairs room put it? "Usin' the sacred trust of the votin' public to get next to a bit of skirt."

Too damned close to the mark.

As he listened to Murphy describe his schedule for the rest of the week, his stomach began to tie itself into a knot. He had to finish up this business with her as quickly and quietly as possible. He had campaigning to do. No more public "persuasion," no more wrenching excursions into poverty and injustice . . .

The more he thought about it, the more he realized that her precious "bank" just might be the answer. If he helped her get her blasted charter—discreetly, of course—then he would be free of his obligation to her. Free to concentrate on his campaigning. And once the campaign was done and he was a U.S. Congressman— he smiled to himself—there would be plenty of time to get better acquainted and, just perhaps, change her mind about men and romance.

FOURTEEN

BEATRICE HAD BEEN closeted with accountants and financial specialists for the better part of two days and was still working on her bank proposal for the next day's board meeting, when Priscilla came home that evening. There was no explosion in the hall this time. No tantrum. No tears. Her niece exchanged a few words with Richards, handed off her hat, then climbed the steps to her room looking a bit forlorn.

Soon Dipper and Shorty appeared in the doorway for their nightly report.

"Well, we ain't in the kitchen anymore," Shorty told her.

"We got a 'pro-ject' now." Dipper took over the explanation. "Puttin' together th' new women's dormitory. And they'd be doing right well"—he glared at Shorty, whose neck disappeared into his collar—"if *Master Jeffrey* would ever turn his hand."

"He's right—them things in the attic is junk," Shorty declared.

"That little bureau was just like one my old ma had

back in th' old country," Dipper countered. "With a mite o' soap and water—"

"An' who's gonna use that soap an' water?" Shorty argued. "Us. And our hands is parboiled as it is." He held out his water-reddened hands in evidence.

"Aw, quit yer bellyachin'. You're gettin' to be just like him." Dipper turned to Beatrice. "He's always duckin' out, old Jeff . . . he was out in the yard, playin' kick ball when he was supposed to be taking out th' slops."

"A fellow's got to have a rest now an' then," Shorty protested.

"What gets me is th' way he's always flirtin' with the young gals." Dipper crossed his arms and looked down his nose in disapproval. "Always got a smile for this one and a wink for that one. And don't think *she* don't see it."

"Well, if she did somethin' besides glare at him an' nag . . ." Shorty laid out his charge's viewpoint: "She's always checkin' up on him, and whenever he gets a little frisky, she gets all mad an' hoity-toity." Shorty sniffed with indignation. "He's a'ready *got* a mother."

"Well, if he was any kind of a man he'd talk to her reasonable . . . help her get things done . . . instead of sneakin' out and dodgin' ever bit of work that—"

"Thank you, gentlemen," Beatrice broke in forcefully, intent on avoiding fisticuffs in her drawing room. "I can see you take your work quite seriously. And I appreciate your efforts."

Through the open drawing-room doors came the sounds of someone at the front door. Alice, who had just come down the stairs, spoke briefly with whoever it was, then hurried into the drawing room carrying an envelope. She stood by anxiously while Beatrice opened it.

"What is it?" Alice asked. "It can't be good news, this time of night."

Beatrice broke into a beaming smile and read it aloud. *"Mrs. Von Furstenberg. You have a lawyer. You'll soon have a bank. C.B."*

Her eyes twinkled as she showed the note to Alice. "Just in time for the board meeting tomorrow." Then she looked back at Connor's terse message and hurried script and chuckled. "The man does have a way with words."

ARRIVING AT THE Consolidated Industries offices on Sixth Avenue the next morning, Beatrice went straight to her office and closed the door. She stood looking at the great desk that had been her husband's and thought of all he'd taught her. "Never go into negotiations unless you're willing to give as well as take." "Never let them see you're worried." And "in negotiations, if you can get your opponent to concede something small early on, you can get him to concede something larger, later."

She drew a determined breath. She would need all of those lessons today if she were to get the start-up money she needed to organize her new "Barrow State Bank."

She removed her stylish hat and checked her man-tailored charcoal pinstripe suit in the mirror behind the door. Deciding that she looked as businesslike as it was possible to look without resorting to male trousers, she tugged down her jacket and headed for the boardroom.

The large, walnut-paneled boardroom was slightly overheated and smelled faintly of mentholatum and mustard . . . which said clearly that reedy old Leonard Augustine and choleric old Ben Haffleck, both contemporaries of her late husband's, were having their seasonal maladies and were likely to be short on patience. As she proceeded to her seat at the head of the table she passed portly, ruddy-faced William Afton and was assaulted by a powerfully astringent cologne mixed with brilliantine. It was a relief to reach the peppermint schnapps emanating from N. T. Wright, the secretary of the board, and the merciful lack of odor surrounding Wilberforce Graham, the vice president.

As she took her seat, only two directors remained standing . . . Harry Winthrop and Archibald Lynch, two recent and frequently contentious additions to the board. She asked them to take their seats so the meeting could begin and they did so . . . very slowly.

"The first item will be amendment of the agenda, which is on the top of your meeting notes," Beatrice began, ignoring their discourteous behavior. "Under new business, we will consider the proposal Miss Henry is now distributing to you."

Scowls appeared and murmurs arose as the title of the proposal and the identity of the sponsor were noted.

"What is this, madam president?" Archibald Lynch asked as he took his copy from Alice and continued to stand behind his seat. He was joined instantly by Harry Winthrop. "Why weren't we sent copies of this with the agenda?"

"I realize this may seem a bit irregular," she said with a confident smile, "but I have worked with our own accountants and banking experts to develop a proposal that warrants special consideration. And there is a time factor to be considered. The state committee that approves applications for charters will meet in two days' time. Now . . . if you gentlemen will be seated, we will hear a motion for approval of the minutes of the last meeting and move on. . . ."

There were a few, barely perceptible shrugs and silent sighs. Lynch tossed the proposal onto the table and sat down, and Winthrop followed. There was the "first concession" she had been looking for.

Her smile broadened.

Old business, including the presentation of a very favorable quarterly earnings report, went smoothly and quickly. Beatrice took pains to point out the exceptional large cash balance being maintained in the corporate coffers and the other directors, even Lynch and Winthrop, seemed pleased. By the time new business and her proposal were introduced, the directors were primed to consider ways to invest that sizable amount of ready cash.

"Funding a chartered bank would clearly be in line with our investment strategy. We have spoken numerous times about having a pool of reserves for development. This bank would serve that purpose as well as provide interest income from loans."

"But we've always gotten whatever capital we needed and done our company business through Chase-Darlington," old Augustine said.

"And Chase-Darlington has charged us enough to give themselves a fat twelve percent profit margin. Twelve percent that we could be saving."

"But initially, there would be more cost than profit," vice president Wilberforce Graham said, generating considerable agreement. "Why would we want to venture into this area? There are already plenty of banks out there."

"Not for everyone," somehow slipped past her own internal censors. She waited breathlessly, and sure enough, it caused a general reaction.

"Another bit of social *reform* in the making, Mrs. Von Furstenberg?" Winthrop demanded irritably, sitting forward. "What is it this time?"

"This is a simple business matter, gentlemen. There is money out there"—she pointed to the windows and the world beyond—"that is not working for its owners. Money stuffed in hatboxes, under mattresses, and in cracker tins. Money that many small investors do not have a place to deposit."

"I don't know of any bank that would refuse to take money on deposit," Lynch declared.

"Well, I do," Beatrice said, turning to Alice, who looked suddenly like a rabbit caught in a circle of hounds. "My secretary, Alice Henry, has an account at the Chase-Darlington and recently tried to make a deposit. They all but refused to take her money."

"Well," Harry Winthrop said with a smirk, "she is a woman, after all. How many women have bank accounts?"

"Precisely," Beatrice said tartly, folding her arms. "Women are a huge, untapped source of investment income."

"They're also a huge, untapped source of *headaches*," Winthrop declared.

"Pennies and nickels . . . we'd spend a damned fortune on counting clerks," declared old Ben Haffleck.

"Women in the bank all the time, clogging up the teller windows," William Afton grumbled. "Have you ever seen a woman in a bank? You have to explain every little—"

"You admit it would be a small return," secretary Wright broke in, "and yet you insist we incur the expense and tie up a great deal of our liquid capital."

"There will be large accounts as well, beginning with mine," she said. "And there are other men and women of substance willing to invest."

"Name one," Lynch demanded hotly. After a heartbeat's pause, he produced a fierce smile and stood. "You cannot, and for good reason. You'd have a damned time getting anyone with half a brain to deposit money in a *woman's bank.*" He turned to his fellow board members. "That's what this is about—you see that don't you? She's trying to coerce us into backing her 'women's rights' nonsense. She's using Consolidated as if it were her own change purse . . . and us as if we were her political shills." He turned on her. "What next Mrs. Von Furstenberg? A *children's stock exchange?*"

"One thing at a time, Mr. Lynch," she retorted, feeling her blood heating. "If we take care of the women, *they'll* take care of the children."

There was a groan from old Ben Haffleck. "Not that again. It's poor children this and starving urchins that. We've lost more deals because of your stand on children in factories . . ."

"And women . . . and ten-hour work days . . . and safety guards on machines . . . and union rights," thick-lipped William Afton said with clear disgust. "Everything's a big moral issue."

"Exactly!" Winthrop bolted to his feet, shoulder-to-shoulder with Lynch. "And we cannot permit this board to become a vehicle for the political agenda of one person, no matter how powerful."

Beatrice was taken aback. This was by far the most direct and serious challenge she had faced in years. She looked around the table, growing alarmed that not one pair of eyes met hers.

"It has always been our policy—not to mention a point of pride—that Consolidated does not acquire companies that misuse workers or maintain unsafe working conditions."

"A policy that has cost us dearly," Winthrop declared, starting for the head of the table. "We lost out on the

Reynolds buyout, the Watersea Textiles acquisition, the Dandridge Knitting Mills purchase. . . ." Then he struck the personal blow she sensed was coming. "We can no longer afford such sentimentality . . . not in our policies or in our *board president*."

"You call making decisions not to exploit women and children sentimentality?" Righteous fire spread through her. "I call it taking a moral stand . . . against abuse and injustice . . . against turning ourselves into profit-hungry vultures."

"Ah, yes," Lynch said, joining his partner near the head of the table. "The high moral ground. Our president would like us all to believe she is a permanent resident of that territory. That she never leaves it." He leveled a fierce look on her. "Not even for a side trip to . . . say . . . the *palaces* of the *Orient*."

It was such an odd turn of phrase that it took a minute for his insinuating sneer and the impact of his words to register. The palaces of the—Orient—the—*Oriental Palace*?

She blinked, unable to believe it. He knew about the Oriental Palace? How could he?

"Notice that she makes no rebuttal," Lynch continued with a vicious smile. "Because it is impossible for her to deny that she is interested in the *bottom* line. In spite of her prim ways, she takes great pride in her *attractive bottom* line."

She felt the color draining from her face, felt her hands going icy. They *knew*. She looked down the table at Winthrop's lidded eyes and sharklike grin. They knew she had been at the Oriental Palace. Lord, they knew about Punjab's humiliating treatment of her! But, how could they?

"What do you say, madam board president?" Lynch

inched closer. "Doesn't our common interest in a *very fine bottom line* change your mind about your *female bank* proposal?"

She was being blackmailed in front of her entire board of directors and every lawyer on her staff. She struggled to remain outwardly calm. If Lynch and Winthrop succeeded, if she gave way to their bullying, she would be handing control of Consolidated over to them, and the company would lose every vestige of decency and social responsibility she had worked so hard to instill in it. She looked from the silent herald of victory dawning in Lynch's face to the fierce glow of pleasure in Winthrop's.

It struck her like a nine-pound hammer: She had played right into their hands. They had used her proposal to rouse slumbering resentment of her policies and leadership. What could she do? Her stubborn pragmatism asserted itself. She could *never* give them power over herself or her companies.

"No," she declared, her hands curling into fists, "it does not change my mind. Consolidated Industries has a responsibility to the world it profits from. We will conduct this company's business ethically and responsibly as long as I am president of this board."

The sparks in Lynch's gaze ignited to a full flame.

"Well, that condition may be easily changed." He wheeled on his fellow board members. "I call for a vote of 'no confidence' in the current president and for her *removal* from office!"

There was a moment of shock before the lawyers shot to their feet.

"Point of order!" one lawyer yelled above the confusion breaking loose.

"There are procedures to be followed!" another admonished, brandishing an open set of bylaws. "Section two, paragraph nine, point seven . . ."

After a few minutes, she grabbed her gavel and pounded the table.

As the noise subsided, Lynch echoed her action with his fist, stealing the floor.

"Gentlemen . . . I had hoped to spare the board and Mrs. Von Furstenberg the revelation of a tawdry and humiliating incident . . . had hoped to make this change of management as painless as possible. But her arrogant and intractable behavior forces my hand. I am left no choice but to reveal the sordid truth as Mr. Winthrop and I observed it." A hush fell over the boardroom and every eye turned to Lynch.

Through a frantic jumble of emotion, she heard Lynch declaring that he had seen her enter the "notorious house of ill repute" known as the Oriental Palace.

"Shocked and dismayed, scarcely able to believe my own eyes, I was driven to follow her inside," he proclaimed. "There, in that foul den of depravity, I was subjected to the spectacle of Mrs. Von Furstenberg"—he flung an accusing finger—"in shameless dishabille . . . upended over the shoulder of a giant of a man . . . being manhandled and put on display for the titillation of the drunken and depraved patrons!"

Beatrice watched in horror. How could she counter what he said? The truth would only sound preposterous and contrived; it was difficult enough for her to believe and she had lived through it!

Gasps and glowers were aimed at her from all around the table. But her dismay equaled theirs. She had worked with many of these men for a dozen years, but they were willing to accept at face value the story of a man with an obvious ax to grind against her. Could they resent her leadership so much? Her humiliation began to turn to a deep and wounding sense of betrayal.

"My sense of outrage quickly gave way to distress," Lynch continued. "In horror and revulsion, I was driven to send for Harry Winthrop. He joined me and also witnessed her degraded revels among the denizens of that den of iniquity."

Winthrop stepped forward and nodded. "I must attest to every ugly and objectionable detail of this account. Mrs. Von Furstenberg was indeed there . . . cavorting with that monstrous giant . . . yelling, laughing, and baring herself . . ."

One by one, the directors turned to stare at her in horror and disgust . . . which only deepened as Lynch went on: "I assure you, gentlemen, her behavior was so notorious and so blatant, that there was quite an audience. It would be no problem to locate any number of men who would recognize her."

Fighting the panic rising and constricting her throat, she suddenly realized in a desperate flash that for the moment it was their word against hers.

"I have never heard such vile and ridiculous slander in my life!" She shot to her feet. "If you truly intend to defame me, you could at least come up with better stories. Why not that I practice black magic? That I frequent opium dens? Or that I'm really a man in disguise?" She wheeled on the rest of the directors. "I have never, *ever* participated in 'degraded revels.'"

"Of course she denies it," Winthrop declared with great indignation.

"I have known for some time that you resented my leadership of this board"—she glared at her pair of accusers—"but never in my wildest dreams did I suspect you would sink to such vicious personal attacks."

"Every word is the truth," Lynch insisted, his face now crimson.

"Every word is self-serving drivel," she countered. "Where are these witnesses you claim exist? Why didn't you bring them with you? Or didn't you think you would need to bother with a little thing like *proof*?

"Well, I demand to see this 'proof' of yours. Here and now." She sat down with regal fury, her arms tightly tucked and her spine rigid. "Go on. Send for your witnesses." When he made no move for the door, she looked up and down the table, seizing and holding each man's gaze until he looked away. "While you are at it, perhaps you should invite a few of the women who ply their trade in that awful place . . . the unfortunates who are forced to serve the lusts of wealthy men. It would be most interesting to discover just who in this room *they* might recognize." Her smile was suddenly fierce and her eyes sparked with defiant energy. "Perhaps they could even tell us just what Mr. Lynch and Mr. Winthrop were *truly* doing in such a place."

She paused to let that sink in and scarcely drew a breath until, one by one, the directors began to squirm in their chairs. A few began to redden beneath their collars. One or two glanced angrily at each other.

"As Lynch told his story, did any of you question how he happened to be 'passing by' this Oriental Palace? How many of you, in your minds, translated 'happened by' into 'was there for an evening's sport'? Ask yourself . . . if I were a man, would such a story—even if it were entirely true—have been anything other than cause for a good laugh, told over a round of Scotch at the Pantheon Club?"

Several of the directors started at her reference to their hallowed club and looked with alarm to Lynch and Winthrop.

"Don't you see what she's doing?" Lynch demanded stalking down one side of the board table. "She's trying to divert attention from her own depraved behavior by indicting you in your own thoughts? Are you going to stand for it?"

Sensing the tide turning, she rose and took the other side of the table, walking slowly, pausing behind each director to let her presence be felt.

"You know me. I have worked with this board for twelve long and profitable years. We have faced crises and weathered financial storms together . . . have taken risks and celebrated many more victories than losses. I have proved both my devotion to moral principles and my fitness to lead this company." Her mind raced to find examples that would link her to the men around the table.

"The teamster contracts in eighty-nine . . . remember, Haffleck? The way we avoided a strike at the Connecticut dye works—you were there, Augustine. We went without sleep for two days and nights to negotiate import agreements with the South American countries . . . to insure the native farmers would receive their share . . . didn't we, Graham? In every case I insisted on ethical dealings." A few heads began to nod agreement. "And I have conducted my personal life with the same standard of decency and integrity."

"Enough of this harangue. I call for the question," Lynch declared desperately, striding back to his seat with Winthrop in tow. "A vote of no-confidence. If you would remove Beatrice Von Furstenberg and her brand of hypocrisy from this board, vote with me."

He lifted his empty water glass and with a flourish turned it upside down on the tabletop. Winthrop followed suit, and together they looked expectantly to William Afton.

He drew his neck into his thick collar, folded his arms and burrowed back in his chair. But after a moment, he too turned over his glass.

Beatrice held her breath as all eyes transferred to old Ben Haffleck. After a moment, he reached for his glass and turned it upside down with a smack. Graham, the vice president, left his glass untouched and N. T. Wright, the board secretary, also voted to retain her. Then treasurer Martin Welgoe and member Barton Kern left theirs upright.

The final and deciding vote was cast by old Leonard Augustine . . . who scowled, sniffed irritably, and turned his face away . . . leaving his glass untouched.

"Five to four," intoned Consolidated's head attorney, who stood at the head of the table to observe the voting. "Mrs. Von Furstenberg is retained as President of Consolidated Industries."

Lynch was instantly livid.

"What's the matter with you? Can't you see what she is?" The others refused to meet his contemptuous gaze, so he turned it on her. "You think you've won, Von Furstenberg, but you're wrong."

He stalked to the door and snatched his hat from the rack. Winthrop quickly gathered up their papers and joined him, and the pair were soon joined by portly William Afton. "The rest of you"—Lynch's hand trembled visibly as he pointed at the directors who had supported her—"you'll rue the day you cast your lot with that witch. She'll take you and this company down with her!"

The three strode out and the sound of slamming

doors wafted back into the open boardroom. The silence that descended was deafening.

She felt their eyes on her, searching and mistrustful, and it was all she could do to keep from railing at them for their lack of faith in her. How could they think her a loose and immoral woman? How could they treat her so shabbily?

At length, she forced a deep, calming breath and reached for her gavel.

"We still have a quorum present and I believe there is a motion to approve a banking proposal before the board." With that statement and the tap of the gavel, a shocking air of normalcy descended. "Is there further discussion?"

The directors looked at each other. She seemed to expect them to continue business as usual, even after the charges they'd heard leveled against her.

"Maybe you *are* a man in disguise." Old Augustine gave a crusty laugh. "You sure got the brass for it." He leaned forward, squinting, scrutinizing her heated face. "All right. In your proposal you say you'll need one and one-half million to fully fund this bank." He paused to look at his fellow directors. "I say . . . you need to show us something. Get yourself a state charter. Convince those boys at the statehouse that you're serious, and *if* they give you a state charter, then we'll give you your first million. The rest is up to you."

"A million dollars?" old Ben Haffleck shook his head. "That's crazy."

"Not if she has to raise or to put up the other half million herself," old Augustine said with a canny expression.

"I agree," vice president Graham spoke up. "If she gets a charter and raises a half million, she gets the rest from us. She'll have her capital and we'll have assurance that there's enough outside interest to make the thing profitable."

The murmurs and side conversations around the table came to reluctant agreement. It was a devil's compromise, but the looks on their faces made it clear that a hard compromise was all she would get.

Half a million dollars was a formidable amount of money to raise for such a project and they knew it. She had been prepared to invest a hundred thousand dollars herself, but the rest of her personal wealth was tied up in companies, stock, and properties. That meant she had four hundred thousand dollars to raise.

True to her pragmatic nature, she squared her shoulders and told herself she could do it. She had a chance. She would just have to make good on it.

"Thank you, gentlemen. You have handed me a challenge that I gladly accept. I promise, you will soon see the Barrow State Bank not only in operation, but also registering in black on your quarterly reports."

When the last director had left, she sat staring at the empty seats around the table, remembering those shocked stares.

Over the years she had faced challenges and locked horns with powerful opponents, but never had she been so close to losing all she had worked for. How could the board's confidence in her be so vulnerable to the word of Winthrop and Lynch, two men who thus far had contributed nothing to the company but discontent?

She was still unsettled when she left the offices. Despite the early-autumn sun, she felt cold when she stepped out onto the sidewalk. Once in the carriage, she crossed her arms to hold in what warmth she possessed, but found it did little good. Inside she felt raw and empty.

For the first time in a long, long time she felt an aching need to confide in someone, to tell someone everything that had just happened.

Her eyes filled with moisture and she turned to stare out the window, unblinking, afraid that Alice would notice. It was bewildering to her that the someone she wanted to see and to share with was Connor Barrow.

What the devil was happening to her?

FIFTEEN

BY THE TIME Winthrop, Lynch, and Afton reached the street in front of Consolidated's offices, they were red-faced from anger and exertion.

"The bitch didn't even bother to deny it," Winthrop said, matching his partner's furious stride, "and they still voted with her!"

"She just climbed on her high horse and took off—dragging the lot of them with her," Lynch ground out. "They've been following her around so long, they've forgotten how to walk without their noses stuck in her bustle."

"And you—where the hell were you, Afton?" Winthrop demanded, catching the arm of the third member of the party and jerking him to a halt. "You could have spoken up . . . supported us."

"I didn't see anything at the Oriental." Afton jerked his arm free.

"You want her out as much as we do," Lynch snarled, "but you're too lily-livered to stand up to her."

Afton reddened furiously and his eyes and voice both

tightened. "You're not a married man, Lynch. I am. I'll support you, all right . . . when you give me something to support." He wheeled and headed quickly down the street.

Lynch watched Afton's retreat for a moment. "Henpecked bastard." He turned to Winthrop with the cogs turning in his mind. "She made fools of us . . . used her own priggish reputation to . . ." He halted and his eyes darted here and there as he collected pieces of a new plan. Then he grabbed Winthrop's arm and dragged him toward the curb. "Come on. By the time we get through with her, she won't be able to show her face anyplace in the five boroughs." He hailed a passing cab.

"Where are we going? What have you got up your sleeve?"

Lynch began to smile as they settled back against the cab's worn leather seat. "There are at least half a dozen newspapers in this city that would kill for a juicy scandal involving one of the richest women in New York. She may have an ironclad arse in the boardroom . . . but in the rest of the world, her 'very fine bottom' is just bustle stuffing. Maybe it's time she was reminded what the rest of the world thinks of a woman who tries to live like a man."

WHEN BEATRICE ARRIVED home that afternoon, Richards greeted her with news that she had a caller who had insisted on waiting. Stepping into the drawing room, she stared at a familiar broad back and dark head. Her rigid posture softened and her knees went a little weak.

Now, of all times. Had her thoughts in the carriage somehow conjured him in her drawing room?

"Mr. Barrow," she said, startling him as she strode

across the room. "This is a surprise. And just in time . . . I have some wonderful news."

"Good." He met her halfway, snagged her elbow, and propelled her back out into the entry hall with him. "You can tell me as you pack."

"Pack?"

"We have to be in Albany by tomorrow afternoon and it's a long ride. Pack light. We'll only be gone two days . . . three at most."

"I'm not going to Albany!"

"You have to go . . . it's your bank. I drew up the charter request, but they'll have questions about the funding and the accounting . . . all the facts and figures."

"I'll give you the documents containing that information and you can study them on the train up to Albany."

"Look, if I can take three days out of my campaign schedule and mislead and evade my own campaign manager about where I'll be and what I'll be doing in order to secure your cursed bank . . . then the very least you can do is come along and help with the groveling and pleading."

She felt her face heating as he pursed one side of his mouth and looked her up and down. His eyes widened in understanding, then narrowed sharply.

"Of course, if you're *afraid* to go with me"—that cursed Irish music crept into his voice again—"afraid you cannot control your lustful urges toward me . . . that you might forget yourself on the train and throw me down and have your wicked way with me . . . I suppose I can understand that. I am a mighty temptation to women." Just as she was ready to give him an outraged shove, he leaned closer to stare into her eyes and produced a smile that would have kept St. Catherine from qualifying for canonization. "But, you're not reckoning with my steely nerve and legendary self-control."

"Don't be ridiculous!" she said, struggling to think against the embarrassment rising in her. "I simply don't see why you can't go alone. The committee is the only real deadline. You could present the proposal to them and still have plenty of time to wine and dine legislators afterward."

He drew a long breath and his face sobered.

"I know some of the people who sit regularly on the committee," he confessed. "They're my grandfather's cronies and they take a rather dim view of anyone who abandons their precious banking profession and their financial world." He straightened. "Now do you understand?"

THREE HOURS LATER, Beatrice was climbing onto the platform of the New York Central's Express to Albany. With her, she had Alice, two books, a stack of corporate reports, and the vivid memory of Priscilla's unhappy face as she watched her aunt's baggage being loaded into the carriage.

When she and Alice were settled in the first-class compartment of the train, she closed her eyes and tried to catch her breath. But the arrival of another passenger, who brushed her skirts more than once, caused her to open her eyes. It was Connor . . . stowing his valise and settling into the seat across from her.

They exchanged few words as the train got underway, and by the time the train got up steam, both he and Alice had nodded off.

She tried not to stare, but something drew her back

again and again to his dark hair and dangerously hand-some face. For all she knew about him, he was still something of a mystery to her. She was putting the fate of her bank and ultimately her position at Consolidated in his hands, and she wasn't even sure she could trust him to tell her what day it was.

If only she had some clue as to what was inside him . . . what he truly believed, how he truly saw things. Could he be trusted with things that mattered to her? How could he have any honor or integrity and still be the darling of Tammany Hall's bosses with their blatant use of graft and patronage? Most of all, she wanted to know why he was sitting across from her on a train bound for Albany. Was concern about the committee the real reason he insisted she come with him?

She looked out at the darkening countryside passing by the window and tried not to think about what the real reason might be that she had agreed to come.

Some time later, the funding documents he had been reviewing slid from the seat beside him onto the floor. She bent to pick them up, just as he leaned forward to retrieve them. They bumped heads and she grabbed her hat and looked up to find his face a mere inch from hers.

She knew she was in trouble when she didn't straighten instantly and slide back into her seat with a sniff of indignation. If he kissed her, she was going to kiss him back; that much was clear. And it was only going to complicate things even more.

She heard Alice stir on the seat beside her and shoved the papers into his hand. He tucked them securely on the seat beside him. For the rest of the train ride, he wore a small, annoying smile that said he knew how susceptible she was to the idea of kissing him.

They arrived at the train station quite late. The hotel, the finest in Albany, was unable to offer them more than mediocre accommodations since the legislature was in session and business was brisk. It was late and they were exhausted, so they gladly accepted two rooms at the rear of the hotel's third floor, overlooking a public livery. Beatrice and Alice were required to share a room, though not a bed, and they all had to use the common bathing room at the end of the hall. Beatrice wasn't pleased with the arrangements, but told herself as she slipped between clean sheets that night and felt every bone in her body ache with gratitude, that it would help procure her bank charter.

She was considerably less appreciative the next morning, as she stood in a line with other hotel guests wrapped in robes and dressing gowns, waiting for a turn in the bathing room. And she became downright annoyed when she heard Connor's voice in her ear bidding her a good morning, and found he had worked his way up the line to stand directly behind her. She pulled her dressing gown together at the neck and refused to look at his tousled hair, sultry, sleep-softened eyes, or his bare chest, with its dark hair, visible beneath his half-opened shirt.

At least she and Alice were able to breakfast in peace; Connor declared he had an early meeting with someone from the legislature and disappeared.

The charter committee met in an office building near the capitol, which housed several governmental departments and bureaus. The air in the paneled room was close and the aged wooden furnishings gave off a faintly vinegary smell. That odor combined with the heavy must of uncirculated air made them decide to wait in the hallway. Stationed by the door, they could watch for the committee's arrival and for Connor, who was supposed to join them.

Promptly at two o'clock, the committee members filed in to take seats at a long table on a low dais. Beatrice winced as she peered through the doorway at them. Connor was right; not one of them looked a day under seventy. With their dark clothes, bent shoulders, and bowed necks, they reminded her of aged vultures.

As they sank into their seats, the room filled with a dry rustle, like the sound of leather brushing leather. Beatrice swallowed hard as she eyed the smaller table set before the dais, where petitioners pleaded their cases. She imagined a huge pile of bones beside that table and . . .

Alice pulled on her sleeve. Connor was coming down the hallway toward them with a firm step and a determined expression.

"Where have you been?" Beatrice demanded in a loud whisper as he took her by the elbow and ushered her through the door.

"Doing my job," he whispered back . . . then stopped dead, staring at the committee members.

His face drained of color. She followed his gaze to the dark, beady eyes of a black-clad old fellow with white hair and a formidable scowl.

An instant later, Connor turned and strode straight back out the door. Beatrice ordered Alice to save them seats and followed him.

"What's gotten into you?" she demanded when she caught up with him.

"My grandfather," he said as if the words inflicted pain.

"Your grand—where?" Then she knew. "You mean, on the committee?" Putting together his grim expression and the gossip she'd heard about his break with the old man alarmed her. "You think he would try to make it difficult for us? To block our charter?"

"He's waited ten years for this very opportunity," he ground out. "Of course he'll make it difficult."

There was a sinking sensation in her stomach. She had been so sure that Connor was what she needed to get them past the committee and through the legislature. Now it seemed he might be their greatest obstacle!

"Perhaps if I went in alone," she said.

He scowled and rubbed his forehead. "He's already seen me with you. I can't back out now, or he'll make it impossible for you. We both have to go back in." He flexed his shoulders like a gladiator preparing for battle. "You'll have to do the talking. Whatever you do, don't talk about women and how they need this blasted bank. Keep it strictly business. Talk profit. That, they'll understand."

Profit. Her recent experience with Consolidated's board came back to her. If the charter committee's attitude was anything like her board's, she had her work cut out for her.

The afternoon dragged on as proposals for charters, most made in absentia, were stripped to mere bones and cast aside. The old gargoyles went over every aspect of each proposal with an eye for weaknesses. And with each failure, Hurst Barrow glanced at Connor to see if that rejection sparked a reaction. He seemed to be searching for the matter that had brought him face-to-face with his rebellious grandson for the first time in years.

It wasn't until late in the afternoon, almost five o'clock, that Beatrice's charter request came before the committee.

She approached the table, motioning Alice and Connor to come with her. The clerk read "Proposed: the 'Barrow State Bank'." Old Hurst Barrow's wiry eyebrows shot up and he sent his grandson a disgusted look. Connor's objection to her use of his name on the future bank now took on an entirely different significance. It must seem to Hurst Barrow and the rest of the committee that they were using the name to curry favor.

Beatrice identified herself as the president of Consolidated Industries, in whose name the charter was sought. She was instructed to be seated.

"Von Furstenberg?" Hurst Barrow squinted and leaned forward to get a better look at her. "You mean to say you're old Furstie's widow?"

"Yes, I am Mercer Von Furstenberg's widow," she said, trying to read in his reaction whether that relationship counted for or against her.

"You run through all his money?" another of the old codgers demanded. "And now you're lookin' to get your hands on other peoples'?"

She tensed but felt Connor's hand on her arm, beneath the table.

"I am supplying a good part of the initial capital for this bank myself," she said calmly. "The rest of the reserve will be provided by a stock offering and by Consolidated Industries. The money has already been approved by the board of directors."

There was a murmur as the committee conferred . . . resulting in a noise that might have been a rumble of either displeasure or gastric distress. When they resumed, Hurst Barrow took the lead.

"Who would run this bank?" he demanded, scrutinizing Beatrice. "You?"

"As has been the case with each of Consolidated's other subsidiaries," she said evenly, "we expect to hire well-qualified managers and officers, who will report directly to Consolidated's board of directors."

Hurst leveled a glower on Connor.

"And what's *your* piece of this plum?"

It was her turn to seize Connor's arm.

"I am here to offer Mrs. Von Furstenberg and Consolidated Industries legal counsel and political advice," Connor declared.

Hurst snorted and turned to Beatrice. "If you get a charter . . . I hope you do a better job choosing bank personnel than you've done choosing legal help."

She reddened and would have spoken, but Connor's hand stopped her. She looked up to find his face frozen into a mask of composure.

"There are at least thirty different banks and savings associations already in New York," another committee member declared. "What makes you think yours will make a go of it in that kind of competition? What makes your bank any different from the others?"

She was about to launch into a litany on innovative policies and underserved populations when Connor whispered into her ear: "Trick question. Bankers *hate* things that are different."

"In the kinds of service offered and general banking procedures, there will be no difference. Only time-tested, tried-and-true business practices will be followed," she announced instead. "There is throughout the Von Furstenberg companies, a deep respect for tradition and integrity . . . which combines effectively with a dynamic vision of the future and a quest for innovation. In that regard we plan to investigate new ways of—"

A hoot of rusty-sounding laughter stopped her. Old Hurst Eddington Barrow leaned forward and pointed at Connor.

"Did *he* tell you to say that?"

"*He* told me to be as forthright and sincere with the board as possible," she said succinctly. "*He* said you would appreciate candor, competence, and brevity."

"*He's* always been full of horse manure," Hurst declared.

"A family trait, it seems," she said on impulse.

In the shocked pause that followed, something in the old boy's testy manner and age-faded eyes triggered a memory of Mercer in a mood, and she responded the way she sometimes had to her aged husband—with a smart, saucy smile that was some part confidence, some part defiance, and some part invitation to return to reason.

Connor stared at her brazen, faintly flirtatious smile in horror. What the devil was she doing? Trying to charm the old boy? He could have told her, from long experience, that appealing to his grandfather's heart was a lost cause. The old vulture didn't *have* one!

"Perhaps, Mr. Barrow, the name of our proposed bank should be explained," she continued.

He groaned softly. Not *that*! But she sat abruptly forward to prevent him from seizing her hand.

"It was chosen to honor the man who suggested its development . . . congressional candidate, Connor Barrow. He was visiting a settlement house with me and hearing the heartrending stories of the residents . . ."

Connor shrank inside from the horror of what was happening and twisted internally in silent agony. There was nothing that could rouse the old man's contempt faster than a sob story—especially one involving his way-ward grandson.

". . . said they didn't need a vote, they needed a bank," she continued. "And I had the good sense to realize he was right. It seemed only fitting to honor him in the bank's name."

The old boy scrutinized Beatrice with a look that he generally reserved for separating meat from bone. But to Connor's amazement, she simply smiled back. He closed his eyes. She was halfway down the vulture's throat and she didn't even know it . . .

"And the fact that for three generations the name *Barrow* has been widely associated with banking in New York never crossed your mind," he said.

Connor opened his eyes in alarm to find that her prim smile and air of confidence remained unshaken.

"Well, I am a businesswoman, after all." Her smile broadened and her cheeks colored slightly. "And none of the Barrows themselves seemed inclined to use the name on an institution."

For a moment Connor wasn't certain whether his grandfather was choking or strangling. The noise was more of a gurgle than a laugh, but as it gained volume it became clear that it was indeed a venting of pleasure.

"Damn me if you don't have more brass than a spit-toon factory," Hurst Eddington declared, his face settling into a wry expression.

Connor blinked, looking from the old man to Beatrice and back again.

"I learned from a master, sir," she said simply. But there was a world of meaning in those words and Connor experienced a startling flash of insight into her life and her character. Had her husband been cut from the same cloth as his grandfather? If so, she had indeed learned from a master. And her first and most powerful lesson had been in control. She soon confirmed his conclusion.

"It is my personal policy to leave as little to chance as possible. I assure you, this bank will be well funded, well structured, and well run. And I expect that this committee, composed as it is of legendary financiers and bankers"—she nodded to include the others—"will see the thoroughness of our care in planning and will give our proposal a fair and responsible hearing . . . untainted by personal considerations. I am also confident that this committee means to render its decision in a wise and impartial manner, with the welfare of the business community and the citizens of the state of New York in mind."

It was such an unprecedented and ladylike affront to the committee's authority, that the old boys were momentarily taken aback.

In the silence that followed, the rest of the committee looked to Hurst Barrow. Connor could feel his grandfather assessing the space between him and Beatrice. After a moment, a canny look spread over the old man's gaunt but still powerful face. The old boy glanced briefly at Consolidated's proposal, then with a sweep of the hand so casual it might in any other context have been deemed accidental, tipped it off the table and onto the floor beside the dais.

There was an audible gasp in the chamber. Every spectator present understood that the old man was telling her where he believed her proposal and her demands belonged. Connor's gut tightened and he started up, but she pulled him back down into his seat. Without a perceptible change of mood or manner, she rose, retrieved the proposal, and placed it firmly on top of the papers in front of Hurst Barrow.

"I believe you will need this." Her voice was oddly devoid of injury or irritation. "The committee has not yet rendered a decision on it."

His gaze locked with hers.

She returned to her seat, folded her hands on the tabletop, and waited patiently for Hurst Barrow's response. Connor watched in disbelief as the old man picked up the proposal, considered it with an inscrutable expression, and then tucked it under his arm.

"I've had enough of upstart financiers for one day," he declared, turning to his fellow commissioners. "I can't rule on anything until I've had a bite of supper and a glass of port. We'll recess until ten o'clock sharp tomorrow morning."

As the committee rose with him and filed out the side door, Connor turned to Beatrice with emotion boiling up inside him. All he could think about was getting her someplace private. . . .

"Have you gone completely mad?" he whispered as they exited and headed for the lobby.

"It worked, didn't it?" she answered quietly, though he noted that her hands trembled when they weren't gripping the portfolio she carried.

"He threw the damned thing on the floor, for God's sake!" He grabbed her arm and turned her around to face him. "Do you honestly think he intends to give you a hearing of any kind?"

"Yes, I do." She pulled her arm free and scowled up at him. "He took the proposal with him and will probably read it over supper tonight. By tomorrow he'll have a few—"

"*Thousand* good reasons not to recommend a charter. You're dead in the water, right now."

She stepped back and looked at Alice, who had stopped several feet away trying to pretend she wasn't hearing every word.

"No, I'm not," she said with a determined tilt to her chin. "He's going to go over it with a fine-toothed comb tonight and will grill us mercilessly tomorrow . . . after which—I'll give you odds—the committee will vote to give us a charter endorsement."

"Oh? And how do you know?"

She tapped her cheek just below her eye. "I saw it in his eyes."

"In his—*Jesus, Mary, and Joseph*—she saw it in his blessed eyes!" He rubbed both hands down his face, as if trying to wipe the thought from his mind. But when he raised his head, it was clearly still there. "You and your precious female intuition—you honestly think you can read the old bastard that easily? All right—fine—put your powers to work again." He lurched closer, shoved his face into hers, and pointed to his eyes. "What do you see in these?"

Beatrice refused to retreat and in a heartbeat found herself engulfed in that searing blue gaze and fighting her way past the suspicion, irritation, and disbelief that he insisted she acknowledge, to another, deeper set of feelings and responses . . . raw and shockingly naked emotions . . . things she had never imagined she would see in a man's eyes.

Riveted by that overwhelming intimacy, she was suddenly awash in estrangement, childhood wounds and hunger, a furious struggle for personhood, and fierce conflict that had never been resolved. Each brief impression found a corresponding niche carved by experience in her own heart. She was looking at her own struggle, her own past in his eyes, and that moment of stark, intense self-confrontation left her momentarily without words.

He felt it too, she realized as he withdrew and fell back a step. For the first time in memory, she couldn't reclose those protective inner doors that had shielded her from the world for so long. With one molten blue stare he had bared all of his inner secrets to her, but it was she who now felt exposed.

"So . . . what do you see?" he said, his voice constricted.

"Loss. Confusion. Disappointment. Battered hopes." Her voice grew hushed. It felt more like a confession than an observation.

"He's responsible for all of that." He swallowed hard, shaken and clearly struggling for control. "He's a master of manipulation and deception. He'll have it his way or die trying. And believe me, *his way* won't even leave you room to breathe."

She was staggered by the depths of his resentment and the pain he hid so completely beneath layers of glib talk and easy Irish charm. It was a moment before she could recover herself and respond.

"I know it seems crazy, but you have to trust me on this. He may be a hard man, but he's not impossible. I believe we can still get our charter."

"You mean, if you bat your eyes, giggle, and flatter him some more?"

She blanched and fell back, stinging and embarrassed by her hurt.

"I'm in dire need of some fresh air, Alice." She

wheeled, put her arm through her secretary's, and headed for the front doors. "It's getting hard to breathe in here."

Connor was in turmoil as he watched her walk away from him. Should he abandon the entire project with a vehement "good riddance," or haul her back and sit on her if necessary to make her see reason?

After several deep, calming breaths that allowed him to find his bearings, he thought of the supper invitation he'd received earlier from the legislature's Democratic party leadership. He headed through the lobby under a full head of steam. It would feel good to be back in the relatively sane and predictable company of politicians. At least they could tell when they were swimming in water filled with sharks.

On the pavement outside, as he looked up and down the street for a hansom cab, he turned and came unexpectedly face-to-face with none other than Hurst Eddington Barrow. For a moment, Connor felt like he'd been punched in the gut. He could hardly draw breath.

"So you came crawling back," the old man declared, "just like I knew you would."

Connor reminded himself he was not twelve years old and his grandfather was no longer his omnipotent guardian. When he managed to focus his thoughts beyond the emotion roiling in him, he was jolted by the old man's appearance at close range. His skin was sallow and waxy, there were dark circles beneath his eyes, and his cheeks had begun to sink. His eyes, once a simmering silver gray, were now age-dulled and flat, and his hands were thin-skinned and bony. There were still remnants of the titan he had once been, but in truth, Hurst Barrow looked old and surprisingly frail.

"I am not crawling. Nor am I 'back,'" Connor responded in savagely controlled tones. "I am doing my duty . . . practicing my profession . . . the same profession you chose and prepared me for."

"Still ungrateful and defiant. And still got your nose stuck in a bustle, I see." The old man produced a smirk. "But at least your taste is improving. Old Furstie's widow. Who'd have thought it? Tell me, boy"—the smirk was replaced by a sneer—"what the devil does she see in *you*?"

"Something you never did," Connor said as he turned away. "A man."

SIXTEEN

THAT EVENING AS Beatrice and Alice were being seated for dinner in the hotel's fashionable restaurant, Alice asked her opinion of the day's events.

"Do you think that we have a chance?"

"I doubt the wine is from France," Beatrice responded absently, her eyes fixed on the centerpiece and the menu limp in her hands.

Alice frowned and tried again.

"Do you think there will be problems with that old man?"

"Old ham? I don't believe I see any ham."

In truth, Beatrice wasn't seeing or hearing much of anything just then. Her air of distraction only hinted at the massive internal dislocation she had suffered in her encounter with Connor that afternoon. Every part of her felt disconnected and out of joint—missing the mundane linkages that permitted the power of speech, hearing, and simple verbal comprehension. Alice gave up and concentrated on her meal.

Later, in their room, under Alice's concerned looks,

Beatrice tried reading. The words may as well have been little black bugs scampering across the pages. She tried making an entry in her diary and had difficulty producing a coherent sentence. By ten o'clock, she was relieved to prepare for bed . . . putting on her night clothes, brushing her hair, and making one last trip down the hall.

The gaslights in the passage had been dimmed, making the austere, painted walls seem a bit less stark. But there was no source of heat to reduce the chill in the hallway as she stood waiting outside the occupied bathing chamber. She heard a noise behind her and turned.

Connor stood several yards away with his arms crossed, leaning a shoulder against the door to his room. His tie and collar were undone, his hair was slightly rumpled, and his face looked dusky in the lowered light. As he strolled closer, she caught a whiff of spirits.

"You've been drinking," she said, looking past him down the hall and finding it empty.

"Of course," he said with a lazy grin. "I've just had dinner with my fellow graft-mongers and influence peddlers . . . the Democratic party leadership of our fair legislature. We always have a wee bit o' the 'Irish gargle' after we finish our nefarious plotting and dividing up the spoils of office."

"Well, I hope you made good use of the time and liquor," she said, pulling her dressing gown higher and tighter around her neck, to cover her thudding heart, "and got your precious democrats to agree to support our charter."

He seemed a bit startled, then laughed.

"Damn me. You are something." He paused four feet away and looked her up and down. "You never let up, do you? You never take time off. You never forget for a minute that you're a living, breathing corporation."

"I've made it a policy," she said breathlessly.

He took in her ruffle-trimmed dressing gown and the way her hair was brushed into a thick fall down her back, and remembered what lay beneath those soft tresses and that frothy silk. When he raised his gaze, her eyes were emerald-dark and luminous. It seemed the most natural thing in the world for him to close the distance between them and pull her into his arms.

"Make a new policy," he growled as he lowered his head.

The minute his lips touched hers, some disengaged part of her slid back into its proper slot. And with every shift of his mouth over hers, with every new combination of touch and movement, another connection was reestablished in her fragmented self. He was healing, making whole, rejoining parts of her she hadn't realized had been separated. She lapped both arms around his waist, embracing both him and the changes happening in her. Then without a single thought of surroundings or consequences, she gave herself up totally to his kiss.

Walls swayed and light and darkness blended as ordinary reality retreated to the edges of her consciousness. After a time, the sound of a door slamming in the distance brought her back to her senses and she looked up to find that it was the door to a room. His room. She pulled back enough to look at him.

In the moonlight coming through the window he seemed made of silver and shadow, with shimmering eyes and desire-darkened features. He seized his tie and pulled it so that it unwrapped slowly, sinuously from his neck, without his eyes ever leaving hers. It was a simple movement that expressed a complex question. She could stay or she could go. And if she stayed . . .

The impact of what she was about to do descended on her. She stiffened, looking at the four-poster bed. The moonlight slanting across it created a sharp line between darkness and light . . . a line as defined as the one she must now cross in her mind and in her heart. And for the life of her, she couldn't have said whether at that moment she was already standing in light, yearning for the darkness or standing in darkness, longing for the light. All she knew was that everything in her, even the well of her fiercest yearnings, resonated with a simple truth: She had never wanted anything as much as she wanted him.

He waited, watching, sensing the decision she was making and knowing that it was hers alone to make. And choosing, she had never felt freer. When she held out her hands to him, there was moisture in her eyes.

He took her hands with a grin and used them to pull her fully against him. She raised her mouth for a kiss, but he paused to look at her first.

"Beatrice fits you in a boardroom, but in a bedroom . . . Bea? Bets?"

"Bebe?" she offered. "It was something my sister used to call me."

"Bebe." He grinned. "I like it." He began to nibble his way down the side of her neck, peeling back her dressing gown. It fluttered into a pool around her feet and she responded with goose bumps and a shiver. He felt tension rising in her and paused.

"You haven't done anything like this in a long time, have you?"

She stiffened. "I'm not certain I've done anything like this . . . ever."

When he chuckled softly and raised her chin, she had difficulty meeting his gaze. Despite her knowledge of the way of men with women, she felt embarrassed and awkward. Her occasional contact with her aged husband had given her little confidence in her ability to give pleasure to a man. And she wanted so badly to please him.

Connor noted the embarrassment darkening her cheeks.

"Well then, lass"—that emerald satin entered in his voice again—"we'll have to do something neither of us has done before." He shed his coat and then unbuttoned his vest.

"This wouldn't involve whips or ropes or a ship's wheel, would it?" Her eyes widened as he slid his suspenders from his shoulders.

"Will you be disappointed if it doesn't?"

"I think I can cope."

He pulled her toward the wardrobe at the edge of the window, positioning her so that she could see her reflection in the aged mirror on the front of the door. Then he stood behind her and placed his hands on her half-naked shoulders. "Rest yer mind, darlin'. This won't hurt a bit."

"Oh?" She was anything but convinced.

"I'm going to sing your clothes off. Every blessed stitch."

"You're what?" She started to turn, but his grip on her shoulders prevented it. "Connor—"

"Shhh—just stand still." He began to hum as he lowered his head to her shoulder and the vibration set her skin tingling where he touched it. By the time he reached the edge of her shoulder, he had indeed broken into a soft melody. " 'Women are angels witho-o-out any wings . . .' "

The song was an old Irish drinking song, to which Connor added words perfect for warming up a nervous suffragette. He unbuttoned her nightgown, phrase by phrase, and peeled it down one arm, singing softly into every inch of skin that was bared. He could feel her sharp breath and tiny quivers as he paused at her elbows. Then he sang her other shoulder free, and she caught the gown before it could fall past her breasts. When she refused to relinquish it, he gamely sang through the thin silk . . . kneeling to glide down the side of her hip . . . alternating kisses and melodic phrases that produced a nervous giggle.

"Hold still," he ordered.

"It tickles." She shivered massively. "And you're off key."

"Am not."

"Are too."

He looked up at her with narrowed eyes. "The music's not the point here, darlin'."

"I'll say." She realized she was staring at him over her half-bared breast and quickly crossed her arms over the pair, reddening. His expression softened.

"Do you have even the slightest notion of how lovely you are, Beatrice Von Furstenberg?"

She flushed and glanced away. "I'm not a beauty. I'm not even in the first bloom of . . ." She took a bracing breath. "Connor . . . I'm *thirty* years old."

"Aged to perfection," he said, sliding his hands up and down her silk-clad hips. "You're a beautiful woman. Don't you know that? There's not a spot on your body that I'd not wish to kiss and feel grateful for the chance to do so.

"Look . . ." He rose, stepped behind her, and nudged

her toward the mirror. She resisted and tried to cover more of herself—or at least look away. He wouldn't allow it. "Look at you, Bebe." The sweet-talking Irishman was gone. This was pure Connor. The real Connor. "Look at us." He wrapped his arms around her waist and smiled into their reflection. "Your strong shoulders and fine legs . . . hips just made for bearing. Look how my arms just fit around your waist and how your head just fits under my chin. This is the way men and women were meant to be. Together." She turned in his arms and looked up at him with a tangle of emotions visible in her face. "Does that scare you?"

He could feel the hammering of her heart against his chest.

"Yes," she whispered. "It scares me to death."

He smiled ruefully.

"I'll confess, it scares me, too. But if there's one thing I've learned in this life, it's that fear and love cannot abide in the same place at the same time. And if I have to choose, I'll take love." He ran his hand up her back to cradle her head. His eyes were dark with a need that just now seemed far more than physical. "Love me, Bebe. And let me love you."

Love me.

Sparks ignited in her eyes and her arms came up around his neck to pull his head down. She claimed his lips with all the joy and passion she possessed, and in that enthusiastic and increasingly steamy kiss, both her gown and the last of her inhibitions melted away. She raised his undershirt, unbuttoned his trousers, and as he shrugged out of his remaining garments, she replaced them with warming kisses and exploring hands. Both were now trembling with eagerness, hungry for sensation and experience.

Desire, banked since they reached the room, now ignited between them. Somehow they made it to the bed and sank down into a feather ticking covered by fresh sheets. Their bodies blended naturally, shapes molding together, limbs shifting, bodies seeking more intimate contact. She parted her thighs and he fitted himself against her, arching his back, rubbing, caressing her with every part of his body.

When he joined their bodies, it seemed paradoxically the most natural and the most remarkable thing that had ever happened to Bebe. She welcomed him, wrapped her legs around him, reveling in the heat and fullness inside her, in his power and in her possession of him. As he moved within her, she felt herself climbing a tightening spiral of response, approaching the purest limits of human sensation.

Their bodies grew damp and feverish, their breath came hard and fast as they strained together, clinging hard to each other, as if they could by force of will merge into one flesh. Then suddenly the bright, brittle limits of arousal shattered within them, freeing them from their individual boundaries.

She lay beneath him afterward, weak with surrender, open in ways she had never imagined possible. Aftershocks of pleasure shivered through her, and he showered brief kisses on her damp face and down her chest as he slid to the bed and curled protectively around her. When she turned her head to look at him, he was blurred by tears. She had no idea why she was crying, except that she was overwhelmed, and grateful beyond words to be in Connor Barrow's bed and in some part of Connor Barrow's heart.

He soothed and stroked her cooling body, nuzzled and kissed her as if memorizing her with each of his senses.

And when her tears dried, she looked up to find his eyes glistening strangely. It was that beautiful expression, that acknowledgment of wonder and connection that filled her mind as her eyes closed. Then, just as she drifted to sleep she heard him confess:

"You may as well know . . . I'm thirty-*two*."

CONNOR'S BREATHING WAS slow and deep. Trying not to awaken him, Bebe slid gingerly from under his arm, peeled her body from his, and slid toward the edge of the bed. Alice was undoubtedly wondering what had happened to her.

Climbing from the bed, she located her gown, robe, and slippers and shivered her way into them. Then she came to the edge of the bed and stood for a moment watching him sleep. He was so gentle, so careful of her, and so sure about the rightness of their loving. He had made it so easy for her to open herself to him, to forget who and what she was and lose herself in the passion he stirred within her. She was tempted to drop a kiss on his ear, but he shifted in his sleep and she refrained. If he awakened, she wouldn't be able to leave him.

She slipped out the door and down the hall to her own room. There, she found the door unlocked and Alice sitting in a chair facing it . . . fully dressed, sound asleep, and holding tightly the stout parasol she sometimes carried for self-defense.

Bebe gently awakened her and suggested she climb into bed instead of passing the night in the chair. Alice was too sleepy to do anything but comply. Bebe heaved a huge sigh of relief as she snuggled under the covers. Her secret rendezvous with Connor was still secret.

The next morning, however, Alice was tired, unchar-
acteristically cross, and clearly suspicious of Bebe's explanation for coming in late. And when Connor joined
them at breakfast in the hotel dining room, Alice
watched with a discerning eye as he gallantly kissed
Bebe's hand and she blushed.

Bebe told herself she didn't care what Alice thought.
But it wasn't true. And as they headed for the banking
department and the committee meeting, she felt pulled
between the propriety and camaraderie she shared with
Alice, and the passion and intimacy she had shared with
Connor. By the time they reached the meeting chamber,
she was beginning to feel guilty that she had thought so
little about her purpose in coming to Albany.

Then she glanced up at Connor, who slipped her a sly
wink as they settled into seats in the committee chamber, and felt a refreshing release of tension. Whatever
happened today, she understood with a knowing deeper
than logic, that what had happened last night was indeed
a gift of love for both of them.

"WE WENT OVER this proposal," one of the committee members announced, beginning the morning's pro-
ceedings, "and one thing puzzles us. Several places refer
to a policy of making loans to *all* customers. Surely you
can't mean that. You can't expect to go about giving loans
to just anybody."

"Anyone who qualifies," she answered. "We intend to
see to it that loans are available equally to men and
women, based solely on their ability to repay."

"Did you say women?" Hurst sat forward, glowering at
her. "You intend to loan money to *women*?"

Connor's hand tightening on her arm beneath the table reminded her of yesterday's warning that she avoid talking about her stand on women's rights. She glanced at him and his expression was taut with caution.

She gave the committee her most confident smile, but not one of their stony faces cracked with a response.

"If they qualify for loans, certainly," she said. "Why wouldn't we take advantage of every possible source of revenue?"

"There are a number of banks that have made loans successfully to women customers," Connor put in.

"With their husbands' signatures," Hurst said, eyeing Beatrice. "But I get the feeling that's not what you mean here. Am I right?"

"Once again, Mr. Barrow, you show an admirable grasp of nuance," she responded. "We will not require husbands' signatures. Women's applications will be considered the same as men's, on their own merit and ability to repay. The interest charged also will be the same, depending on the size of the loan."

"Then who will vouchsafe these loans?" another of the committee members demanded. "You've got to have cosigners. Women must have someone sign for them."

"We will certainly reserve the right to ask for collateral and cosigning," she said, choosing her words carefully, "for any loan we feel needs guaranteeing."

"That implies you intend to loan money to women *without* a husband's signature," Hurst declared.

"Some women, myself included, have no husbands." She smiled tightly. "And some of us 'husbandless' women have thriving business and will make good any loan we contract for . . . just as a man would do in the world of commerce."

That statement caused frowning and muttering amongst the committee. She felt her stomach knotting as Hurst Barrow leveled a dour look at her.

"You're one of those women's rights-ers, aren't you?" he said with deepening conviction. "Should have seen it straight off. It would have saved us all a helluva lot of time." He tossed the proposal from the table with open disgust, and transferred his glare to the other applicants in attendance. "Next!"

"Oh, no!" Connor shot to his feet. In one movement, he scooped the proposal off the floor, jumped onto the dais, and slammed the document down in front of his grandfather . . . pinning it to the table with his fist.

"What the devil do you th—" The old man started to inflate with outrage.

"You're going to pass this proposal and recommend a charter. And you're going to do it today," Connor declared. "This is a damned fine proposal . . . for a bank that's damn well funded and will be damn well run. It will be a credit to the state of New York, and you know it. It doesn't matter what she thinks about women—or what you think about me—or even what I think about you and your high-handed, controlling ways." He flung a finger back toward Beatrice. "She and Consolidated deserve a charter for this bank—and you're damn well going to give them one."

"Or what?" Hurst pushed his chair back and rocked to his feet.

"There is no 'or what.' You're just going to do it."

They stood face-to-face across the table, each filled with old hurts and old grudges, each grappling for the upper hand in a battle that had been joined two decades before. The intensity of the moment recalled a similar conflict, ten years earlier, regarding Hurst's opinion of another woman. . . .

"It's obvious . . . she's planning to use this bank to—" the old man blustered.

"Make money," Connor finished for him, "like any other banker. Just because she has a conscience and a heart doesn't mean she's a fool."

"Making unsponsored loans to women—what's that, if not foolish?"

"Canny. Insightful. Forward thinking. Courageous. Determined. Compassionate. Anything *but* foolish. She has the best head for business old Mercer Von Furstenberg had ever seen," Connor continued, his voice hoarse with compressed emotion. "She wasn't just his wife, she was his student, his protégé. Why do you think he left a total of twelve companies in her hands?"

Hurst trembled as he glared at his grandson, then at the woman for whom his grandson was willing to do battle with him. After a pause, he planted his hands on the table and shoved to his feet. But even standing, he was not tall enough to look his grandson straight in the eye. Scarcely a breath was taken in the room as he pulled his gaze from Connor and looked at his stunned fellow committee members.

"Do what you have to do," Hurst snarled at them. "You already know what my vote is."

Then he made his way to the side door. It was a moment before the click of the latch registered and there was a collective exhalation of tension.

Connor snared the gaze of each remaining committee member, leaving no doubt that what he had just said to his grandfather was meant for them as well. Then he retreated from the dais to his chair beside Beatrice, feeling charged and coiled inside like a watch spring. All he could think was that the old man had withdrawn. He looked at Bebe with his questions in his eyes. What did it mean? Hurst's vote, it seemed, had already been cast. Was the decision already made?

The four remaining committee members turned aside to confer in heated tones. More than one member turned away in exasperation, then came back to the group for more glowering, snapping, and pointing.

Beatrice looked at Connor. From his grave expression and the shake of his head, she gathered that he had no more idea of what was happening than she did. Alice was pale as she reached for Beatrice's hand and squeezed it. There was nothing to do but wait.

In those never-ending minutes, Beatrice kept hearing Connor's description of her echoing in her head . . . canny, determined, courageous, and compassionate. Was that truly what he thought of her? Was that what she was?

Then something even more dire occurred to her. What if they didn't get the charter? What if she had to return to the board empty-handed, having failed to meet one of their conditions for funding the bank? In their current suspicious mood, how long would it be before her failure with the bank tainted the rest of her work in their eyes? How long would she retain the presidency, membership on the board, or even controlling interest?

In her mind's eye, she could see the committee casting negative votes and she squeezed her eyes shut.

By the time they resumed their seats, the committee members were red-faced, agitated, and clearly out of patience with the entire situation.

"If it were up to me, young woman," the spokesman for the group declared with furious glare, "I would pack you off or lock you up, and see to it you had more to do than gad about the countryside dreaming up ridiculous schemes to put money in women's hands." He shook an age-knotted finger at her. "It is pure idiocy—not to mention against the very natural order—to have women out buying and selling, making decisions, and handling money. It's an affront to the authority and responsibility of men everywhere!"

Beatrice's face burned, her heart beat erratically, and her throat filled with tears she refused to show. It was bad enough to be refused a charter and to know that she had to go back to her board a failure. But to be attacked so personally. . . . She stiffened and without quite realizing it, shoved to her feet. She was trembling . . . torn between fury and hurt . . . scarcely aware of Connor and Alice rising to stand with her.

"It is with great pleasure that I will watch this accursed bank fail," the spokesman continued. "And when it does, I shall personally request to testify at the trial for fraud, malfeasance, and larceny which shall undoubtedly follow." With that, he gathered up his papers and stalked from the chamber . . . pausing just long enough to send her one last, hateful glare.

Another of the committee members quickly followed his lead, withdrawing from the chamber in a huff.

Beatrice turned to Connor in confusion. "What does that mean? What's happened?" Seeing he had no answer, she turned and called out to the two remaining committee members: "What does this mean? What was the vote? At least tell us that."

One of the old boys struggled to his feet and pinned her with a dark look.

"Three to two," he said, gathering up his things. "It looks like you'll get yourself a charter."

"What?" She couldn't seem to make sense of it. Three

to two? They had gotten their recommendation? They had *won?*

"We did it," Connor said in a tone of disbelief. "*You* did it."

Beatrice heard only bits and pieces of the admonition that followed . . . the gist of which, according to what Connor reported later, was that the state banking department would be watching her very carefully, and she had better mind every jot and tittle of the bank's business.

She hurried to the dais to thank the committee, assuring them that the bank would have her total attention and that she would validate the trust they had just placed in her and in Consolidated Industries.

By the time she reached the hallway, it was beginning to sink in—she had their recommendation and after a legislative vote the charter would be theirs!

"We did it!" she said, tears of joy and relief spilling down her cheeks as she pulled Connor around to face her. "*You* did it!"

Then she hugged him . . . hugged Alice . . . and hugged herself, laughing through her tears. Then Alice hugged her again, laughing, and Connor picked her up and whirled her around the lobby, heedless of the shocked stares of onlookers.

By the time she had her feet back under her again, she was wiping away those tears and already thinking of the next step.

"Goodness"—she pressed a hand to her breast—"what a fright that gave me." Then she straightened with fresh determination. "Now, all we have to do is get one or two hundred *more* men to agree that our bank is a wonderful idea."

Connor rolled his eyes at Alice. "She never quits, does

she?" When Alice just grinned, he looked bewildered. "How do you put up with it?"

Alice laughed and tossed Beatrice a faintly conspiratorial look.

"She gives me a raise every other week."

THEY CELEBRATED WITH a luncheon at a fine restaurant, then paid calls on several key legislators who agreed to introduce and shepherd the bill of charter through the legislature. Later, as they walked back to the hotel in the cool autumn sunshine, Beatrice stole glimpses at Connor's profile. How could his grandfather possibly ignore his many fine qualities and continue to disparage him? He was a good man . . . persuasive . . . clever . . . courageous . . . and determined to act on his convictions.

When they stopped at a restaurant for coffee, Alice yawned and declared that she had had enough excitement for one day. Beatrice and Connor walked her back to the hotel so she could rest, then resumed walking. Beatrice felt completely at ease with him, contented to be in his company.

"Thank you for speaking up today," she said finally.

"You don't need to thank me. It was my job, after all. Wait until you get my bill."

She laughed, then grew serious again. "If you hadn't spoken up, I don't know if we would have gotten the charter." She caught his gaze. "And the things you said . . ."

"Only the truth," he assured her. "And one hell of a risk. Three to two. It very well might have gone the other way."

They reached the capitol green and found a bench under a tree that was turning autumn colors. As they sat in the lowering daylight, he grew reflective. "The last time we saw each other we argued, too." She realized that he was referring to his grandfather. "Over another woman." He expelled a heavy breath. "My wife. He didn't want me to marry 'shanty Irish' like my father had . . . he said he'd disinherit me."

"And he did," she supplied, bracing her elbow on the back of the bench and resting her cheek on her hand. He nodded. She needed to know more. "Tell me about her."

"Are you sure . . ."

"I'd like to know," she said. "I think she must have been very special."

"She was. Erin. Bright and beautiful . . . with flame red hair and a temper to match. We were well suited, despite what my grandfather thought. She was both an anchor and a rudder for me. She grounded me and yet made me want to touch the stars." He closed that vivid memory and gave her a short, rueful smile. "It took me a long, painful while to understand that I wouldn't die, couldn't die just because she did. It's been seven years and though I still love her, I no longer feel married to her. I don't know if that makes any sense to you." When she nodded, he paused and propped his elbow on the back of the bench, leaning toward her. "Your turn."

She blushed, touched unexpectedly by the fact that he wanted to know her story, too. She told him, haltingly at first, about the circumstances of her marriage to Mercer. "My parents were ambitious socially and financially. They panicked when my older sister Caroline— Priscilla's mother—eloped with a penniless Italian count. She was my best friend, my confidante, the one thing that made my life in my parents' house bearable. I was crushed when she ran away with her Dominic. My parents were furious at us both and decided to marry me off quickly, before I got silly romantic notions myself."

"So, insanity runs in the family, then," he quipped.

She raised one eyebrow and continued. "Mercer was getting older and his advisers were concerned that he have an heir—someone to take up the reins of the businesses when he could no longer run things. But, we were unable to have children." She shrugged. "So I became a combination daughter and wife. He tutored me in business and made special legal arrangements for me to step in as head of the companies when he died."

She paused and stared off into the distance, thinking of the board meeting and how narrowly she had avoided being replaced as head of the companies. "I probably should have told you . . . when I presented this bank idea to my board of directors, they weren't impressed either. Things got a bit ugly." She smoothed her skirt over her lap, deciding how much to reveal. She wanted desperately to share it, to have him know what had happened to her. "They called for a vote of no confidence in me and tried to remove me as president of the board."

"What?" He straightened sharply. "They tried to kick you out?"

She nodded. "Two of the board members knew about my being in the Oriental Palace and tried to blackmail me into resigning. When I didn't cooperate, they described to the board in vivid detail, seeing me in 'depraved and immoral revels' at the Oriental. They called me a hypocrite for my 'high-and-mighty' stand on fair wages and labor standards, and demanded I resign."

"How could they have known about the Oriental

Palace?" He took her hands in his. "I didn't tell anyone and I'm sure Charlotte wouldn't have said anything about it."

"They said they saw me there." She gradually relaxed under his touch, grateful to be able to talk about it. "Punjab carried me up and down the main stairs several times. They might have seen me." The more she thought about it, the likelier it seemed. "I guess they must have seen me."

"But you said they failed to oust you."

"I had to do some fast talking." She looked up with a wry grin. "I just pretended I was you. I demanded that they produce more witnesses and finally reminded the older board members of all we'd done together." She grew more thoughtful. "What surprised me was how quickly they were willing to turn on me. I guess they must have resented Mercer's choosing me to run the company more than I thought. I had always considered them my friends as well as my business partners." She raised his hand and rubbed her cheek against it. "A contradiction in terms, I now realize. A woman in business has no friends."

A rumble of understanding came from his throat. "Sounds like politics. You never quite know who your real friends are." His voice trailed off, along with his thoughts. After a minute or two, he set those dismal thoughts aside.

"We've had quite a day." He leaned close and whispered, "How about if we make dinner tonight just as memorable?"

She smiled up at him. "I believe I could be persuaded."

When they arrived at the hotel, she stopped by the

front desk to check for her messages. There was nothing of consequence and she started up the stairs to her room while Connor consulted with the hotel manager to make arrangements for a special dinner. As she reached the mezzanine of the lobby she heard a voice that sounded alarmingly familiar. But before she could place it, she came face-to-face with its owner on the steps: Hurst Eddington Barrow.

"You." He glanced past her, looking for Connor. "If I'd known you were staying here, I'd have changed hotels." Then he pinned her with his steely regard. "I suppose you think you've won."

"We got the committee's recommendation," she said calmly, glancing over the railing to see if Connor was coming. He wasn't in sight. "I'll get my charter and my bank."

"Enjoy it while you can. You've gotten all you'll ever get from *him*."

Something in his tone caused her to look more deeply at him. What she now saw in his craggy face was pain and illness. He was an old man who had been too alone for too long with his grudges and regrets.

"You're wrong about him. He's a good man. He's generous and caring . . . strong and compassionate, and thoughtful . . ."

The old man snorted disgust.

"He's slick. He's too damned clever. And he looks out only for himself."

"If you really believe that, then you're shortsighted *and* foolish," she said irritably. "You're determined to hate him because he rejected your fortune and your control of his life. But when I see what your kind of life has done for you, I believe he made the right decision."

The old man produced a bitter smile. "He may have sweet-talked you into believing he's a saint, but you'll learn the truth soon enough." He moved closer to her on the steps and shook a bony finger. "He'll turn his back on you . . . just when you need him most. You mark my words."

She stood for a moment, torn between anger and pity, watching the old man's knotty figure thumping down the steps. To have had so much wealth and yet be so poor in love, compassion, friendship, joy, and family . . . the things that make life meaningful. Hurst Barrow was a sobering lesson in what was and was not valuable in life. He had spent his entire life in a quest for control . . . of his business ventures, of his vast fortune, of an entire industry . . . of his associates and employees, his competitors, his family . . . his only grandson.

Control. Insight blew with gale force through her, causing her to clutch the railing to steady herself. That was what her life had always been about, too . . . controlling her expectations, her circumstances, her businesses, and her fortunes. And that growing need for control had inevitably extended to her associations . . . her suffrage work . . . her desire to wrest power from arbitrary and incompetent rule makers in society or on her own board . . . even her fierce control of her niece's future. And her successes had culminated in the ultimate exercise in control . . . suppressing her hopes and her dreams, her deepest needs and passions. How different was that from what Hurst Barrow had done in his life? His loneliness, his anger, his bitterness . . . was that what she had been headed for?

Had been. Past tense.

It was in that moment, standing on the hotel stairs,

watching Hurst Barrow barreling and bruising his way through his loveless world, that Beatrice understood how much had changed in her life. Thanks to Connor, Priscilla, and Jeffrey—she was being given a second chance at things she thought long lost or destined only for others.

SEVENTEEN

WHEN BEATRICE AND Alice arrived in the private
dining room Connor had arranged that evening, they discovered that their celebration included a half dozen legislators who would be key in the passage of their bill of
charter.

"Surprised?" Connor murmured as he held her chair
at the linen-draped table.

"Very." Her pleasure was somewhat forced.

"I'm learning to use every political opportunity to the
fullest." The twinkle in his eye said he had taken that
particular lesson from her.

Dinner was splendid and the conversation lively. All
too soon the time came when ladies were expected to retire and leave the gentlemen to their brandy and cigars.
Beatrice rose like the hostess she was and circled the
table, greeting and chatting with each legislator, thank-
ing him for coming and for his support in the coming
days. One by one, the men headed downstairs to the
smoking room, and Beatrice and Alice gathered their
wraps and started for their room. Connor reappeared as

they were halfway up the stairs and seized Beatrice's hand.

"Some of your new friends suggested you join us for brandy and cigars."

"What?" She gave a puzzled laugh. "Don't be silly . . . it's not done."

"I was under the impression that you make your own rules." He raised one eyebrow. "Aren't you the least bit curious about how the other half lives?"

She glanced at Alice, who was no help at all: "I won't tell."

Truth be told, it was tempting to be offered a place among the state's elite. "All right, I'll come," she said, handing off her purse to Alice. "But only if I get to try a cigar."

He chuckled, and as they hurried down the stairs he tossed Alice a cheery "Don't wait up" over his shoulder.

He escorted her down to the lobby and through the main parlor toward the paneled smoking room marked with a standing sign declaring "Gentlemen Only." But instead of entering, he veered to the side and down a short hallway to a side set of stairs.

"What are you doing? The smoking room—"

"Is empty," he declared, pulling her up the steps with him.

"But you said . . ."

"They all went home," he said, pausing on the first landing. "I thought we might use the time for a bit more personal celebration." He circled her waist with one arm and pulled her against him. "What do you think?"

She couldn't decide whether to be delighted or scandalized. It was damned assuming of him. On the other hand—she felt his hard body pressed against hers—it was exactly what she had wanted earlier.

"I think," she said, warming quickly to the idea, "I could be persuaded."

He led her onto the second floor, despite her protests that their rooms were on the third, and pulled her into an elegant suite furnished in Chinese Chippendale and blue and white damask. The floors were covered with silk rugs and there was a marble fireplace set with silk chairs stuffed with down. In the center of the spacious room sat an elegant four-poster draped with blue willow print damascene and gauzy silk tulle. She blushed when he caught her staring at it and pulled her into his arms.

"This"—he reached behind her to throw the lock—"is now my room."

"Oh, my," she exhaled on a breath,

"Yours, indeed," he said just before he kissed her senseless. Her knees buckled and he caught her tight against him. "Very definitely yours." He slid his hands around her waist and up her back, caressing her. "Any way you want me."

The sense of what he said finally penetrated the steam enveloping her rational processes. She pushed back lightly in his arms to look up at him. The light deep in his eyes invited her to test that offer of control.

"Even if I decide"—she thought of the tantalizing possibilities she had glimpsed at the Oriental Palace—"you need a bit of time with a strict schoolmistress?"

A spark flared in his eyes. "Absolutely."

"Or if I decide . . . you should pose like an artist's model for me?"

His smile was slow and irredeemably sinful. "You catch on quickly."

Her eyes glowed with mischief. "I have it on good authority that congressmen require a strong hand."

"A strong hand." He pressed her hand against his

chest and directed it down his body. "Ummm. By all means, use a strong—" He looked down at her. "What authority? Who do you know that 'handles' congressmen?"

"Diedre, I believe her name is," she said, narrowing her eyes.

He frowned, unable to place . . . Then he thought of the other things she had just mentioned and realized where she must have come into contact with such a creature. "It seems you made good use of your time at the Oriental."

She laughed softly and slid both hands over his body, exploring him through his clothes, collecting impressions, seeking the satisfaction of a hundred little curiosities roused by postures and movement. She pressed his vest and shirt taut against his chest and then rubbed her cheek against them.

"Take them off," she said, stepping back to watch. He slid his coat from his shoulders, unbuttoned his vest, and removed his shirt. By the soft glow of the oil lamp, she circled him, dragging her fingertips over his hard frame and sleek skin, memorizing every slope and mound of him.

"You're so beautiful," she said, her voice thick with discovery and desire. Then, testing the control he had put in her hands, she leaned close and whispered, "Take your trousers off, too."

"If I do," he said with a tremor, "your skirts will come off next."

"Is that supposed to be an objection?"

A moment later he stood naked before her, astonishing her with his ease. He behaved as if it were the most natural thing in the world. And perhaps it was. For as she ordered him to take her clothes off and he obeyed, piece by piece, she felt gradually lighter, freer. By the time they stood naked together, she found herself thinking that indeed this was the most natural and honest way for men and women to be with each other. No pretense or artifice. No evasion or deception. All she was and all he was . . . revealed . . . offered . . .

She waited for him to accept and take her into his arms, but he stood silent, eyes hot and body thick and ripe with desire. Suddenly she understood. He was waiting for her . . . putting control in her hands . . . giving her the power she wanted and needed. She looked into his eyes and saw inside the desire and longing, a glint of understanding. He knew about her. He knew what she needed to feel safe and to be free.

"Take me to bed, Connor. And love me," she said, uncertain whether she had spoken aloud until he grinned and scooped her up into his arms.

With unhurried care, he laid her gently amidst the pillows and pristine linen. She had time only for one self-conscious shiver before he joined her and began to cover her with kisses and caresses. As he slid slowly over her, she brought her knees up to cradle him between her thighs, and luxuriated in the heat and weight of his body against hers.

Opening to his kisses, she first sought and then demanded more. Nibbling kissing . . . discovery accompanied each breath, each touch, each motion. Every particle of her being came to life, craving that life-giving sense of communion.

She welcomed him into her body, trembling as he imbedded himself in her and began to move with exquisite deliberation. Years of maturing and restraint had brought control to his loving and now each simple movement created pleasures of infinite meaning and complexity for both the giver and recipient. She understood with a wisdom beyond her experience that his touches and caresses, his kisses and sweet, hot whispers were far more than just an exercise in pleasure. They resonated with caring and delight in discovering a part of himself in another . . . his counterpart.

A sweet fever seized them as their bodies blended and molded to each other. They submerged in a sea of heat and sensation that grew steadily more intense and compelling. Each knew where it was leading and both gave themselves over to the drive for completion that propelled them sharply upward, until they reached a shattering climax.

For one breathtaking moment, there were no boundaries, no bodies, no separation of self, and no end to that lush, drenching pleasure.

In the gentle calm that followed, as their hearts returned to normal and their breathing slowed, she looked at him with new eyes. And as they lay together, luxuriating in a delicious lethargy, she understood that something fundamental had changed for him also. He was letting go, releasing his own expectations and demands, allowing her to be who and what she was.

When she awakened, some time later, he was padding back to the bed, bringing her a glass of wine. "Thank you." She sat up against the pillows and pulled the sheet across her midsection. While she sipped, he settled onto the bed with his back against the footboard and began to run his hands slowly up and down her calf.

"What are you doing?" She gave him a quizzical look.

"Something you'll like," he said with a small, seductive smile.

Slowly, he began to draw his fingers up her arch and

around her ankle in a repeating pattern. Every nerve in her body began to hum as he pulled her foot onto his lap and began to apply his thumbs to the sole of her foot in circular, kneading motions. Up her arch, down her arch . . . rubbing pressing, massaging . . . until she closed her eyes. His touch was subtly erotic, but also contained elements of comfort and caring that left her both stimulated and relaxed.

Leave it to him to find a way to sweet-talk without even using words.

When he paused for a moment, she opened her eyes and wiggled her toes, urging him to continue.

"If we keep this up, we may turn you into a romantic," he said with a laugh, watching her eyes begin to glow with warmth and arousal.

"Me?" She gave a huge sigh and settled back contentedly into the pillows. "Well, I suppose there are worse things to be. Horse thieves, white slavers, ax murderers . . ."

The rumble in his chest somehow sent a pleasant hum up her leg.

"Dangerous company we romantics keep," he said.

"Romantics *are* dangerous," she said, looking up at him. "Romantics dare to dream. And dreams are what inspire innovations and reforms, and even revolutions."

"Sounds grim. I don't believe I've participated in any revolutions lately."

"Oh, yes you have."

"I have?" He tucked his chin down to look at her. "Where?" It struck him. "Oh, the charter committee and my grandfather. To be honest—"

"Not there," she said quietly, searching him, deciding how much was safe to say. Then she smiled ruefully at her stubborn habit of seeking control. She was never going to be "safe" again, especially around him. And she'd better get used to it.

"In here." She tapped her temple, then she tapped her chest above her heart. "And here."

He frowned while smiling, confused for a moment. Then he met her gaze and seemed to understand what she was saying.

"You've stirred things up in me, made me think about things in a different way. I'm not the same woman you met in Charlotte Brown's Dungeon."

He ran his knuckles down the sole of her foot and gave her a look of such feeling and compassion that her heart seemed to pause and then to race.

"Oh, I don't know," he said, eyeing her half-naked form appreciatively. "You look pretty much the same to me. Minus the whip and cane, of course." He grinned. "And you certainly give orders the same."

"Only when you ask me to," she said, sitting up, her eyes shining.

"Oh?" He sat up straighter. She definitely had his attention now. "And what if I want to give orders?"

"I . . . might be persuaded to . . . cooperate."

He laughed at her careful choice of words. "Obey" was apparently not in her vocabulary.

"And what would I have to do to *persuade* you?"

"Well, let's see." She looked around the sleeping room, thinking, and came up with something suitable. "You could tell me what the devil Charlotte Brown's customers use that ship's wheel for."

He hooted a laugh, and squeezed her against his side.

"I could tell you . . . but, why do that when I can show you instead?"

She grimaced as he slid from the bed and pulled her up with him.

"No, really—" She tried to bring the sheet with her but failed, and was forced to grab the next available thing—his shirt lying on the nearby chair. "I have a very good imagination," she said, struggling to don the shirt with only one hand, "just tell me."

"Ohhh, no. Come on . . . you may even like this." He stood her at the end of the bed, with her back against the ornately carved footboard. She squirmed, feeling a bit exposed in his unbuttoned shirt.

"Onboard ships, the wheel was the symbol of the captain's authority and as such was sometimes used for disciplinary purposes." He propped her hands out on the footboard, on either side of her, ordering her to: "Stay there." He grabbed up her belt and his tie and began to lash her wrists to the bed.

"They would tie the offender's hands to the ship's wheel . . ."

"Hey!" She jerked her hands back. "You're not going to—"

"Demonstrate? I most certainly am. Do you want to be 'persuaded' or not?"

The glint in his eye and the sensual heat beginning to radiate from him convinced her it might prove worth the risk. After a moment, she laid her hands back on the bed rail. He waggled his eyebrows as if to say she wouldn't be sorry, then, lapping the restraints loosely, he bound first one wrist, then the other.

"They meted out punishment before the entire crew. Lashes, usually."

Her eyes widened as she looked at his sensually dangerous expression, then at her loosely bound wrists. All she had to do was lift her hands and she would be free, but she found herself grabbing onto the top of the foot-board and hanging on.

"L-Lashes?" she said distractedly. "With what?"

"A whip, a cat-o'-nine-tails, a bamboo cane . . . the usual." His gaze slid over her and settled on the gaping front of the shirt she wore. "Of course, there are other possibilities . . ." His eyes narrowed in concentration, then he strode over to the writing desk near the window and opened the drawer. She found herself bracing as he returned and from behind his back he drew an old-fashioned writing quill.

"What are you going to do with . . . oh . . . ohh . . . ohhhhh. I see."

He had knelt by her feet and was stroking the feather back and forth up her legs, beginning with her ankles . . . Going slower, lingering longer the higher he rose.

It began to arouse her. She bit her lip and shivered. Then the feather slid under the tail of the shirt and she whimpered as it reached sensitive skin. He pushed the side of the shirt back to bare her body to him and continued that exquisite torture. The strokes of a feather. It did indeed seem like punishment . . . mostly because he was looking at her bare body and watching her try to contain both her embarrassment and arousal.

"So," he said with one eyebrow raised, "you've been a naughty girl."

"Ummm . . ." She could hardly stand still as the feather raked up her abdomen. "Sure. I suppose. I mean, probably. I—I c-can't remember."

"Well, we only punish *naughty* girls." The feather withdrew.

"Naughty. Yes. That's me. Absolutely."

She writhed as the feather reached her breasts and

began a delicious stroking of her nipples. She closed her eyes and dropped her head back, abandoning herself to those wildly erotic sensations. Back and forth . . . the slow, tantalizing rasp of the feather's tendrils on the taut, aching tips of her breasts. She arched her back to thrust closer to that hypnotic friction . . . more than just yielding . . . seeking. She could barely breathe for the desire filling her throat.

Then she heard a groan and a moment later the feather was replaced by his mouth. His arms clamped fiercely around her, and she squeezed her eyes tighter shut and gasped as waves of pleasure crashed over her. She could barely feel the bed rail she gripped so tightly. There was only room for that compelling pleasure in her consciousness.

She was dimly aware of him lifting her up and bearing her back onto the bed. She grabbed what she could of him, his hair and his shoulder, and pulled him fiercely down on top of her. With moans and whimpers of need she wrapped his hips with her legs and drove him into her. She was frantic each time he withdrew partway and groaned satisfaction from deep in her throat each time he thrust inside her.

Over and over their bodies came together, hot and demanding, straining together, as the boundaries between self and other melted, and their senses filled with pleasure too intense to hold. Claim and possession fell away . . . all attempts at control failed . . . there was only the time from breath to breath and sensation to sensation. Now. And each other. And when their bodies and hearts could bear no more, the last fragile threads of restraint shattered and soaring pleasure carried them into regions known only to those who attain the rarest truth . . . that there is no difference between conquering and surrender.

It was some time before their senses cleared and they returned to ordinary time and place. Empty of words, swept free of tension and expectation and even desire, she curled up beside him and yielded to the languor of complete satisfaction. Strangely, she did not sleep. She heard his breathing deepen and felt his chest slowly rise and fall beneath her cheek, and smiled. She had given him something she had not voluntarily given anyone since she was eighteen years old. Control. He had understood, as no one else could, the value of that gift. And he had proved worthy of her trust. Tears burned her eyes but did not fall.

It was some time later that he awakened to find her propped on one elbow, watching him sleep. He grinned and yawned and opened his arms. Before she crept into them she frowned thoughtfully.

"Men really come to the Oriental Palace to do that?" she asked.

"Some do," he responded, running a finger down the valley between her breasts and watching her shiver with an echo of pleasure.

She caught his hand and nibbled his fingertips, one after another, while watching his eyes darken with pleasure.

"Then it's just as I suspected. Men *do* get to have all the fun."

THE TRIP FROM Albany took most of the night. The sky had just begun to lighten and the lamplighters were extinguishing the gas lamps in the older sections, when the cab bearing Connor, Beatrice, and Alice arrived at her Fifth Avenue house. Connor exited first, helped them down, and then insisted on carrying their bags inside. Before Beatrice could object, he had waved the cab off.

"Madam! Miss Henry!" Richards greeted them. "We were quite concerned—we expected you yesterday."

"We decided to stay another day, for the vote in the legislature." Beatrice saw her butler staring at the way Connor held her hand and quickly pulled it free. "We got the charter!"

"Excellent, madam." Richards took their wraps, hats, and gloves.

"It was late when the session ended and we had to take the late train down from Albany," she continued. "We've been riding most of the night and we're desperate for some coffee."

"Not me," Alice said, heading for the stairs. "I'm desperate for a bath and a nap."

"And some breakfast, Richards," she said as the butler strode toward the kitchen. "I invited Mr. Barrow for breakfast. We'll be in the morning room."

The butler nodded, then hurried off to see to it.

She turned to Connor, took his hands in hers, and said, "You will stay, won't you? Our cook is a wizard with eggs and morning pastries." He had a sleep-heavy look about his eyes that reminded her of the previous morning, when she'd awakened in his arms and he'd made love to her a second time, in the rosy light of dawn. He smiled as if reading her thoughts and she colored pleasurably and led him toward the morning room. Halfway through the entry hall, Priscilla's voice stopped them in their tracks.

"Aunt Beatrice?"

Beatrice looked up in surprise to find Priscilla, dressed for work at Woodhull House, hurrying down the stairs. She dropped Connor's hand a second time and edged away, fearing that no amount of distance between them could prevent Priscilla from detecting the air of intimacy between them. She looked up at Connor, who radiated satisfaction, and groaned silently.

"I waited up for you, and even had Rukart take carriage and wait at the train station. He came back with it empty at midnight, saying you weren't on the last train." Priscilla's eyes narrowed suspiciously on her rumpled garments. "Are you just getting home?"

"Yes—did you need to talk to me? Is something wrong?" Beatrice asked, hoping to divert Priscilla's curiosity with an air of parental authority.

"No. I just wanted to know how things went in Albany." Priscilla turned a dark look on Connor. "I didn't imagine you'd have a guest at *this* hour."

"I was helping your aunt and Miss Henry get a charter for their new bank," Connor inserted. "We were successful, but it took a bit longer than we . . . I . . ." He ground to a halt under Priscilla's hostile stare and turned to Beatrice. "I appreciate the offer of breakfast, but I think I'd better head for my office. This trip set my entire schedule back. I have a mountain of legal work to do and I need to check in with my campaign manager."

"The least I could do is provide you some coffee . . . after I made you pass the night sitting up on a train," Beatrice said with a hint of nervousness.

"No, thank you. I'll get back to you . . . later today or tomorrow on . . . that . . . stock offering we talked about."

They both winced inwardly. Could they have been any less credible? She extended her hand and he took it briefly, then exited.

Breakfast was the longest, most uncomfortable meal

Beatrice had endured in years. Priscilla stared at her for some time, then finally spoke up.

"Really, Aunt Beatrice, you should be more careful about who you associate with. And your hours. Coming home before six in the morning, in a gentleman's company, is . . . is . . ." She paused, trying to find a "proper" word and failing, then blurted out: "Indecent."

"Priscilla!" Beatrice dropped her fork with a clang. "Whom I associate with and when I arrive home are none of your concern."

"They are my concern. You're my guardian and my aunt and you're *supposed* to be my example. And here you are, cavorting around with a man who is Irish *and* a politician, *and* consorts with all manner of lowlifes and riffraff. He's little better than a crook."

"I was not cavorting, I was on a business trip . . . *with* Alice. And Connor is a good and decent man. He's running for the United States Congress," Beatrice declared hotly, gripping the arms of her chair.

"That just means he's a *successful* crook." Priscilla picked up her hat, glaring resentfully, and fired one last salvo before stalking from the room.

"No wonder you have trouble with the board of directors. You certainly aren't *behaving* like a company president."

Beatrice sat listening to the sounds of Priscilla's departure, feeling irritable and disarmed by her niece's criticisms. How had Priscilla learned about her troubles with the board?

Perhaps she wasn't acting much like the president of a company . . . indulging her desires, spending her passions without any assurances or guarantees, or regard for society's sanctions. Strangely, she didn't feel a bit of guilt. She had devoted her life to upholding the highest

standards of morality and integrity . . . despite the fact
that, again and again, she had found herself straining to
force her beliefs and behavior into two utterly divergent
molds: woman and business executive. How was it that
her feelings and behavior with Connor seemed to fall
outside every boundary she had observed in her life, and
she still felt somehow right about them?

She thought of her nights in Albany and couldn't help
smiling. Then it struck her: She was acting like a board
president—a *male* one!

Men got to cavort and consort with the opposite sex
and visit places like the Oriental Palace whenever they
pleased, and no one said a word about it. Let a woman
try to exercise the same prerogative, and she'd be condemned and hounded out of decent society.

Her irritation drained and she propped her cheek on
her hand and stared down into her poached eggs.

It wasn't that she wanted to "cavort," exactly. She just
wanted to spend time with Connor. Her eyes unfocused
as she recalled the sight of his face dusky with passion
and his eyes black with need. She sighed. He was so
strong. So male. And so utterly irresistible.

CONNOR TREATED HIMSELF to a long walk and a
huge breakfast at a small restaurant near his office, just
off Union Square. Along the way, he stopped to talk to
the produce company hands who were unloading their
fruit and vegetables and paused to chat with shop owners unrolling awnings. All the while, he struggled to hold
on to the sense of ease and satisfaction his time in Albany had brought him. As he had seconds of eggs and
heaped jam on his biscuits, he thought that the conver-

sation in the restaurant seemed livelier and that everything tasted especially good this morning. There was a spring in his step as he headed for his law office. But the minute he entered his office building, he lost that buoyancy.

Standing in the small foyer, leaning one thick arm on the newel post of the stairs, was Del Delaney. And he did not look happy.

"Where the hell have you been?" He stuck his unlit cigar back in the corner of his mouth and launched himself for the door, snagging Connor's elbow along the way. "Never mind—the boys would like a word with you."

Connor didn't resist. He'd been out of touch—*gone*— for three days. Murphy was probably having fits. He spent the rest of the short, silent walk to Tammany Hall going over his reasons and drafting points to raise with his campaign overseer. He'd been doing legal work for Consolidated Industries . . . and meeting with some of the boys in Albany. He'd very likely picked up a new endorsement or two . . . By the time they trudged up the steps to the meeting room where "the boys" were waiting, he felt reasonably prepared for their criticism and even their irritation.

What he was not prepared for was the icy silence that greeted him as he entered . . . and the presence of Tammany's boss, Richard Croker, police chief Thomas Byrne, and city aldermen McCloskey and Burke, in addition to his campaign manager Murphy. To a man, they leveled searching looks on him. One by one they transferred those stares to the numerous copies of the morning papers that littered the large table before them.

"Where the hell have you been?" Croker said, his tone flat and cold.

"I was upstate . . . Albany . . . doing some legal work and some politicking."

"So you were," Boss Croker said, picking up a newspaper that had been folded back to highlight a specific article. "The question is, for who?"

The pause indicated they expected him to answer and he did.

"Consolidated Industries, actually. I did some legal work for them . . ."

"For that bank you had *nothing* to do with?" Murphy said, crossing his arms and tilting his head to view him from a skeptical angle.

Connor glanced from Murphy to Croker, then to the newspaper on the table. "After we spoke, Consolidated retained me to—"

"Don't you mean Mrs. Von Furstenberg?" Murphy inserted. "That is her name, isn't it? The president of Consolidated?"

"You know . . . your *suffragette* friend," Croker added.

Connor swallowed hard. "As I was saying, I was asked by Consolidated Industries to help them secure a state charter for a new banking venture."

"Her new 'Women's State Bank,'" Murphy clarified.

"The Barrow State Bank, actually." Even worse. Connor felt his face reddening. There was no plausible way to deny a connection with the venture, no matter how many distinctions he tried to draw. His name was on the damned thing. "It was named after my family . . . without my consent. I requested that they change it. I believe I can still get them to see reason. . . ."

"Too late," Croker snapped, sitting forward, his face suddenly crimson. "Whatever you want to call it, you're in it up to your damned eyeballs!" He opened the copy of *The New York World* in his hands and slammed it down on the table. There on the front page, was a heart-stopping headline:

BARROW MAKES GOOD ON PROMISE:
BANK FOR WOMEN CHARTERED!

Connor felt his feet go numb.

"The damned newspapers—I didn't even think about—" He snatched up the paper and stared at the print, unable to comprehend anything more than the horror of the headline. "How the devil did they find out about the charter? It was only voted on yesterday morning."

"You can't even belch or fart unnoticed in a state-house, Barrow. You know that. The place is crawlin' with news writers," Croker said, rising and pacing angrily back and forth.

"You'd have gotten less notice if you'd just put up bill-boards, hired criers, and taken out advertisements in the blasted *Daily News*," Murphy declared.

Connor's mind flew, trying to figure out who would have drawn the reporters' attention to his participation in the process. But in truth, Croker was right—there were probably at least a dozen news reporters hanging around the statehouse—and he wasn't exactly an unknown commodity in political circles. Just because he hadn't seen *them*, didn't mean they hadn't seen *him*.

"Look, it's not a *women's* bank," Connor said earnestly. "It's just a bank—a commercial venture—it's got nothing to do with women's suffrage."

"That's not what the paper says," Police Chief Byrne put in, pointing at the article. "New policies, it says. Special treatment for women customers. Women won't have to have a man's signature on the papers." He glanced around the room at the others. "Sounds like that 'female rights' crap to me."

There were strong murmurs of agreement and Connor tried to think how things said in the committee room could have ended up in the papers.

"I'm telling you," he said in his most persuasive tones, "it's just a *bank*."

"No, it's not." Murphy stalked over to him. "Come on, Barrow, you're smarter than that. It's a bank started by and associated with a woman who is known to be in the thick of this move for suffrage and women's rights. She challenged you on it at the debate and has used this 'bank' business *twice* to drag you in and associate you with their cause in the newspapers."

"Now, she's got you workin' for her, and is making political hay off your name," Croker declared, planting himself squarely in Connor's face, hooking Connor's gaze and probing his motivations. "But what worries me is, you don't seem to see anything wrong with that."

When the boss turned away, Connor felt as if his world were tilting and he struggled for balance. Everything they said was the truth. But there was so much more to the story. Of course he was working for her—she had blackmailed him into it. And of course she was using his name—she was a tough, savvy businesswoman who was used to seizing every advantage . . .

A chill raced through his heated thoughts. He hadn't thought about it like that . . . her using him . . . at least, not since . . .

When had he lowered his guard and abandoned his own best interest with her? He had gone to Albany to discharge a debt—a blackmail debt at that. And he had ended up not only arguing her case, but seeing things through her eyes, defending her, and making, mad passionate . . .

The blood drained instantly from his head.

Love. Dear God. He was in *love* with . . .

"This Von Furstenberg woman must be some piece of work," Alderman McCloskey said with an insinuating smirk.

"Must be," Alderman Burke agreed with a sneer. "She's got him hooked so hard he can't see nothin' but her petticoats."

"That it, Barrow?" Boss Croker pinned him with a stare. "You involved with this woman?" When Connor didn't answer straightaway he drew his own conclusion and turned aside, giving the air a furious punch. "Damn it! You finally get a candidate you can run with, and along comes a slip of a skirt and the bastard goes straight to rack an' ruin on you!" He turned to the others. "It's the curse of the Democratic party!"

"Look, I'll fix it." Connor jolted back to his senses, but his head still felt spongy and everything seemed to be far away. It was as if his whole world were turning inside out. "I'll talk to her . . . get her to change the name of the bank—"

"No you won't." Croker wheeled on him. "You won't go near that woman or her 'shriekin' sister' friends. You're goin' to campaign hard, keep your nose clean, and keep your pants *on*." He looked at Murphy, who drew a long, quiet breath. "Maybe—just to make sure you keep your mind on the campaign—we should have somebody move in with you for a bit."

"I can take care of this myself," Connor said, feeling

more lucid and grounded as he grew more irritated. "I don't need a nursemaid."

"The hell you don't," Croker snapped. "This is the second time it's all over the papers that you're cozy with suffragettes. Once, people forget. Twice, people take note. Three times, people take it for a *fact*." He stabbed a blocky finger into Connor's chest. "There ain't gonna be a third time. You got that?"

Connor's heart was pounding and his mouth was dry. In the silence, the depth of their anger struck deep and he scrambled for a response, while he tried to reconcile his personal feelings and convictions with Croker's demands.

Give up Bebe? Lose the woman he loved for a second time in his life?

"Come on, it's not that big of a deal," he said with a smile so forced that it made his face hurt. If ever there was a time for sweet-talking . . . "It's not like I ever said I would support votes for women. My personal feelings—"

"You still don't get it, do you?" Croker said, stepping closer, shoving his face into Connor's. "You're in no position to decide what you'll support and what you won't. As long as you're on the Democratic ticket, you'll do what we tell you to do. You won't have any part of women voting or women banking. And you'll stay the hell away from that Von Furstenberg woman. You got that?"

The declaration was nothing short of an ultimatum.

Had Murphy been right? Would they really go so far as to kill his candidacy over his relationship with Bebe?

"I believe I am beginning to understand," he said tersely.

Croker took that statement as submission to Tammany's larger wisdom. "Good. Now we'll have to get a—

whadda ye call it when ye take it all back in the papers?"
Croker snapped his fingers in Murphy's direction for
help.

"A retraction. But I don't think that's necessary." Murphy supplied, watching Connor carefully. "Claiming our
candidate is *not* for women's suffrage might just call attention to the charges that he *is*. On the other hand, we
can pass the word informally and make a fuller explanation at the second debate. We don't want to look arse
over elbows on policy."

"Ye think that's enough?" Croker demanded.

Murphy nodded. "I'll take care of it."

Croker started for the door, then paused by Connor to
issue one last warning. "Tammany can make you or
Tammany can break you. Think about it, son."

Connor had his answer.

EIGHTEEN

THE DAYS AFTER Beatrice arrived home from Albany
were a whirlwind of activity. She spent long hours at her
offices, consulting with the company's lawyers on setting
up the stock offering that would fund the remaining part
of the capital she needed to raise.

She recruited Lacey and Frannie to call on the suffrage association members who might be interested in
helping fund a woman-friendly bank, and paid calls herself on Susan Anthony and Elizabeth Cady Stanton. She
notified every individual and agency she thought might
be interested in the project, and made lists of "favors" to
be collected. Each evening she arrived home late, had a
cold supper in her room, and fell into bed. It wasn't until the third day, when things slowed enough for her to
catch her breath, that she began to wonder why she
hadn't heard from Connor.

He had campaigning to do, she told herself. Three
and a half days out of his schedule, at this point in the
campaign, had been a sacrifice. He had warned her that
he would be busy for the next several days, but she

couldn't help feeling disappointed that he hadn't found time to pay even a brief call.

She couldn't help wondering what he thought of the newspaper articles announcing Consolidated's new bank. They couldn't have asked for better publicity. Even the controversy over the new bank's policies would eventually work to their advantage. Before long, everyone would know that there was one lending institution in the city that respected and served women.

A NUMBER OF velum envelopes were hand delivered to the Oriental Palace that evening. In the midst of the gaiety and revelry, Mary Katherine, Annie, Pansy, Eleanor, Millie, Tessa, Jane, and Diedre opened engraved invitations to participate in the initial stock offering for a new financial institution: The Barrow State Bank. Even more impressive, was the short, handwritten note from Beatrice Von Furstenberg in each envelope, assuring them that their money would be entirely welcome at the new bank.

After most of the trade slowed that evening, that select group collected in Mary Kate's room on the third floor, invitations in hand, and talked excitedly about the first genuine printed invitation any of them had ever received. Then as they clutched those precious envelopes, things grew quiet in the room and more than one woman lowered her eyes to hide the moisture in them.

"She wrote us," Annie whispered. "I ain't never got a letter before."

"Me either," Pansy said. "An' a proper invite. Like a regular lady."

The others nodded and Mary Kate began to smile through her tears.

"That Bebe . . . she's a good one, all right. A real lady."

"She's better than that," Diedre said forcefully. "She's a real *woman*."

ON THE FIFTH morning after her return from Albany, Beatrice was standing in an empty office building with a building contractor, discussing the best locations for tellers' windows, desks, accounting offices, and the new steel and concrete vault. Plans for the physical facilities of the bank had been developing in her mind for some time, but only the previous afternoon had she learned that the building she wanted on Broadway was available and in her price range. She sent instantly for the construction engineer she had used for work on several of Consolidated's properties, and after a close inspection, he had agreed that the structure was sound and that the desired renovations were possible.

As he took his men down to the basement level to check footings and space for a vault, Beatrice stood in the large, empty space and tucked her arms beneath her cloak and around her waist. Exciting as seeing her dream take shape was, she had imagined a good bit more pleasure and satisfaction in this day. She walked around the space, listening to the echo of her heels on the wooden floors. It sounded as empty as she felt inside. She still hadn't heard from Connor and had finally sent him a note the day before, along with one of the invitations for the stock offering. There had been no reply.

She worried as much about her reaction to his absence as she did about the absence itself. This, she told herself, was why she had kept people at a distance for so long . . . this uncertainty, this anxiety, this ache beginning deep in her heart. There were any number of reasons he might not have called; she defended him in her thoughts. No doubt he was very busy with the election just over three weeks away. Two days ago there was an article in the paper reporting his visits to a labor congress and a Democratic rally on the Lower East Side. He had a lot on his mind. He was tending to the business he had neglected to help her.

She sighed sharply and went to the front windows to take in the view her bank patrons would have while waiting. To her surprise, she saw Alice hurrying toward the front door. She went to meet her.

"Here—" Alice shoved a letter into her hands and braced against a stone pillar to catch her breath. "This just came . . . it's important."

Beatrice saw that Alice had already opened and read it, as she did all of Beatrice's business correspondence. It was from the Vice President of Consolidated Industries. Just two short sentences. "There will be an emergency meeting of the Board of Directors of Consolidated Industries on Thursday morning, promptly at ten o'clock." and "Your presence is required." She looked on the back and all over for more . . .

"No reason? Just come to an emergency meeting?"

Alice, pale except for two bright red spots on her cheeks, thrust the newspaper she was holding into Beatrice's hands.

"Page four . . . at the top . . ."

The headline struck her like a hammer:

SCANDAL ROCKS CONSOLIDATED—
WOMAN PRESIDENT FACES MORALS CHARGE!

Beatrice's eyes widened in horror as she skimmed the article. "Eyewitnesses charge that the female president of Consolidated Industries, wealthy financier and suffragette Beatrice Von Furstenberg, has been observed indulging in obscene and immoral acts at a house of ill repute known as the Oriental Palace . . ."

Her stomach slid to her knees as she read the inflammatory prose detailing how she had been observed "performing" for the drunken patrons with one of the brothel's male employees. The article went on to associate her with the anti-marriage, "free-love" contingent of the women's rights movement. It further stated that more men would undoubtedly come forward to "unmask her as a hardened devotee of the pleasures of the flesh." The scurrilous piece ended by saying that these charges had resulted in "a call by mortified board members for an emergency meeting tomorrow morning" and it was "expected that they will immediately remove Mrs. Von Furstenberg from the presidency of Consolidated Industries."

Beatrice couldn't seem to expel the breath she had taken as she read that vile bit of yellow journalism. Bracing against the wall, she struggled to maintain some semblance of control. Now, of all times. What was she going to do? Then Alice asked her the same question.

"What are you going to do?"

For Beatrice, there was only one possible response.

"Fight. What else?"

THE NEXT TWENTY-FOUR hours were shrouded in a fog of disbelief for Beatrice. One minute she was basking in the glow of accomplishment and the memories of shared loving . . . the next, she was beset by a storm of visitors waving newspapers and demanding to know if she were indeed the Jezebel of Wall Street.

That afternoon, vice president Graham and secretary Wright from the Consolidated board arrived at her house to be sure she would attend the emergency board meeting. Soon afterward, Lacey Waterman and Frannie Excelsior arrived to offer support. Then came Martin Harriman from the Chase-Darlington bank, followed by Susan Anthony and Carrie Chapman Catt who came in the interest of fairness, to learn the whole story.

Just when she thought she might have a moment's peace, a brace of lawyers arrived from a law firm that represented Consolidated in some ongoing business negotiations. Each visitor brought a copy of the article from Joseph Pulitzer's *New York World,* and each stayed long enough to pry—slyly or oafishly—and outrage Beatrice. The one person she didn't hear from was the one she was increasingly desperate to see . . . Connor.

After dinner that evening, when she had retreated to her rooms with Alice she paced, going over and over her possible courses of action. The truth was an option, of course, but that would mean revealing Connor, Priscilla, and Jeffrey's parts in the absurd happenings. Worse still, the whole truth as she finally told it to Alice, sounded every bit as far-fetched in her own ears as she had feared it would.

At last she hit upon the notion of seeking out the writer of the article and learning where he had gotten his information. If she could prove Lynch and Winthrop were the "sources" cited in the article, then she could argue that it was just the same word of the same two men . . . who had publicly betrayed Consolidated's best interests, in an attempt to force their will on the board. That sort of power grab would sit ill with the board members and they might be convinced to back her and ride out the scandal. The risk was, of course, that there might truly have been someone else who saw and recognized her.

Her only other option, Beatrice realized, was to speak a truth and cling to it: She had never "cavorted" or "performed" at the Oriental Palace, nor participated in anything sordid or immoral. She could make that claim in all honesty.

She called for Dipper and Shorty and sent them out to some of the haunts around the newspaper offices on the Lower East Side, to see if they could learn the identity and whereabouts of the news reporter. But as they departed, arguing about which taverns and saloons to check first, she felt less than hopeful about their success.

She lay in bed that night, sleepless and anguished, realizing that more than just her position in the company was at stake. The news writer had taken pains to identify her as a suffragette and a social activist. Everything she had worked for—women's rights, decent conditions for workers, a reduction in child labor, the establishment of a bank to serve women on an equal basis—was at risk of being tainted by the cloud that now hung over her. She needed desperately to talk to Connor.

Where was he? Why hadn't he responded to her note or called on her as he said he would? She tried to imagine what he must have thought when he saw the paper that morning . . . if he saw it. Then she remembered how carefully he had pored over the morning papers when they were in Albany. Of course he had seen it. Surely he knew that the story could have dire implications for him as well.

Her heart began to beat erratically at the awful realization that Connor, too, was at risk. He had been linked with her in the newspapers and anything that tarnished her reputation would sully him and give his opponents ammunition to use against him at the polls.

Was that it? Was he distancing himself from her? A chill went through her. When asked about her story, would he deny it all . . . claim he was her lawyer briefly . . . declare that he had nothing else to do with her? She thought of his defense of her at the charter committee. Could he speak so powerfully on her behalf then and simply abandon her now?

In the darkness of her bed, Hurst Barrow's leathery voice returned to her. *"He'll turn his back on you . . . just when you need him most."* It seemed an eerie portent.

"Oh, please, Connor . . . please . . ." she murmured, pressing her face into her pillow to muffle her sobs. Had she finally opened herself to love and passion and companionship . . . had she finally rediscovered her heart . . . only to have it broken?

It was more than her career that depended on the morning's business, she now realized. It was her entire life.

IT WAS HALF-PAST ten that evening when Connor climbed down out of a cab in front of his brownstone and stumbled up the steps with Del Delaney at his heels. He had spent the afternoon addressing groups of city workers and crowds in Irish clubs and German cultural societies. Everywhere he went he shook hands, joked, cajoled, and sweet-talked his way into a few more votes. Now, he was out of energy, out of voice, and completely out of patience. He turned at the front door to face the burly Delaney with a glare that would have sliced through granite.

"I believe I can take it from here, Delaney," he said acidly, though the effect of his sarcasm was dimmed by his hoarseness. "I doubt I'll run into any wild, rampaging suffragettes between here and my bed."

The veteran ward heeler backed off, but admonished him to wait for his escort before leaving the next morning for his campaign appearance. It was all Connor could do to enter his house without throwing a bare-knuckle punch.

The hall was dark and quiet. As he trudged up the stairs and stood in the doorway of his bedroom, he thought of Bebe and felt a powerful need to see her, to share with her what was happening to him. But after the physical and emotional stresses of the day, he settled for peeling his jacket off and falling facedown across the bed. The smell of the fresh linens reminded him of that first night in Albany . . . the soft bed . . . the feel of her skin . . . He smiled as he closed his eyes and he didn't open them again until the next morning.

Mrs. O'Hara, his housekeeper, had breakfast ready when he came downstairs and as he ate she presented him with a rumpled copy of one of yesterday's newspapers, open to an article reporting his statement after touring a textile factory in the garment district: "Children need schooling more than they need work." Those unguarded, emotional words had landed him in hot water, yet again, with his campaign watchdogs. She lifted her chin and told him that she was proud of him for saying what needed saying . . . no matter what Mrs. O'Shaunessey's housekeeper, Mildred, had to say.

"You just keep doin' what you know to be right, lad," she declared, giving him a motherly pat and returning to the kitchen.

He managed a weak smile, wishing fervently that

Mrs. O'Hara had the vote. Groaning at that thought, he turned the paper facedown and tried to finish his eggs and bacon before facing the words about child labor that Tammany would expected him to eat in public at the next debate.

But he couldn't keep his eyes from that paper and as he drank his coffee, a word on the page finally registered in his vision. He refocused and realized he was looking at "Consolidated Industries." Broadening his gaze, he spotted the name "Von Furstenberg." Galvanized, he snatched up the paper and read the headline on the page opposite the article about him:

SCANDAL ROCKS CONSOLIDATED— WOMAN PRESIDENT FACES MORALS CHARGE!

"Eyewitnesses charge that the female president of Consolidated Industries, the wealthy financier and suffragette Beatrice Von Furstenberg . . ." His stomach contracted into a hard knot as he skimmed the inflammatory prose claiming she had been seen "performing" in a notorious brothel. Then his gaze sank to the end of the article where it was revealed that Consolidated's board would convene an emergency meeting on Thursday morning "to effect the immediate removal of Mrs. Von Furstenberg as president of Consolidated Industries."

He shut his eyes. She had told him about the attempt to oust her as president. She seemed to think that she had prevailed. But what her enemies had failed to do at the board meeting, they were now trying to accomplish in the newspapers. And if that nasty piece of yellow journalism was any indication, they stood a good chance of succeeding.

Apparently, in the world of business a woman's reputation was just as fragile and subject to the judgments of others as it was in society. The scandal could make her a pariah, even if she were proven innocent at the board meeting.

Thursday was today—they were meeting this morning!

"Just keep doing what you know to be right," Mrs. O'Hara had said. Every muscle in his body tightened. What he knew to be right and what Tammany insisted that he do, were worlds apart. They demanded that he cut all ties to Bebe, and turn his back on her and everything she meant to him. For the last five days he had grappled constantly with those demands.

With each empty night that passed, the conflict became clearer . . . between all Tammany had been to him and what it was now demanding of him . . . between the loyalty he owed them and the devotion he felt to the woman he loved. They owned him, body and soul, they said. His opinions had nothing to do with his election, they said. It wasn't up to him, they said.

The hell it wasn't.

He ripped the napkin from his vest and pulled out his pocket watch. Nearly nine. Damn—the board could be meeting already!

He was out in the street in a moment and racing for the cabstand at the end of the block with only a half-formed idea in his head. He had to go to her, had to help her. Bizarre and preposterous as it might sound, the truth was her only hope . . . even if it meant revealing his part in that disastrous elopement-cum-kidnapping. He would have to produce Dipper and Shorty . . . and if he could persuade Charlotte to give her version . . .

It was also time Priscilla and Jeffrey owned up to their misdeeds and took the blame they deserved.

PRISCILLA WAS UP to her elbows in plaster dust, secondhand furnishings, and stacks of newly delivered mattresses, when Connor strode into the new dormitory and ordered her to get her jacket and hat.

"What for?" Priscilla demanded.

"Your aunt needs you." He looked around. "Where's Jeffrey?"

She frowned and looked petulantly at the mess around her. "He's in the kitchen, I think. Maybe the yard. I'm not sure where he went. He's always—"

"We'll have to find him." Connor consulted his watch. "We don't have much time." He looked around the long dormitory room. "Where are Dipper and Shorty?"

"They didn't come this morning. Richards said Aunt Beatrice sent them out on an errand last night and they hadn't come home. I'm the only one who's—what's happened?" Priscilla grew alarmed. "Is Aunt Beatrice all right?"

"No, she's not. She's about to lose control of Consolidated Industries."

"Oh." She backed away when Connor grabbed her short cloak off the pegs and held it for her. "What do you expect *me* to do about it?"

"You and Jeffrey are going to tell the board what you did to your aunt."

Priscilla blanched. "We can't do that!"

Connor towered above her and thrust the garment into her hands.

"Oh, *yes* you can."

Jeffrey wasn't in the kitchen . . . or the rear yard . . . or the linen room . . . or the pantry . . . or any other of his frequent hiding places. Connor consulted his watch once again and declared that they were out of time.

"But . . . I can't go alone," Priscilla said with genuine horror.

"You have to," Connor said, taking her by the elbow and ushering her forcefully to the front doors. "Your aunt needs you, and you're not going to let her down this time." He paused for a moment, his gaze dark and troubled. "*We're* not going to let her down." His voice gentled slightly. "That's what people who love each other do, Priscilla. When one of them is in trouble, the other pitches in and does everything he can to help. And when something goes wrong, they take responsibility for themselves and their mistakes, no matter what it costs."

She felt his gaze boring into her and lowered her eyes, reddening. He watched her struggling with his words and her role in her aunt's difficulties.

"Let's go," she said quietly.

They were just climbing into the cab when Dipper and Shorty hailed them from down the block. Connor whirled and beckoned them to hurry.

"Where the hell have you been?" he demanded as they lumbered up, out of breath from running and looking like they'd slept in their clothes. "Never mind—I've got a job for you."

A BRISK TOUCH of frost tinged the air as Beatrice arrived at Consolidated's offices at half-past nine the next morning. In keeping with the gravity of the situation, she had chosen to wear a severely tailored black wool dress with fitted jacket and a small black hat. She had spent a long, sleepless night preparing herself for the coming fight. She was ready, she told herself, for any witnesses or allegations that Lynch and Winthrop might throw at her. What she was not prepared for was the presence of a number of her friends from the suffrage association in the reception area of the offices.

Lacey, Frannie, Carrie Catt, and Belva Vanderbilt hugged her and told her they believed in her, offering to besiege the board in her behalf. Frannie even offered to chain herself to something or someone in protest. Beatrice's determined composure was nearly undone by the warmth of their support.

Blinking, refusing to allow tears to form, she led them down the hall to the boardroom, where the sergeant-at-arms refused entry to all but Beatrice and Alice. Her suffragist friends, out of consideration for her, declined to make a scene and took up a vigil just outside the boardroom doors.

As she entered the cavernous, paneled room, the clumps of men gathered around the long board table lowered their voices to whispers. The company lawyers were seated along the wall behind the chairman's seat and at the far end stood Winthrop and Lynch, talking with Afton.

She could feel their hostile stares like needles pricking her skin. She had been in worse spots before, she told herself. She headed for her usual place at the head of the table, but vice president Graham intercepted her. With an apologetic look, he informed her that since she was the subject of this meeting, he would be presiding in her stead.

"I see," she said, refusing to show how that hurt. "Of course."

It seemed a dark omen. She moved to the chair immediately to the right of the chairman.

"Let's get straight to it, shall we?" Graham declared as everyone settled uneasily into their chairs. "You know the reason for calling an emergency session . . . the recent revelations in the newspapers regarding our board president."

"News*paper*," she corrected him. "Only *one* newspaper carried those scurrilous accusations."

"*The New York World*," old Augustine reproached her. "The city's *leading* newspaper."

"In the interest of fairness," Graham quickly continued, "we must offer Mrs. Von Furstenberg the opportunity to address these charges before taking action."

He turned to her and nodded, giving her the floor. She looked around the table, seeing only fixed expressions and set minds.

"The facts of the situation have not changed, gentlemen," she said.

"And just what facts are those, Mrs. Von Furstenberg?" old Haffleck interrupted, leaning forward. "I don't recall getting any facts from you at the last board meeting. You made your case based on your record at the reins of the company and we were willing to accept that. But now, in light of the public accusations and additional charges—"

"But, these are not additional charges," she declared. "You heard Winthrop and Lynch's threat when they left here that day. They said you and I would pay for not going along with their nasty little grab for power. Clearly, they are the anonymous 'sources' the news writer quoted in the article. No one else claims that I frequent brothels."

"Have you any proof of that?" Lynch demanded, rising and looking at the others. "She might have been seen by any of dozens of patrons of the place."

"Put her to the question," Winthrop said eagerly, shooting to his feet. "She prizes *honesty* so . . . ask her point-blank if she has ever been to the Oriental."

Every face in the room turned to her. She summoned all of her courage.

"I will *not* answer such a question. Not unless every man here is forced to submit to the same hideous request about his own personal life."

In the uncomfortable silence that followed, Graham visually collected a consensus from the board and turned to her.

"It has gone beyond the personal, Mrs. Von Furstenberg. However it began, however unfair it seems, it is now a matter of public discourse and affects the good name and fortunes of this company. Our stock prices are teetering even now. You must answer the question or we shall be forced to conclude that you cannot answer except in the affirmative."

"I—I—" Whatever she said would seal her fate. She looked around the room with dwindling hope. "I will not deny that I was in the Oriental Palace once."

The murmur that went around the room sounded like vultures' wings.

"There, you see—from her own lips—she admits it!" Lynch crowed above the turmoil that was unleashed.

"I move that Beatrice Von Furstenberg be removed as president of Consolidat—"

"Stop!" The commotion that was growing in the hall outside burst through the double doors.

A motley contingent of people came tussling and shoving into the boardroom, with Connor Barrow at its head. "You need to hear what we have to say!"

Beatrice was stunned. Behind Connor came Priscilla, Lacey, Frannie, Carrie Chapman Catt, and Belva

Vanderbilt, followed by several news reporters. The women pushed past the sergeant-at-arms, who managed to halt the reporters at the door.

"What the devil—this is a private meeting!" Graham insisted.

"No, this is a *trial*." Connor strode furiously to the table.

"And womanhood itself is in the dock! None of this would be happening if Beatrice Von Furstenberg were a man!" Frannie Excelsior declared with an upraised fist, before the others pulled her back against the wall with them.

"We've come to give evidence," Connor continued, "and if you want the truth, you'll hear us out."

"Get these people out of here!" Lynch ordered, glaring at Connor. "They're trespassing!"

"Testifying," Connor corrected, taking in Winthrop's and Lynch's presence but turning quickly to the other directors.

Beatrice felt her heart beating in her throat. They had come—he had come—to testify to what they knew? To help her?

"Who are you, to come bursting in here?" Winthrop demanded anxiously.

"Connor Barrow, attorney." From the number of nods around the table, the name was familiar to a number of the directors. "I don't know what these men have told you"—he pointed to Winthrop and Lynch—"but Mrs. Von Furstenberg is totally innocent of the charges leveled in the *World* yesterday."

"He has no right to be here," Lynch snapped, pointing at Connor. "He's that politician she's involved with—the one in the newspapers. He'll say anything to protect her."

"Is that so?" Connor looked around the table, folded his arms, and spread his feet. "Then I won't say anything, and let others speak for themselves." He nodded to Priscilla.

He was here. Beatrice could hardly see anything but Connor as she struggled to keep her composure. She had no time to think about where he had been for these last troubled days or how he came to be here. She had to maintain her focus; too much was at stake. They had come to testify . . .

"Priscilla?" Her voice was suddenly thick with emotion.

"It's all right, Aunt Beatrice." The girl's voice quivered and she clamped her hands together as every eye in the room turned on her. "It's partly my fault and I want to tell what I—"

"We got to see Mrs. Von Furstenberg!" It was Dipper. He and Shorty were alternately dragging and shoving someone into the room with them. "We found him. A little bit ago—snoopin' around outside!"

Squeezed between Dipper and Shorty like a sausage in a casing, was a scruffy, undernourished-looking fellow in a worn gray suit, sporting a battered bowler hat and the beginning of a black eye. Dipper's blocky face beamed as he and Shorty hauled the man to the table, opposite Beatrice, and held him in place with no little force.

"This is the reporter?" Beatrice had to steady herself on the table.

"Artie Higgins, he calls hisself," Dipper announced. "Of that *New York World*."

"This is absurd—what is he doing here?" Lynch motioned to Higgins.

"He didn't want to come," Dipper said, as everyone

eyed the bruise darkening around Higgins's eye. "But we persuaded him it wus the right thing to do." He looked at the reporter. "Tell 'em what you told us."

"Ohhh, no!" Higgins jerked free unexpectedly and rushed for the door, but Dipper and Shorty caught him and forced him, struggling, back to the table. "This isn't right—you can't make me talk! I'm part of the free press!"

"This has absolutely no relevance—" Winthrop began.

"It has every relevance," Beatrice declared. "You've said that there could have been any number of sources—men who saw me cavorting at the Oriental. I say there were only two." She turned to Higgins. "Please, Mr. Higgins . . . tell us how you got the information for the story you wrote."

The reporter glared furiously at her and pursed his lips.

"Cat got yer tongue?" Dipper said, tightening his grip on Higgins's arm. "He sung like a bird a little bit ago. Said he got the story from a fella . . . came to him at the Pressman's Bar, up on Thirty-fourth Street."

"I suggest you tell us what you know, Higgins, and help us get at the truth," Graham spoke up. "Libel suits against newspapers can cost hundreds of thousands of dollars, and newspapers don't employ reporters who cause them expensive legal trouble."

The reporter looked from Graham to Lynch with a furious glare. Finally, seeing no hope of rescue, he snapped: "All right," and shook free of Dipper and Shorty's hands.

"It's true," Higgins admitted. "A man came into the bar and asked the bartender if he knew any reporters. The barkeep pointed me out to him, and he came over and said he had a story . . . asked if I was interested."

"Is that man in this room?" Beatrice asked.

He still hesitated, until Dipper and Shorty looked like they were about to seize him again and then he nodded.

"Who is he?"

Another pause occurred before he raised his gaze and nodded to Lynch. "It was him . . . over there. Archibald Lynch."

There was some consternation at that, but Lynch lifted his head above the other board members' hostile stares. "That's not how it was. I was in a restaurant—he came up to me and asked questions—"

"Did you talk to any other witnesses before you wrote the story?" Beatrice asked the reporter, ignoring Lynch. "Did you talk to anyone from the Oriental Palace?"

"I checked it out," Higgins declared defensively. "I asked if he knew anybody else who could back up his story. He gave me a name and I talked to him, too. That fellow agreed it was all true, so I wrote it up."

"And the name of that man?" Beatrice was twisting into knots inside.

"Him." Higgins nodded to Lynch's partner. "Harold Winthrop."

"Anyone else?" she demanded, over Winthrop's sputtering and the other directors' growing outrage. "Did you talk to anyone besides these two men before you wrote that story?"

When he shook his head, she nearly melted with relief.

"There were no other witnesses. Just Lynch and Winthrop," she said to the board. "Do you see what they've done? They couldn't *persuade* you to vote with them, to oust me, so they thought they'd *force* you to do it. Once the story was made public, you would have no choice but to remove me." She turned on the pair. "Then

what? Who would you have smeared next in your quest
for power? Graham? Wright?"

"This is absurd—she's guilty as sin, and the only way
she can defend her immoral behavior is to attack those
who know the truth about her!"

"Then give us the names of other men who saw her at
the Oriental," Graham declared. "We'll call on them ourselves, for verification."

Lynch looked desperately at Winthrop, who reddened
but said nothing. Then he looked around at the anger
and accusation in his fellow board members' faces, and
realized that they had withdrawn whatever support he
once had.

"We're waiting, Lynch." Graham rose. "The names of
these other witnesses you claim to have. Winthrop?"

"So our word isn't good enough," Lynch said furiously,
dragging Winthrop by the arm toward the door. "Go on
to hell in a hand basket . . . with her. I've had enough.
I'm getting out. Don't come running to me when your
precious stock prices take a dive!" He and Winthrop barreled past Connor, past the sergeant-at-arms, and
through the clutch of reporters and employees collected
just outside the door.

For a moment everyone stared at the door where they
had disappeared. Then the silence burst and Graham
hammered for order as everyone began talking at once.

Beatrice wasn't certain where these revelations left
her. She looked around the board table, then at her suffrage friends, Priscilla, and finally, at Connor. Would
they still have to tell the board what happened? And if
they did, what would that do to him . . . to her . . . to
them?

"Gentlemen!" Secretary Wright pleaded for order. "I
think it may be drawn from their response that Winthrop

and Lynch attempted to override the board's authority by going public with a story we had already dealt with and voted on. They knew the story could damage Consolidated's credibility and force us to rescind our prior decision. Whatever their motivations—"

"Their motives should be perfectly clear," Connor inserted. "Their malicious allegations against Mrs. Von Furstenberg were part of a scheme to gain power and influence on the board." He paused to look at Bebe. "Mrs. Von Furstenberg could never behave in an immoral or unethical manner."

Beatrice couldn't speak. This was the second time he had vehemently defended her at no small risk to himself.

"Yes, well," Graham began, clearly uncomfortable with what came next. "We could certainly accept that explanation for the charges against Mrs. Von Furstenberg . . . if she hadn't already admitted to being at this 'Oriental Palace.'"

"What?" Connor looked to her with a frown.

"Yes, I . . . I have admitted that I was at the Oriental Palace . . . on one occasion." She cleared her throat. "It is not a particularly proud moment in my life, but it hardly represents a great moral failing."

"I can tell you why she was there." It was Priscilla, who had stepped forward.

"No!" Beatrice hurried around the table to intercept her niece. "*I* will tell you why I was there." She looked down into Priscilla's huge dark eyes, forbidding her to speak. "All of this began when I foolishly—"

"When she foolishly decided to do a bit of 'missionary' work in my establishment," said a bold voice from the doorway. "And I'm *not* talkin' about positions, here."

The figure in the doorway was swathed in dramatic black and red velvet and an enormous feather-trimmed hat, with her arm outstretched and propped against one of the door facings.

Beatrice was shocked speechless at the sight of Charlotte Brown standing on the threshhold of her boardroom. Behind the notorious madam stood several of the girls from the Oriental, dressed to the nines and grinning and winking at Beatrice over Charlotte's shoulders.

Around the table, jaws dropped in astonishment.

"Hello, Congressman," Charlotte Brown said as she swayed into the room and paused to survey those present. "Hello, Mrs. Von Furstenberg." She let her gaze linger on more than one of the red-faced board members. "Hello . . . *boys*."

As she looked around the table, her smile started small and slow and broadened to suggest the volumes of illicit knowledge she possessed.

"Me and my 'Oriental' seem to be in the news of late." She assumed a pained look as she continued. "Limelight is bad for business. It's time I set the record straight. 'Beatrice' here was at the Oriental exactly *one* time. She entered without my knowledge or permission and spent time with some of my girls."

She glanced at Beatrice with a wince of disgust.

"Tried to 'reform' them. Talked to them about bein' seamstresses and shop girls." She gave a snort of amusement. "As if any of my girls would trade 'the life' for Mrs. Von Cluckenberg's deadly dull respectability."

Beatrice stiffened but clamped her jaw tight, resisting the urge to bite the hand that seemed to be rescuing her.

Charlotte swayed farther around the room, past the suffrage contingent with their matronly dark dresses and prim white collars, dismissing them with a faint roll of her heavily kohled eyes.

"I discovered her on my premises and asked her to

leave. She was less than cooperative. I had to have my servant—Punjab—remove her physically from the place." She smiled and looked up as if remembering fondly. "He picked her up and carried her out arse over teakettles—with her screamin' bloody hell the whole time. Her petticoats turned inside out and her respectable 'garters' were viewed and enjoyed by all."

"Really, Mrs. Brown!" Beatrice could no longer contain herself.

"Really, Mrs. Von Footsieberg," Charlotte said, going to stand by board member William Afton and drape her arm with great familiarity over his fleshy shoulders. "I will not have my reputation as a professional sullied by rumors that I present *amateur* entertainment." She transferred her insultingly thorough gaze to the men now literally at her fingertips. "Now, *boys*"—her voice dripped with honeyed warning—"do we have any questions?"

The board members avoided eye contact with her and with the girls waving and blowing kisses at them from the doorway. She ruffled Afton's thinning, brilliantined hair, then smiled and released him.

"Good. I would never want to be accused of tellin' tales out of school." She headed for the door.

Her bustle swung more noticeably as she passed the tight-lipped line of suffrage-minded females. Looking them over, she muttered just loud enough for them to hear: "Oh, yeah. We'll be in business for a good, long time."

As soon as she disappeared out the door, the gasps of indignation from the suffrage contingent were matched by the covert sighs of relief from the men around the board table. Graham called their attention back to the business at hand.

"So, Mrs. Von Furstenberg," vice president Graham

said, dabbing his forehead with a handkerchief, "it seems that you went to the Oriental to do 'rescue' work. A most ill-advised venture, however noble your motives. You might have told us this story and saved this confusion."

"Would you have believed me?" Beatrice did her best to look suitably aggrieved. "As I said before, the incident is not exactly something that makes me proud." She glanced at Connor. "It ended in disaster all around. And the humiliation it caused just seems to have no end."

"Well, it has ended as far as this board is concerned," Graham declared, with an eye on reporter Higgins. "I believe there is nothing more for the board to consider. I will entertain a motion for a vote of confidence in Mrs. Von Furstenberg as president of Consolidated Industries."

Graham called the roll for the vote that yielded a unanimous decision . . . to keep her as president of Consolidated.

Beatrice scarcely heard the vice president's declaration that the meeting was adjourned and barely heard the rumble of relieved voices as board members stopped to greet her before hurrying out. Her attention was riveted on Connor, who stood smiling at her. In that moment she realized she was deeply, earnestly, and thoroughly in love with Connor Barrow.

Wonder bloomed in her as she was embraced by Lacey and Frannie and Priscilla and Alice and Carrie Catt.

She moved through a sea of sensations and responses until she reached Connor and held out both of her hands to him. He took them and held them tightly.

"The gov, there—" Dipper said, intruding, "it was him that sent us for Charlotte Brown." He nodded toward Connor.

"We wasn't sure she'd come," Shorty said earnestly. "She acted right huffy when we told her what was happenin'."

"What if she hadn't come?" Priscilla said.

"Then we'd have resorted to something really desperate," Connor said, lowering his voice, "like the *truth*."

Beatrice felt Connor's hands tightening around her own and realized how narrowly they had averted disaster. A deep and unprecedented calm settled over her. He was there. With her. That was all that mattered.

She introduced him to her friends and watched him enduring with grace their flattery and their questions. He was not only charming, he was entirely respectful to them and they responded in kind.

It was only as he was taking his leave that she noticed how drawn and tired he looked.

"I have to go . . . I'm already late for a campaign appearance."

"Can you come for dinner tonight?" she asked quietly, for his ears alone.

He shook his head.

"I have to work with my campaign manager on my speeches for tomorrow." The pressure of his hands increased for a moment. Then he said to all of them: "I have a debate tomorrow night at Irving Hall. I hope to see you all there."

The minute he was gone, the women turned to Beatrice with wide eyes.

"He's wonderful, Beatrice," Lacey said.

"He has such warmth, such charm," Belva observed.

"But that woman—that 'Charlotte Brown' creature," Frannie said.

"Hardly the sort you'd expect to come running to help

a suffragist." Carrie Catt turned to Bebe. "How on earth did Mr. Barrow know you had been at that awful place?"

Beatrice was caught off guard. "I suppose she told him." Then when she realized the others were staring at her in dismay, she hastily explained: "I believe she was one of Mr. Barrow's legal clients."

"In her business," Lacy muttered, "she needs a good lawyer."

"In her business," Frannie added, "she needs a *priest*."

NINETEEN

BEATRICE HAD LUNCHEON with Priscilla at a restaurant near Consolidated's offices. Despite the air of relief between them, there were still long silences as both sat lost in thought. When the final coffee came, Priscilla looked up at Beatrice with her eyes glistening.

"I'm so sorry, Aunt Beatrice. I didn't mean to cause you so much trouble."

"I know, Prissy." She laid her hand over her niece's on the table. "Let this be a lesson to you. You never know what the outcome of your actions will be." She smiled. "I confess, I was ready to strangle you when I found out you were responsible for my kidnapping. But, seeing how things have worked out, perhaps I should hug you instead."

"Hug me? For what? For nearly getting you kicked off your own company's board of directors?"

"That wasn't entirely your fault. Lynch and Winthrop were behind that move. I was surprised that the gentlemen of the board still resent the way Mercer left the reins in my hands. No matter how much money I've made them, they still don't like the idea of a woman running things." She shook her head sadly. "It's the price a woman pays for doing business in a man's world. They hold us to a different standard, Prissy. They're like spoiled children. To a lot of men, women are little more than possessions or playthings. To others, women have to be saints up on a pedestal . . . pure and loving and all-forgiving . . . like their mothers. Heaven help us if we prove to be merely human, like they are."

She looked off into the distance and her expression softened.

"But, there are some men, special men, who see us for what we really are. And they come to respect and care for our strength and intelligence."

Prissy watched her wistful look with a frown.

IT WAS MID-AFTERNOON before Priscilla returned to Woodhull House. She and Dipper went straight to the dormitory to start work, while Shorty headed for the kitchen to find Jeffrey and bring him upstairs. Shorty needn't have bothered; Jeffrey was already in the dormitory, propped on a stack of mattresses with his feet up and his eyes closed. At the sound of their arrival he started up and rolled from his perch, dragging his hands through his hair.

"Where in the blazes have you been?" He intercepted Priscilla halfway across the room.

"We might well ask the same of you. We looked everywhere for you before we left." She gave him an icy look. "All of your usual hiding places."

Dipper backed out the door, saying he would look for Shorty, while she continued unbuttoning her short cloak and went to hang it on a peg.

"I . . . I stepped out with a few of the older boys . . . for some fresh air," he said, bristling. "I was only gone a few minutes, and when I got back you were gone. Not a word about where you went. You just left me here . . . alone."

She scowled at the messy hall that was just as they had left it. "Well, you don't seem to have strained yourself while we were gone."

"Where did you go?" he demanded, even louder. "If you went to ask that McKee fellow for that donation—I told you I'd do that—and I will."

"We went to Aunt Beatrice's offices, at Consolidated. She was very nearly booted off the board of her own company today because somebody found out about her being in the Oriental Palace. Your cousin came to get us so we could tell the board of directors what really happened."

"What?" Jeffrey's face paled and he grabbed her by the shoulders. "You didn't tell them, did you? You didn't mention me?"

"I should have. I should have told them every last detail."

"Priscilla!"—he gave her a shake—"what did you tell them?"

"Jeffrey!" She jerked free and stumbled back with a look of disbelief. "I didn't have to say anything. Your cousin, Dipper and Shorty, and that awful woman from that Oriental place . . . they managed to get the board to realize it wasn't Aunt Beatrice's fault . . . that she hadn't done anything wrong."

"Thank God." He turned away, sagging visibly with relief. But, after a moment, he recovered enough for a cocky toss of his head. "It's probably just as well I wasn't there. If they'd have asked me, I'd have said it was *all* her fault."

"Jeffrey!" She grabbed him by the sleeve. "How can you say that?"

"Because it's true," he said, pulling from her grip. "If she hadn't been such an old dragon—if she had let us see each other—then we wouldn't have had to resort to such schemes to get her to change her mind." His chin set at a stubborn angle. "She was as much to blame as we were. And personally, I think we've been punished enough." He stalked over to a row of dusty chairs stacked by twos and gave one of them a contemptuous kick. "Stuck here in this smelly, godforsaken place . . . having to work like menials . . . day after day . . ."

"Jeffrey, you're being childish."

"Me? Childish?" He gave a stack of mattresses an impulsive shove that sent them toppling. "I'll tell you what's childish . . . playing make-believe at our age . . . hiring men to pretend to rob somebody so we can rescue them. *That's* childish."

"You're just being mean and spiteful," Priscilla said, stinging from his lashing out. She whirled and looked for something to do to hide the angry tears forming in her eyes. She picked up a scrub brush, dunked it in the pail of vinegar water nearby, and began to wash down one of the old bureaus.

Behind her, she heard him walking about, grumbling and occasionally hitting or banging something, but she kept scrubbing. After a few moments, he came up behind her. She could feel him watching her and scrubbed even harder.

"Will you stop that and turn around and talk to me?" he said angrily.

"Somebody has to do the work," she snapped.

"Meaning what? I do my fair share around here, you know. Just because I refuse to turn myself into a drudge like—" He halted before it came out, but the unspoken end of the sentence echoed around the room anyway. *Like you.*

The scrub brush landed in the bucket with a splash. She wheeled and stared at him, seeing him—really seeing him—for the first time.

"How dare you?" She began to tremble as long-suppressed resentments bubbled to the surface. "You've done nothing but wash a few dishes since we got here, and we've heard nothing but complaints about *that*."

"You, on the other hand, seem to thrive on this great, noble work of yours. Little Miss Do-Good. Saint Sober-Sides. You never smile or laugh anymore. You won't let me kiss you or even touch you. You're always keeping an eye on me and ordering me around like I'm some"—he made a dismissive gesture—"*kid*."

"Well, if I treat you like one, maybe it's because you—" She stopped before "*act like one*" came out, but it was as plain to him as if she'd shouted it. "I'm tired of making up excuses for you to Miss Gerhardt. I'm tired of having to do things you were asked to do first, and I'm tired of always having to finish the things you start."

"Well, who put you in charge in the first place? You're not my mother, you know," he declared hotly. "Or my *wife*!"

"Thank God!" It came out before she thought. But once it was out, she realized that it had been lying there, just below the surface for days. *Thank God* she wasn't his wife or his mother . . . or anybody who had to depend on him for something. Thank God she had seen him as he truly was . . . outside of moonlit gardens and darkened carriage houses . . . in the reassuring clarity of daylight.

Everything had to be his way. He only thought about

his comfort, his pleasure . . . *his* precious, water-chapped hands. In the last few minutes he had thrown a full-scale tantrum, kicking and bashing things, behaving—Aunt Beatrice's words came back to her—like a spoiled child. Worse still . . . he said he wouldn't have stood up at the board meeting to tell the truth . . . to own up to his part in what had happened to her aunt. Where was his honor, his integrity? Those traits had been missing all along. She just hadn't wanted to see it.

"What did you just say to me?" he roared at her. His face was red and his fists were clenched. He looked ready to stomp or throw himself down on the floor in a fit of anger.

She backed one step toward the door . . . then another . . . then another.

"I believe I just said *good-bye,* Jeffrey. And good riddance."

ALL AFTERNOON BEATRICE thought about Connor and explored her newly recognized feeling for him. Love. It was everything Priscilla had believed—eagerness, passion, enthrallment—but it was so much more. It was meeting and appreciating another's heart, mind, and soul. It was knowing another's thoughts and feelings without words, and trusting him to care for you and be there to help when you needed it. It was putting another's welfare above your own. It was opening yourself . . . letting go . . . trusting your heart in another's hands. Today she had learned just how earnestly Connor Barrow held her welfare, and the last element of love was suddenly present in her heart.

She loved Connor Barrow, and the intensity of her

feelings for him heightened her awareness of his tension and of the signs of fatigue in his face.

What was wrong? Was it his campaign? Was it something between them? She was increasingly desperate to know. She was preparing to leave the house that evening, intending to stop by his office and then his home, when Priscilla arrived.

"You're early," Beatrice said, noting the high color in her niece's face.

Priscilla's eyes flashed as she jerked the gloves from her fingers.

"I'm through with him. Absolutely through," she declared. "You don't have to worry anymore about me marrying anytime soon, Aunt Beatrice. I wouldn't have a man if you handed him to me on a platter!"

Beatrice halted in the middle of drawing her gloves on.

"What's happened?"

"You were right." Priscilla unpinned her hat. "Men are all beasts."

Beatrice frowned. When had she said that?

"Something did happen." She took Priscilla by the hand and started for the drawing room. "Come and tell me."

Priscilla pulled her to a halt. "Jeffrey has showed his true colors, that's what's happened. He's arrogant, high-handed, and selfish in the extreme. He has no more idea what life and love are about than a five-year-old child has." She freed her hand and drew herself up straight. "I've given it some thought, Aunt Beatrice. I intend to finish out my sentence at Woodhull House"—she lifted her chin—"because that is what a woman of integrity must do. But please, I beg you, shorten *his* sentence, so I won't have to see him anymore."

Beatrice thought about it for a moment, then nodded. "If you're sure . . ."

"I'm positive."

IN THE CARRIAGE, Bebe thought about her part in Priscilla's break with Jeffrey. A few weeks ago she would have been overjoyed at the demise of Priscilla's romantic illusions. But now she felt an unexpected and unsettling regret. Priscilla's shedding of illusions was accompanied by a loss of innocence; she would never again view men or love in quite the same way. And it involved a failure of hope . . . that things with Jeffrey would change . . . that love would find a way. What if this experience caused her to become bitter and angry? What if she never fell in love again?

Beatrice winced inwardly, thinking of the emptiness of the years her own heart had lain fallow. Did she really expect Priscilla to follow the same lonely path? It struck her that, from her niece's birth—to two impetuous romantics—Priscilla's life had been very different from hers. Perhaps she was destined for love and fulfillment much earlier in life.

She thought of the passion and joy she had experienced with Connor. She had never felt so whole or alive as she did in his presence. It was a pleasure even to argue with him. Could she, in all conscience, deny such joy to Priscilla?

Connor's offices were dark and empty. As they drove by Tammany Hall, she thought of stopping to look for him, but she had Rukart take her to his home instead. There was a light on inside, and the door was answered by a short, apple-cheeked woman with a motherly air, who introduced herself as his housekeeper, Mrs. O'Hara. Connor wasn't at home, but was expected before long. Summoning her nerve, Beatrice asked if she might wait inside for him.

The housekeeper looked at her fashionable clothes, glanced at her carriage, and said she couldn't imagine it would do any harm.

It was more than an hour before there was a rattling of the lock at the front door and she heard voices. It was Connor, but he was with someone. She froze, regretting her impulsive decision to wait for him.

"Ye missed a fund-raisin' breakfast this mornin'—the second one this week, that's why," came a deep male voice with a heavy Irish accent. "My orders is to not let ye out of my sight 'til after the election."

"Fine, Delaney"—Connor's voice sounded ragged and angry—"stay or go, I don't care. But if you stay it won't be inside. I'd advise you to go home."

"An' leave ye to yer own devices, I suppose. So ye get into more trouble. Where were ye this mornin', Barrow? Off with yer lady friend again? If the boss finds out, yer nuts'll be in the grinder. I told ye to leave that skirt alone—ferget women until after the election."

"Dammit, Delaney—" Connor raised his hand to point toward the door. At that moment, he caught sight of Beatrice standing in the parlor. The next instant he was pushing the beefy, red-faced Delaney back down the entry hall and out the front door. "Out! Now!"

"Wait just a damned minute," Delaney demanded, trying to see around him. "Who is that? Is that her? Is—"

The door slammed shut, cutting off the rest of his remark. Connor threw the lock and lowered the shade over the oval window in the door.

"Who was that?" Bebe asked.

"Del Delaney . . . ward heeler and Tammany watchdog," he said.

He stared at her with a hunger that seemed as much emotional as physical. After a moment, the pounding on the door penetrated his awareness and he ushered her into the parlor, closing the door behind them. "Don't worry about him . . . he'll give up and go away."

"You're in trouble," she said anxiously. "I sensed something was wrong this morning, and I was right."

"Nothing I can't handle," he said.

"Or manhandle," she countered.

"It seems I'm not on Tammany's good side, just now. They've decided I need a bit of encouragement to stick to the party's program."

"Encouragement?" The exchange between Connor and Delaney began to make awful sense. "It's because of Albany, isn't it?" Her eyes widened. "And me. You've been linked with me in the papers, and half of New York seems to think I'm the Jezebel of Wall Street."

He settled in front of her and ran his thumb over the curve of her cheek. "It has to do with what I believe in and whether I intend to run my own life or to allow them to run it."

"How diplomatic of you. So, it does have to do with me. Then perhaps I should leave and—"

"Don't even consider it," he said. "There are some things in my life that aren't negotiable." His intense gaze said she was one of them, and she wasn't sure if that made her feel better or worse.

"But I don't want to make trouble for you, Connor."

"You should have thought of that *before* you started blackmailing me," he said with a half smile.

It was true, she thought. She had been appallingly shortsighted and selfish in her demands. He had tried to tell her about the pressures he faced and she had refused to listen. Now the forces she had unleashed were bearing down on him.

"Tell me what's happened." Her heart was suddenly pounding.

"I don't know if it's me who's changing or if it's Tammany . . . or maybe both." He ran a hand back through his hair. "Until now, I've made speeches, brought in votes, and kept up my law practice . . . pretty much lived my life as I wanted. Then, a couple of news articles come out . . . one mentioning suffrage and one your bank . . . and suddenly I can't do anything right and I can't go anywhere without a watchdog. I'm told where to go, and who to see, and who *not* to see."

"They don't want you to see me," she said, stunned.

"They don't want me to see anyone or anything that might prove a distraction." He smiled ruefully. "And you are one powerful distraction."

"You're running for Congress now," she said, feeling a towering wave of guilt. "They have to protect their investment. The stakes have gone up."

He nodded. "Not just for them. These last few days, I've been doing a lot of thinking. There are a lot of things I want to do—things I want to do to help change and improve things—and this is my chance. I've worked for years to be in this position. I'd be crazy to throw it all away."

"And?" She felt something awful coming and braced.

"And so I won't throw it all away." He grinned, turning on that patentable charm of his. "I'll make it work."

"How?" She knew he was using that charm to close

off discussion of how he would deal with the pressure Tammany Hall was applying, but he seemed so certain and was so irresistibly determined . . .

He waggled his brows and pulled her close, aiming for her mouth.

She was putty in his hands, she told herself. She should be ashamed of allowing herself to be sweet-talked and distracted. These were important issues, major problems. But by the end of that first kiss, she couldn't think of anything horrible enough to eclipse the sheer joy of that moment, of being in his arms and feeling his warmth and vitality all around her. When it became clear where their second kiss was leading, she summoned what was left of her melting resolve and resisted a third.

"Maybe we shouldn't do this."

He pulled back slightly to look at her in exaggerated horror.

"Maybe we should wait until word of Consolidated's decision has been announced in the papers and the scandal has had a chance to fade."

"Maybe you should just quit talking." He lowered his lips to her throat.

"But—"

"And quit thinking."

"But—"

"And quit worrying."

His hands glided over her back and around her waist. Her eyes closed. It would be so easy . . .

She forced her eyes open, but it was a minute before they would focus.

"Seriously, Connor," she said, her voice thick with desire as she pushed back. "What are you going to do?"

He paused for a moment, searching her determination. The light in his eyes began to twinkle like stars in a midnight sky.

"I've noticed you don't take 'no' for an answer very often," he said as he slowly claimed her lips. "Whenever I find myself in trouble, I'll just pretend I'm *you*."

THE NEXT MORNING, the front page of *The New York World* carried an article titled:

CANDIDATE DEFENDS JEZEBEL —
IT WAS "RESCUE WORK" IN A BROTHEL!

But neither Connor nor Beatrice saw it. In her Fifth Avenue mansion, Beatrice slept late, after her late evening, and she had always disliked the smell of newsprint with her tea and marmalade. Across town, Connor was roused early by a testy Del Delaney and had made two separate breakfast speeches before he had a chance to eat breakfast himself, much less read a newspaper.

But others saw it and its companion piece on the front page . . . a dry, somewhat officiously worded announcement from Consolidated Industries. Both articles contained the same information: The Consolidated board of directors had met the previous day, exonerated their board president, and given her a vote of confidence. But the "Jezebel" piece contained juicy details . . . such as the accused's admission that she actually had been in the brothel and the appearance of an infamous madam and a delegation of her "employees" to attest to the accused's purpose in being in said brothel. The madam was quoted as saying that as the accused was being removed from the premises, her garters had indeed been "enjoyed by all." Also prominent in the "Jezebel" article was the morsel that congressional candidate Connor Barrow had been present and asserted Mrs. Von Furstenberg's innocence and outstanding character.

Fortunately for Connor, most of the voters at the Elkhorn Brotherhood Lodge breakfast and the Gemutlichkeit Bakers' Association breakfast did not bother with newspapers . . . nor did the factory workers who attended a Democratic rally that noon in a square nestled in an industrial area of the Lower East Side.

After making a speech that drew sustained cheering, Connor descended from the bunting-draped platform, drew the first beer from the barrels that Tammany had provided for the rally, and began to walk around the square. He shook hands everywhere and paused to talk with workers eating their lunches out of battered metal pails or the old newsprint used by street vendors. They grinned at him and gratefully sipped their beer. He listened and laughed and commiserated, noting their concerns with a heightened intensity and earnestness that endeared him to them. And when the whistles blew, calling the workers back to their jobs, they waved and called good-bye to him as if he were a friend.

He watched them go back to work with an odd constriction in his throat. He wanted desperately to represent these people, to help make their lives better. And he found himself wondering if Boss Croker still felt—or had ever felt—this desire to be *of service* to the people.

While Delaney was busy directing the beer wagon drivers and the teamsters who were dismantling the speaker's platform, Connor caught sight of a coach barreling down one of the side streets, headed straight for him. He watched with growing dread as it entered the square and stopped a few feet away. The door flew open and Boss Croker appeared in the doorway, furiously chewing a cigar.

"Barrow!" he shouted at the top of his lungs. "Get in here!"

Connor strode over to the coach and spotted Charles Murphy and Mayoral candidate Thomas Gilroy inside. The instant the door closed behind him, the coach lurched into motion.

Croker was red-faced, Murphy was grim, and Gilroy was smacking a rolled-up newspaper against his palm in agitation.

"You damned fool!" Croker roared as soon as they were underway. "What the hell did you think you were doing? I told you to stay away from that woman—I told you to keep your nose clean—and damn me if you didn't go and get involved anyway!" He was so angry veins stood out at his temples and in his neck. "Years of work teeterin' on the brink . . . all because you can't keep it in your pants!"

"Look, if you're angry about Delaney—" Connor began.

"Show him!" Croker ordered Gilroy, who unrolled the paper in his hands and shoved it at Connor. Croker rocked forward and jabbed the middle of the front page. "Look at this mess! Look at it! What have you got to say for yourself?"

Connor felt his insides go cold. The title of the article said it all. Once again, his relationship with Bebe was splattered all over a piece of newsprint, and once again, he was being called to account.

"I went to offer evidence I believed would help them arrive at the truth," Connor said in tightly measured tones.

"Truth?" Croker snatched the paper from him and

pointed it at him. "The only truth you need to know is that you're about half an inch away from gettin' kicked out of this congressional race on your arse!" He slammed back in his seat and stewed visibly for a moment as he looked out the window. He was still breathing hard when he pinned Connor with a javelin of a look. "What is it with this bit of muslin? She's got you droolin' and stumblin' over your own ballocks like some lovesick boy, and you can't see what she's doin' to you."

He leaned forward and bit out every word. "Let me give ye a sound bit of advice, Barrow. One piece of tail's the same as another in the dark. Go find yourself a cute little whore and work it out of your system."

Connor felt as if he'd been stripped of skin . . . left with every nerve ending he possessed exposed. And Croker was grating on all of them. Until that moment, he hadn't imagined Croker—genial boss, canny politician—capable of some of the stories he'd heard noised about. Croker the gang tough. Croker the enforcer. Croker the vindictive power-monger. But now, his capacity for baseness and bullying were all too clear.

A woman was simply "tail" to him. Whether she was a chippy bought for two bits on the street or a woman of education, breeding, and integrity . . . she had only one value. And that included Beatrice Von Furstenberg. His wise, strong, generous, and courageous Bebe was merely an inconvenient "piece of tail."

"Tell him," Croker ordered, giving Murphy a jab with his elbow.

Connor's fists clenched in his coat pockets as he looked to Murphy, whose distaste for the job he had been given was obvious. But if Murphy was anything, he was a good soldier, and good soldiers always follow orders.

"We're going back to Tammany Hall," Murphy said in

a flat, matter-of-fact tone. "We've assembled a number of news reporters in the reception hall . . . every major paper will be there. You're going to deny any and all ties to suffrage organizations and denounce the women's rights organizations as dangerous factions that are trying to mislead women and undermine society." There he paused and glanced at Croker, who told him gruffly to get on with it.

"Then, you will deny any personal involvement with this Mrs. Von Furstenberg and say that you were misled as to the nature of the banking venture you were asked to represent. You will state that you have severed all ties with her and her company." He paused again, seeming uncomfortable with this next part. "And you will do exactly what you say. You will not see her again."

"Do what you have to do to end it. Tell her whatever you want . . . hell, tell her the truth, that we're making you do it," Croker commanded. "Just do it." He glared at Connor. "You got that?"

"Loud and clear," Connor said, struggling to maintain some semblance of calm as he scrambled for what to do. In a few minutes, he would face a dozen reporters with Croker and Tammany Hall breathing down his neck. If he wanted to save his career, his political future, he had to deny and denounce the very thing that had put joy and meaning back into his life.

What astounded him most was that they fully expected him to do it. They counted on him to submit to this raw exercise of power. That was how they saw him . . . ambitious, talented, and utterly, shamelessly malleable. He would take whatever shape they required of him. And they saw him that way because, for a number of years now he realized, that was exactly the way he had been.

The good soldier. Going along with the platform. Always cooperative and accommodating. Always making excuses for Tammany's excesses and deficits. Always the sweet-talker.

And the one he had sweet-talked the most was himself.

He sat with his head in his hands, as the coach rolled to a stop. One by one, the others climbed down out of the coach, until he was the only one left.

"Come on, Barrow," Croker said darkly. "Let's get it over with."

Moving through a haze of anger and despair, he descended the steps and crossed the pavement to the doors of Tammany Hall. With each step he took down the center hall and toward the reception room, he grew more agitated inside. Someone took his outer coat and someone else went over his suit coat with a brush. And the moment was upon him.

The door swung back and through the opening he saw more than a dozen news reporters. They were here to watch him unravel his soul in the service of Tammany Hall and his own ambition. And as he moved into that doorway, he felt a strange sort of calm descend. This was his greatest fear. The moral choice. The turning point. The one situation he couldn't sweet-talk his way out of. He closed his eyes briefly, then opened them and stepped into the room.

He was hit instantly with a barrage of questions, all of which he ignored on his way to the small wooden podium at the end of the room. He held up his hands for quiet and declared that he intended to make a statement first and would take questions afterward. He paused to look around the room, took a deep breath, and pretended he was Bebe Von Furstenberg.

"Gentlemen, you have been called here to hear a position statement necessitated by recent events, and to hear my response to an article printed in this morning's *World*. It has been charged by my opponents and suggested in the newspapers that I have not only flirted with, but have actually embraced the burgeoning women's rights movement. It has been suggested that I have been persuaded to support, both personally and publicly, the vote for women. Further . . . my involvement in securing a state charter for a bank which intends to serve women customers on the same basis as men, has been cited as evidence of my growing involvement with both women's rights and a certain lady . . . Mrs. Beatrice Von Furstenberg.

"I have come here today to state finally and unequivocally that every one of the allegations, suspicions, and suggestions I have just mentioned . . . is absolutely, undeniably, and irrevocably *TRUE*."

It was a testament to his verbal sleight-of-hand that every person in the room believed for a moment that he had indeed just issued a denial. It took a full minute for what he had truly said to register, by which time he began speaking again, to a shocked and reeling audience.

"Over the last month I have indeed come to believe in equal rights for women. I have seen firsthand the injustices women in our world must endure and I believe something must and will be done about them. I believe one of the best ways to address these injustices is to grant women the right they should already possess as humans . . . the right to vote."

The gurgling, choking sound that had been coming from behind him, suddenly erupted in a hoot of nervous laughter. Boss Croker appeared at his side wearing a forced grin, and clamped a hand savagely on his arm.

"A more wicked wit ye'll not find in the city of New York," Croker said with a frantic edge to his mirth.

"Wicked indeed," Connor retorted, ignoring the vicious pressure on his arm. "And finally, I must say that I am pleased to be involved both with the Barrow State Bank and with the remarkable woman who not only conceived it, but who is working diligently to bring it into being. I have nothing but the greatest admiration for Beatrice Von Furstenberg." He produced his infamous and beguiling smile. "And I expect that as time goes on, the rest of New York will come to feel the same about her."

There was only a faint titter of nervous laughter from the back. Everyone else was holding their breath, watching Boss Croker, and preparing for an explosion. They didn't have long to wait.

"That *isn't* what you intended to say, though, lad. A fine joke it was. But now, tell the boys what ye called 'em here to say." His eyes were blazing with a dual promise . . . clemency if he repented fast, and retribution if he didn't. Connor was being given one last chance. The carrot or the stick.

He had been here before. Ten years ago he had faced a similar ultimatum. The easy way or the right way. Submit to another's control and give up what he loved and believed in, or lose every hope he had of a comfortable or important future. It was all happening again. And being the man he was, now that he had found his center again, he couldn't pretend his heart, his values, and his convictions didn't exist.

Connor jerked his aching arm free and stepped back with determination in every particle of his being.

"That is exactly what I intended to say," Connor declared with fierce calm. "Every word of it."

"One last chance, damn you!" Croker shouted, above the chaos breaking out around them. "Tell 'em what we agreed!"

"*No.*"

Up came a fleshy finger in Connor's face.

"You're off the ballot!" Croker roared. "Hell, you're out of the party!"

Murphy and Gilroy grabbed Croker to keep him from launching himself at Connor. And Connor felt a curious sense of power—to be so in control of his responses, while his opponent was so out of control.

"Fine by me," he said fiercely, and turned and strode out.

TWENTY

IRVING HALL WAS awash in red, white, and blue bunting that night, and the outside was brightly lit and covered with banners proclaiming the virtues of the two congressional candidates featured in the evening's debate. But as Beatrice, Lacey, Frannie, Alice, and Esther Rose approached the hall, they noticed a profusion of newsboys hawking papers, and that everyone who approached the main entrance paused briefly, then walked away. It was only when they reached the steps that they realized people were reading a notice posted on the doors. It was the back of a playbill, hastily inscribed with ragged letters: DEBATE CANCELLED — BARROW OFF BALLOT.

Beatrice stared at the announcement, thinking that this had to be the cruelest joke Tammany or anyone had ever played. Then Frannie rushed up to the doors and pounded furiously on them until an aged usher answered and confirmed for them that the debate had indeed been canceled, and for the reason stated. When the group badgered him for details, he snapped "buy a paper" and slammed the door.

They grabbed the closest newsie, bought a paper, and stood under one of the building's large gas lamps to read the thin special edition. The account in the paper unfolded with details they discovered later were devastatingly accurate. Lacey took over the reading as Beatrice's hands began to tremble, and soon everyone was staring at her.

"He publicly declared his support for suffrage," Lacey muttered in awe, looking at the others.

"All right!" Frannie punched the air with a fist. "We've got a candidate!"

"But he's off the ballot," Esther Rose said. "What good does that do us?"

"They kicked him off the ballot." Lacy scowled. "Can they do that?"

Alice took the paper from Lacey and finished reading.

"How could they do this to him?" Beatrice's throat tightened. "Kick him out of Tammany Hall and drop him from the ballot, after all he's done for them and their precious Democrats?"

"Damned *men*." Frannie shook her fist at the notice on the doors. "They never know a good thing when they've got one!"

Beatrice swayed and the others reached out to steady her. They asked Alice to reread parts of the article and expressed outrage at the ruthlessness of Tammany's political machine. Beatrice heard only one word in three.

What had happened was all too clear. He was no longer Tammany's man . . . no longer Tammany's candidate . . . no longer a Democrat . . . no longer on the ballot . . .

The combined weight of all of those drastic changes came crashing down on her in a suffocating wave. He had just lost his platform, his chance for a role in national politics . . . just as he had found fresh conviction in his political course. His work, his affiliations, his entire world had turned upside down. And it was all because of her.

Dear God. What had she done?

Connor's connections, his friendships, his future—his whole life lay in shambles. And she was responsible.

Her eyes burned dryly as she struggled for composure. From the edge of her awareness came Frannie's voice saying: "We can't just sit here. We ought to *do* something."

She certainly did have to do something.

Abruptly, she lifted her skirts and bolted down the steps, heading for the cabstand on the corner. The others rushed after her.

"Beatrice, wait!"

"Are you all right?"

"Where are you going?"

"To find him!" she called out over her shoulder.

ARMED WITH LITTLE more than hope, Beatrice headed first for Connor's office and then for his house. He had to return home sooner or later, she reasoned, and she intended to be there when he arrived. On hearing her story, Mrs. O'Hara agreed to let her wait again and even made her a cup of tea.

For the next two hours, Bebe sat in his dimly lit parlor, watching the front door and imagining him in all sorts of dire situations: lying in a gutter somewhere, attacked and robbed . . . venting his hurt and anger in a barroom brawl . . . drowning his miseries in Irish whiskey.

When she could bear those possibilities no longer, she

turned her thoughts to what would happen when he came home. Would he be furious to see her here? Would he rage and blame her for what had happened to him? What could she possibly say to him?

I wish I had never involved you in all this . . . I never guessed Tammany would go so far as to kick you out . . . I'm so sorry I wrecked your life . . .

He had every right to order her out of his house and refuse to set eyes on her again.

She thought of her future without him and could imagine only a long succession of bleak, silent days and cold, empty nights. Nothing . . . not his anger, his humiliation, or his rejection of her could change what was in her heart. Whatever happened between them, she would always be wholly and irrevocably in love with Connor Barrow.

He was infuriating and intoxicating and passionate and unpredictable, and probably every bit as dangerous for her as she had proved to be for him. The thought of losing him, after just finding him, was nothing short of devastating.

What was she going to do?

It took some time, but she finally understood that the real question was—what were *they* going to do? This involved both hearts, both lives. They had to find a solution together, or not at all.

She was dozing, curled on the settee, when the front door opened and closed. She bolted upright and wiped the sleep from her eyes as Connor appeared in the doorway. His clothes and hair were damp from the light drizzle that had begun outside. His face was taut and his eyes burned like blue flames. She shot to her feet so quickly that she was momentarily dizzy.

"I heard what happened," she said, taking two steps

toward him . . . stopping when she had difficulty reading his turbulent mood. "We went to the debate and they had posted it. I wouldn't believe it . . . until we got a newspaper. . . ."

He headed for the small liquor cabinet in the corner and poured himself a whiskey before responding.

"Well," he said with a sardonic edge, "I finally declared for women's suffrage. It seems I am a man of my word, after all."

She watched him raise his glass to her, then take a drink and brace for the impact the liquor would make on his stomach.

"I'm so sorry, Connor. I never meant for anything like this to happen." She took a single step closer. "I knew how much this election meant to you. And still I pushed and badgered and demanded . . . It's all my fault. I wouldn't blame you if—"

"*Your* fault," he said, coming toward her then stopping abruptly an arm's length away. "*You're* to blame for it all?"

She bit the inside of her lip and nodded. The weight of that responsibility made witnessing the pain and anger inside him almost intolerable.

Connor stared at her for a moment without speaking. Her hair was mussed, her eyes were red, and there was an imprint of pillow fringe on her cheek. He had just spent hours walking the streets, thinking, sorting it all out in his mind and heart. And now as he saw the caring and pain in her face, he felt a poignant warmth surging through his veins.

"You're right. You are to blame."

Her stricken look made his chest ache. He took a step closer, but she shrank back.

"If I hadn't met you . . . if I hadn't felt your passion . . . if I hadn't witnessed your conviction and your courage . . . I might never have had to wake up and face what I had become. I might never have realized how much of me I had given away.

"I walked out on my career, my future, my hopes and dreams today. And for what? It wasn't women's suffrage, or bank policies, or even political convictions. I'm ashamed to say that none of that was important enough to me to bring me to the brink of rebellion. It was the thought of losing you and everything I feel for you that finally was too much.

"Tammany pushed me to make a choice. Them or you." He took a bracing breath and gave her a pained smile. "To tell the truth . . . they might have gotten me to recant women's suffrage. They might have made me withdraw from your bank and they might have even dictated every word I uttered on the campaign trail."

He had said all this and more to himself in the hours he had walked the streets. But hearing it aloud, confessing it to her, had a drastic impact. Shame gripped his throat so that his voice became forced and ragged.

"But they could never have made me deny my love for you. I lost one love. One heart. I know how rare and precious love is. And to be given a second chance? I love you, Bebe." He winced as if expecting her to recoil from his admission. "And that love seems to have affected everything else in my life. I can't keep my eyes shut or my conscience asleep anymore. You make me want to change and reshape the world . . . make it a better place. You make me want to go out and single-handedly force Congress to recognize women's God-given rights . . . to change every bad law . . . to rescue every needy woman and child."

He reached out to touch her cheek and felt her trembling. It was all he could do to keep from pulling her into his arms.

"I wish I could offer you a future . . . a life . . . a reason to be proud to say you love Connor Barrow." He had spent seven long years planning and preparing. Right now he couldn't even imagine a future outside those long-cherished political dreams. "But I have no future to share, no career, no wealth or achievement."

"I don't need money, Connor," she said, seizing his hands. "And I don't care about Tammany Hall or the election, or you making me a place in the world. I already have a home. What I need and want from you makes all of those other things pale by comparison."

"You still don't get it, do you?" He loomed over her, his expression bleak. "I don't have anything to give you. I don't have anything of value left."

"That's not true," she said, refusing to release his hands when he tried to pull away. He backed one step, then another, but she still would not let him go. Then she said the words he both dreaded and longed to hear. "You have me."

Connor watched the softening in her, the love shining in her liquid emerald eyes, and felt as if he'd been slammed against a wall.

"You have my love, Connor, and you have thousands of tomorrows ahead . . . in which anything and everything can change . . . except that."

He pulled her into his arms and held her tightly against him, letting the warmth and strength of her love combat the chill created by his excruciating self-awareness. She loved him. He raised her chin and kissed her with such tenderness and passion that their tears mingled to season that kiss with salt.

When he finally drew back, she looked up at him with joy and pain both visible in her face.

"Together"—she caressed the side of his face—"we can do anything. We can remake the world . . . change the way people think . . . we can even win back your place on the ballot."

He recoiled from the mention of his failed congressional bid, and a moment later withdrew his arms from her.

"Connor, you could still be elected," she said anxiously. "We could find a way."

"Give it up, Bebe." He turned aside; the sight of her was painful. "It's a lost cause. It's over. After what I did at that news conference, no party in its right mind would take me on. I burned too many bridges." His features hardened. "And if Tammany asked me back on bended knee, I wouldn't go."

"We'll think of something," she began. "We'll find a way to—"

"Look"—he grew agitated—"I'm off the ballot. And all the commiseration and sweet talk in the world won't change that."

"You know people all over the city," she said. "Surely some of them would be willing to help . . . to see that you stay on the ballot."

She didn't want to let it go, he realized. She couldn't bear the thought of being involved with someone without a future, so she was determined to see possibilities where there were none. The thought caused his chest to contract around his lungs, making it hard to breathe.

"What's done is done, Bebe. The sooner we both face it, the better."

"I can't give it up, Connor. For your sake. We

can't walk away from something that means so much to you."

Anguish erupted in the core of him.

"You mean, something that means so much to *you*."

He had to get out of there. He had to clear his head . . . and maybe his heart. He wheeled and headed for the front door.

"Wait! Connor—"

She ran to the door, but his shape was already disappearing into the darkness down the street. She felt as if part of her had been crushed. He believed he had nothing left to fight for, nothing left to give. She couldn't believe that and couldn't understand how he believed it . . . until she remembered that this wasn't the first time his life had come crashing down around him.

Despair threatened to overcome her as she stood in the dimness, holding the sight of his hopeless expression in her mind. But as the new love in her faltered, the seasoned businesswoman in her roused to take control. She loved him and he loved her. But they would never have a life together until he had a future . . . a place in the world to call his own.

She had to do something. She had to find a way to keep him on the ballot, to get him to run . . . and to help him win.

First—her mind raced desperately—federal elections were in the federal jurisdiction. She needed someone with the authority to . . . a judge . . . a federal judge . . . who could be persuaded to do the right thing. And then she needed to grab Connor by the heartstrings or the pride, and convince him to throw himself back into the race.

After a few minutes of pacing and hand wringing, it came to her. She knew one person with enough clout to persuade a federal judge and enough grit to goad a stubborn candidate into running.

IT DIDN'T TAKE long to learn where Hurst Barrow lived, but getting there was another matter. He had withdrawn from the rigors of the city into a baronial house in the countryside, north of the city. As she was admitted through the iron-bound doors into the cavernous main hall, the house seemed more a fortress than a dwelling. The stone walls were more than a foot thick, the interior was heavily paneled with dark wood, and the furnishings seemed massive and immovable. The air had a musty, unstirred smell, and through the arches flanking the entry, she could see that the drapes in the rooms on either side were still drawn. It was midday and sunny, but in Hurst Barrow's house lamps had been lit.

The butler returned with word that the master was busy and could not be disturbed. Beatrice looked the imperious old retainer in the eye, then barreled past him, straight down the hallway from which he had emerged, looking for the old man. She tried one door and then another, and finally found the old boy ensconced in a dark, book-lined study . . . his thinning hair wiry and disheveled . . . one foot wrapped in gout paper and propped up on a stool.

"What the devil—" He slammed down the magnifying glass he was using to read and began to bluster.

The butler made profuse apologies and tried to drag her from the room, but his squeamishness at setting hands to a female gave Beatrice an edge. She wrestled free and made it back to the desk Hurst was now crouched behind.

"What are *you* doing here?" he demanded, waving the old butler away.

"I've come to"—she instinctively changed *ask for your help* to—"make a deal with you."

"A deal?" He gave a rusty harrumph that passed for sardonic pleasure. Deal making was his lifeblood. "You already run aground with that bank of yours?"

"Not that kind of a deal," she said, analyzing him and his surroundings.

"Why would I want to deal with you? You haven't got anything I want."

"Oh, but I do," she said, her eyes narrowing cannily. "Do you want to be respected, revered, even adored? Want to be a part of life again, instead of a lonely old prune rattling around"—she gestured to the house—"in a musty old mausoleum?" She leaned impulsively over his desk, her eyes glinting with challenge. "Want to turn back the clock ten years and undo the stupidest thing you've ever done?"

The old man drew breath for what she sensed would be a vitriolic attack, but for some reason, as he met her gaze, he did not launch it. At least five different responses became visible in his face as she waited and every one strengthened her belief that this might work. Finally, he thrust back in his massive leather chair and shot a penetrating look at her.

"You got more balls than ten men," he said flatly.

She straightened, unaffronted. "So I do."

"You can't deliver," he charged.

"Oh, but I can." She smoothed the peplum of her jacket. "If *you* deliver."

He studied her for a moment, his eyes growing more lively as they darted over her.

"Deliver what?"

"A judicial ruling. A little federal muscle. Tammany Hall has kicked Connor out and said he's off the ballot. They don't have the legal right to do that—I checked—but they'll do it, just the same. And we don't have time for a court battle to get him reinstated. We've got to have a decision, right away. If anybody has the clout to get a federal court ruling in less than a week it's you."

"Why would I want to help that insolent pup? He walked out on me—"

"He was pushed," she countered. "You pushed him out with both hands."

"He chose his bed, let him lie in it," he grumbled.

"He chose to be a man, instead of a doormat."

"He threw in with that bunch of Irish crooks at Tammany Hall. He deserves what he gets."

"He has walked out on those crooks at Tammany Hall . . . for the very same reason he walked out on you. Because he's a man." She straightened and spoke right from the heart. "A good man. A strong and principled man. The kind of man this world needs."

Hurst scowled, but the deepening furrow in his brow and the subtle slumping of his shoulders said that her words had fallen on fertile ground. Her reading of heavy regret in the old man's eyes had been right on target. And she hoped one last nudge would bring him kicking and thumping back into the land of the living.

"We're a lot alike, you and me," she said, allowing her compassion to rise into her voice and face. "We've both spent our lives seeking control of the things and people around us . . . only to learn that the things worth having are the things you can never really control. Love, in all of its guises, is a gift. You can't make another person give it to you . . . you can only offer it to them in hope." She lowered her voice and tried very hard to keep the Irish out of it. "I'm making you that offer, Hurst Barrow. And this may be your last chance."

When the old man turned his stubborn gaze on her, she could have sworn there was moisture in his eyes.

IT WAS LATE the next night before Connor turned the key in the lock of his front door and let himself in. He had spent a good part of the day walking the streets to avoid both his house and his besieged legal offices. Then, after the reporters had grown tired of waiting and left, he had crept up the fire escape to catch a few winks on the settee in his office. After that, he had a late supper in a small Italian-run café off Broadway and then began the long walk home.

There was a light burning in the parlor, but he quickly discounted the possibility that Bebe would be there again. He'd be damned lucky if she ever spoke to him again after he had walked out on her last night. He had needed the time, the space, to do some serious thinking. He hung up his hat, removed his rumpled coat, and hung them on the coat tree in the hall.

When he entered the parlor to turn out the lamp, he stopped flat . . . staring at his leathery, age-hardened gnome of a grandfather, who was dozing in one of the wing chairs by the hearth. The old boy had taken the wool lap blanket from the window seat to cover his knees and had made himself completely at home.

His first impulse was to flee, his second was to toss the old boy out, and his third—and most civilized—impulse was to wake him up and see what the devil he was doing here. Besides the obvious.

"Come to gloat, have you?" Connor said in a strong

voice, startling the old fellow awake with a snuffle and a grunt.

"Huh—what?" Hurst came abruptly alert.

"How did you get in here?" Connor demanded.

"Your housekeeper." The old boy wiped his mouth with a withered hand. "She's gullible. You ought to fire her."

"She let *you* in . . . I probably should." Connor planted himself in the middle of the room with his hands on his hips. This time *he* was not going to be the one to leave. "What do you want?"

"A new left foot, better hearing, and about ten more years than I probably have left. But, that's neither here nor there," Hurst snapped as he tossed the lap blanket aside. "You may as well know: It wasn't my idea to come. It was that damned infernal female. She made me."

He could only be talking about Bebe. They didn't have any other "damned infernal females" in common anymore. Connor scowled.

"Why?" he demanded. Why on earth would Bebe inflict his miserly, combative, crotchet-ridden old grandfather on him at a time like this?

"She's got some damned fool notion about mountains and Mohammed. Says you and I've got some business still to do. Silly romantic nonsense if you ask me." He huddled irritably. "She's your bit o' fluff—you figure it out."

Connor clung tenaciously to the tenuous equilibrium he had achieved in the last twenty-four hours. It was probably that recovering sense of self-possession that allowed him to actually see the absurdity in the old boy's grousing. He had called Bebe a bit of fluff. There wasn't an epithet in the entire English language less suited to her. And *romantic*? Connor couldn't help the way his mouth quirked up on one side.

Hurst looked up at him with a much-practiced scowl. "So they tossed you out."

"I walked out."

"Figures," the old man said, looking away in disgust.

"They sat on me. I couldn't live like that." He braced, expecting a stinging retort. To his surprise, the old man drew a heavy breath and then gave a snarl of impatience.

"I always said Tammany was full of idiots. A damned convention of idiots." Then he looked up at Connor with a narrow, assessing gaze. "What are you going to do?"

Was that what this was about? Connor wondered. The old man swooped in to catch him in a weak moment and haul him back into the family lair?

"I have no idea." It hurt to admit it.

"Well, I do," the old man said, studying the way Connor tensed. His drooping mouth lifted so that it actually made a straight line. He looked like an expressionless old turtle trying to smile. "You should run for Congress."

Of all the things the old man might have said to him, that was the least expected. Connor stiffened all over at the impact of it.

"What?"

"Run for Congress. Take the damned seat away from those bog-trotters and show 'em how government should be run."

Connor stared at him, blinked, and opened his mouth to speak without producing a sound.

"That's what I said," came Bebe's voice from the door behind him. He turned and found her holding a tea tray and leaning against the doorway, watching. "Campaign hard, take the congressional seat from them in a landslide, and make them come to you on bended knee." She carried the tray in, set it down on the table, and stood studying it for a minute before looking up. "I can't guarantee this tea. It's my first attempt." She caught Connor's gaze. "But I can guarantee that you'll make a better congressman than anybody else they can come up with. And I know you can win."

"You've caught something . . . the pair of you. And you're delirious with fever," he said, staring at her clear, emerald eyes and seeing in them a polished glint of certainty. He felt a startling rush of warmth flowing over him. She was there. Now. Dirtying up his kitchen and giving him her unguarded, unflinching support.

"I'm off the ballot . . . or hadn't you heard?"

"Not necessarily," Hurst declared, drawing a folded paper from his pocket and waving it. "Once you're on the ballot . . . they can't get rid of you that easily . . . unless Tammany rigs the printing of the ballot. It may take a bit of work, but we can prevent that. We did a little checking this afternoon." He looked at Beatrice with a conspiratorial squint. "I've got a federal judge willing to rule and guarantee your place on the ballot in two days. It'll be spread all over the papers and we'll be watchdogging the election commission. Your name will be there . . . if you want it to be there."

Connor was stunned. He looked from his grandfather to Bebe with a dozen questions on his lips. "But I don't have an election machine . . . I don't have posters or venues or ward captains . . ."

"Connor," Bebe said, coming to take his hands, squeezing them as if trying to force some fighting spirit into them. "What have you been doing these last six months? Campaigning, right? People have heard your name. They've heard you speak and debate. They've shaken your hand. They've told you their problems. And they've liked what they saw. If your name is still on the ballot, a lot of people will vote for you. You've already done the hardest work of the campaign . . . the 'grass-roots' things. You have a chance, Connor." Her eyes began to shine. "Take it."

"But the mess in the newspapers," he said, feeling his throat constricting.

"Piss on the newspapers," Hurst said with an irritable wave of the hand. "How many people read 'em anyway? And how many people *believe* what they read. Use your head, boy." He tapped his temple. "Tammany may get print, but anybody can get print . . . for a price. Even us."

Us? Connor studied the old man as he pushed up from the chair and shuffled stiffly toward him. Bitter ground was giving way under his feet and it astonished him that a decade's worth of grudges and pain seemed to be irrelevant just now.

"How bad do you want it, boy?" Hurst asked. "How hard are you willing to work?"

"You believe I can do it?" Connor asked, knowing that he was asking about far more than his political chances.

"I never once doubted your ability, boy." The old man's voice grew thick with unaccustomed feeling. "Nor the rightness of your heart. And as I get older, I can't remember what I thought was so much more important than those two things." He gave a heavy sigh that spoke volumes. "If you run, you'll win."

Connor felt Bebe's hands on his arm and looked down at the hope and expectation in her face.

"You really think it can be done?" he asked her.

"Me? I'm the one who convinced your grandfather it was possible."

Connor had a hard time swallowing the lump in his

throat in order to speak. "I must be losing every shred of intelligence I possessed." He took a deep breath and felt his gut tighten in anticipation. "I'll do it."

Bebe grabbed him and hugged him, laughing. When he looked up from kissing her, his grandfather was watching them with a jaundiced eye.

"You won't get elected doing that kind of nonsense," Hurst said, shoving the paper containing the court date into Connor's hands and heading for the front door, grumbling all the way. "I got a campaign to fund."

Connor saw the old man turn at the doorway for one last glimpse, and thought he saw a quirk of a smile on that withered face. Then the sound of the door closing reached them and he looked down at Bebe. Her cheeks were wet and her lashes glistened.

"You came back," he said, brushing her hair back along her temple.

"Did you doubt that I would?"

"Well . . ." He reddened. "I wasn't exactly—"

"In any frame of mind to hear about possibilities?" she supplied. "I realized that later. Sometimes it takes a little while for your heart to recover enough to begin to hope." She reached up to cradle his face between her hands. "You're the most precious thing in the world to me. It broke my heart to think of what those bastards did to you. And when you walked out, I realized that when I saw you again . . . I had to have something to give you . . . some course of action, some reason for hope."

He felt his own eyes burning, and blinked.

"You didn't have to go to all that trouble. All you had to do was be here . . . looking at me like that . . . with love in your eyes. That would have been enough. I love you, Bebe. And I want to give you the world. But right now, all I have is this house, the promise of a lot of hard work, and a pair of arms that will never get tired of holding you."

"More than enough." She raised her lips for a kiss. "You sweet talker, you."

TWENTY-ONE

FOUR DAYS AFTER Connor's disastrous meeting with news reporters at Tammany Hall, the newspapers were still full of the story, its aftermath, and implications. Speculation ran wild on who Tammany Hall's new candidate would be, and the more daring newspapers raised questions about whether or not it was possible to legally place his successor's name on the ballot at such a late date. Wags commented in cartoons and in prose that Tammany Hall never had trouble with legalities . . . it simply changed the laws to accommodate whatever it wanted to do.

The bombshell of the week, however, came with the news that Connor might contest his removal from the ballot in the courts. Those rumors were followed quickly by confirmed reports that the federal court had ruled that Connor was indeed a certified candidate and must be included in the voting. Tammany reacted by quickly anointing City Alderman Bert McCloskey as Connor's successor on the Democratic ticket, and by sending a pair of beefy new "clerks" to work in the election commission office.

When Connor and Beatrice delivered the court papers ordering that his name must appear on the ballot, the new "clerks" snatched the papers from the commissioner's hands before Connor and Beatrice made it out the door.

"Just as I figured," Hurst said when he met them at Connor's house that evening and they told him what had happened. His ancient turtle smile appeared, but with a crafty twist. "You leave the ballots to me."

"What are you going to do?" Beatrice asked.

The old man swallowed another dose of gout medicine and shuddered as it hit his stomach.

"You don't want to know."

"Nothing illegal . . ." she said, scowling intently at him.

Hurst looked up at Connor with thinly disguised impatience.

"She's new at politics, isn't she?"

BEATRICE'S FIRST PRIORITY was to establish a headquarters for the campaign. On a suggestion from Alice, she arranged to rent some rooms in Woodhull House for their use. They moved into rooms in the new annex below Priscilla's dormitory and set about organizing furnishings and securing some of the printed campaign materials Tammany Hall had already ordered. Beatrice put Priscilla to work checking the newspapers each day and clipping all articles related to the campaign. They sent invitations to reporters to come and visit their new headquarters, and Beatrice met informally with them and arranged lunches and dinners for Connor with various reporters. Beatrice also met with the leaders of the National American Woman Suffrage Association, and persuaded them to endorse Connor publicly and to provide him with campaign volunteers.

Lacey Waterman and Frannie Excelsior arrived the very next morning with a platoon of women eager to help. Beatrice gratefully handed them stacks of freshly printed posters and pamphlets, and bags of campaign buttons to distribute. The women left in an adventuresome mood, but they straggled back in mid-afternoon looking rumpled and dazed, telling horrifying stories of being trailed by gangs of toughs who tore down every poster they put up and who intimidated them physically.

"Damned bullies!" Frannie staggered in with a rip in her jacket, a scrape on her cheek, and her felt boater hat squashed beyond recognition. "Too cowardly for a fair fight." She held up two wiry fists. "The buzzards came at me four at a time . . . yanking the posters out of my hands . . . pushing and shoving. And not one man came to help me or even yelled at them to stop!"

The others commiserated, deeply shaken and angered by their treatment.

"That's men for you," one declared caustically.

Beatrice couldn't fault them for their attitude; she was just as shocked as they were. But she had to refocus their anger and put the blame where it belonged.

"It's not *men*," she said, rallying the troops. "It's Tammany Hall. And whether we like it or not, they'll keep doing this until the election. If you're game, we'll try again tomorrow." They reluctantly agreed, and she forced a smile. "Don't worry, we'll think of something."

Connor was furious at what had happened to their volunteers. Tammany was known for using strong-arm tactics in elections, he said, but to his knowledge, they had never stooped to intimidating and abusing women.

It was little comfort to think that they had reduced Tammany to a desperate, new low.

"If they won't respect us as competitors, you'd think they would at least respect us as women," Beatrice said irritably.

"Well, beggin' your pardon, ma'am . . . them bein' your friends an' all . . . but they don't exactly look like regular women," Dipper said with a wince. "You can tell they're 'shriekin' sisters' from a mile off."

"Just because they don't carry frilly parasols, mince steps, and bat their eyelashes . . ." But Dipper was right. Most of the NAWSA women wore tailored clothes, spectacles, and masculine-looking hats. An idea began to form.

The next morning, when the women arrived, she presented them with a pile of borrowed clothing, mostly flowered dresses and ruffled aprons. The volunteers quickly got into the spirit of what they were being asked to do and donned the oversized dresses and put extra silk flowers on their hats. Then Bebe pulled out a stack of pillows donated from every bed in Woodhull House and began stuffing them under the ladies' dresses. The women, some of whom had white hair, thought the idea outlandish but gamely went along. Shortly, an army of very "pregnant" women emerged from Woodhull House to cover the streets with posters and handbills and "Barrow for Congress" buttons.

Beatrice joined them dressed in a noisy red-and-white print and a hat sprouting silk poppies. As she waddled along the streets, putting up posters, she passed a number of suspicious-looking clumps of men who eyed her but, seeing her bulging "belly," left her alone. Impending motherhood was still sacred, it seemed, even among Tammany's thugs.

The headquarters rang with laughter as the others returned and told their experiences with gangs of men confounded by a sudden rash of expectant mothers.

"It won't work forever," Beatrice told them, grinning, "but if it gets us through the next week, that will be good enough."

Then, as they were removing their disguises, a pair of women appeared at the headquarters door . . . women whose style of dress and movement left no doubt as to their profession. When the newcomers swayed into the room on a cloud of French perfume, the ladies of the NAWSA backed away as if afraid of contamination. Beatrice heard the noise drop and hurried to investigate.

There stood Mary Kate and Annie dressed in flashy satins, exaggerated bustles, and picture-book hats . . . one dripping with ermine tails and the other with feather boas. Beatrice watched the volunteers pull back as the pair entered and was momentarily at a loss. What could they be doing here?

"Hiya, Bebe!" Mary Kate called, and Annie greeted her with similar buoyancy. "Dipper come by the other night. He said you an' th' congressman could use a bit o' help. We tho't we'd come an' offer our services."

"That's most civic minded of you. We'd be grateful for the help." Ignoring the mutters of her suffragist friends, Beatrice gave the Oriental's ladies a broad smile and gathered up some printed materials. "I should warn you. We've been having a bit of trouble with some of the city's rougher element. Tammany's toughs have been harassing our workers and ripping down our posters."

Mary Kate grinned and glanced at the poker-faced suffrage contingent. "Ye just 'ave to know how to *handle* men. We'll get 'em *up* for you."

As the pair sauntered out with their arms laden with

campaign materials, Annie paused by a suffragist still wearing her pregnancy disguise and gave the woman's padded belly a tap.

"There are ways to keep that from happenin', ya know."

The next afternoon, there were two campaign forces at work for Connor Barrow on the streets of the Fourth District, and they couldn't have been more different: soiled doves and mothers-to-be, traditionally the opposite ends of the feminine spectrum. Occasionally, members of the two groups came together on a street corner with only one lamppost, and it was a standoff to see who would get the privilege of posting the handbill. In the end, there were far more posters and handbills put up than torn down, and once again, "Connor Barrow for U.S. Congress" was being seen all over town.

Connor himself, however, was having difficulty being seen anywhere. He tried to keep his planned schedule of appearances, but Tammany gangs knew where he would appear and caused disruptions wherever he went . . . tossing catcalls and rotten vegetables at Connor and the first punch at their fellow spectators. Twice, full-scale brawls broke out, preventing Connor from saying much of anything. The second time it happened Connor was angry enough to climb down off the scaffolding and throw a few punches himself. He arrived back at Woodhull House with a bruised jaw, a smashed lip, and a foul mood.

Beatrice ordered him into a chair and sent Priscilla for iodine and bandages . . . both of which he refused. "It's not that bad," he told her, testing his battered lip from inside and out.

"Yes, it is. It's monstrous," she declared, fierce with

protective impulses she had heretofore associated only with Priscilla and Consolidated.

"You forget." He looked up at her with a pain-filled smile. "I've seen these things from Tammany's side. They have to be really desperate to use this much muscle. We must have them worried."

"Hurray for us," she said, scowling. "By that logic, when they beat you to a bloody pulp, we should break out the champagne."

"Exactly," he said with a wink at Dipper and Shorty, who chuckled.

It was no laughing matter for Beatrice, however. Over the next week she watched the disruptions escalate and saw the toll they were taking on Connor. She found herself holding her breath each time he left the headquarters and growing quietly more frantic each time he was late returning. She tried dispatching Dipper and Shorty with Connor. All three came back with bruises, gashes, and wrenched muscles. She tried having Dipper and Shorty recruit a few fellows who wouldn't mind enforcing order at Connor's speeches. They made a difference—briefly. The disrupters returned in even greater force and a sizable donnybrook ensued.

"Where were the police?" Beatrice demanded as she and Alice and Priscilla tended the minor wounds inflicted on their security force.

"In Croker's back pocket," Connor said darkly.

Beatrice felt a chill as she looked at his grim face and realized how thoroughly Tammany possessed the city. There was no agency or authority in the entire city that operated without its influence . . . not even the police. No wonder Connor had been reluctant to take them on. He knew better than anyone what an uphill battle they faced.

Then, to everyone's surprise, Priscilla came up with a suggestion.

"Aunt Bebe . . . remember that young man . . . that detective . . . Mr. Blackwell? Maybe he could get us some police help."

Bebe regarded her with nothing short of amazement. Since Priscilla's break with Jeffrey she had been moody and unpredictable. It was encouraging to have her take an interest in the success of Connor's campaign.

"What an excellent idea," Beatrice said, putting her arm around Priscilla. "Why don't you and Dipper pay the good detective a call and invite him to come and see us?"

The next day, Detective James Blackwell arrived early at their campaign headquarters, with two patrolmen in tow. When he heard what was happening, he looked from Bebe to Connor to Priscilla and he smiled.

"Well, it's always in the best interest of the city for campaign appearances to stay orderly. I think I can get my captain to agree to assign some men to it."

Priscilla stood a bit straighter as she returned the young detective's smile, and Beatrice could have sworn that she blushed.

That very afternoon, a dozen uniformed police appeared at a rally where Connor was scheduled to speak. At the first sign of disturbance, they moved in to quell it and hauled off the ringleaders, and Connor was able to finish his speech for the first time in a week.

Judging by reports in the newspapers and the escalating resistance from Tammany Hall, they seemed to be making headway. Then, after two major newspapers came out with re-endorsements of Connor, things became markedly more tense. Shopkeepers with "Barrow for Congress" posters in their windows found those windows broken. The newspapers who had backed Connor suddenly found their papers stolen off the streets and ripped from their newsboys' hands. Woodhull House was splashed with paint and several halls where he spoke were damaged under cover of night.

After visiting a dry-goods store owner who had been terrorized and warned to stay away from the polls, Connor agreed they would need additional muscle on election day, to make certain their voters could get past Tammany's shoulder hitters and into the voting booths. He sent Dipper and Shorty out to recruit additional help.

Just six days before the election, on a bright and frosty morning, they awakened to a story in the early editions telling of a gang caught attempting to steal the ballots for the upcoming election. The men, all Irish immigrants and well known to the local police, had been caught red-handed. They claimed not to know who had hired them, but Connor said it was clearly Tammany at work. The newspapers seemed to agree. For the first time in quite a while, editors took pens in hand to call for election reforms and for an end to Tammany tyranny at the ballot box.

Tammany took out large advertisements in the newspapers and printed up handbills disclaiming responsibility for the dastardly attempt to sabotage the election. Connor said they were a lying bunch of hypocrites and was ready to call for an audit of the ballots, to be certain they were properly printed. But Hurst Barrow, who had stopped by to inspect their headquarters, eyed his grandson's indignation and pulled him aside.

"No audit. The ballots are just fine," Hurst assured him.

"And what if we walk into the voting booths on election day and my name isn't there?" Connor demanded irritably.

"It's there, all right. Now." The old man's eyes twinkled with mischief and Connor came alert and studied him.

"What do you mean, '*now*'?"

"Police never pay attention when somebody is putting something *into* a locked room. They only notice when somebody's taking things *out*."

That was all he would say, but it was enough. Hurst Barrow had somehow made good on his promise to take care of the ballots. Connor met the old man's gaze and for a long moment they stared at each other in the way of men who know each other well enough to need few words. It was then that Connor realized that the old man truly wanted him to win.

In that moment, both began to release the pain, recriminations, and estrangement caused by what had happened between them years ago. They had a second chance, both realized, and in the rich silence that followed they agreed to finally forget the outcome of the first one.

ELECTION DAY DAWNED clear and unexpectedly cold, but nothing short of a blizzard would have deterred the public from turning out in record numbers. By ten o'clock in the morning, the streets fairly crackled with the electricity of democracy in action. Every group in the city with an ax to grind turned out into the streets on election day; from charity mavens to sidewalk evangelists . . . from temperance advocates to union organizers . . . from immigrant cultural societies to nativist groups protesting immigration.

Adding to the charged atmosphere were the beer and Irish whiskey distributed freely to voters who had done or were about to do their civic duty. As the voters exited the bunting-draped polls, they were directed to the beer wagons parked nearby, and many of them could be seen heading back into the voting line after a few beers. The growing crowds were laced with pickpockets, streetwalkers, sleight-of-hand artists, election odds-makers, and roving gangs of youths. With such a volatile crowd about, it was little wonder shops around precinct polling places had closed for the day and shuttered their premises.

The National American Woman Suffrage Association planned their customary election day march to end at the precinct where Connor would make an appearance and cast his own vote. The women arrived at Woodhull House mid-morning and donned sashes and put together placards touting both their candidate and their cause. Connor watched them preparing and turned to Beatrice, who had just pinned a red-and-white sash proclaiming "Barrow for Congress" diagonally over her dark blue wool jacket.

"Are you sure this is a good idea? I mean, it could get a little rough. McCloskey votes in the same precinct, and Tammany will undoubtedly turn out."

"I don't think you have to worry about this group. They're no strangers to marches or to election day celebrations," Bebe assured him, straightening his tie and pausing to admire him. He looked quite "congressional" in his black cutaway coat and charcoal pinstripe trousers. "Besides, Detective Blackwell has asked for every available patrolman to be assigned to the area, and Dipper and Shorty have stationed men at every polling place to make sure your supporters get through. If we need them, they'll be there."

Connor pulled her down the hall, into Ardis Gerhardt's office, and into his arms. For a moment he just held her, looking at her, his face filled with tension. There had been so little time for the two of them these last two weeks. He had to pray that sacrifice would be worth it in the end.

"I want you to know, Bebe," he said tightly, "that whatever happens, I'll always be grateful for your love, your help, and your faith in me. I love you more than I can ever say."

"I love you, too," she said, trying to speak past the tears collecting in her throat. "And you're going to win."

"I know," he said with a flicker of uneasiness. "But if I don't . . ."

She kissed him to stop him from saying any more. They were together in this, her kiss said. They were both lovers and partners. They remained in each other's arms for a few moments . . . Bebe listening to the reassuring thud of his heart beneath her cheek . . . Connor inhaling her along with the scent of her hair. There came a discreet knock on the door and they released each other . . . both achingly aware that the next time they embraced, their hopes would have been either fulfilled or dashed to pieces.

Out in the street, the women of the NAWSA formed ranks, five across, behind a huge horizontal banner, proclaiming "Send Barrow to Congress to Work for the Woman Vote!" Connor took up a place just behind that banner along with Bebe, Alice, Lacey, Frannic, Esther Rose, and Carrie Chapman Catt. More than fifty women followed as they marched down the street toward the polls.

Five blocks later the street narrowed appreciably due to stopped wagons and carriages and milling crowds of people. They had to narrow ranks and wait at times for the street to clear. It was about that time that they were joined by a number of women in flashy clothes, carrying placards supporting Connor. When Beatrice turned to see how things were going in the rear, she spotted Mary Kate, Pansy, Millie, Annie, and Eleanor in their ranks, waving at her.

By the time their group reached the polling place, a lofty old brick building called Veterans' Hall, they had attracted quite a following. Some people smiled and waved, others booed and yelled at them to go home and tend to their children. Connor waved to his supporters, then took Beatrice's hand and pulled her up the crowded steps with him toward the voters' entrance.

They were bumped and jostled by a number of inebriated voters and somewhere in the press of the crowd, she stumbled and lost her grip on his hand. When she righted herself and looked up, he was nowhere to be seen. She heard him call her name, but had difficulty locating him . . . until the noise and movement buffeting her abruptly lessoned. Standing on tiptoes, she caught a glimpse of a huge beer wagon drawn by massive high-stepping horses approaching Veterans' Hall. Atop that wagon sat Boss Croker, Charles Murphy, and a number of other men she took to be Tammany dignitaries . . . they, like Connor, were dressed in elegant top hats and swallowtail coats.

"Here's our man . . . Bert McCloskey! Come to do his duty and vote," Croker roared, in a bald play to the appreciative crowd. "I wonder who he'll vote for!" There was a cry of approval from the Tammany supporters present. Then Croker looked down and spotted Connor standing on the middle of the steps. "Would you look at that." He pointed at Connor with a sneer. "These days they'll let just anybody vote!"

"Not just anybody, Croker," Connor called above the noise of the well-lubricated crowd. "There are a lot of people here who want and need the vote, but don't yet have it." And the women of the NAWSA let loose a cheer. At the front of their contingent, Frannie raised a fist and began a chant in a cadence quickly joined by the others: "We won't rest 'til we get our vote!"

A male wag in the crowd shouted back: "And we won't rest if you _do!_"

Connor was stopped at the doors by several beefy shoulder hitters blocking the only way inside. Connor asked them to move, but they crossed their arms and refused. Up out of the crowd came Dipper and Shorty, who beckoned to their boys. A number of equally brawny longshoremen shoved their way up out of the crowd to stand at Connor's back. The odds were nearly even, and the prospect of an evenly matched fight was enough to give Tammany's thugs pause.

It was a stalemate until Croker huffed and panted his way to the top of the steps. "Well, well . . ." He halted not far away, glaring at Connor through bloated, froglike eyes. "There's garbage on the steps."

"There certainly is," Connor said, returning Croker's scrutiny. "You've hit a new low, Croker. Blocking your opponent from even casting his own vote."

After a tense moment, Croker jerked his head and the men blocking Connor's way melted to the sides to allow him to pass. Croker turned to comment to the crowd, "One more vote won't make him any difference."

"One more vote may be all it takes to bring you down!" came a woman's voice from the crowd. Frannie Excelsior broke free from the NAWSA delegation and charged up the steps with her placard in her hands. But before she was halfway up, she was met by a Tammany shoulder hitter who tried to wrestle the placard from her. She yielded it to him and while his hands were busy trying to break up the placard, she belted him in the midsection. He grunted and went reeling.

Like a spark landing in dry grass, that one quick burst bit of violence was all it took to ignite the crowd. Instantly, the pushing and straining going on all over the tightly packed crowd became earnest shoves and punches. Out came billy clubs and shillelaghs, blackjacks and old-fashioned cudgels. The hours of beer and boredom had taken their toll and the crowd erupted in a massive brawl.

Connor's first thought was of Bebe, lost somewhere on the steps in the churning mob. But a shove from one of Tammany's enforcers sent him flying back out the door and from that moment, he only had time to defend himself and those near him who were being shoved and trampled underfoot. Dipper and Shorty tried to reach him, but then found themselves under attack and had to retreat under a barrage of blows. In a moment, it was nearly impossible to tell who was on which side; everyone simply sided with those they knew and defended themselves as best they could.

Dazed from a blow and galvanized by the pain in his reinjured lip, Connor spotted a thick form dressed in black top hat and tails, and headed for it. He grabbed Croker's arm and spun him around . . . planting a savage right fist squarely in the boss's porcine face. Croker flailed and went down with a cry of pain and a gush of blood. Connor's satisfaction was cut short by a vicious blow he didn't see coming.

Suddenly, everyone was fighting. Young and old, male and female, Tammany and independent, tavern keepers and temperance society members, trade unionists and management stoolies, Irish immigrants and nativist bigots. The NAWSA contingent and their uninvited guests from the Oriental wielded their signs and placards with every bit of their strength against antisuffrage forces. Hats went flying, placard poles cracked and splintered, and when those were exhausted, the members defended themselves with purses, shoe heels, empty beer steins, and even planks torn from police barricades.

Above the chaos, the high, shrill sounds of police whistles could be heard, distant but growing closer. Those on the fringes of the fighting began to retreat. But those in the middle of the brawl kept throttling and thrashing until they were rushed by a swarm of black-uniformed officers.

One by one, then three by three . . . then a dozen at a time . . . the brawlers were subdued, arrested, and hauled away in paddy wagons.

DIPPER AND SHORTY had traded a number of punches before reaching the edge of the chaotic mob.

"Where's Miz Von Furstenberg?" Dipper yelled to his panting, doubled-over partner as they leaned against the corner of a building. "We gotta find her!"

They plunged back in, dodging fists and bottles and billy clubs, as they tried to locate their employer and pull her to safety. Instead of Beatrice, they spotted Mary Kate and several of her Oriental Palace friends wielding broken parasols and borrowed clubs with surprising force. They managed to help the women retreat to the safety of a nearby alley . . . just as the sounds of police whistles filled the air.

Familiarity with that chilling sound sent the entire group running for cover. It wasn't until the last paddy wagon hauled its batch of rioters away that they emerged to survey the damage. The square looked like the aftermath of the world's worst St. Patrick's Day celebration.

"What a mess," Dipper said, scowling at the debris, then turning to his cousin. "You girls all right?" Mary Kate nodded and adjusted her bodice with an irritable yank.

"Looks like they got the gov," Shorty said, testing a couple of loosened teeth. "It ain't fair. He didn't even get to vote."

Dipper looked around them and spotted a wagon full of half-drunken voters being carried *to* the polling place, not away from it. "Tammany's already back at its old tricks," he said, punctuating his disgust with a spit. "This e'lection is as good as lost."

Mary Kate came to stand by her cousin and join him in glaring at the men being unloaded and herded toward the voters' entrance.

"It ain't right," she said bitterly. "Th' congressman deserves to win this ballot. He's the finest man I ever *didn't* know."

Annie, Eleanor, and Pansy agreed with her. Then a glint appeared in her eye. She jerked her corset down a smidgen and headed for the voters' line. The other girls watched at first, then one by one began to grin at each other and straighten their hats and plump their bustles.

Just before Annie joined her friends doing some politicking of their own on the voters' line, she caught Dipper by the lapel and whispered into his reddening ear.

"I got a message for you to deliver to the girls at the Oriental. . . ."

THE LIGHTS OF the city hall police station were merciless . . . just like the sickly, toiletlike odor of the filthy holding cells. Beatrice was herded with at least thirty other women into a large cell with two brick walls painted a noxious pea green and two walls made of stout iron bars. Her hat was gone, her Gibson-girl coif now hung askew, and her sleeve was torn partway from her jacket. There was a patch of scraped skin on her cheek, and she felt battered and sore all over. She kept seeing in her mind the way Connor fell to the steps after he'd been blindsided by a blow from one of Croker's thugs. She was haunted by the thought that he might be still lying there, bleeding and gravely injured. She called to the jail guards, reaching through the bars to attract their attention, but they ignored her the way they ignored the twenty other women yelling at them. Then from a far corner, she heard her name being called. It was Lacey, standing on one of the narrow cots that lined the walls.

They embraced as if long-lost sisters, both in tears, then found a place to sit together on one of the cots, leaning back against the painted bricks.

"It's my fault," she muttered through her tears to Lacey. "I insisted he run. I thought he really had a chance to win." Every inch of her handkerchief was soaked and she had lifted her skirts and started to use her petticoat.

She couldn't remember ever feeling this helpless and despondent. But, then, she had never suffered such a catastrophic failure before. Connor's political future had just been beaten and battered to a pulp . . . done in by a drunken mob, a political machine, and her own stubborn naiveté. She had wanted so much to help him—as he had helped her. What on earth made her think they could win against the corrupt power of Tammany Hall?

"Poor Connor . . . he didn't even get to vote in his own election. If only I hadn't pushed so hard," she said miserably. "I'm sorry I got you into this, Lacey."

The veteran suffragist smiled ruefully. "Well, it's not like it's my first time in jail." When Beatrice looked at her in shock, she added: "I once went to a 'Women United in Labor' rally with Frannie. We did three days."

Beatrice tried to smile and Lacey put an arm around her. Not long afterward, the lights were turned out, and it seemed that all hope went with them. Despite Lacey's company, Beatrice's had never felt so alone. It was the darkest, longest night she could remember.

"What's she blubberin' about? She scared?" came a coarse female voice. When they looked up there was a huge, raw-boned woman staring down at them.

"Leave her alone," Lacey said fiercely. "She's not scared . . . she's just worried about someone."

"Connor." Beatrice sniffed. "If I only knew for sure that he's all right."

To their surprise, the woman's hardened face softened in the dimness. "This 'Connor' . . . he get pinched, too?"

"I hope so," Beatrice said, thinking to herself that her world must be standing on its ear for her to be praying that Connor was well enough to be arrested.

"Well, honey"—the woman made something akin to a smile—"there's ways of findin' out things, even in here." She turned to a woman who had posted herself in the corner closest to the next cell. "Hey, Goldie! See if there's a . . ."

"Connor Barrow," Beatrice supplied his name.

"See if there's a Connor Barrow in one of the men's cells."

Goldie contacted a Mary Jean, who contacted a fellow named Boxer in the nearest men's holding cell. Boxer called up and down the alleys, trying to locate him. And after what seemed like an eternity, word came back that he was indeed in the jail, in a cell block on the next level down.

Beatrice's heart began to beat normally again. At least he was alive. She gave the woman responsible for getting the information a grateful smile.

"Thank you."

"In here," the woman said, glancing around them, "we're all sisters."

The return of light was of little help the next morning. The effects of the beer and the brawl had mostly worn off and it was a drooping and subdued bunch who now waited for release. They were allowed morning relief and were given cups of jailhouse coffee and chunks of bread, but there all attempts at humane treatment ended. The jailers refused to listen to Beatrice's demands that they send for her lawyer and they went about their grim business as if she hadn't even spoken.

Then mid-afternoon, the jailers came through, calling names, and Beatrice and Lacey were among the first. They were led out to the main sergeant's desk where prisoners were being processed and released.

There stood Alice and Priscilla. They rushed to hug Beatrice.

"We would have had you out last night, but they made everyone wait until morning," Alice told Beatrice.

"Are you all right, Aunt Bebe?" Priscilla asked urgently. "Those beastly men didn't beat you or mistreat you?"

"I'm fine, Prissy." She stroked her niece's anxious face, then turned to Alice. "But, Connor—he's here somewhere—we have to—"

"Already done," Priscilla said with a smile, nodding toward a door on the far side of the station house. Detective Blackwell was just leading Connor out of the detention area. "We gave James our volunteer list and he's helping arrange everyone's re—" She halted, staring in surprise at the person exiting just behind Connor. It was Jeffrey Granton.

Connor had a bruise or two and his cut lip had been reopened; otherwise, he looked hale and well. When he spotted Beatrice he rushed toward her, then slowed as he looked her over with his heart in his eyes.

"Bebe." He opened his arms and in a heartbeat she was in them and hugging him so tightly he groaned. After a long moment, she looked up with wet eyes and met his kiss . . . full on the mouth . . . there, in front of God and everyone.

It was like coming home. She gave herself over to it . . . allowed it to sink into the deepest recesses of her heart and her being . . . surrendered that last, guarded bit of control . . . and let love take her wherever it wanted.

"Are you all right?" she said, touching his lip and then the dried gash on his forehead. "I was so worried."

He grinned, even though it hurt like the very devil. "I'm fine. In fact"—he took a deep breath—"I don't think I've ever felt better."

"Connor, I'm so sorry. I never imagined it would be so rough and dangerous. I saw you fall and couldn't get to you—"

"You don't have to be sorry." He put his finger against her lips. "Maybe a clout on the head is what I've needed to help me see things clearer. I've had a long night to think about it, and I realized that I have everything I want right here in my arms . . . right now. Losing this election may be the best thing that ever happened to me."

"Are you sure? Connor, you didn't even get to vote."

"True." He chuckled. "But I have it on good authority that Dipper and Shorty each voted several times. I'll just consider one of their votes mine."

Priscilla came face-to-face with Jeffrey for the first time since their parting, that day in the dormitory. He had his battered coat over his arm, a bruise on his cheek, and a tear in the knee of his trousers.

"What are you doing here?" she asked, glancing past him to the jail door he had just exited. "And what happened to you?"

"I was there to see how the election was going. When I saw Cousin Connor go down . . . well . . . nobody treats a Barrow that way."

"Jeff, here, got in a few good punches," Connor put in with a smile, and Jeffrey straightened, clearly pleased. "Call it one last fling . . . before he leaves for France."

"France?" Priscilla said, surprised.

"My father is shipping me off for a grand tour. Starting in Paris."

For a moment, Priscilla and Jeffrey came eye to eye, wary and yet hungry for some resolution of the conflict between them. After a meaningful pause, Priscilla lifted her chin and produced a taut but genuine smile.

"I hope you'll have a wonderful trip, Jeffrey. I really do."

With a visible relaxation of tension, he returned her smile. "Thank you, Priscilla." He squared his shoulders as if a weight had just rolled from them. "I'll send you a picture postcard from Paris."

"That would be nice," she said with a nod.

As Jeffrey tipped his hat to Beatrice and Connor, and struck off down the street, Priscilla turned back to her aunt and cleared her throat. "Are we ready to go? The carriage is outside and I have a ton of work to do. I suppose I'm going to have to be the one to clean up that mess at Woodhull House and shut down our campaign headquarters." She gave a long-suffering sigh. "A woman's work is never done."

"Unless . . ." Detective Blackwell put in, watching Priscilla with a twinkle in his eye, "Mr. Barrow would like to keep it open. He's probably got a great head start on the *next* election."

Connor groaned and clapped Blackwell on the shoulder. "By all means, close it down." He looked at Bebe. "Who knows where I'll be in two years. I could just be the head of the largest and most profitable bank in the city. Or I might be a husband." He gave Bebe a squeeze. "I might even be a *father*."

"Let's go home." Beatrice beamed up at him. "And tonight we'll have the biggest, best *loser's* dinner ever."

"Sounds wonderful to me," he said.

And as they stepped outside, into the glorious autumn sunshine, they were both determined, for the first time, to let life take them where it wanted.

BY THE TIME they reached the carriage, they spotted a small crowd of people headed their way, with a dark-clad figure hobbling along at their head. They paused long enough to realize that it was Hurst Barrow, leaning heavily on his walking stick and waving a newspaper with his free hand. They looked at each other, puzzled, and turned from the coach to meet him. As the group drew closer, they could see the infamous Artie Higgins and at least a dozen other news reporters firing questions at the old man . . . whom they left in the dust the instant they spotted Connor.

"What do you think, Congressman?" one shouted as he ran toward them.

"How does it feel?" another wanted to know, rushing up to him.

"How does what feel?" Connor asked, pulling Bebe protectively against his side.

"Don't you lot say a word!" the old man bellowed. "I want to tell him!"

Connor looked over the reporters' heads to where his grandfather was barreling through the group to reach him. "What is it?" he asked, as the old man caught his breath. "What's happened?"

"You won!" Hurst panted out, brandishing the newspaper as proof. "Look for yourself. You won!"

"I did?" Connor said, grabbing the paper and opening it to bold headlines declaring that he had won by a mere handful of votes. Tammany Hall was furious, charging every sort of malfeasance imaginable and demanding a recount. "How the devil did that happen?"

"There he is! Hey, gov!" came a familiar voice, approaching from the other direction. They discovered Dipper and Shorty hurrying up with Dipper's cousin, Mary Kate, swaying along behind. "Did ye hear? Ye won!"

Connor shook his head in disbelief. "I just heard! I can't imagine how."

"It was yer volunteers, Congressman." Mary Kate sauntered up and struck a pose, straightening her spine and raising her shoulders to make the most of her world-class cleavage. "Some of us just know how to get out the vote."

Connor stared at the gleam in Mary Kate's eye then looked to Bebe, who bit her lip, but then burst into a grin anyway.

As the reporters' pencils poised to take down his every word, Connor looked down at Bebe with a wondering smile. "If I really have won . . . and I'll wait for all of the results of all of the challenges to be certain . . . then I'm pleased that the people have placed such trust in me. And I'll do my best to be worthy of the opportunity they have given me to serve and to lead."

Life, apparently, was taking them to Washington. Together. Bebe's eyes were shining, but he remembered too well that it was dangerous to make assumptions about her.

"And I want to say one more thing." He turned to her and took both of her hands. "Beatrice Von Furstenberg, you're the most outrageous, stubborn, courageous, scandalous, and flat-out dangerous woman I've ever known. And I won't rest until you agree to marry me."

She laughed, surprised. Then she realized. "You're serious."

"Absolutely."

"Well . . ." Her eyes twinkled. "I suppose I could be persuaded . . ."

EPILOGUE

New York, Present day

"ARE YOU SURE it's up here, Nana?" Courtney Barrow waved away a billow of dust and picked up the battered lamp shade she had knocked down onto the attic floor. Then she planted her hands on her hips and looked around her at the collected domestic surplus of six generations. "I never would have asked if I had known it would cause this much trouble."

"What trouble?" Colleen flashed her granddaughter a grin and wiped a wisp of graying hair back from her moist forehead. "I'm sure I saw it up here last year when we were moving things up from the spare bedroom. Now where did we put . . . oh . . . over there." She pointed to a stack of chests, crates, and barrels stuffed back under the eaves.

They located, between the chests and the wall, several large, ornate pictures stacked together on their sides. Colleen squinted into the gloom, trying to make out if the picture she recalled was among them.

"I think that's it." She pointed to a sizable frame bearing fading gilt.

Together, they pulled it out and carried it over to the attic window. Colleen wiped the dusty glass with the heel of her hand. The dark-clad figures of a man and a woman stared back at them. At ease. Domestic and yet somehow dignified. The woman was seated in a Victorian-style chair and the man stood beside her with his hand on her shoulder.

"Happy-looking pair, weren't they?" Courtney said dryly.

"Well, you can't always tell by looking," Colleen said.

"Oh, yes you can." Courtney gave her grandmother an authoritative look. "They were Victorians. The men waxed their mustaches and sniffed women's gloves for turn-ons, and the women wore fifty-pound bustles and fainted at the thought of somebody seeing their ankles. This pair probably did it . . . how many kids did you say they had?"

"Four."

"Okay, they did it four times. Maybe *five,* for good measure."

Colleen laughed and shook her head. "You kids . . . you think you have a lock on love and passion."

"So that's Beatrice," Courtney said, staring at the woman's light eyes and Gibson-girl coif. "Lord—look at her waist. Must have been a heck of a corset. Women used to have ribs removed so they would have waists that small." She curled her nose. "Whatever would possess a woman to do that to herself?"

Colleen looked at the row of gold rings up the rim of her granddaughter's ear and bit her tongue.

"And that was the congressman," Colleen said, tapping the glass above the man's face. "He only served two terms, then went back into the family business. Banking. Handsome devil, wasn't he?" She smiled in admiration.

"Yeah. Probably had his share of honeys on the side. The old Victorian double standard. It's *her* I'm interested in." Courtney wiped more of the dust and cobwebs away. "I was so excited when I found her name on an old membership roster of the NAWSA. A real family connection to my thesis work on the history of the women's suffrage movement."

"Here—let's take this downstairs and clean it up," Colleen said and shifted it to take more of the weight. But as she carried it toward the stairs, she brushed the back of it against an old bed frame and heard a rip.

They stopped and looked, but there didn't seem to be any damage until they reached the better light of the upper hallway. The heavy brown paper glued over the back of the picture was ripped and inside it, they saw something that looked like newsprint.

It was only when they turned the picture upside down on the dining-room table to assess the damage, that they realized the paper inside the back wasn't just stuffing . . . it was tied with a faded ribbon . . . something put there to be preserved.

Gingerly they removed what appeared to be a packet of news clippings. And as they unfolded and read the brittle newsprint, their jaws dropped.

BARROW FLIRTS WITH WOMEN'S RIGHTS.
BARROW MAKES GOOD ON PROMISE:
BANK FOR WOMEN CHARTERED!
SCANDAL ROCKS CONSOLIDATED—
WOMAN PRESIDENT FACES MORALS CHARGE!

CONGRESSMAN DEFENDS 'JEZEBEL'—
IT WAS 'RESCUE WORK' IN A BROTHEL!
BARROW OFF BALLOT—
BREAK WITH TAMMANY OVER WOMEN'S RIGHTS!
BARROW BACK ON BALLOT
BARROW WINS CONGRESSIONAL SEAT!
VON FURSTENBERG-BARROW NUPTIALS.

After an hour of poring over their discovery, Courtney sat back and looked with fresh respect at the pair in the picture that was now faceup on the table.

"He was a feminist and she was . . . a wild woman." She looked at her grandmother with surprise. "She ran her own company and either romped around in a brothel or tried to 'rescue' prostitutes, depending on which account you want to believe." She smiled and shook her head. "I guess you can't *always* tell by looking."

Colleen's eyes sparkled.

"Imagine that."

A muffled electronic chirp came from the overstuffed backpack propped in a nearby chair. Courtney lunged for it, unearthed a cell phone, and punched a key to answer the call.

"Courtney Barrow," she said in clipped tones. The voice on the other end of the line brought her to her feet in an instant. "Just a minute, Nana," she said aside to Colleen, "I have to take this call." As she hurried out into the entry hall, her voice softened markedly.

From the quiet dining room Colleen caught a single word.

Jeffrey.

Smiling, she rose and carried the portrait to the grand buffet set against the wall. Propping it up amongst the silver serving pieces, she was arrested by something about the painting and paused, staring intently at the honored pair. Then she glanced through the door at her granddaughter's flushed and glowing face and back to the serene and loving countenances in the painting.

"Some things," she said with a wry laugh, "never change."

ABOUT THE AUTHOR

BETINA KRAHN lives in Minnesota with her two sons and a feisty salt-and-pepper schnauzer. With a degree in biology and a graduate degree in counseling, she has worked in teaching, personnel management, and mental health. She had a mercifully brief stint as a boys' soccer coach, makes terrific lasagna, routinely kills houseplants, and is incurably optimistic about the human race. She believes the world needs a bit more truth, a lot more justice, and a whole lot more love and laughter. And she attributes her outlook to having married an unflinching optimist and to two great-grandmothers actually named Pollyanna.